D0197060

THE EIGHTEENTH CAPTAIN

NAUTICAL FICTION
PUBLISHED BY MCBOOKS PRESS

BY ALEXANDER KENT
Midshipman Bolitho
Stand into Danger
In Gallant Company
Sloop of War
To Glory We Steer
Command a King's Ship
Passage to Mutiny
With All Despatch
Form Line of Battle!
Enemy in Sight!

BY CAPTAIN FREDERICK MARRYAT
Frank Mildmay OR *The Naval Officer*
The King's Own
Mr Midshipman Easy
Newton Forster OR *The Merchant Service*

BY W. CLARK RUSSELL
Wreck of the Grosvenor

BY RAFAEL SABATINI
Captain Blood

BY MICHAEL SCOTT
Tom Cringle's Log

BY A.D. HOWDEN SMITH
Porto Bello Gold

THE
EIGHTEENTH
CAPTAIN

NICHOLAS NICASTRO

MCBOOKS PRESS, ITHACA, NEW YORK

Copyright © 1999 by Nicholas Nicastro

All rights reserved, including the right to reproduce this book
or any portion thereof in any form or by any means, electronic or
mechanical without the written permission of the publisher.
Requests for such permissions should be addressed to
McBooks Press, 120 West State Street, Ithaca, NY 14850.

Book and cover design by Paperwork.
Cover painting by William M. Benson.

Library of Congress Cataloging-in-Publication Data

Nicastro, Nicholas.
  The eighteenth captain : a novel of John Paul Jones / by Nicholas
Nicastro.
    p. cm.
  ISBN 0-935526-54-4 (pbk. : alk. paper)
  1. Jones, John Paul, 1747-1792—Fiction. 2. United States-
  -History—Revolution, 1775-1783—Naval operations—Fiction.
  I. Title.
PS3564.I193E35 1999
813'.54—dc21   99-19233
                                              CIP

Distributed to the book trade by
Login Trade, 1436 West Randolph, Chicago, IL 60607
800-626-4330.

Additional copies of this book may be ordered from any
bookstore or directly from McBooks Press, 120 West State Street,
Ithaca, NY 14850. Please include $3.00 postage and handling with
mail orders. New York State residents must add 8% sales tax.
All McBooks Press publications can also be ordered by calling
toll-free 1-888-BOOKS11 (1-888-266-5711).
Please call to request a free catalog.

Visit the McBooks Press website at http://www.mcbooks.com.

Printed in the United States of America

06 05 04 03 02 01 00 99
10 9 8 7 6 5 4 3 2 1

This book is dedicated to
Mary Rutland, with love.

THE EIGHTEENTH CAPTAIN

I.

At 30, man suspects himself a fool;
Knows it at 40, and reforms his plan.
                    —EDWARD YOUNG, *Night Thoughts*

~

PAUL JONES conquers worlds at night, but would rather sleep.

Writing useless letters, you have wasted your last candle. Now you are sentenced to a torment of closely watched darkness.

He has been contemplating his invasion of India for many weeks. He spends hours sitting on a bench in the Luxembourg Gardens, thinking about the project. Crossing the Rue de Vaugirard, it occurs to him that the best route to the subcontinent is the ancient one—the one through Egypt. Jones stops, smiling to himself, oblivious to the manure cart bearing down on him, missing him by inches. The driver turns to curse at him in French, so he does not understand.

Fool! You have lost the capacity to navigate street traffic, much less the blue.

There would be war between England and Russia. Those powers, one pre-eminent at sea, the other on land, must try conclusions for the mastery of Europe. The man who contrives the plan to strip John Bull of her Asian possessions would earn the lifelong gratitude of the Empress Catherine. That monarch, if she be rational, must instantly restore his flag rank and furnish him with the fleet he needs. That slander about a rape in St.

Petersburg would evaporate like mist before the sunshine of his strategical genius.

But where will you get the money to post the letter to St. Petersburg?

Jones is dressed to go out by 7:30. At table, his porridge lies like wet plaster troweled upon his tongue—he has lost his capacity to taste his food. Instead, he sits there in his little apartment on the third floor, upstairs from an insurance clerk, next door to a composer of sentimental snuffbox inscriptions. He eyes himself in the mirror, wondering how the material of his stock came to be so dull, and how the lapels of his admiral's uniform coat happened to be of different widths—or are they? Jones stands up, steps closer to the mirror to see. Apparently, an optical illusion. It is only twenty to eight! He sits again, his eyes still on the mirror, and turns his head first to the right, then the left. From a distance of eight or nine feet, he fancies the gray hairs multiplying at his temples are barely discernible. He coughs—hack hack hack—and swallows. Egypt. (This only takes a few seconds.)

You think of everything but the Woman, don't you? But you see, you've thought of her just now! Her married hands lay in yours, years before, in some toilet at Passy with a coffered ceiling. How thin married hands are, how fragrant and trembling! To have that oh-so-aristocratic, perfumey knuckle beneath your nostrils again, and her married lips on the other side of a short space traversed by your quickening breath—La Vendahl! The woman was nothing to you. You must write a letter to her and explain.

With the tactical advantage of his plan, seven or eight ships of the line would be all he'd need, with an additional handful of frigates, of course, to bear his messages and convey his intelligence. Seven ships, less than five thousand men, and he would pry the lid off an Empire!

But I am so sick of the sea and ships!

It is 9 o'clock. Assuming he walks slowly, he could contrive to appear at the American legation just as Gouverneur Morris arrives at ten. He leaves his apartment and descends the stairs, noting, with some annoyance, that the buckles on his shoes have lost their shine. On the street, he stops and checks his pockets for his handkerchief, but finds he has forgotten it. No matter: there is a large Revolutionary rosette of blue, white and red on the curb, left there no doubt by one of the political processions that occasionally rattle his windowpanes and disturb the course of his thoughts about the likely occupation of Pondicherry. He plucks the rosette off the ground and uses it to buff his shoe buckle to a presentable luster, then drops it back in the gutter.

He encounters Morris some distance from the legation. Jones smiles, grasps the man's hand. Two old friends. Two men of quality. But there is an expression on Morris's face, an inertial disposition of his body away, away. . . . He still grasps Morris's hand, shaking it, smiling, smiling, and then coughing, choking, bending in two with the pain of it. Morris steps forward, alarmed. But what pleasantly cool weather for July, yes! They must surely dine together again soon, yes! Morris, reassured that his visitor is not suffering an inconvenient death, is once again receding, gravitationally attracted to the mass of the legation house. But Mrs. Morris is fine, yes! And you will surely receive your back pay by the next vessel over, yes! Busy, busy, must read over the day's dispatches. Barbary situation worrisome, dangerous. . . . But Jones has a plan for that, too! Just three or four sloops of war would do nicely, slipping into Tripoli with a handful of fire ships, but . . . what? No time to hear it all now. Well, now they have something to discuss over dinner, yes!

"By the way, might you slip this in with the pouch to St. Petersburg?" Jones finally asks, holding forth his sealed invasion plans for Empress Catherine.

A cloud passes over Morris's brow. They look at each other for a silent moment. The pretense hangs in the balance—two old friends, two men of quality—until Morris, with a heaviness suddenly afflicting his arm, takes the letter in hand.

"I'm in your debt, old man."

Morris responds only with his eyebrows, knitting them in a gesture that might be understood as either salutation, or puzzlement. Then he has turned away, waving faintly, and is gone . . .

But wait! They have forgotten to set the date and time for dinner!

Jones resolves to drop by the legation again later.

For the moment, he makes his way down the street, idly fingering the tasselled cord on his cane, picking his way around the rude barricades left there for no reason but to commemorate the thuggery of the mob. He has the whole day ahead of him, and he has already stopped in once to see Morris! He really must organize his time more wisely. He really must . . .

It is July the sixth. You barely remembered the date yourself!

A pang of self-pity taps his soul and descends, weightless, to the pit of his empty stomach. He knew no one else in Paris who would care. So he sets himself the task of whiling away, alone, the burdensome hours of his forty-fifth birthday.

II.

. . . We are not practiced rioters, we Parisians . . . nor have we settled
in our minds the difference between disturbance and revolution.
          —Louis-Sébastien Mercier, *Le Tableau de Paris*

~

CAPTAIN JOHN SEVERENCE could thank the changes of 1789 for his luck with Mlles. Nathalie-Anne Thierry and Thérèse Gualbert. Very early in their meal together, he placed one of his big buckled boots on each woman's slipper, under the table. He put them there before the soup was served, and had not removed them straight through the veal service. He showed no sign of changing his position as long as the beauties refused to acknowledge the weight on their toes. He was an American.

The condition of the women's apartment could only have encouraged his forwardness. They had struggled to prepare the way for him, cleaning the rooms themselves, curtailing meals to raise money for a reasonable cut of meat, making due with a minimum of fresh flowers. Thierry's out-moded lévite, and the frayed hems of Gualbert's English gown, could hardly have escaped his eye.

With no money to pay night servants, they were forced to serve the food before his arrival and let it sit, waiting for him. The conspicuous lack of domestic help was as obvious a signal as waving a white handkerchief in the face of Severence's scavenging manhood. Sensing their desperate poverty, he peered over the lip of his glass and cast suggestive looks. The women grew bored waiting for the inevitable proposition.

"I accepted your invitation with great pleasure," he finally said. "Might I suggest . . . an unconventional liaison, to consolidate our friendship?"

Gualbert looked to Thierry, who muttered, "*À trois?*" Her friend closed her eyes, nodded. The pressure on the women's feet increased. None of the three would meet the eyes of the others.

Severence imagined it was their modesty he was probing; in fact, they despaired only of their fee.

Mlles. Thierry and Gualbert had, after all, been intimately attached to the persons of Abbé Joseph Jean-Baptiste Abrimal, Second Deputy-at-Court to the Powdered Wig, and Botaniste-Royale Georges Busson, respectively, and had once enjoyed all the privileges, responsibilities and honors of courtesanship in the Outer Court.

Granted, Abrimal and Busson were only members of the *noblesse de robe*, talentless and unremarkable, and, accordingly, had been granted the honor of purchasing government posts at the going rate of one hundred thousand *louis d'or* each. Typically, these honors brought such debt on their two households that the men were obliged to recoup their investments by accepting cash "vocations" for particular services. Abrimal sold access to the treasurers Turgot and Necker, and was even known to drop helpful suggestions into the ear of Louis himself. Busson entertained a relentless stream of requests from gentlemen-scientists bent upon childish researches. In this way, these servants of the state trust became as rich as ever, and set about the project of finding mistresses appropriate to their wealth and station.

This was exhausting business, not unlike the pursuit of public office itself, entailing many hundreds of tiresome dinners, operas, and liquor-leavened anecdotes from notorious libertines. These latter each possessed road maps to the vices of Paris, high and low, and the wise shopper was well advised to seek those places where the maps agreed.

In Abrimal's case, the task was complicated by a peculiar and remarkable condition of abbreviated foreskin that made erection painful and intercourse impossible. The malady was not unknown in France: the King's own case had kept Queen Marie Antoinette herself waiting for seven years before the consummation of the royal marriage. It was eminently correctable, in fact, with a simple surgical procedure, but Abrimal was afraid of both blood and unconsciousness, and would not undergo the cure. His condition therefore called for a *demi-mondaine* of special talents, one versed in the arts of patient, contemplative arousal leading to satisfaction within the bounds of restful detumescence. (His wife, the legendarily devout Madame de Orvilles *(née)*, alas required a more vigorous bucking than he was prepared to mount.)

His relief was suggested to him by no less than Bishop Talleyrand. A tireless epicure, His Holiness referred Abrimal to one Nathalie-Anne Thierry, a small-town draper's daughter of such prodigious beauty she was coveted and deflowered by a local seigneur at the age of ten. Entirely ruined, she was turned out upon her own devices at eleven, and immediately prospered.

Abrimal duly invited Mlle. Thierry to a large and public supper. After slyly encouraging Mme. Abrimal to festoon herself with her most conspicuous jewels, he made certain the former was seated across from his wife, where these advertisements of his worth would shine suitably in the candle flames.

Mlle. Thierry's powers of observation did not disappoint him.

By machinations too lengthy to report, Abrimal supplanted the competition and made his way into Thierry's bed. In the full glory of sensual disarray, his new odalisque's true beauty blazed forth in facets he could only gaze upon in rising exasperation—eyes of almost oceanic greenness, amber ringlets about naked shoulders, an amply graspable bosom.

In minutes, Abrimal was on the floor, his culottes around his knees, squealing with the agony of his rigidness. Mlle. Thierry, a quick study, immediately comprehended the situation. Seizing a bowl of iced fruit, she dispensed with the fruit and poured the ice in Abrimal's lap.

Thus relieved, he then learned the full truth of Talleyrand's praises. Improvising a special method for Abrimal's "release," Mlle. Thierry dressed, powdered, and equipped herself fully, as if for a turn in the garden, then reversed the procedure in a slow and teasing manner. All the while, she kept vigil on Abrimal's member, slowing her progress or making disparaging remarks to control its stirrings. Abrimal achieved a state of gratification without a hint of pain. She was hired.

Thierry was also instrumental in ending Busson's search for a respectable adulteress of his own. Her acquaintance, Mlle. Gaulbert, was such a relentless competitor for their limited market the only peace possible between them was one of tactical friendship. Gualbert's coloring, as black and shining as a blackbird's, made the women chromatic complements to each other. (They had occasionally alternated in the beds of aesthetes rich enough to afford them.) It was not ordinary practice for such businesswomen to help each other, but their equivalent loneliness and ambition gave the women similar tastes. Busson was, in any case, happy for the referral.

Unfortunately, the scheme of their employment did not take into account the untimely Death of Leisure. Abrimal and Busson had taken close notice of the propitiating "reforms" launched by the Crown, from the liberation of the serfs on royal properties to the prohibition of tortures useful in obtaining confessions, to Louis's public stand against the *corvée* tax and his inexplicable tolerance of lies published by trash pamphleteers. They worried when he called the first Estates-General in more than 150 years, then grumbled at his further specification that the bourgeois Third Estate would send as many delegates to the gathering as the nobles and the Church combined.

At length, Mlle. Thierry's special talents became moot. Abrimal's mind could focus on nothing other than what he had heard at the Hôtel des Menus Plaisirs. Sitting with other members of the minor aristocracy on the outskirts of the auditorium, he found himself situated next to a wall, through which he could hear the speeches underway among the rabble next door. Voice after angry voice followed each other, hour after hour, punctuated by joyous yelps of exultation, applause, animalistic growls. The pox-faced Robespierre delivered two- and three-hour oratories fraught with verbs like "strike," "seize," and "universalize," and nouns like "tyranny," "emancipation," and "freedom." Abrimal lost his color for hours at a time; Thierry only had to utter the word *"égalité"* to keep his rising organ in check.

France was already an alien country to them by the time the demagogue Camille Desmoulins ignited the events of that awful July from atop a café table near the Palais-Royal. The Bastille itself meant little to Abrimal, Busson or even to the King, but its violation by the mob rudely deprived them of consoling rationalizations: to wit, the Duc de La Rochefoucauld-Liancourt's reply to the royal question, "Is it a revolt?"

To which the redoubtable Duke replied, "No, Sire, it is a revolution."

As if to underscore this, on the way back from the prison, the marauders happened upon a well-heeled gentleman, kicked him to death and stuck his severed head on a pike. According to horrified witnesses, the victim's clothing was scarcely ostentatious—plain-colored silk frockcoats were hardly seen anymore, and bagwigs were most definitely not *à la mode*. It was frightening to contemplate what the mob would do to a truly well-dressed man.

Suddenly, to the annoyance of our heroines, Abrimal and Busson rediscovered the rising value of their wives' extensive foreign holdings. The decision to take flight from the country was simply out of their hands, the men shrugged, since such important matters were always the preserve of their wise and beautiful spouses. Within two months, Abrimal, Busson, their wives, children and moveable assets were removed, to Austria. Neither man had offered a goodbye to his faithful mistress. Neither left behind so much as a *sou*.

It was a singular position for the two women. Ever since their mid-teens, they had had little difficulty in supporting themselves, but the atmosphere had changed. Suddenly, the social calendar was less and less marked by affairs at which they could advertise. Had they been practical, they would have fled to the revolutionary salons of Madame de Gondorcet or the Marquise de Chabonas, where they could be pawed by churlish intellectuals and bourgeoisie drunk on new power. Unfortunately, they were not only pampered whores, but patriotic ones, and could not stomach such men. Meanwhile, famine and shortages of available males added competition from the low end of the market. For the first time in the women's lives, their fortunes began to decline.

Stubbornly refusing the attentions of anything less than a Marquis, they tried to make due. Since they would not relinquish their apartment in the well-placed Left Bank neighborhood of Faubourg Saint-Germain, on the Rue des Petits Augustins, they alternated in offering their favors to the landlord's assistant. The carving work on their panelled dining room had to stop short of the completion of the over-door trophies (dedicated to poetry and the marital virtues, respectively). The laurel, peacock, and vole arabesques in their bedrooms were never finished. Instead of crystal, they had to make due with a nine-candle chandelier of plain, patinated bronze. They could not even afford to buy the yards of books they needed to decorate their new shelves.

History continued to turn on its head. Mlles. Thierry and Gualbert were bewildered witnesses as thousands of common women from the bakeries, butchershops, fruiterers and nutsellers marched past the Tuileries on the way to deliver their demands to the King at Versailles. Demands! Our heroines were still more bewildered the next day when these women returned, not only with their necks unstretched, but with the King himself and an escort of National Guard. Parisians cheered as wagons laden with flour followed the royal carriage into the city. Truth be told, Gualbert could not help but be infected by the surging republicanism, and went so far as to pin the tricolor rosette to her bonnet. Later, with the crowd no longer behind her, she threw the device in the trash. Moments later, she reconsidered and fetched it out.

They could not afford their scruples for much longer. Their courtly wardrobes were falling farther and farther behind the new, classically inspired fashion, and they could scarcely meet the expense of buying fresh ostrich feathers for their hats. They fought like common charwomen over the least expenditure, but, in fits of contagious self-pity, bartered jewelry and furs on evenings at the theatre and bouts of boozy despair. They were used to better, after all. It simply wasn't fair.

At last they compromised, resolving that new patrons could qualify for their services merely on the basis of income. Their financial straits eased throughout 1790, permitting them to improve their condition from free-fall to merely steady decline. They could eat, stay out of the rain, and purchase what minimal accessories were necessary to their trade, but little else. They began to consider marriage.

Just when they were sure they must settle for either twitchy bourgeoisie or callow Revolutionary officers with manure on their boots, they were reacquainted with the species of true Man. Gualbert saw him first, as he came out of the Hôtel de Ville in a most agreeable green carrick coat and Pennsylvania hat, grasping a cadogan cane not unlike Busson's. Closer, and she spied long black lashes beneath a high and handsome brow, a square chin, and lips curled in a shadowy smile as his rich blue eyes swept over her. More thrilling, he sported a most virile scar, a veritable *gouge,* from the bottom of his left eye down the angular span of his cheek. Who was this man, Gualbert wondered, who dared dress so well, so openly?

Acting on impulse, not calculation, she immediately threw a glove to the ground and waited for this vision to demonstrate his breeding.

"Is this yours, dear Lady?" Captain Severence inquired, caressing the glove as if her hand were still in it. She was careful to reply with a most encouraging blush.

Ordinarily, Gualbert's procedure would have next entailed a precise probing of the stranger's income, cash holdings, stocks, commissions, executorships, bonds, accounts, investments, degrees, associates, real equities, prospective inheritances, outstanding debts, gambling patterns, club memberships, recent invitations received, connections of influence, cut of clothing, and deportment of his footmen (if ascertainable). But these were not ordinary times. In her current desperation, she judged only on the basis of the glad chirping of her own heart—and his perfect manicure.

Without the taste and inclination to mount the barricades in search of the times' finest men, our heroines were starved for reputable male society. Severence was therefore invited to the Rue des Petits Augustins, ostensibly for late supper and conversation. Gualbert allowed her eyes to promise a bit more.

Surging into their elliptically shaped dining room precisely at half past eleven, he took an appropriate unnotice of their still-ungilt beechwood chairs, their console tables topped with second-rate marble, their tulipwood commode with unlaundered doilies. Instead, he reserved his sailor's interest for the Bassement wall clock/thermometer adorned with Cupid astronomers. He even correctly attributed the instrument's decorative inspiration to the 1769 transit of Venus.

"That was the very night of my conception!" Gualbert informed him.

"I understand, in fact, that Venus is at her greatest elongation this very evening," he added with careful indelicacy.

"You surprise me," Thierry chided him, "by hinting at the dessert course before the main is done. Are you Bostonians always such poor guests?"

Severence colored a bit, then smiled.

"Mlle. Thierry, I can't describe to you my astonishment at how often I am called a 'Bostonian' by otherwise educated Europeans. I myself am from New-York—from the green isle of Manhattan, in fact. But I believe the term you seek is American. That is what we are properly called."

"How fascinating!" trilled Gualbert. "A geographical trivium!"

"A trifle," Thierry corrected her.

"Just so."

Severence smiled into his glass. "You ladies speak the English better than most titled ladies I have known."

"Of course," said Thierry. "We are capitally educated. You might also be amused to hear our German: *Wir sprechen auch perfekt Deutsch, nicht wahr, Nathalie?*"

"*Wenn wir mit unseren deutsch Kunden sind,*" her friend replied.

"So you see, we are ladies of quality. You cannot just eat our food and then fuck us."

"He should not," Gualbert amended, her eyes dancing over his.

Severence looked down, thought a moment. The women felt the pressure lift from their slippers. Thierry was relieved to rub her numbed toes against the back of her calf.

"You are most surely in the right, Miss Thierry. My actions tonight have betrayed my rearing, which was in fact quite respectable. You must forgive me—I have been at sea almost constantly for the last dozen years. The trade has ruined me. I have lived with the language, smells, and manners of men. I have slept in bunks no bigger than two chairs lashed together. I have been obliged to see blood and piss through the hawse more times than any man should. My dear mother would not know me. I believe I have entirely lost myself."

His face lacked the slightest hint of irony as he made this admission. Gualbert looked to Thierry, who shrugged. Severence merely sat and drank, adding nothing more.

"Well," said Thierry at length. "It is well you say these things. It has been a long time since we've been regaled with such stories."

"Yes! Tell us of the sea! Tell us how you came by that scar!" Gualbert enthused, clapping her hands together.

"Not just of the sea," Thierry charged him. "In these times—in this age of little men—I want to hear of men of stature. Tell us of the heroes you've known. Tell us well—and you will get everything you came here for."

Severence glanced up, startled by her offer. Even Gualbert was obliged to stare.

"Nathalie! You might have thought to ask me before making such pledges!"

"Your position regarding Captain Severence has been clear all evening," Thierry replied. "Besides, I make no promises. He must first tell his story well. The verdict of the judges must be unanimous." She cast her cold eyes at Severence again, not hiding the quality of haughtiness she had learned from Abrimal. "Tell us then, Captain. Do you take up the gauntlet?"

He raised an eyebrow. "I wonder why I am being challenged to win the prize, when it is widely known to be for sale."

"It is for sale," said Thierry, "but not for money. Not tonight."

The women were staring expectantly at their guest. Severence drained his glass deliberately, as if to pique their impatience, then reached into the Canabas wine cooler beside his boot, lifted the decanter, and offered it to each of the women.

"*Merci, non,*" said Gualbert.

"Yes," Thierry responded.

When she was suitably topped, he sat back in his chair and crossed his legs absently. His recitation began quite unexpectedly:

> *While o'er my limbs Sleep's soft dominion spread,*
> *What through my soul fantastic measures trod*
> *O'er fairy fields; or mourn'd along the gloom*
> *Of pathless woods; or down the craggy steep*
> *Hurl'd headlong, swam with pain the mantled pool;*
> *Or scaled the cliff; or danced on hollow winds,*
> *With antic shapes; wild natives of the brain?*

He stopped, drank some more. Thierry narrowed her eyes.

"Poetry," she said. "Whatever is possible, in English."

"It is from a work of Edward Young, called 'Night Thoughts.' A poem much admired by the only hero I can confess to have known in his person. Have you ladies ever heard of Paul Jones?"

"The pirate?" asked Thierry.

"The lover," asserted Gaulbert. "I walked past him once at Versailles, as he stood at the Bassin d'Apollon looking at the Grand Canal. I remember he was quite gallantly outfitted in a blue uniform faced with white, and a single gold epaulet, in the style of the Bost—American navy. He was legendary at sea and in the boudoir. All the women spoke of him, but he was taken with a married woman—that Bourbon flirt, married to a general, whose name I can't recall—"

"Madame la Comtesse de Lowendahl," Severence reminded her.

"That's the one." Gualbert continued. "They were standing together, looking over the water as the sun set behind it. As I passed, I overheard her telling him there used to be a man o' war afloat on the canal—a frigate of thirty guns—set there just for the amusement of Louis XIV, like a toy. I remember Jones was quite indignant at this. He said something like, 'I spent half my career bringing honor on smaller vessels than that.' Then she laughed at him, and touched his chest with her hand, and he blushed. And that's all I saw."

Thierry smiled at her friend. "No one could see more making a casual pass in a garden."

"Was he wearing that medal of his?" Severence asked.

"It shone quite prominently in the sun."

"I don't doubt it. He may even have calculated the best angle to catch the rays."

"You clearly have very definite opinions of the man," Thierry said, impatient. "Tell us, then."

Severence would not be rushed. Whether it was because of the weight of the story or the promise of the prize, neither woman could say.

"You may be interested to learn that he resides very close to here, on the Rue de Tournon, almost broke and very certainly alone."

Gualbert frowned. "It seems hardly possible he should be forgotten, especially here, in Paris!"

"I'm afraid the years have not treated him well," he replied. Severence inserted a pause here, patently to cultivate an air of mystery. Thierry ruined it for him by waving her hand and insisting, "Well then, go on!"

"Before I begin, a warning. In the main, my association with Paul Jones was early in his career at war. Though there is heroism in those months— as much as in the entire lifetime of an ordinary ship's master—I can't claim to have known him during the cruise on the *Bonhomme Richard*, or in Russia. If you care to hear the well-known stories, you may consult any parlor historian. But at the risk of immodesty, I can say that no one knew him better during his first months in Europe, when the foundation of his fame was laid."

"A fair caveat. As long as you don't disappoint us," said Thierry.

Seeking a more sympathetic judge, Severence rested his eyes on the umbral charms of Gualbert. "A proper introduction to Paul Jones must begin some time before I encountered him," he began. "Even then, my career was influenced by his."

III.

FIRST, you must understand that I am a seaman by circumstance, not by nature. My original lieutenant's commission was issued by that polity that became New-York State after the War. Even this was something of an accident, as I preferred the smart uniforms of the British infantry to the rags of rebel service. I quite simply wanted to fight, without regard to the details of political allegiance.

...

Thierry frowned at this. "You cared nothing for your freedom? For the ideals of your revolution?"

...

At first, no. But there are worse sorts of men—such as the "sunshine patriots" Thomas Paine wrote of, who roar like lions when seated beside a warm hearth and bleat like goats in the face of real hardship. On the contrary, the more fighting I did, the more I came to care who won.

You cannot know, from this side of the blue, how many Americans bore allegiance to neither side. For my father, bless him, it did not signify whether tyranny ruled from Hampton Court, or Philadelphia. The assurance trade, our family's business, would hardly be affected, he told me. Indeed, many in loyalist New-York felt in this way.

I informed him of my desire to enlist in the King's Provincial Artilleries on the turn of my nineteenth birthday, November 12, 1775. For my trouble, I was immediately locked in a pantry until my intention should reverse. Twelve hours later, I was brought out before my father again.

"Are you still bent on such foolishness?" he asked me.

"I am," I replied and, on a spiteful impulse, added, "I am now further determined to cast my lot with the Continental Army. Long live General Washington!"

At that, my father's fists clenched and his face took on the aspect of a boiled lobster. I was ordered back to the pantry, and was compelled to stay there for the next three days. I had all the provisions I could use, to be sure, but my other bodily functions were ill-served by the pickle jar I used as a chamber pot.

Called before my father again later in the week, I was unwashed, unkempt . . . and unbending.

"Whence this stubbornness, boy?" he demanded. "Quickly, render an account of yourself before you return to your cell!"

This was, my dear ladies, a singular opportunity for a son such as me, tied by blood to a father such as him. I thought for a moment, and spoke the answer my heart had proclaimed many times from the pit of my despair, but had never before escaped my lips.

"You ask why I seek to serve? Very well, I will tell you. Come closer."

My father was, at that time, quite close to deaf, and had soothed his annoyance with his own disobedient faculties by sporting an absurdly fine cherry-wood hearing trumpet. He leaned forward in his chair, holding the vain instrument toward me. I bent to speak into it.

"For nineteen years, I have countenanced being your son, Sir. I have been your son despite the manifestly little regard you have for my sense and my value. I have mattered less to you than the account books you keep in your bed with you by night. I have held my tongue with news of my accomplishments, knowing you didn't care to hear about them. I have pretended to listen to you, however. I have known what little love you bear for me since the death of my mother, yet I have stayed your son. Of late, I have even entertained the plans you have laid for me without once inquiring of my opinion.

"These past months, I have learnt of another tyrant that claims me as his blood. He is no more harsh than yourself, I might assure you, no more sparing in his compassion. I can expect no kinder fate from him than from a career spent in your service. He may even kill me, but you will undoubtedly do so. He calls to me now."

As I said these things, I watched my father's face tumble to ruins. My words seemed to have all the effect of poison poured directly into his ear. When he spoke, it was a lowly sound, carrying no more force than the whisper of dead leaves blowing across a churchyard.

"And who is this man who seeks to steal my only son?" he asked me.

I grinned with all the cruelty typical of young hearts—a simpering destroyer pouring forth the wages of vengeance. "MARS is my real father!" I cried with appropriate melodrama. "I embrace him utterly! Let me fly to him, imposter! Release me from this detestable place, beast!"

Before I could even finish this declaration my father had his eyes averted, waving me away. I was escorted directly to my pantry again for a term I plausibly believed would never end.

Shoved and sealed within, my only relief was Esmeralda, our Jamaican housekeep. I had, in fact, mainly been raised within the protection of her bony arms—her protuberant cheeks and wise eyes were very possibly the first I saw as a babe. As she'd done for me a thousand times before, I expected her to smooth the way between myself and my father or, barring that, at least take revenge on him for me.

"Please, Emmie," I entreated her. "Cast a spell on him!"

"Now why do ya think Esmeralda knows de odeah?" she asked me.

"Because you're from down there."

"Oh, you're very, very bad lad, young boss. Why don' ya go down and tell de man you're sorry—for me?"

"Never!" I cried.

"What a foul mon! You're gonna live to regret that stubborness, boy."

"So be it."

And with that, she closed the door. My only solace, then, was that she had emptied and cleaned my pickle jar.

Scarcely eight hours later, I was pleased to see the door open, and light pour in from without. "Come on now, young boss," I heard Esmeralda speak to me. In the uneven light, I could see the gleaming of tears in her eyes.

"What's wrong with your eyes, Emmie?" I inquired brightly, relishing my apparent triumph. She was silent.

I rose, followed her, and found myself suddenly laden with hat, jacket, a packet of cakes, and a single, thin envelope.

"What's this?" I asked her. "Where is Father?"

"Your trunk is coached on de outside," she told me. "Th' young boss is to leave now."

I allowed her to tow me toward the door. Meanwhile, I opened the envelope and found a bank draft inside. The figure on it read 500 pounds sterling.

"Your inheritance," she said, her voice shaky. "To God wi' ya, now."

I was standing in the street. I turned to inquire further, but Esmeralda shut the door.

Need I emphasize my shock? It was the single major surprise of my young life, and I had brought it entirely on myself. I pounded on the door with my fists. I shouted up at the windows. I sat in the mud of Broad Way for an hour, waiting for a reversal. Just as she said, there was a coach there with my trunk loaded on it; the coachman watched my antics with a pronounced lack of impression, as if he'd seen it all many times before.

In my desperation, I made the further error of proceeding to my only other blood relative in New-York, my paternal aunt, Hope. She lived her spinster's life in a small house on the post road to Boston, across from the Common, where I had known her to live all her life.

I did, at the time, still cherish certain memories of afternoons spent there as a child, after my mother died. Aunt Hope was particularly talented in the realistic modelling of gingerbread cakes—she would make astonishing gingerbread soldiers, gingerbread horses, gingerbread ladies, gingerbread warships. One day, after my father had deposited me off there on the way to his offices, she prepared for me a tin of portly gingerbread bankers, each with the sort of swelling bellies and pothandle ears that suggested—I was giddy to recognize—my own dear father!

"Is it him?" I asked her.

"I don't know," came her reply as she virtually smirked into her apron, the accustomed paleness of her still-young face then driven away by crimson daubs of mischief and shame. "Do you want it to be?"

My response, even as a boy of five or six, was impossible to misapprehend. I placed one of the cakes flat on Aunt Hope's great oak table, balled my little fist, and smashed it to crumbs before her very eyes. Then I looked up for her approval.

"No, you devil-boy. That isn't any way for a proper young gentleman to behave. Watch me."

Aunt Hope then seized a cake of her own and, to my delight, dared to bite my father's head off! Still smiling, she then proceeded to chew him up very slowly.

She was, from that moment onward, my favorite relative. As I knocked at her door with my fist (her fine brass knocker had long ago been requisitioned for melting down by the rebels, like all the others in New-York), it was to me an absolute surety she would give me asylum. I was already busily plotting my independent career, and my revenge against my father, as I waited for her to come to her door and throw her soft, unconditional arms around me.

Instead, her housekeep came out and handed me a note, addressed to me in my dear Aunt's hand. Puzzled, I opened it and read the following lines:

"MY DEAR BOY," it began,

> *Let there be no question of the Tenderness I hold for you. I would like nothing better than to take you into my house now to serve as its Lord and Master, as is your proper Destiny. However, you must agree that without respect for our mutual esteem and Love, Concord with your own Father must take Precedence. Indeed, what purpose would be served in Perpetuating the Strife between you by offering you soft and easy Asylum? Better that you take this moment for most deep Reflection, and the guidance of Providence, to see you back to your Father's bosom, and the proper and necessary Reconciliation. For this reason, and this reason solely, I cannot open my door to you.*

And this was signed, I noted, with her full name of "Hope Elizabeth Severence," as if to make emphasis on her hateful gens, the source of all my grief!

I looked up at what I knew to be her bedroom window, and—yes!— could see the lace of the curtains move, and the silhouette of her figure in the candlelight, standing there above me, watching! Resentment surged through my body, and I cast her letter aside contemptuously, adding the dramatic exclamation, 'Et tu, Spes?' This gesture evidently had its effect, for the silhouette shrank momentarily from the window, and it did shake and bend noticeably, as if convulsed with emotion.

...

Gualbert shook her pretty head in a manner she calculated would show the bounce of her natural curls to best effect. "The poor woman. Her situation was impossible."

"No doubt your father sent word not to admit you," Thierry speculated. Severence appeared skeptical.

...

Perhaps. In any case, I was determined to make her suffer for taking my father's part. To wit: there was a small churchyard across the street from her window. Marching inside, I found a grave set in full view of her window, and with full theatrical effect, reclined upon it with my boots upon the foot-stones, my arms across my chest. There I remained for some four hours as night fell and the carriage driver swore and the neighborhood swine came by to sniff at me. I am fully convinced my Aunt, who made a kind of hobby of suffering, never took her eyes from me there. Finally I felt raindrops on my face. I briefly considered remaining on my plot nevertheless, but the instinct to comfort prevailed.

I rose from the grave and returned to the carriage without sparing a glance at my Aunt's window. My only command to the driver was to take me to the nearest rebel militia. I had resolved that would be the last day I would see either my father or my aunt while they lived.

A career of money-counting and self-loathing had rendered me a poor physical specimen, and my first days in the Continental troop were not auspicious. On my first day on the training green, our corporal, a devil by the name of Riggs, found it necessary to teach me the difference between my right and left foot by tying a red handkerchief around one boot. When this didn't work, he taught me by pounding on my toes with the butt of his firelock.

"Maybe we'd best send Severence over to the Provincials, since his soldiering would do them more harm than us good!" Riggs jested, humiliating me as I stood in the ranks. For a child of privilege who could have bought and sold every man in the regiment several times over, these were bitter lessons.

But the months spent in learning to march straight, load cartridge, and dig breastworks still didn't free me from my father's influence. No sooner had I struggled to earn my place as a private of the line when I was informed there was an officer's commission waiting for me in the captain's tent.

There could be no doubt whose perverse intelligence was behind this. At one stroke, my compatriots would become my subordinates. But I accepted the commission, in part because the uniform was more seemly, and in part to work my revenge for Mr. Riggs's cruelties. For the rest of his term under my command, I addressed him as "Corporal 'kerchief," and obliged him to wear a red hankie around his foot. Sometimes, I even placed him in charge of shining the boots he had once insulted.

Two months later, I received a note from Esmeralda. My father was dead, from pneumonia. She told me she expected no credit for his passing, because she knew no black magic. My father's dying wish, in any case, was that I not be permitted to attend the memorial. On that score, we were agreed.

...

Severence paused, staring into his empty glass. It was Gualbert's assumption that his tongue was silenced by the intensity of his emotion. Instead, he burped.

"I'm sorry," he said, realizing this *faux pas.* "I must remind myself I am no longer on the gun deck."

"I must tell you, you handled this affair with your father most ungraciously. You probably planted him in his grave," Thierry told him.

Gualbert laughed at her. "That is hypocrisy untypical even for you, Nathalie. When was the last time you wrote to your own father? How easy has it been for you to forgive and forget?"

"I make no claims to an exemplary life," came the sullen reply. "It was only an observation."

The Bassement clock struck nine. Under the hothouse gaze of the device's patinated Venus, a mechanical Cupid traversed the porcelain heavens trailing his quiver. Severence inspected both of his watches, both hanging from the fobs at his vest, and compared their progress. He nodded, replaced them, looked up again.

...

My first months of service in the Continental Army gave me ample experience in two faces of battle—defeat and retreat. At Brooklyn Heights, we withdrew before we were even engaged. At White Plains, I commanded a battery of field cannon but received only enough powder to find the proper range and run dry. We could only stand there, with cannon and ample shot, but no way to deliver it, as the King's brick-red formations swept us from the field. My mother city was now under occupation.

These were dark days, but not hopeless. The enemy's plan was obvious. We knew they would try to bear down from Canada while the forces in New-York would push north along the Hudson. If they linked, the united colonies would be disunited by a river of redcoats. Our strategy was equally clear—to stop them by whatever means possible.

That summer I was ordered north with a detachment of foot to deliver the same battery of cannon—still without powder—to Continental forces on Lake Champlain. Once there, I would place myself and my men at the service of our greatest military tactician, General Benedict Arnold.

...

"The traitor?" Thierry gasped.

"The same," replied Severence.

"And you trusted him?"

...

Be assured, Miss, that at the time of my tale General Arnold's crimes lay years in the future. By unanimous acclamation, he was the single greatest hero of our war. His march through the wilderness after the siege of Quebec was an enviable piece of generalship, not to mention a display of American frontier vigor sure to strike fear into any lobster-back fool enough to march into the wood after him. The keenness of his mind was matched only by his contempt for the predictable. Coming up from Saratoga, I was puzzled to see many sizable trees in the forest beyond Crown Point freshly reduced to stumps. Closer, I found Arnold's men were stockpiling many tons of green wood. You see, instead of pursuing the obvious strategy of erecting a series of cross-firing fortifications along the shoreline, Arnold intended to oppose the enemy's lake fleet with a scratch-wood flotilla of his own. The General was determined to draw his inspiration from the victory of the Roman "instant navy" against the Carthaginians in the Punic Wars—the passage of twenty centuries notwithstanding!

Upon reaching Arnold himself, I found he had little patience for civilized discourse. He was standing with several adjutants on a hill overlooking the lake, facing north. Only after I had introduced myself and my mission to him did he turn, a maneuver that revealed the famed limp he had derived from his action in Quebec. His face had a kind of long, pinched nobility about it, with a handful of chins and a nose that looked more appropriate for resting in the crease of a book than sundering the walls of Ticonderoga.

"Bear you any relation to the New-York Severences?" he asked me.

"I do."

"Capital," he said, and looked to his secretary. This bespectacled fellow immediately opened a vellum-covered tablet and read several names to me.

"The *Washington*. The *Enterprise*. The *Liberty*. The *Revenge*. The *Trumbull*. The *Repulse*. The *Lee*. Stop me when you've picked one, Lieutenant . . ."

"Excuse me?"

The man glared at me. "You have experience commanding water-craft, do you not?"

"I most assuredly do not."

The general looked at his boots, clucked his tongue, but said nothing. The secretary pressed, "You have at least travelled by water, eh? Observed naval operations *in situ?*"

"No more than the next man, I'd gather . . . "

"Then you are as expert a man as we have," Arnold snapped. "You will command the *Repulse*."

"General, my qualifications leave me far short—"

"You will load your ordnance aboard the galley the moment it is built," the secretary instructed. "Cut extra gunports as needed. Your vessel will be rated two 18-pounders, two short twelves, and six 4-pounders. We sail on August the 24th."

Then, just as you please, the man turned back north with his general, and said nothing more to me. This left me not a little vexed. In point of fact, I sensed the hand of my father in this new unwanted honor, though how he could reach forth from the grave to once again disorder my life was beyond my powers of explanation. "General Arnold," I began, "I must protest a charge that will inevitably be disastrous for the vessel and the seamen under my command—"

"We have no seamen to spare you. Your troops will serve as crew," Arnold explained without turning. "You are dismissed, sir."

"Then this is whole lunacy."

"You are dismissed!" he roared.

I walked away from him, seething, entirely wanting in the sort of discipline I could have had if permitted to climb the ranks on my own merits. In my instant antipathy for Arnold, I could perceive only the certainty of failure, not the magnitude of opportunity he was extending me. I never exchanged another word personally with him again.

Over the next few months, I began to apprehend the extent of the general's peculiar madness. Alas, this was no navy he was creating, but a rafted penal colony manned by the detritus of every militia in the vicinity. Only a very few of the men—the ones who had sprung from fishermen stock, for instance—had any experience afloat. Still fewer knew anything useful about rigging, navigation, or naval tactics. Indeed, the only corps of professionals among us were the carpenters and sail makers Arnold had had sent up from Boston, Providence, New London. These last constructed a fleet of a half-dozen stout, handy, if not sizable galleys mounting less than ten guns each, and a somewhat greater number of shallow-draft gondolas less than 50 feet in length and bearing three light guns each. Unfortunately, these very competent craftsmen would not be accompanying us into battle.

Against this pitiable force the British planned an overwhelming battery. Our agents in St. John reported that General Guy Carleton had at his disposal a ship of three masts with eighteen 12-pounders, a radeau with six 24-pounders, two dozen gunboats, and several ocean-going schooners he had ordered disassembled on the Richelieu River and portaged overland to the lake. His seamen and marines were professionals, and outmanned us two to one.

The only possible advantage available to us was tactical surprise, and Arnold was determined to have it by launching his fleet first. Every pair of hands in Crown Point was employed in one shipbuilding capacity or another. I knew nothing of the trade, yet found myself laying keels, bending sails and stepping masts, all under the strict direction of our imported experts. True to Arnold's word, our fleet sailed on August 24—a full month before Carleton was ready to move south from St. John.

And what a sorry sight it must have been, this motley armada working its way north, its captains lubbers all. I "commanded" the *Repulse*, but only in the loosest sense of the word. I led with a manual in my hand, issuing orders I had learned the moment before. It was fortunate Arnold waited until the wind blew from the south to sail—most of us knew nothing of tacking or running close-hauled. Still, even running directly before the wind, we suffered mishaps. The gondola *Revenge*'s bow gun was knocked loose from its slide in a collision with the *Liberty* in the straits of Split Rock. This piece plunged directly through the strakes, making a hole big enough to swallow three men. The craft sank in two minutes. All forty men aboard were saved, but three more precious guns were lost with the hull. I'd have wagered sovereigns to coppers Arnold's screaming reproofs could be heard from one shore of the lake to the other.

By our leader's uncanny foresight, our galleys were rigged with comparatively simple lateen sails that promoted, albeit by painful degrees, the improvement of our seamanship. We learned how to tack, or take a zig-zag course to sail in the direction of the wind. We learned how to "wear ship," or circle with the wind for emergency maneuvers. Before long we could adjust our sails for more or less immediate stops, and crack on sail to accelerate, until we could at least avoid collisions with friendly craft. My crew—the column of forty light infantry I'd commanded from Saratoga, complemented by thirty convicts from Albany granted amnesty in exchange for volunteering in the cause of Liberty—exercised the guns against Indians who dared show their faces onshore. According to Arnold, most of the local tribes were on the payroll of Carleton's agents. Even if they were not, I feared our habit of taking target practice against them was incentive enough for the savages to assist in speeding our destruction.

The purpose of our cruise that September was more than instructional. Arnold made good use of the time surveying the field of the coming strife, looking for a place from which to ambuscade the enemy fleet. He finally settled upon the west side of Valcour, a wooded island commanding the path of descent on Crown Point. Our force would dispose itself in a rough crescent stretching from the island to the western shore of the lake. Since the enemy would most likely pass on the east side of Valcour, the mass of the island would shield our presence until long after they had passed to our south. At that juncture, either we would surprise them from behind and most likely annihilate the lot, or they would detect us too late and be forced to beat back against the wind to engage us. Arnold reserved for himself, in either case, a positional strength out of all proportion to his meager firepower. I could not discount the pleasing subtlety of this plan.

By the end of September, our entire flotilla was assembled and set in position. The *Repulse* was placed far to the right, near the mainland shore. Arnold's flagship, *Congress,* anchored the center. Our force had magnificent command of the channel south. Our trap was set; all we counted upon was God's blessing and the arrogance of the British.

At first, both stood us in good stead . . .

...

Severence paused, suddenly looking around the table as if he'd lost something. Thierry and Gualbert could barely tolerate the interruption.

"Come along now, what happened?" urged Gualbert. "Did you triumph?"

Instead of answering, Severence stuffed his mouth with cherries before the women's startled eyes. Thierry only began to see his purpose when he spat the pits into his palm and arranged them in a rough crescent between the salt cellar and the edge of his knife. She emulated him with several plums, further befuddling poor Gualbert, who feared this communicable fruit-ravening madness would strike her next.

"Enough," Severence said finally. He had before him more than twenty cherry pits, laid on the white table cloth after the fashion of the American forces at Valcour Island. Meanwhile, a half dozen British plum pits were gathered some distance beyond, their sharp ends pointed in the opposing direction. ...

We were there for more than two weeks when we finally spoke them, their backs to us, more than a mile down the channel. It was an odd feeling I had at that moment, a fear that I was about to encounter something I never had before in uniform—victory.

But if anything is typical of the British character, it is the compulsion to watch their backs. The Scots and the Irish have taught them that. They sighted us when they were barely two miles beyond the island, and sent a mass of row gunboats at us . . .

...

One British plum pit peeled off the south-running formation and doubled back at the cherry pits.

...

Arnold, in the *Congress,* took the *Royal Savage* and two other galleys out to serve these boats a hot greeting. They began to exchange fire at 500 yards. Meanwhile, the British radeau and square-rigger had begun their attempt to tack into the action, but the wind was in their faces, and they were slow. The gunboats were finally reinforced by one of the British schooners . . .

The American cherry pits formed an arc around the lone plum pit. Another plum pit zig-zagged laboriously toward the action, until there were two plum pits facing the cherries.

...

The heavy British guns, and the aim of the British gunners, were taking a heavy toll on *Congress* and *Royal Savage*. The former was pierced in the hull three times. The latter lost half her rigging to British bar shot. The American fire was flying off in all directions. Arnold ordered a withdrawal, but in such a narrow stretch of water, with shredded sails, the *Savage* was unmanageable. She ran aground on Valcour. I was watching as her men struggled to get free of the wreck—and were immediately set upon by Indians hiding in the woods on the island. The Americans were exhausted, soaked to the skin, and mostly unarmed. They were slit like pigs by the enemy's tomahawks and knives. The *Savage* was, by the way, our stoutest, most heavily armed vessel . . .

...

Severence picked up one of the pits, dropped it in the cherry dish.

...

After witnessing this, our gunnery improved. The British schooner was hulled several times, and one fortunate shot even carried away her stern cable. This was important, because it takes two such cables, one forward and one aft, to keep a man o' war's broadside in one direction. Anchored at only one point, the schooner swung around on the wind until her bow faced us. Since she carried no bow gun, we could now rake her—bombard the length of her without facing any return of fire. This we happily did, reducing her to wreckage until a gunboat finally crept up and towed her out of range.

...

He lifted a plum pit, deposited it in the plum bowl.

...

Not long after, another big British vessel, the square-rigger, beat up within 500 yards and dropped anchor. This felt like quite a different thing, I will confess: there is no quality of fear quite like the one that comes when facing such a floating wall, studded with the mouths of cannon about to discharge. At Brooklyn and White Plains, the fighting had not lasted long enough for me to know fear. Here, I truly faced the prospect of eternity. On balance, I found the sensation to be rather disagreeable.

Immersing oneself in the exercise of fighting, I discovered, was the only remedy. I manned one of our 18-pounders myself.

The square-rigger dealt a heavy fire, working much mischief among our galleys. My *Repulse* was struck twice above the water-line, and one of my crew, an Albany cutpurse, was struck by a ball and cut clean in half. Before we dumped the shivering pieces of this man over the gunwales, I noticed his stumps were most curiously browned with heat, like those of a roasted goose.

Our fire sank one of their gunboats, theirs sank one of our galleys. By nightfall the enemy set the wreck of the *Savage* aflame, lighting the action with a most cheery orange glow. More feathered Indians came out of the woods to slaughter any Continental survivors escaping to shore. I remember the buckskin rascals squatting there on the beach, knives hanging between their knees, waiting. Our crew took to singing "Sweet Chastity sit by me a-while," as we wormed our guns, rammed the cartridges home, shotted, primed, aimed and fired, over and over again, until the stars came out:

> *Sweet Chastity sit by me a-while*
> *A-while beside me*
> *'Til the sun do rise up*
> *Yer dress fairly rough*
> *And a devil grow strongly inside 'ye!"*

"Scandalous," said Thierry.
"Delicious," replied Gualbert.

By early evening the Indians grew bored and left. The pyre of the *Savage* faded with only a ruby glow marking the resting place of her sturdiest timbers. As if by mutual agreement, both sides broke off and retired for the day.

At that moment, I did believe the battle would resume the next morning. Once fear is mastered, I'll warrant there's no sensation more thrilling in a man's life than that of working the engines of war on other men. I was almost sad to see the day end, and heartened when the signal was flown for a conference of commanders aboard the *Congress*. I dashed into the *Repulse*'s little quarter boat and rushed across the water to receive my next lesson in naval tactics from our little lawyer-Caesar. I was beginning to think the sailor's life agreed with me.

My ignorance of the true situation was breathtaking. The other surviving captains looked more like dead men than live victors. Most reported their vessels were taking on water. Powder and shot were running low. Arnold appeared the worst of all, with powder burns pitting his face and blood soaking his sleeves to the elbow. He spoke quietly and with much soberness, explaining that we'd yet to face the enemy's best, that the radeau would surely beat into the action tomorrow, and the three-master too. We would not survive, he said, as much more than charred flotsam and trophies for the savages waiting to pick over our bones.

There was no time to delay our escape. The wind was still at our backs, and with stealth we could slip safely along the western shore and back to Crown Point. The order was given, and as the meeting dispersed, I recall being clapped on the back for a fine fight, a good shot, or whatever. But I was aghast at my own foolishness in believing the scrap was going well so far, if not actually won! I returned to the *Repulse* with such a different air about me my men looked askance at the moody humors of their captain.

As I related before, much of my crew was comprised of furloughed prisoners with a patriotism much fortified by self-interest. Though pressed for hands, I had to assign five of my men to act as sentries against desertion, sabotage, or any such mischief criminal minds could conceive. When I explained our escape would take the galley back to the south, in the general direction of their Albany prison, some of the felons grew restive, daring to dispute their orders. As instructed by Arnold, I dealt with such insubordination in a quick and decisive manner. Their disposition beyond the end of our duties upon the lakes was not my concern, I told them. For the moment, their fate rested squarely with their cooperation and, above all, their quiet.

The operation began as soon as the moon had set. The *New-York* led the way out, her lanterns shaded to shine only in the direction of escape. The rest of the flotilla followed past the sleeping British, until it was the turn of the *Repulse*. I opened my mouth to give the order to put the tiller up—and found it stuffed full of another man's fist.

General pell-mell broke out around me as the convicts engaged in either a loosely organized mutiny or well-planned panic. The struggle was regrettably violent and tragically noisy. A half dozen prisoners leapt into the icy water and swam for shore, Indians be damned. One of my troops compounded the problem by firing off a pistol at the foolish deserters. By the time I had regained control of the deck, Arnold, on the *Congress,* had been forced to slip through before me. We were the last galley left facing the entire British squadron.

I took the helm myself and doused our lantern completely as an extra precaution. According to orders, no one moved on deck unless necessary for the operation of the rigging, and no one dared speak. The vanquished prisoners were laid up in the hold, where they kept up an ungodly racket that I hoped would be too muffled to attract attention.

We glided south, through the enemy's line. I steered as straight a course as I could, and cursed even the whisper of the wake behind us. We could see the masses of the vessels around the *Repulse,* looming up darker than the night sky, British chat and laughter audible on their decks. A half dozen gondolas fell behind us, and we looked up in awe at the great radeau, its 24-pounders nodding with the lake swells, and the square-rigger's masts reaching into the sky, tracing great circles around Cassiopeia's chair.

The end came abruptly. The quiet was shattered by a smashing sound at the hold-door, as if the prisoners had set to work on it with hammers and axes. Unfortunately, we had neglected to remove the repairing tools from the hold before imprisoning the mutineers there. As they set to regaining their freedom, I made straight for shore, hoping to beach the galley and escape into the forest with enough arms to ward off the Indians.

But the British are no strangers to stealth. Still a hundred yards from shore, we collided with a gondola running with her lanterns draped. We stopped, the drapes came off, and there was a beacon as fine as the Pharos Light marking us. My men asked if they might escape over the beam, but I forbade it, wishing to see no unnecessary loss of life. Another gondola rowed up, and a schooner. I suspected my sailing days had reached an end.

"*Mon dieu,*" breathed Gualbert, grasping Severence's hand in sympathetic alarm.

"Your Arnold must not have been the genius you thought," Thierry said. "His defeat was total."

...

Then consider this: General Carleton chased the rest of our fleet at first light, and with the wind at their backs they made excellent sail. All the American galleys that escaped that night were either run aground, destroyed by enemy fire, or scuttled. Arnold and his staff fled into the wilderness, leaving all of Champlain to Carleton.

Yet this "defeat" of Arnold was perhaps his finest moment. By building and using his toy navy, Arnold had cost Guy Carleton an entire season of campaigning. By late October it was too late for him to push on to retake Fort Ticonderoga before winter. Instead, he had to wait for spring, giving our defense time to prepare. The lobster-backs met Arnold again, a year later at Saratoga, and the outcome was far different. It was, if I recall, the Continental victory that brought France into the war on our side—thank you most kindly.

...

He nodded in the direction of Gualbert, who acknowledged his tribute with a gamely aristocratic inclination of her head.

...

IV.

. . . beings, deathless as their haughty lord,
are hammered to the galling oar for life;
And plough the winter's wave, and reap despair.
Some, for hard masters, broken under arms,
In battle lopp'd away, with half their limbs,
Beg bitter bread through realms their valour saved . . .

—YOUNG, *Night Thoughts*

CONSIDERING the history of hostilities between your two nations, I trust you ladies of France despise the British as much as we Americans do. I have acquaintances on either side of the ocean who believe utterly that there exists no more duplicitous race of men on the Earth, none who maintain such airs of arrogant civilization, yet want for the merest trace of civilized instinct.

Gualbert shrugged. "You must excuse the ignorant opinions of women such as we. I have found British gentlemen to be quite courteous and quick. Several have been generous to a fault."

"Generous! Ha!" Severence slapped the table, scattering his cherry pit fleet. "Ask the survivors of Danbury about the generosity of the King's agents. Go up to Falmouth, or to any peaceable and industrious Yankee who saw his village or farm fired by the cowards, and inquire after British quickness. Marry, ask any American seaman taken prisoner on the high seas by the Royal Navy! General Washington's men—bless them—were a desperate lot who lost many a battle, but at least the Briton respected them enough to exchange prisoners one-for-one. His Britannic Majesty considered the high seas, however, as reserved for Himself only, and regarded any American captured serving on a ship of the Continental Navy not as an exchangeable belligerent, but as a common criminal! Look for British 'civilization' among the poor souls of Mill Prison, dear lady, where the authorities take sport in baking ground-up glass into the prisoners' bread, and jeering the wretches' painful death! Or among my colleagues on the *Jersey*, set to rot on that cursed hulk to gnaw in hunger on their knuckles, befouled by their own droppings—!"

As he sketched these things in broad and graphic strokes, Severence noted well that excited flush that came to the women's faces, the titillated shortness of breath, the sheen of perspiration that betokened the complete and total engagement of their decadent tastes—

"Your point is taken," Thierry stopped him at last. "Please remember our sex has no ear for such talk."

"Quite right. My apologies. You have my promise, from this moment forward, to try to render the horrors I have seen with some degree of art."

"Thank you," said Gualbert.

"You are welcome."

"Your sudden passion puzzles me," Thierry observed. "The first part of your account led me to believe you didn't care who won your war. Now you place George the Third some number of circles below Beelzebub in the Inferno. Come now, are you a patriot or not?"

"Mlle. Thierry, the subtlety of your mind continually impresses me. Alas, that is a question you will have many occasions to ask as my account unfolds. I am, if I might bore you with a personal confession, of a rather philosophical turn of mind. Unlike Paul Jones, I understand both the anger of the Americans and the political expediency of British policy. I can stake either side in polemical discourse and argue with equal passion. Rather, in telling my story, I am sometimes shamefully guilty of divers tonal embellishments, entirely for dramatic effect."

"I understand," Thierry pronounced. "In truth, as long as I am confident you are sticking to the facts as you know them, I pay such effects little mind."

Gualbert touched his hand again, shaking her head. "No. Do be dramatic! Nathalie's facts are like the tart without the fruit!"

"Understand me, ladies, I am entirely committed to the satisfaction of both your respective tastes."

...

To resume, we were taken prisoner aboard the British man o' war *Inflexible* in the morning of October 12, 1776. As soon as the last American galley was either destroyed or scuttled by her crew, the rascals saw fit to take us out of the ship's hold and parade us across the quarterdeck for the amusement of the officers. You must understand, Arnold's escape from their fleet was a grave embarrassment to them, as were the high number of casualties sustained aboard their schooner, *Carleton,* which we had the pleasure to rake several times. Indeed, the damaged vessel was named after the great and vanquishing General Sir Guy Carleton himself. He appeared to us then, shining and resplendent in his accoutred rotundity. He was in an evil mood.

"Your lives were forfeit the second you took up arms against the Crown, your master," he informed us. "You have my promise, upon my personal honor, that you all will be hanged at the earliest pleasure of a loyal court!"

As senior officer present, I presumed to step forward and plead our case before the British conscience. I informed Sir Guy of my name and commission, of my respect for his tactical skill, and of my generally high regard for British customs, letters, and architecture. I assured him that, indeed, my grandmother often regaled me at bedtimes with readings from *Samson Agonistes.* In addition, I reminded him that the Continental Army held a number of British prisoners who would be equally ill-served by dangling from ropes.

"Treasonous churl!" he spat at me. "The Continental Army has no bearing upon this affair. Since you were taken on the water by men of the Royal Navy, you are pirates and have no such belligerent rights."

To which I replied: "Far be it for me to gainsay such legal subtlety. But the fact of our attachment to the Army is attested simply by our uniforms."

"A simple matter of dissimulation," came the answer, and he nodded at the ship's captain, who relayed the gesture to the master-at-arms and thence to the master-at-arms's mates.

Pikes and cutlasses were brandished, and we were ordered to strip. My men looked to me for deliverance from such humiliation. "This treatment is unbecoming of a civilized nation. Imagine, if you will, the state of degradation Christian warfare would fall to if every power treated prisoners—"

"You will be hanged!" he raged at me, and disappeared to his stateroom below.

My entreaties exhausted upon deaf ears, we were obliged to exchange our poor Continental uniforms for still poorer smocks and rags. Thereafter, the fifty of us were shut up inside a chamber in the hold no larger than twelve feet square, with a narrow grate and a pair of armed Marines set above us, for the entire week's voyage back to St. John. The pattern was repeated for the journey on the Richelieu River, bound for where we could not say, except that we were joined by thirty more prisoners from a letter of marque ship taken on Lake Erie. As we were marched to our next floating torture, I noted that several members of the *Inflexible* crew were sporting Continental uniform coats and breeches.

After four weeks on the second vessel, the stench of men fouling themselves had dulled my wits. Several of my men died on their feet and were not noticed until the burden of their leaning weight became a matter of argument for their unlucky neighbors. At first, lice were chronic pests. Later, these insects became treasured delicacies beside the weevil-ridden biscuits and rotted pork fed us as "food."

After a month at sea, the survivors of this devilish voyage were hurried up the gangways at the points of pikes and into full sunlight. Blinded by the sudden transit from almost total darkness, some of the unfortunates stumbled, and were rewarded by several lashes of the cat o' nine tails for their "clumsiness." Opening my own eyes at last, I was surprised and relieved to find myself in familiar waters, with the Battery of Manhattan abaft the vessel, and the green heights of Brooklyn on my right hand. But of the line of dark craft lined up in Wallabout Bay, out amid the tidal mudflats, I could conjure no recognition.

Since my absence from New-York, a fleet of British prison hulks had been established in the harbor to accommodate colonial prisoners. They were mostly old 64's with their armament, masts, and rudders removed, netting fitted along the rails, and a row of tiny air-holes cut through the sides to tantalize the prisoners' lungs. Anchored in the center of that fetid body of tidal back-wash, the hulks were notorious pest-filled holes—overcrowded, dank, virtually impossible to escape from. Stories of their horrors had long circulated among Yankee soldiers and sailors. I do not exaggerate to note that, by the contest's end, thousands of American prisoners died on the *Jersey* and her sister craft, for no more reason than the cruelty and neglect of their jailers.

...

"Oh, horrors! Horrors! How did you survive, *chéri?*" breathed Gualbert.

...

On the hulks, one does not "survive" as much as die more or less slowly. There are no words in the English or French tongues I could use to describe what awaited us there. Perhaps images alone will suffice: a thousand cadaverous creatures, clothed in rags, squatting in the dark, with all pretensions to civility ended, deprived of the faith in Providence to resist theft, buggery, murder. In the rain, dirty water seeping down on the prisoners, some of them already delirious with fever. The food—biscuits laced with red worms, beef rank enough to appear gelatinous, flour alive, if we were lucky, with nutritious maggots and aphids. Typhus and rickets lashing mercilessly through our ranks, tormenting the victims and subverting the sanity of the survivors. Elsewhere, prisoners organized into discussion societies or classrooms to ward off the madness, the incessant moaning, with absurd discourses on the nature of Utopia, or the teaching of foreign languages. One moment, men would converse genteelly after the fashion of the Platonic Academy of Athens, the next, they would contend like apes for a scrap of stringy meat or a husk of corn. In the four months I lived on the *Jersey*, I aged ten years. Even now, when Americans remark upon the early maturity of my face, I allude to my time on the hulk, and they entirely understand.

The guards were mostly Hessian mercenaries who would run us through with lances sooner than understand a word of English. The officers in charge were British, however, and upon reflection, I realized their lives were also sadly remote from the congress of humanity. Shut up on that human ant-hill, amid a stench so acute it was detectible a mile downwind, they occupied themselves with sundry pointless hobbies. One man, a warrant officer and a Liverpudlian, had a knack for carving entire model ships out of human bones. His work culminated in an ossuary version of the *Golden Hind* he could not resist displaying proudly to the assembled corps of prisoner-skeletons. The warden of the vessel was something of a gourmand, and used the ship's boats to fetch such things from the Manhattan inns as quail, venison, artichokes, cocoa, and oysters. I know this because prisoners with officer's commissions occupied the aft section of the prison deck, just a thin wall away from the warden's storerooms.

Sometimes, holding my ear to this bulkhead, I could hear the stewards moving about the larder, tapping tierces, sampling the wares, groaning with sensual pleasure. Through my beclouded brain, a compelling goal took shape: to breach that wall, to share the warden's unwitting hospitality, and to live!

As I remarked, the hulk was old, almost to say falling to pieces. An enterprising prisoner could, if so inclined, find himself a rusty nail unseated partway in some loosening plank and, if persistent, work it free. This I did, and though my little sabre was too small to be useful as a weapon, it was ideal for the fine work of prying open the temporary boards that separated me from my goal. Since there was no such thing as privacy in our floating hole, I recruited five of my former subordinates in the New-York troop to stand watch against the eyes of the guards and other curious prisoners, motivating them with promises that, under the circumstances, must have sounded like a description of the wonders of Old China: roast beef, mutton and hams, fresh vegetables and nuts, pound upon pound of fresh cod and haddie, sardines, cheeses, olives, eggs, pies, cream and biscuits, peaches and apples and grapes and mulberries and raisins and pomegranates and, best of all, Jamaican rum!

Our conspiracy took its hushed form in the darkness, and held firm through long nights of picking and prying through the hulk's aged flanks. Mornings, I awoke from the throbbing of my own bloodied fingers, regarding them with puzzled horror, like a stranger's appendages at the ends of my wrists. The nail itself, the slender metal reed on which sat the weight of our collective hopes, bent many times this way and that, but it never broke. At last, one charmed midnight, I felt the board shift, and worked it free!

In the enormity of my madness, I conceived that moment to be the happiest achievement of my life. Sniffing the air in the larder, after a month of smelling nothing but the odors of dying men, I knew my promises to my cohorts were not exaggerations after all. Yet still I was thwarted—the space cleared by my days of toil was still too narrow for my shoulders to slip through! My heart sank with the realization that I would have to work on, even with the prize just inches from my grasp, and the possibility of detection rising with every loose shaving and servant's errand.

Or—I could attempt a strategy I rarely preferred. I could trust someone. Mind, this was no small decision; if my agent happened to drop something in the larder, or through carelessness left some trace of his visit, punishment would fall heavily and indiscriminately on us all, and close the prize to me forever!

But the temptation was too great. Groping in the dark, I found a Richmonder to be the smallest of my co-conspirators and, with a clutch of solemn warnings, sent him through the boards. By the light of a solitary moonbeam, I watched the ecstasy of his expedition—the pickles, the cakes, the beer, the rum! The Richmonder became almost delirious, it appeared, with the sudden infusion of nutrients into his punished form. He sat down on the deck with a heavy THUMP!, a jug of Spanish port in his hands, cackling recklessly as I entreated him to return quickly—and with some morsels of food for his mates. I expected a steward to be attracted by the noise at any instant.

"I don't care. I'm dead if I come back anyway," he told me.

"If you return now, you can return again tomorrow," I promised. "And the day after that. You won't die. You'll thrive, maybe until the war ends, and maybe long enough to see your family again, your friends. You have land? What will it look like the day you walk down the lane, a survivor? What songs will the birds sing? What colors will the flowers bloom? What will your wife be wearing, what ribbons in her hair? How sweetly shall she kiss you, thanking Providence for your return at last? Think of that!"

The Richmonder looked at me, apparently stunned at this turn of dungeon eloquence, and, to my surprise, took a last gulp of port, and rose to return.

"Pickles, man! Don't forget the pickles!" I begged.

So began my second career on the grim old *Jersey*—that of gastronome, of bon vivant! After our initial feast of port and pickles, we set about perfecting our ruse, practicing the shipping and unshipping of our gate until it was well nigh silent, and virtually undetectable to the casual eye. Thereafter, every night, our Richmonder stole into the larder and took whatever fare pleased our fancy, and albeit that the meat was wet and raw, I've never known any culinary sensation to compare with it since. We took care, of course, never to exhaust a stock entirely, or to remove provisions likely to be noted the next day. I do believe that, given the rate at which the warden replenished his stocks, we could have lived on his largesse indefinitely.

Yet even with our perfect thievery, this bounty was not without additional risk. It was not long before the guards began to notice an improvement in our color. Flesh was beginning to conceal our ribs again, and musculature reappeared upon our bony arms. To the further befuddlement of our jailers, this renaissance was confined to just six men with no apparent connection between them (we took the precaution of disassociating ourselves during the daylight hours to blunt speculation of conspiracy). Regarding our robust good health, the British shook their heads in wonder at the imperishable Yankees, thriving (even growing fat!) on less than a rat's portion of condemned food. We heard speculations abound on the nature of this new, indomitable sort of frontier man— speculations we were happy to encourage by falling with delight upon every scrap of rancid meat and fungal bread served to us. Licking our fingers, we were sure to thank the stewards for the generous repast. Some of the Hessians took to eating prison fare too, hoping to derive a similarly healthful effect.

...

"Did it ever occur to you," Thierry asked, "to share the benefits of your cleverness with more of your fellow prisoners?"

Severence frowned. "You touch upon a delicate issue. This was, in fact, a point of contention between members of our cabal. Four of them suggested the very matter you raise. Myself and the Richmonder agreed with the sentiment, of course, but reasoned that the amount of food necessary to feed a thousand men would certainly be missed by the stewards. Feeding any number less than the total would in principle be no better than the current arrangement. In addition, feeding more mouths also meant more mouths could betray our trust."

"Of course. A most compelling argument." said Gualbert.

"Hmmm," Thierry turned away, skeptical.

...

In the end, my term aboard the *Jersey* was cut short by a most unexpected circumstance. One day in February, while we prisoners were treated to a few frigid turns up in the open air, we watched a cutter come up from the shore and land an officer and two soldiers on the hulk. A message was whispered to the warden, who regarded the officer with no small degree of incredulity, shaking his head. Taking a position at the break in the quarterdeck, the officer then read an announcement to the prisoners:

"By order of the Right and Honorable Board of Admiralty, by whose merciful beneficence you have hitherto been maintained in comfort and safety, in spite of the seditious and dishonorable nature of your deplorable crimes, a general clemency has hereby been granted, this day of February 15, 1777, for twenty-seven of your number. The names of the amnestied will read as follows—"

And he commenced to read names from the paper, one after another, of men who would immediately know freedom again. Some of these blessed souls were so dulled by their ordeal they did not understand the nature of this miracle, and had to be pushed forward by their kind but heartbroken comrades. Others fell to the deck and shed shameless tears, then had to suffer the agony of parting the frozen bond their flesh instantly made with the icy timbers. But this pain was trifling. They were led down to the cutter straight away, eyed enviously by the rest of us.

"Number twenty-four, Hopkins, Elijah J.," the roster continued, "Twenty-five, Peterson, Samuel A.; Twenty-six, Severence, John L.; Twenty-seven, Thiel, Robert Anthony. So ends the list. May God Bless King George III!"

The British offered up three half-hearted cheers, and someone grasped my shoulder. Turning, I regarded the Richmonder, who pulled me along with him.

"That's us, mate! We're free! Come on, now!"

Indeed, I did think I heard my name called near the end of the list. But what were the chances, with only twenty-seven picked out of a thousand? It was most suspicious.

...

"Suspicious? Who cares? You won your release!" Gualbert cried.

"That was the curious aspect of my reaction," he said, his eyes flitting to the passing carriage lanterns outside the women's dining room window.

...

I believe I was rendered incapable by the depth of my ill luck to appreciate my immediate good fortune. Instead, I suspected the hand of my father in it all! I sat in the cutter with the others, and to their surprise, did not exult or weep over my freedom but instead cursed my patrimony, my very name! There I was, surviving so very well, I dared to think, and what befell me but an untimely release? I was mad. It was several moments before I remembered that my father was dead after all. My thoughts settled—I began to laugh out loud. No one dared sit beside me for the rest of the run to shore.

My last glimpse of the *Jersey* was from several hundred yards away, its outlines squatting grimly in the water under a stretch of dour cloud. I could see the day's detachment of prisoners filing out on the mud-flats under guard, pushing a barrow filled with a tangle of gray bodies. They rolled the barrow direct to the cemetery and set to picking at the sodden ground. The rank airs of muck at low-tide, dead fish and farting corpses moved the guards to tie handkerchiefs around their mouths and noses. Just as our cutter reached shore, the detail upended their barrow over a shallow trench, and I saw the night's toll of patriots tumble free.

V.

*I may be wrong but in my opinion a Captain of the Navy ought to be
a man of Strong and well connected Sense with a tolerable
Education, a Gentleman as well as a Seaman both in Theory and
Practice—for, want of learning and rude Ungentle Manners are by
no means the Characteristick of an Officer.*

—John Paul Jones, in a letter to Joseph Hewes, 1776

NOW BARRING some unlikely fit of common conscience afflicting the
Admiralty, there was no plain reason for them to spare themselves the
pleasure of reducing 27 men to a wasting death through some notion of
"merciful Beneficence." Putting aside some supernatural agency, I began
to inquire after an earthly reason as soon as my health made such an inves-
tigation practical.

Fortunately, Esmeralda still resided on my father's farm on Broad Way.
Clad in *Jersey* rags, whiter than a shade, I knocked on the door and presented myself as "John Severence, orphan of primogeniture." The good
woman's eyes widened, looked me up and down, and resumed the weeping she'd begun the night of my ejection. She cried as she led me within,
and cried as she warmed the kettles for my bath. She did this, though she
was least to blame for the circumstances of my departure. Despite my
father's acts, and the mantle of self-pity I had spun for myself, I could
never truly deny I had ever known kindness.

The largesse of the hulk's larder helped to shorten the term of my
recovery, and before very long I felt capable of resolving the mystery of
my unexpected freedom. Esmeralda made a startling confession:

"I'd be mor'shamed to own it, young boss. I know ya were comin' up from de papers, but was much afraid to see ya, knowin' ya sufferin' aboard Sat'n's ship un' blamin' me for it."

"Blaming you? Why?" I laughed at her.

"They be comin' back different men. Their heads go soft."

"My head's no softer than usual. Tell me now, what papers did you read that told of my release?"

She went off and returned with a handbill, doubtless issued by some local separatist press, reporting that a prisoner exchange was in the offing due to the success of a certain Continental vessel (which remained prudently nameless) in intercepting a British transport before it could berth with a load of winter uniforms for the Canada army. In addition, some four dozens of captives were taken, including several British soldiers and their families! My appreciation of this action was tempered only by my burning curiosity to find out the identity of the brave captain who had finally turned the tables in our favor. Of this, there was no clue, except the propagandist's boast that "said vessel will sally forth again, to mete out further measures of punishment on British shipping from Block Island to Nova Scotia."

This theatre of operations clearly suggested a base in New England, most probably New London, Boston, or Portsmouth. To Esmeralda's sorrow and relief (she could occasion both, being of a puzzlingly intricate mind), I informed her of my intention to depart the next day to make contact with the brave Continental Captain who had won my freedom for me.

She extracted a folded letter from her apron. "If ya be gone soon, I might give this to ya now. It's been left far ya forever 'n a day, after ya left. Aunt Hope sent it over, but I dare not show it t' the Old Boss. So I hold it."

She held it out to me. It was most considerate of Esmeralda to assure the proper delivery of Aunt Hope's letter, I knew. I even retained some thimble's measure of warmth toward the old woman, despite her betrayal. Unfortunately, I retained a full measure of anger as well.

I thanked her and stuffed the packet in my coat with full intention to dispose of it later, out of Esmeralda's sight. I also took with me, out of a chest of my father's worldly possessions, his cherry-wood hearing trumpet. This I kept less out of residual affection than a desire to win some trophy from the years of enmity and struggle with my nemesis. Of course, I could not at that moment envision the use I would finally find for the device.

The next day I set out to rejoin my regiment at Fort Montgomery in the Hudson Highlands, and thence on temporary convalescent leave to New England. Upon making inquiries after my savior captain in Providence, Rhode Island, I was directed to Boston, where I was told I might find the ship of war *Alfred*, lately under the command of one Captain John Jones of Virginia.

I then set my mind to the problem of securing passage to that city, in spite of the British blockade of our ports. An overland journey would have been a lengthy ordeal, possibly longer than I could stay away from my post. As an officer of some experience, I was of no small value back with my regiment as soon as possible.

With disappointment, I contemplated giving up a personal meeting, and instead sending a suitable letter of gratitude to Jones in care of the Navy Board in Philadelphia.

Yet I had not counted on the certain peculiarity of the mariner's world. In port, that world is an exceedingly small one, confined to the coast cities and, in some cases, just a handful of city streets close by the wharves. Acquaintances, though rostered on different ships, will meet time and time again if the ships frequent the same ports, often without design. The phenomenon was about to strike me as well, with regard to this man, John Jones.

I was walking back to my inn in Providence, my mind entirely occupied by thoughts of the return journey before me, when my attention was compelled by what sounded like a street melee. Pushing my way to the front of the collected onlookers, I found three men in the center: one, a hulking figure in an old tricorn hat, with stains of perspiration running down the front and underarms of his blouse, bearing a short bludgeon; the second wiry, dark-suited, bearing a clutch of documents; and the third, a short fellow, dressed in the blue and red-faced uniform and single gold epaulet then standard among captains of the Continental Navy, brandishing a sword.

"We bear the court's warrant! You must desist!" exclaimed the dark-suited man from behind his hulking comrade. This coward was undoubtedly a lawyer.

"Come down now, Cap'n Jones," the man with the bludgeon said, a strain of weariness in his voice. "I'm only about to do my right duty."

At the mention of this name my mind flew immediately to Captain John Jones of Virginia—but it seemed too unlikely a happenstance—

"Th' man who touches me begs t'be clipped!" replied the defiant little Captain, his voice marked by a trace of a musical Scot's burr (an accent Jones strenuously sought to suppress, I later learned, but that still rang though on occasions of great emotion). The crowd responded to his threat with a hearty cheer and a cry for blood.

"Oppose this man at your peril! He is a King's officer!" the overwrought lawyer cried. The crowd laughed at this dubious honor, those days outright dangerous in a town of virulent separatists. The Captain quickened, surged forward. "A King's officer, eh? By God, I have a commission t'run him through then!"

"He lies! He lies! I ain't no King's officer!" jabbered the other, raising his bludgeon to cover himself.

The lawyer dashed his papers against his comrade's back, shouting "Blast him, why don't you take him?" to which the "King's officer" retorted, "The devil—don't you see his poker?"

At that, the latter turned his back on the captain and pushed free of the crowd, leaving the lawyer to face his quarry alone. This confrontation did not last long, as Jones cut the air with his sword this way and that, and the other did turn tail and run for his life, but not until the captain had landed a blow with the flat side of the blade direct upon the lawyer's rump.

The crowd derived much humor from this Punch and Judy show, and the captain earned congratulations from many a low-born admirer as the audience dispersed. But he did not appear to notice these, concentrating rather on the perfection of his sword-blade, and its proper sheathing in the scabbard. When I placed a hand upon his arm, he suffered a startle.

"Mark me, sir, my sword cuts all points o' the compass!" he threatened, his posture defensive again, his hand partly withdrawing the weapon.

"Nay, nay, my business is peaceable!" I assured him, opening my empty hands before me. He glanced at them, my uniform, and up at my face (for he was a good six inches shorter than I), but still did not take his ease.

"State yer business!" he demanded, most disagreeably.

"Know then, sir, I am Lt. John Severence, lately of the Third New-York Artilleries, more lately of the prison hulk *Jersey*, from which I won my release with the help of Captain John Jones of Virginia. If you are he, I would offer my thanks, and the thanks of 26 others, for the valor of that action. But I now doubt you could be anything like the gentleman responsible, much less himself, so I will vex you no further."

He frowned more deeply. Much frustrated by this behavior, I turned away from him and continued my journey to my inn. Before I took six steps, I was halted again by a hand on my arm. Jones had run after me.

"Accept a gentleman's apology, Lieutenant. I am the man you speak of, and your words are a tonic to me. It was just that . . . the pass was awkward."

Strangely, the man before me then seemed entirely transformed. Where, during our last exchange it had appeared sharp, focused, impossible to faze, its natural angles were now much softened with solicitousness, even fear that I would prove offended by his action. The lowborn burr in his voice was suddenly gone. His small body seemed charged with nervousness— the eyes that had before flashed green fire at his enemies now smiled amber contrition. Indeed, I had many occasions later to puzzle over changes in this aspect of his coloring, where a good fight made him look dark as a Moor, social intercourse brought out the blonder, more honeyed Jones.

I shrugged. "It is forgotten."

He grasped my hand and shook it with almost fraternal warmth, a great smile of relief on his face.

"Then you will dine with me this evening? At my rooms?" he asked, adding, "I'm much interested in the war news from the interior."

As my coach did not depart until noontide next, I saw no grounds to refuse this offer.

"Good!" he said, clapping me on the shoulder. "You're a Severence, aye? Is that of the New-York Severences?"

To spare his confusion, I limited to a simple nod my reaction to this damnable question.

...

"I must own, dear ladies, that I was not disposed to thoughts of friendship with the man on the evidence of our first meeting," Severence said. "At worst, I judged him a bully and perhaps even a coward;

at best, a fool. Later, there was no question of his courage, yet my ambivalence persisted throughout the years of our acquaintance.

"How ungracious!" Thierry asserted. "You owed your liberty, if not your life, to him!"

Gualbert looked at him sadly, laid a soft hand on his sleeve. "Yes, *chéri*—your heart is hard—"

Severence smiled into his lap, then looked up at them with an air of bemused tolerance. "You don't know Jones," he told them. "I was not alone in my sentiments: indeed, I stood as his champion on more than one occasion. But I did not love him. No one did. Mark this fact well, and know, if you were confronted with him as well, you could not love him. Among men, the best Jones could expect was acquiescence; among women, girlish celebration of his heroism. I say this, fully knowing the measure of the man—in battle, I would gladly twist the tail of Satan on Paul Jones's order. Yet there were times I fervently desired to take a simple liking to him, and struggled."

"These are subjectivities," Thierry said, wearily.

"Tell us about your dinner with him!" encouraged Gualbert.

...

Two hours before the appointed time, I received a note from Jones at my rooms. This, I assumed before reading it, would be a cancellation of his hasty invitation. But I was wrong: rather, I broke the seal and found myself gazing at a note, set down in a most agreeably skilled hand, to the effect of begging my pardon, but would I mind if an additional party took dinner with us that evening?

Though I appreciated the care Jones took to apprise me of the guest list, I was surprised to find such conscientious formality, such a feminine refinement of manner, taken not by a diplomat or a dandy, but by a man employed in the business of making war! I tried to frame my reply as elegantly as his question, but failed utterly, my skill with the pen clearly much the inferior of his, despite (as I learned later) my advantage of formal education.

Arriving at the appointed tavern, and shown into the private dining room Jones had reserved for the evening, I was immediately surprised at the appearance of Jones's guest. She was an African Negress of gracile form, thin hands folded before her, her dark and thoughtful eyes flitting about the room in evident nervousness. When her eyes rose to meet mine, they instantly fell to the floor in one of the characteristic mannerisms of racial servitude. This made her presence at the table doubly puzzling.

I have seen your French custom of banishing certain inferiors from your tables, based upon the circumstances of class and birth. In America, we do not seat ourselves with blacks—or more precisely, with slaves—but the distinction hardly operates. Though I had known Esmeralda, my father's domestic, all of my life, I had never once witnessed her taking a meal, much less broken bread with her myself! I fully expected this young miss to excuse her momentary presumption and depart for the servants' quarters. Instead, Jones rose to greet me.

"Lt.-Severence-of-the-Manhattan-Severences!" he sang out, clasping my hand with unaffected zest. As ruffled as he appeared before, in the street, Jones fairly gleamed now, his aspect meticulously neat, his uniform impeccable, the hilt of his sword polished to a high sheen, his hair swept back perfectly and tied behind (except for a solitary lock, a dash of characterizing unruliness, curling over his brow). Again, his refinement shamed me, with the flecks of road mud peppering my crumpled uniform, my arrival a half hour late as well! Worse, I was ashamed to find myself grasping his hand lightly, like a woman.

He turned to introduce me to the Negress, who had risen to her feet. She wore a simple dress of white linen.

"Lt. Severence, I've the pleasure to present to you the celebrated Phillis Wheatley, poetical prodigy and favorite of the Nine!"

I looked at her again. Indeed, this Phillis Wheatley's reputation had reached New-York and far beyond with the publication of her elegy to the memory of George Whitefield, much beloved preacher of the Great Awakening, some years before. I am no judge of such things, but I recall a general sense of astonishment that such verse could course from the pen of a young girl, much less a girl new to the English tongue, still less a Black one. Her renown came to the attention of George Washington, who received her for thirty minutes, and spread even across the Ocean to the literary salons of London and Paris. She was, in a phrase, the most accomplished of her race in all the Continent. But what was she doing there, with Captain Jones of Virginia?

I extended my hand, which she was too modest to presume to touch. However, her eyes were bright and mirthful, and it was with some familiarity that she looked to Jones and entreated, "Might I sit at the side-board this time, my cruel Captain?"

"I won't have it," he pronounced. "You will take your privileged spot, rather, at the head of my table!"

At that moment, all in the room—myself, the poet, the serving boy— except for Jones exchanged such worried glances we might have been engaging in something outright illegal, not merely eccentric and outrageous. The Negress, for her part, obeyed him with the most reluctant stiffness, and touched only the merest morsel of her food. To her credit, she knew her station better than her overweening host, and evidently possessed the greater measure of wisdom.

I was still most interested in the feat of gallantry Jones had performed to compel the Admiralty to trade away seamen prisoners. Jones obliged with a ninety-minute narrative of his capture of the British transport ship *Mellish*. Though the exploits he described as captain of the Continental frigate *Alfred* were worthy of pride, he related his tale in plain, dry fashion, betraying even a note of disappointment that he did not capture more enemy ships, destroy more enemy strongholds. When I asked him what the British did to frustrate him so, he scowled.

"I was charged at the outset to accomplish two simple objectives: first, to strike at Cape Breton in Nova Scotia, where American prisoners were forced into coal mines to dig with their bare hands, and second, to intercept the convoy of colliers upon which the enemy army in New-York depended for winter fuel. En route, we were blessed to capture not only the *Mellish,* with its load of British officers' wives and their children, but also a fully laden brigantine, and a snow bearing fish oil to the West Islands.

"But instead of finding courage in these successes, my crew petitioned to return immediately to Boston, as if they were thieves content with their share of ill-gotten loot! I appealed to their humanity by describing the travails of their American brothers toiling in the filth and darkness of the coal mines. Alas, the meanness of their hearts blinded them to these facts. Moreover, I was stunned to witness polls and straw votes being taken, as if decisions on a vessel of the Continental Navy were made in the manner of a Massachusetts town meeting! My patience exhausted, I thereby made our course to Cape Breton an *order.*

"It was a sullen and mutinous crew that I took into battle in enemy waters, having learned from the captain of one of our prizes that three British frigates were sweeping the waves to find us. We pressed north, blasted by storms, anxious lest an ambitious prize crew would make off with one of our three captives in the dark. We were, in actual fact, most foully deserted by the one other American vessel in our little squadron, the sloop *Providence,* under cover of a snowstorm. After this betrayal, every hand on deck and below quailed pathetically at every piece of flotsam we had occasion to see. The panic was general when one of our topmen finally sighted three strange sails on the horizon, making toward us.

"Their fears proved false. When these vessels were hull-up, I could plainly see these were no British frigates, but the very colliers we'd been sent forth to capture or destroy! What's more, their escort had somehow 'come detached, leaving them without defense. We came to and approached them, flying the British ensign. Fortunately, they stayed together, and a few shots across their bows were enough to induce their surrender."

"Bravo, brave Captain! Another virtuoso performance!" exclaimed Miss Wheatley. He did not respond to this, apparently ill-used to accepting compliments.

"We were now charged," he continued, "with guarding not less than six captured vessels. The snow and the brigantine I right away sent to Rhode Island with their prize crews. The *Mellish* was too valuable to trust to luck. Besides, my crew was reassured by the spectacle of all that prize money floating nearby, and would not stand for letting it out of their sight. Yet another betrayal lay in store when I questioned the colliers' mates in preparation for our raid on Cape Breton. Apparently, our American patriots-in-chains, the focus of all our struggles, had escaped the coal mines to freedom after all—by becoming the newest recruits in the enemy's Navy.

"Not unusual, given the choice," I commented. I was accurate, but this earned me a chilly glance from Jones. He then continued his tale like a man determined to follow through on a distasteful chore.

"Our errand mooted, we turned back. Our luck brightened somewhat when we intercepted and captured *John*, a letter-o'-marque mounting ten guns. We again had the happy problem of holding more prizes than we could possibly defend. More seriously, a new sail appeared, and this one was indeed a British frigate, one we later learned was H.M.S. *Milford*, 28 guns. This ship had the capacity to deprive us of our prizes most handedly, being more than a match for poor *Alfred*, much less with our guns and crew spread over five other vessels. Accordingly, I showed the British ensign again, and informed the ship's master to conduct our vessel in the manner of a Royal Navy escort.

"To the *Milford*, we appeared to be conducting the three colliers to resupply General Howe in New-York. Our ruse succeeded for some hours, until her captain brought her too close to the *Alfred*, and I was forced to detach myself and attempt to bait the enemy away from the prizes. Unfortunately, these could not make good their escape before the British captain perceived the deception, and bore away. Turning, I poured a broadside into her, then ordered all reefs shaken out and made a dash for Boston. The *Milford* pursued, but by Providence we made better sail. We were more than three leagues ahead when the enemy abandoned the chase and, casting about, found *John* coming up lazy from astern!

"I had, much earlier, ordered the midshipman I'd placed in command of that prize to drop back and count the enemy's broadside, so I might better anticipate whether we could best him, or he us. But that order was plainly countermanded by circumstance. The boy's plain incompetence and unwillingness to defend his command cost us a perfectly good prize."

"But you still compelled the exchange of the *Jersey* prisoners, and returned with four other good prizes," I reminded him.

"It might 'o well been five."

"Captain Jones will never be satisfied while there are any British ships still on the water," Miss Wheatley observed.

Jones shifted forward. "England commands more than 130 ships of the line, one hundred frigates, forty sloops of war. Against which the colonies can range—what?—a few dozen motley craft, some converted merchantmen."

"You make the task sound hopeless."

"On the contrary!" he replied, now quite animated. "Large as the Royal Navy is, her commitments are larger. She cannot be everywhere at once, protecting all of her vital interests with adequate force. Where she is not, on that bare stretch of jugular vein, that is where you will find me."

He was clearly in earnest as he stated this. Truly, at that moment, watching the pure, untroubled, elemental determination on Jones's face, the thought occurred to me that, with men like him, we could not lose the war. We simply could not. It was a curious impression that had nothing whatsoever to do with confidence, bravado, or such. I sensed he was simply willing, by whatever genius of destruction moved him, to test conclusions to their ultimate end.

"I gather I will either end my life with some measure of fame—or die in pursuit of that same object," he remarked, adding a modest smile to deflect suspicions of boastfulness. But I did not believe he was boasting. This was a forecast made more in the manner of an impersonal observation, regarding a distant acquaintance.

Miss Wheatley broke the silence:

> *Proceed, great Chief, with virtue on thy side,*
> *Thy ev'ry action let the Goddess guide.*
> *A crown, a mansion, and a throne that shine,*
> *With gold unfading, JONES! be thine.*

"Your ode to Washington," Jones said. "You honor me."

She bowed her head reverentially to him. I inquired of the origin of their acquaintance, and she reported that it was Jones who sought her out, after her book *Poems Various* arrived in Boston. (It was, he concurred, his happy habit to acquaint himself with the leading literary figures of the day.) This appeared to me unusual, but Miss Wheatley was quick to inform me that Jones was as felicitous with the pen as he was deadly with the sword, and indeed had cultivated a considerable talent at sentimental poesy. I looked to our host, hoping to hear some evidence of her praise. He modestly demurred.

Instead, Jones saw fit to launch into a lengthy critique of his superiors in the Continental Navy. His comments were cogent and specific, to be sure, and it was difficult to gainsay him on any count. Still, it would not have been a subject I would have chosen for dinner conversation, particularly in mixed company. I nevertheless opted to emulate Miss Wheatley's attitude on this score: patient, obliging, sympathetic—in short, waiting for it to be over.

Jones declared that cronyism and nepotism ruled in Congress, as when (he illustrated) Naval Committee Chairman Stephen Hopkins saw to it that his brother Esek was commissioned as the Navy's first commodore. Hopkins, in his turn, gave his son John command of the fine fifteen-gun brig *Cabot*. Moreover, Jones's predecessor in command of the *Alfred* was Dudley Saltonstall, brother-in-law of Congressman Silas Deane.

Had I been inclined to dispute him, I might have pointed up the difficulty of finding trustworthy men to take over such responsibilities, and, all things being equal, the usefulness of obliging men not only by ties of oath and honor, but by blood relation. I would have said these things, that is, if I did not suspect them to be feeble pretexts: excuses for the fact that my own commission was due to my father's influence.

Jones, unfortunately, was not done with the subject. Very soon he produced a printed list out of his pocket, apparently placed there for the purpose of discussion that evening, of the original captains of the Continental Navy, arranged in order of seniority. Unfolding it, he handed it to me.

"This list was issued by Congress October last. Do you see anything wrong with it, Lieutenant?" he asked me.

Now, over my term of service beside Captain Jones, I had many occasions to hear his displeasure over this damnable little list. For him, it had taken on the proportions of a personal and malicious insult. No matter that it was superannuated almost a matter of weeks after it was issued. No matter that it was compiled purely on the basis of geographical consideration, to assure that each shipbuilding city could boast a native captain as an attraction to local recruits. Time and again Jones pulled this list out (he saved it like his most prized of personal possessions), read the order aloud, and pronounced and ridiculed the names of his rivals. I can now recite the thing entirely from memory:

CAPTAINS OF THE CONTINENTAL NAVY

By Rank of Seniority

As Established by Congress, October 10, 1776

As Follows:

1. James Nicholson, frigate *Virginia*
2. John Manley, frigate *Hancock*
3. Hector McNeill, frigate *Boston*
4. Dudley Saltonstall, frigate *Trumbull*
5. Nicholas Biddle, frigate *Randolph*
6. Thomas Thompson, frigate *Raleigh*
7. John Barry, frigate *Effingham*
8. Thomas Read, frigate *Washington*
9. Thomas Grinnell, frigate *Congress*
10. Charles Alexander, frigate *Delaware*
11. Lambert Wickes, sloop *Reprisal*
12. Abraham Whipple, frigate *Providence*
13. John B. Hopkins, frigate *Warren*
14. John Hodge, frigate *Montgomery*
15. William Hallock, brig *Lexington*
16. Hoysted Hacker, brig *Hampden*
17. Isiah Robinson, brig *Andrew Doria*
18. John Paul Jones, sloop *Providence*
19. James Josiah, no assignment
20. Elisha Hinman, ship *Alfred*
21. Joseph Olney, brig *Cabot*
22. James Robinson, sloop *Sachem*
23. John Young, sloop *Independence*
24. Elisha Warner, schooner *Fly*

"James Nicholson," Jones began, "has no skill or quality of character to recommend him to primary rank except the accident of his high birth." (Surely enough, Captain Nicholson distinguished himself by his quickness in running frigate *Virginia* up on the Chesapeake shoals two years later, and, by his additional failure to fire the hull, allowing it to fall into enemy hands.) "I had occasion to serve under Dudley Saltonstall as first lieutenant on the *Alfred*," Jones continued, "and I have never met a more narrow-minded and dull intellect." (Saltonstall later commanded the disastrous Continental attack on the British fort at Bagaduce, in Maine, and through his inexplicable strategy of delay, allowed British reinforcements to scatter and annihilate his squadron.) "John Hopkins's sole claim to martial fame is the dubious achievement of being the son of Commodore Esek Hopkins. Hoysted Hacker—the devil take him!—cowardly stole away in the night in Providence during our cruise to Cape Breton." (Prior to that voyage, Captain Hacker also made his mark by running his vessel aground in his own home port.)

But Jones appeared particularly incensed at that moment at the assignment of the *Alfred*, the vessel in which he had enjoyed his greatest success so far, to a captain of rank two places below him. Despite his five captures and evident knack for embarrassing the British, Jones was reassigned to tiny *Providence*, a vessel he had commanded six months earlier. The volume and vehemence of his words unfortunately do not bear repeating in the company of the fairer sex—

…

Severence glanced at Gualbert and Thierry. Gualbert winked at his intermittent propriety.   …

At length, Jones remembered where he was. As if to lighten the atmosphere, he then pressed Phillis Wheatley to take his personal copy of *Poems Various* and read one of her own works to us. This she obliged by reciting, without the aid of the book, one poem on her perceptions of the landing of British troops in Boston in 1768, another particularly fine one describing the notorious Massacre in that city several years later, and finally, a scalding rebuke of the Stuart tyrant that included the lines—

> *Already, thousands of your troops are fled*
> *To the drear mansions of the silent dead:*
> *Columbia too, beholds with streaming eyes*
> *Her heroes fall—'tis freedom's sacrifice!*
> *So wills the power who with convulsive storms*
> *Shakes impious realms, and nature's face deforms.*

At this, Jones made a great show of making a toast to his "African

Sappho", filling our port glasses to the brim and making a tribute *ex tempore* to her genius, the substance of which I happily have forgotten. Miss Wheatley, for her part, looked much embarrassed by his attentions, and immediately deflected his praise with a torrent of fine words on Jones's account.

The manner in which the two complimented each other, the Poet and the Captain, quite escaped my powers of explanation at the time. Later, during Jones's service in the Imperial Russian Navy, he made an increasing habit of indulging his morose reflections and did, on several occasions, write to me of "loneliness of my stolen African Princess" and the obscurity of her early death, forgotten as she was by the literary society that had once hailed her genius . . .

...

"Such a prodigy, forgotten?" asked a sad Gualbert. "How can that be so?"

...

I know but a little of Miss Wheatley's history. Before the war, she was held up by some as one of the true miracles of the Christian mission in the New World, and by others, as proof that genius knows no color. She was patronized and supported by her white mistress, who encouraged her talent at letters. Her book was received well, in England particularly, and she was invited there, so that she might be fêted. She had only just arrived in London, unfortunately, when she received a note that her mistress was suddenly taken ill, and ordered her slave's immediate return to attend her sickbed.

...

"That is suspicious," Thierry observed. "The sickness was no doubt a rank demonstration of her mistress's power, or a work of jealousy."

...

No doubt. But Miss Wheatley was nothing if not a loyal and grateful servant, and she prepared to turn right about and return to America. She did this, though her admirers held out to her the prospect of living in fame and freedom in England. She sailed back just a few days after setting foot on European soil.

Her mistress, as it happened, did not die straight away, but lingered for several years with her household poet laureate to serve her. Then came the war—with the typical decrease of interest in things poetical. Miss

Wheatley gained her freedom at last on the old woman's death, but it was a hollow triumph, for her fame had ebbed away, and she was obliged, like many of her sex, to make a bad marriage to survive. Jones corresponded with her very seldom in these years, and the letters stopped entirely some years ago. She was but thirty years old when she died.

"There, but for the grace of God, go I," Jones once told me as we spoke of her. His tone, however, was very far from one comforted by sure knowledge that "the grace of God" was really with him.

That evening, at any rate, Miss Wheatley pointed up that both she and Jones achieved their respective successes despite being recent newcomers to America (another fact Jones would have done well to recall with respect to the Congressional seniority list). She warned me, "You should know that he is not just a soldier, but rather an artist of soldiery. His canvas is the brine, and his paint the blood of the tyrant. Without knowing this, you will never understand him."

"Indeed," I responded, not knowing what to say. Jones, for his part, kept silent.

I came to be quite intrigued by this girl's brilliance and modesty by evening's end, when Jones and I stood at the inn door to see her to her carriage. Taking her dark little hand in his, he made a gallant display of kissing it, thereby drawing the disdainful stares of many around him. He ignored these, instead conveying her to her seat with much conspicuous grace and charm, as if he had a duchess on his arm, and then declaimed:

> *"The riches of the ship is come on shore!*
> *Ye men of Cyprus, let her have your knees.*
> *Hail to thee, lady! and the grace of heaven,*
> *Before, behind thee, and on every hand,*
> *Enwheel thee round!"*

"I thank you, valiant Cassio . . . ," she replied, taking Desdemona's part. And with this closing spasm of literary piety, they exchanged a last affectionate glance, and he spanked her swaybacked horse onward.

We stood together and watched the carriage roll away over the cobblestones, until, with a final wave of her handkerchief, Miss Wheatley disappeared around a corner. When I hazarded a glance at Jones's face, there was regret there.

"That damn list," he said, "has cost me my social graces."

"Hardly," said I.

"Your liberality surprises me. Lower-born men than you would not have sat with her."

"Then they know not their loss."

On this note of pleasant concord, I finally inquired after the nature of the . . . business . . . I had witnessed between himself and the lawyer in that street that afternoon.

"It is of no account," he said. "On cruise with the *Alfred,* I encountered the privateer *Eagle,* out of Rhode Island. It was well known that this vessel had enlisted deserters from the Continental Navy. I boarded that ship and reclaimed the men."

"And they sought to bring suit on that pretext?"

"They did. But that is not the true crime in this matter."

"And what would that be?"

"Let me ask you this, Severence: knowing what I have told you tonight, do you think Commodore Hopkins, our commander-in-chief, would voice his support for the lawful, reasonable recovery of deserters by one of his most loyal officers?"

"Knowing what you have said . . . no."

My unreserved agreement, coming so close by a compliment honestly offered to Jones's breadth of social taste, provoked a manner of awkward silence. This, I later learned, he deployed in defense when surprised by an overwhelming force of kindness. At length, he turned to me and caught my eye with a gratified look that skipped, for that moment, all barriers of temperament, politics, unfamiliarity.

Severence stopped, drank. ^{...}

"You were becoming friends," Gualbert speculated.

Severence shrugged. "I owed him my life."

...

VI.

A friend is worth all hazards we can run.

—YOUNG, *Night Thoughts*

~

THE BASSEMENT clock spoke eleven times. Severence halted to permit the clock's delicate metallic voice to claim the floor, if only for a few moments. While he waited, he again assured himself that his two pocket watches were synchronized, puzzling Thierry and Gualbert with this show of fussy precision. There wasn't anything in his outward appearance that would suggest such a particularity of nature, no part of his personal confessions so far—the only possible hint (thought Thierry) being a father who loved his account books more than his son, his authority more than his happiness or even life itself. How Severence would abhor such an observation, she knew. He would defend himself hotly, denying that he could ever come to be like the father he willfully insisted on hating. Yet didn't the depth of this feeling guarantee the resemblance?

...

I returned to my rooms believing my evening with Paul Jones would amount to no more than an odd anecdote in a military career spent defending my country on land. The sun had barely pulled itself out of the Providence River the next morning when I was up and about, preparing my departure. But someone had been up much earlier than myself: I was surprised to receive a second letter from Jones, written in the same maddeningly perfect hand.

"To my dear friend & comrade-at-arms, Lt. Severence of the New-York Volunteers," read the address. Jones's presumed friendship was odd, even a bit desperate in its quickness, but I must own I put it down to some pleasing aspect of my own character that fired his confidence. (I was wrong.) The letter was, in fact, an invitation as he said, "to address a matter more urgent than the closing of the Hudson" (the arrogance!) "and fulfill my fondest wish for Lt. Severence to transfer for duty aboard the sloop-of-war *Ranger,* presently fitting out at the port of Portsmouth, New Hampshire for an extended cruise against the Enemies of Human Liberty."

How I was taken aback by this invitation! Indeed, there had never been any question of my interest in sea duty during our evening together. The subject was never discussed. In the steady blizzard of Jones's oratory, I didn't have the opportunity to describe the action off Valcour Island to him. I hadn't so much as whispered I'd even taken a jaunt in a rowboat.

"If it serves the Lieutenant's pleasure," the note went on, "Captain Jones will await his visit until ten o'clock this morning, to discuss the above Matter, the quality of the Vessel, and the various Strategms he has planned to bring Honor & not to mention Profit to our prospective collaboration."

Curious, I returned to his hotel to find him at table again, over breakfast, attired this time in an exactly fashionable double-breasted flannel morning gown with padded shoulders. These, I later learned, he preferred for the same reason he craved ever more elaborate epaulets for his uniform—to counter his unimpressively small stature.

He also wore his hair untied, about his shoulders, its sand-hued tints shining in the early light. In his handsome delicateness, he looked more the pampered Dauphin than warrior.

The evidence of his menu, however, implied pure Scottish starch—a few crumbs of hard scone strewn on his plate, a half-eaten bowl of plain oat porridge by his elbow, a glass of lime juice in his hand. It was one of his disagreeable habits to strain the stuff between his teeth.

"You are intrigued by my suggestion," he stated after rising to greet me.

"I am not," I replied coolly. "Rather, I am more curious how you came to think of it. How did you perceive any love for the sea in my character?"

He laughed at me, but it was not a genuine laugh. In the years I knew him, I rarely saw an expression of mirth out of him that was not guarded by a sidelong glance, an appraising distance in his hazel eyes, as if measuring the effect of his emotional display. "Love for the sea? Pray, tell me what is that?"

"You tell me you spend your life on the ocean . . . and you have no taste for it?"

"Ah—a taste is another sort of thing. That I have always had. When the range of my options included a plot of land and a small income in Scotland, only a few leagues from where I was born, or a dull term of apprenticeship in London, or else a career pursuing my fortune on the waves beyond Solway Firth, I acquired exactly such a taste. But I'd sooner plight my troth with a miss of Covent Garden than mistake this choice for love!"

Once again, his explication of this point was clear, strong, well-reasoned—and utterly irritating. To his credit, this time he appeared to sense this, taking care to add, "All of which is to say, it is not necessary to love the sea to make a career of her. Respect—yes. But not love. Tea?"

I shook my head. "Why favor me, then?"

"None less keen could serve as my Commander of Marines."

"Commander of Marines?" I repeated, rather dumbly.

"I dare say there would be few in the service with such evident good breeding," he continued. Then he laughed at me. "Or such manifest love for the sea!"

Already, I had reason to wish the damnation of John Paul Jones. Though he honored me with his invitation, no gesture of goodwill came unalloyed from his mind. Jests cohabited with tribute; he sought to unhinge me with glorious and onerous challenges. He sipped his lime juice, ran it through his fine little incisors, swallowed, and stared at me.

"Robert Morris and I have shared the salt on occasion. I could request a commission in the Marines. By all rights, I should get it for you."

Though I heard these last words, I did not listen. Inwardly, my instincts battled my impulses, my curiosity mocked my pride, and I found myself owning up to the fact that—yes!—the flush of excitement I'd felt in command of the *New-York,* deep in the pell-mell of battle with superior forces, had never ceased to haunt me. The illusion of success, despite the indifference of General Arnold's appraisal, still shimmered before my eyes. It was indescribable—electrical! It was also a pride I was not likely to find again as an anonymous artilleryman in some obscure wilderness battlefield, short of men, short of supplies, without authority to distinguish myself in the fashion I believed I deserved . . .

On the contrary, Jones had offered me ample authority—Captain of

Marines—and the certain prospect of battle under his redoubtable flag.
And yet—

...

Severence paused. "You hesitated," pronounced Thierry, her cynicism thick in her voice as she reached for a plum.

...

I hesitated. These were, after all, matters of some gravity. My experience
afloat was still minor, as would become rapidly evident the second I
stepped aboard a real ship of war. Surely, I would embarrass myself—or
worse, prove a graver menace than all but the most lubberly landsmen. By
God, I didn't know a brace from a stay, a deadeye from a davit! Under
those circumstances, Jones would not, could not, want me.

"And don't run off pleading inexperience," he pressed, anticipating my
rhetorical tactics as well as he would the evolutions of an enemy ship. "No
more than half the officers and men of the *Ranger* will have spent any
more time afloat than you."

"A naval vessel—half-green?"

"If I am lucky, half-green. You must know that the privateers pay better than naval scale, and attract the best recruits. We Continentals scramble
for the dregs—the criminals shipping out just ahead of the law, the children, the diseased, the incompetent, or else those miserable creatures who
sign on in despair, and half hope never to return! As we speak, there are
no less than six new privateers trawling in Portsmouth, stealing the best
men from under my nose, the rascals!"

...

"Privateers?" asked Gualbert, looking from Severence to Thierry.

"A legal pirate," attempted Thierry.

Severence nodded. "Private enterprises, authorized by combatant
governments to harry enemy shipping. As an inducement, privateers
keep all their prize money. On the other side of the coin, at that time
navy crews surrendered one-half a warship's value to Congress, and
two-thirds a merchantman!"

"An absurd policy," pronounced Thierry. "Your Navy did not deserve
to attract crews."

...

Which they did not, as Jones well knew. Later, under pressure from his
applications for reform, and the entreaties from other wise quarters, the

Navy share was adjusted to one-half a merchantman's value, and all of a warship's. But service aboard a privateer was still a jollier business, with plenty of good food, lax discipline, and the luxury of picking and choosing whom to fight. Jones would have to struggle to find 150 men and boys willing to imprison themselves under his iron rule for months. This frustrating state of affairs called for creativity on the part of all recruiting commanders, including such enticements as touring drum-and-fife companies, buskers, and cash advancements. I recall the advertising poster for *Ranger* described a veritable pleasure-cruise "in the most pleasant season of the year"—that is, in November! Indeed, the range of Jones's tactics was not limited to happy hyperbole: when he had described his encounter with the privateer *Eagle* to me in Providence, he had neglected to mention that, along with the two naval deserters, he had also seen fit to "enlist" twenty members of the privateer's rightful crew, by force. In the naval officer's ongoing duel with the insidious enticements of the privateer, Jones had taken the offensive. In my case, however, he played the hapless victim, wishing only to do his duty, seeking to mine a vein of presumptive sympathy.

"Let them take every able-bodied salt in Essex County!" he proclaimed to me. "Give me a complement of peachfuzz, a wardroom of scofflaws, malfeasors, brigands and buggerers! At the very least, my officers will be gentlemen. There will always be my dear Severence!"

How could I fail to appreciate such inventive flattery? In truth, my doubts over my capacity to serve in such a position would have overthrown all temptation—except for the fact that my father had, after all, secured for me an Army commission. A career in the Continental Navy would hardly have been within the old man's power even to imagine. He surely would not have approved. This attracted me.

"What would the object of this cruise be?" I asked him, hoping only to delay a definitive answer to his invitation. But Jones appeared absolutely joyous at the opportunity to field this question.

"It is the best sort of cruise—an Attack! It is our Navy's good fortune that such men as Robert Morris still sit in Congress. He and I have agreed that our numbers are too few to make a consequential defense against the Royal Navy. The best way to drive the Trident from our coast, therefore, should be a program of vigorous offensives against enemy possessions, vessels, cities . . . everywhere. Britannia would be forced to pull her navy back from this hemisphere to protect her other interests. Her army of occupation would be forced to withdraw as well, of course, or else face the death of an amputated rump!

"We will be based in France," he added. "I cannot tell you more particularly, for risk of espionage—not from you, mind, but from prying ears." He raised his arms then, as if to include the whole world among the parties interested in the plans of Captain Jones.

I looked at him, hoping for him to say more. Alas, his answer had been too concise, too brief.

"Captain Jones," I finally told him. "I can scarcely express my astonishment at this invitation. It has taken me very much aback. Might you do me the further courtesy of allowing me to consider it?"

He rose, clapped a small hand on my shoulder. The disparity in our respective heights gave him only a slight advantage over my seated form.

"Of course you may. The *Ranger* is hove down, and undressed. With the shortages, the privateers, and a frigate fitting out, we should not sail until late in the year. By all means, take counsel with yourself—but do strike out with me!"

I left him, walking back to my rooms with my pulse quickened and my brain befogged.

I had, in fact, already decided to accept the commission. This was not patriotism, it probably would not surprise you to know, but an opportunity to launch a fresh offense in my Thirty Years' War with the House of Severence.

The problem then became one of mastering my palpitations, staunching the flow of cold sweat that had already drenched my waistcoat, and quieting the doubting voices within. These described in precious detail the sure death I had determined to inflict on myself, the musket shots that would find my innards, the cutlasses that would separate me from my extremities, the cannon shot that would shiver a mast and shower me with thousands of wooden needles . . .

Just then I turned a corner onto Water Street, and found myself peering through a thicket of idle rigging onto the frowning surface of Providence River. Where on any normal day of business there would be a riot of packets, jollies and barges about on it, and thence into Narragansett Bay, the British blockade had then worked its chilling effect on the local fleets. Only the occasional brave square-rigged snow or brig would run out, loosening sail, on the stiff nor'wester and the morning tide, hoping to conceal her courses in the unsettled overcast. Even some of the clouds, showing up dark like smudges on a parchment of drab sky, seemed stalled aloft, as if afraid to run to sea.

Not many months after, I received a packet at my posting at Fort Montgomery. Jones had done as he had promised: the packet contained a commission, duly signed by the Congressman John Hancock, for my service as lieutenant in the American Marines, and placing me at the disposal of Captain Jones for his operations against enemy shipping in European waters. A check was enclosed, with which I was expected to direct the manufacture of my new uniform. The coat was prescribed to be green with white facings, the knee breeches white and edged with the same green, and garters of black or "material of Hue approximate." I was also directed to purchase a brimmed felt hat, turn it up on the left side, and affix there "an appropriate Cockcade Device." As I was then ill-disposed to such rakish dress, I disposed of the felt hat and substituted a plain black tricorn that would, I trusted, attract far less attention.

...

"Shy of dress? You?" teased Gualbert.

"Under those circumstances, I was. It is a fear I have since overthrown," he replied, fingering one of the large, flat mother-of-pearl buttons on his sleeve.

"That much is clear," said Thierry. "Pray resume."

...

I wasted no time in resigning my Army commission and packing off most of my personal effects (as suggested by Jones) to Esmeralda in New-York. While sorting these, I came upon a letter addressed to me in a hand I recognized from years before. Studying it, I realized I had never disposed of that old letter from Aunt Hope—the same one that Esmeralda had delivered to me after my release from the *Jersey*. Suffering a momentary lapse into sentiment (I was, after all, about to leave my native shores for the first time in my life, perhaps never to return), I tore open the seal and scanned the following lines:

My dear boy—

You have just this moment left my front door in anger. Now I can scarcely keep my fingers steady to grasp my pen, so deeply has this Affair between yourself and your father disturbed me. It is my fear you have hardened your Heart against me now. If that is my Fate, I accept it, in hope that one day you will see fit to Forgive an old woman her foolishness. I do not have much Love in my life. In my own greed & vanity, I have perhaps given you a false impression of my willingness to supplant your dear departed Mother. I cannot. I am sorry.

It was a short note, indeed written in an unsteady hand, and sent off with such dispatch she had forgotten to sign it. Standing there, I measured my heart and, to my surprise, found it slightly too large to crumple her plea in my fist and be done with her. Instead, I sat down to write what I intended to be the last lines I would ever address to an acquaintance in America, to the effect of—

Madam—

The enclosed note was delivered to me only recently. As you must agree, Circumstances have completely overtaken the conditions of its writing. It is no matter in any case: very soon I depart this Continent aboard a Ship of Congress, very possibly to die in defense of Liberty. However questionable we deem your conduct, know that it did have the fortunate Effect of driving me onward, to the reward awaiting all true Patriots.

And I signed it "At your service, Lt. John Severence, American Marine."

...

"True patriot?" repeated Gualbert.

"Liar," pronounced Thierry.

"I believe I am, in truth, something much smaller than either of those things."

Severence looked down. Gualbert, for her part, was at that moment fully and helplessly in love with him . . . but only for that moment.

...

Thereafter I went on to pay brief calls on what friends and associates might

concern themselves with my fate. Among these was Esmeralda, who refused
to wish me luck, but instead tried to convince me to abandon the project.

"Why ya gotta go wi' that mon? What he give you that you can't find
at home?"

"I don't know. But I will find out," I replied.

"I say it's Satan who he is, and he'll make of yer life a hell before he's
through!"

"How can you say that, Emmie, when you don't even know him?"

"I know de ship captains in my time. An' my family know 'em too, long
way back."

I laughed at her. "I assure you, he's no slaver."

"But you be his slave," she warned.

I found my way back to Portsmouth by October of 1777. The *Ranger*
was due to set sail for France 'round about the first of November.

I found Jones once again to be the perfect host: agreeable, expansive,
almost jocular. He gave over almost one entire morning to touring the
Piscataqua docks with me, sweeping his gilded sleeve across that shallow
river, giving me my first instruction in ship recognition and naval architecture.

"Presently," he told me, "there are, in the main, three classes of warship
in service of the best navies. First and most powerful, is the Ship-of-the-
Line mounting from 64 to more than 100 guns, two to three thousand
tons burthen, and manned by eight to nine hundred crew. It is this class
of vessel that, in the evolutions of the great fleets, sails end to end with
its fellows, forming what are in essence continuous broadsides miles in
length and bearing thousands of guns. This is the way that oceans are con-
quered and held—it is the way England propagates her power upon the
waves. The United Colonies could not possibly afford to build Ships-of-
the-Line in numbers. And if they could, they could not find a man the
length and breadth of this continent with knowledge of how to command
such a force."

"Not even you, Captain Jones?" I asked, baiting his vanity. But he surprised me.

"No—certainly not me. I can perhaps hold my own in single-ship
actions, but so far my knowledge of fleet tactics is only theoretical. The
best in which I might hope now is the next inferior class—the frigate of

20 to 56 guns—a vessel fast enough to pursue and capture, or fly and escape. A scourge of commerce—a jackal of the seas—"

His voice trailed to nothing, and he looked quite mournful. I was about to intrude on his reverie when he suddenly revived with a baleful sigh and a toss of the head.

"Certainly a command worthy of Number Eighteen," he said.

Fearful of another discourse on the List, I diverted him by inquiring, "And the last class of warship?"

"A sloop-of-war, like the *Ranger* . . . "

Aptly, we had arrived at the *Ranger*'s slip. A small square-rigger rode before us, not more than thirty yards a-keel, forlorn and abandoned. This was most unlike the atmosphere surrounding the privateers fitting out nearby, which were all veritable hives of hammering, sliding, coiling, heaving, brushing, sawing, grappling, boring, scraping, tying, tarring, shouting, and, in some cases, boisterous wenching and grogging.

By strict contrast, the *Ranger* then appeared as proper and quiet as a chapel on Sabbath. Half the rigging seemed to be missing, and there was but a single man on board—a gentleman of strikingly horizontal features—

...

"Horizontal?" asked Gualbert.

...

Horizontal. This isn't to say obese—he would not have weighed more than thirteen stone—only that his mouth and eyes seemed to run off the sides of his face like drips of wet paint from a wall. The bit of wire holding the glass of his spectacles together must have stretched three inches across the flat bridge of his nose. He was indifferently dressed in buff-colored waistcoat and black breeches, and lounged against the bulwarks in an attitude of studied ease. Indeed, in the weeks I knew him, I rarely ever saw this man on his feet when a chair, or a board, or some bare stretch of floor would support his weight.

When Jones saw him, his eyes and ears twitched in anger. I was forced to rush after as the little Captain descended to the deck in a flurry of clenched fists and flashing eyes.

"Mr. Cullam!!"

Cullam jolted erect forthwith. He had heard that tone of voice in Jones before, no doubt.

"Sir?"

Jones rushed up to him, to a position almost beneath the other man's nose.

"Mr. Cullam, might we break your *nap* to engage your services as the Ship's Master? Or would you prefer to repose in irons, beyond fear o' interrupt?"

That betrayal of his native accent, that "fear o' interrupt," no doubt slipped into his speech due to the extremity of his feelings against sloth. Still, this hint of foreignness did nothing to reconcile Mr. Cullam to his reprimand. He looked down at Jones, and even a stranger like myself could see the mutiny playing itself out behind his eyes, in the quivering of his jaw muscles and in the length of time he took before responding. Clearly, this was not a man used to taking orders, especially ones proclaimed from the miniature Olympian athwart him at that moment. And we hadn't even put out to sea yet.

Alas, Jones saw nothing. To him, there was no difference in the conduct expected from a New England salt, or Jersey farm boy, or a runaway Jamaican plantation Negro. All were expected to display the fealty and obedience more typical of a Berber galley slave than a free American.

"You have my apology, sir."

Jones gave him a short nod and proceeded to introduce me as an old and dear friend who might, judging from the warmth of this tribute, have known him even as a fry on the bonny shores of Scotland. In turn, Jones told me that, as Ship's Master, Cullam was the Warrant Officer in charge of the actual sailing of the ship. Cullam took my hand, and I could see his eyes ask the desperate question, "Are you, God help me, another one like *him?*"

I could only smile, quite certainly deepening the mystery.

"Captain Severence is most curious of our lady," said Jones, quickly adopting a tone of voice more appropriate for steeplechases and lawn parties.

"She's just touched water a few months back," said Cullam, looking to me and apparently hoping for the best. "She'll be poppin' strakes and takin' water all th' way to France, 'til the wood wears. She's got a fine line, haked in the bow, hollow-counter'd astern. Ask for ten knots, and she might give us eleven."

"She is crank," said Jones. Cullam's brows shot up, as if Jones had uttered some surprising morsel of gossip, or impugned the virtue of his own mother.

"Ahhhh—she may be a touch tender in a stiff blow, but—"

"She's got too much canvas to ride straight up in the water," Jones informed me parenthetically, then back to Cullam, "She'll put 'er lee gun-ports underwater for sure. We'll be lucky to see L'Orient alive."

To that, Cullam had no answer. Indeed, this was the first I had heard of Jones's honest appraisal of our chances to reach a safe port in France. But instead of lending reassurance, Jones thought of supper.

"You will dine with me tonight at the Marquis of Rockingham tavern," he told Cullam, delivering this invitation in the manner of a prosecutorial charge. Cullam nodded. As Jones led me away, I could hear the master grumble to himself under his breath.

That evening, with Cullam sitting there more prisoner than guest, Jones discoursed at length on the Navy's poverty of strategic insight in not approving his (no doubt daringly original) plan to raid the British colony at St. Kitts, in the Caribbean, and thence to Pensacola or Barbados. This monologue was cut short, alas, by a Lieutenant Thomas Simpson of the *Ranger*, who begged entrance.

"Your business, Lieutenant?" barked Jones.

"Dispatches have just reached Colonel Langdon," said the other. "Burgoyne has surrendered. Saratoga is ours."

There was a momentary silence. There had been reports from the woods of troop movements—skirmishes—forces shadowing one another—but this, a complete victory, was as unanticipated as it was essential to our struggle. The enemy's bid to split New England from her sisters had failed.

Jones looked to me, and in a sudden fit of graciousness, said, "In that happy case, we must each raise a glass to our compatriot John Severence, who took no small role in defense of the North!" He then lifted a glass of port in my honor, though I had nothing whatever to do with Saratoga— that is, nothing direct—and Cullam and Simpson followed his example. His plan for the subjugation of St. Kitts was entirely forgotten. It was as if Jones sought to snatch the laurels from General Arnold and give them to me.

VII.

IT WOULD severely tax my poor storytelling abilities to attempt to convey to you even a fraction of what I endured in my first hours at sea. Suffice it to say a major impression was a case of seasickness that began just a few minutes after we successfully slipped past the British patrols near the Isle of Shoals. Meeting the ocean currents at last, the vessel began to adopt a long, deer-like, loping gait that amused me at first but only until I realized, with rising anxiety and nausea, that it would not stop until we reached France.

The following miserable hours I passed in what was introduced to me as my "cabin," but what was in fact no more commodious than a broom closet and only slightly more comfortable. If I had seen fit to strap a musket and field pack to myself, I could not have turned around in it. My bunk was some ten inches shorter than my height, and when I nonetheless managed to squeeze myself into a position of sleep upon my back, I was somewhat annoyed to find the mattress (such as it was) stuffed with a thatch of animal hair that set me to a most devilish and constant itching. Indeed, I would have much preferred passing a night on a bed of cobblestones, or in the comparative luxury of a camp-bed on a damp forest floor.

Yet there I stayed for four full days, bent almost in two, my skin worn red from scratching, my stomach turning end over end with every slide of the *Ranger* into that damnable trough of the sea, and inevitably reaching for my bucket when the vessel performed that horror of horrors, a lateral rolling movement simultaneous with the loping up and down, that never seemed to stop no matter what time of day I dared take to my feet, or depth of night I resolved to crawl to the air-holes to exercise my lungs.

Not that I was deprived of unusual entertainments during my confinement. The bulkheads of the officer's cabins, I had the distinct displeasure to learn, were designed to be quickly removed and stored away in times of battle, so that the gun-crews could roll their ordnance into position before the gun-ports. As it happened, this convenience also made the walls quite transparent to sound, rather in the manner of Japanese paper houses. Too often, when I had just managed to accustom myself to the relentless pitching of my chamber, slow my racing heart, forget my nausea and close my eyes to sleep, I found myself blasted awake by the loud yammering of some boatswain's mate or idler, testifying to the questionable virtue of some milkmaid, or the size of the maggot he had once found in his meat ration and dared to chew and swallow.

Such interruptions were not by half as ruinous to my rest, however, as the steady clop-clop-clop of someone pacing on the quarterdeck (Jones?) that usually kept me far from any presumptions to actual slumber.

When I emerged from my exile on the fourth day it was not so much that I was cured, but that I could stand my sickroom no longer. This move in fact served me well—out at last to breathe the fresh breeze of mid-ocean, with an eye firmly anchored on the line of the horizon, I felt my stomach settle. Looking aloft, I saw for the first time the *Ranger* under full spread of canvas, and felt no small measure of exhilaration in the spectacle. Where below the ship had seemed as shut and dank as a coffin, on deck she seemed a miraculous creature of velocity and delicacy—a speeding spider web. Her new sails drank the wind and gleamed such a white in the sunshine I had to shade my eyes. The motion of the hull, so discomfiting to me before, now seemed as natural and essential to me as the turning of the planets in their courses. The *Ranger*'s orbit was carrying her little world before the wind, away from the setting sun.

I then understood why the preponderance of the crew, excepting those asleep or debilitated, strove to spend their time above-decks, even when not on watch. As if reading my thoughts at that very moment, Jones clop-clopped past me and remarked cryptically, "Upper gun deck—and sick—is best." But when I turned to take up my part in the conversation he had so clearly begun, I found he had walked away. I was looking at his back as he paced the quarterdeck, his hands clasped behind him. I pursued, but my salutation was cut off at the roots by his exchange of words with the ship's master.

"Square the mains'l, Mr. Cullam. Helm a-starboard, east by north."

Cullam repeated these orders to the helmsman, a cadaverously thin old salt with a kerchief on his head and a whalebone pick in this teeth. He made the slight adjustment on the ship's wheel, and the sails momentarily lost some of their taut convexity.

"Hands t'the braces—look sharp, now," Cullam whispered.

The crews then seized several ropes that hung down from the yards to the decks (the braces), and re-adjusted the yards' angle. The courses filled again and we were off.

I stood beside Jones as this operation proceeded, but he did not turn to me. This was, to my recollection, the first time since our meeting that he had not greeted me with a yelping proclamation of my illustrious tribe.

Indeed, now that we were at sea many things had changed about my new comrade Paul Jones. Most obviously, he had had a new uniform made for himself and his officers—one with blue coat and white facings, gold buttons, breeches and stockings of white, and, on his own individual person, what appeared to be a mine's-worth of gold piping.

His departure from the authorized attire of an officer of the Continental Navy was a minor puzzle to me at first, signalling (I first feared) a capricious and hypocritical nature. Only later, when I had met and fought the enemy, did I understand his rationale. The new uniform, in fact, was brazenly designed to be well nigh indistinguishable from the British one at distance, and therefore more useful in practicing those arts of deception (or more precisely, of impersonation) in which Jones had a particular talent and interest. The alteration of the uniform was not approved through the proper channels, admittedly, and could still therefore betoken Jones's personal vanity. It nonetheless helped to capture prizes and save our lives on more than one instance, as I will have occasion to relate . . .

More puzzling was the sudden plunge in the temperature of our social intercourse. For now, just a few weeks after our acquaintance and less than a hundred miles east of New England, I might as well have been a stranger to Paul Jones. On the *Ranger*'s tiny quarterdeck, he preferred to restrict the range of his attention to the span of his pacing. If I happened to catch his eye with mine, I saw nothing behind his pupils but a closed dullness, as if he'd retreated behind a door, into a secret apartment in his mind where I, his "compatriot," was suddenly not welcome.

Had I been given to suspicions of persecution, I would have thought about the circumstances of my seduction out to sea, and the rapid turn of my sponsor's demeanor, and believed myself the brunt of an elaborate joke that would end, no doubt, with Jones, my comrades at the Fort Montgomery, Aunt Hope, Benedict Arnold, and my father all coming forth to have a hearty collective laugh at my expense.

...

"How childish of Captain Jones to treat you so cruelly," said Gualbert, seizing the opportunity to touch his hand in sympathy.

"How necessary," Severence replied. "Imagine, if you might, how you would cope with sharing these apartments . . . ," and Severence waved his hand around to indicate the women's rooms, " . . . with a hundred men. Not just to sleep, mind, but to eat and work and play and perform all functions of life. What would you do?"

"I would be sure to befriend them all," came the smirking answer.

Severence realized—and regretted—the opening he had furnished for Gualbert's feeble joke. He smiled, plunged on.

"A sentiment worthy of a generous soul. But even friendships can fail. And imagine further that your crowded apartment is filled with cannon, gunpowder, muskets, cutlasses—a thousand weapons. You begin to see, then, the value of a little space, if only between one's ears, in regaining the privacy one loses in shutting oneself up on a 90-foot sloop with 150 other men."

Thierry shook her head. "It has become a pattern, Captain Severence, for you first to criticize and condemn Paul Jones's manias, then to explain and excuse them. One would think you have no clear opinion."

"A reasonable assumption. Let me defend myself, then, by observing that good opinions require knowledge, and of the latter I had very little in the those first days afloat. In truth, nothing on the *Ranger* was what I expected it to be."

...

The first of my pleasant preconceptions to fall was the notion that, under the circumstances of privation and war, if not the predicament of mutual isolation aboard a tiny vessel lost on an infinite sea, a certain *esprit de corps* would naturally be promoted among the crew. I had, indeed, found occasion to imagine scenes of such joyous heaving and ho-ing, of laughter around the grog tub, of general camaraderie—in short, of all the collegial belonging I had missed all of my life—that the actual case was a great disappointment to me. For despite its small size, the *Ranger* contained a virtual universe of separated castes and sub-castes, with all the tensions attendant to such a condition.

I do not speak here of the standard divisions of rank. These I anticipated fully. Rather, I found the officers divided against themselves, and the crew divided against themselves and the officers, and the captain divided against them all. The seamen, in fact, were distinguished largely on the basis of experience and ability, and achieving some measure of both (the exact degree of which I was never able to determine) were considered "able." Those less able, but still of some considerable competence, were deemed "ordinary." The rest were either green sailors, known as "landsmen," or bad ones, called "waisters." This is to say nothing of the chaos of nationalities aboard, including Acadian, Irish, Swedes, Jamaicans, *ad nauseam,* that Jones was obliged to master and command.

"Able" seamen were further distinguished by age. Those on the near side of thirty were consigned to service aloft, on the three deck masts, furling and unfurling the sails, securing and removing the gaskets, climbing the shrouds, handling the running gear, all such business conducted some three or more stories above the deck. These were our "topmen." Able sailors who were too long in the tooth for such acrobatics were employed forward, on the fo'c'sle, in operation of bowsprit and anchor—the "anchormen." Ordinary seamen, as part of the "afterguard," worked those facilities which were accessible from the main deck, including main-sails, stay-sails, braces, capstans. Everything else that was left to be done—which included most of the unsavory tasks of scrubbing and swabbing, was left to the "waisters" and "landsmen." In addition, all of these castes were immediately halved and assigned to either the starboard (right hand, facing forward) or larboard (left hand) side of the man o' war.

Our officers showed themselves quite adept at fanning these purely administrative divisions into real rivalry, and even hostility. On occasion, Captain Jones would call for "top-watch drill," and the top-men would be obliged to race one another up and down the shrouds—mainmast division versus foremast division versus mizzenmast division—for the prize of avoiding the captain's displeasure. Sometimes Jones would merely withhold grog rations from the slowest squad. Sometimes he would withhold them from the slowest two squads. Now and then he would have the slowest topman in each division—whether his particular squad won the race or not—lashed to a hatch and given a taste of the cat. Whichever permutation of punishment his mind could conceive, it was sure to provoke ill will between the rivals. Fear of "the Old Man," of course, was a given fact of the seaman's life.

Intercourse between officers was hardly more warm. Ship's Master David Cullam, as you have seen, had little reason to love Paul Jones, and was further annoyed by the captain's distaste for any sort of yelling on deck. As a matter of course, a ship's master must communicate with his men aloft, sometimes fifty or sixty feet over his head. To forbid such an officer to yell, even in the interests of maintaining a genteel and efficient atmosphere, was well nigh to deny him the means of doing his job. Cullam was obliged to pass his orders on to the addressed parties by means of spoken relay. To Jones, he hardly spoke at all.

Lieutenant Thomas Simpson was of a different sort. Some ten years older than Jones and a good ten inches taller, he spied out from beneath his hard black eyebrows with a calculation I never could trust. He appeared to suffer Jones's demands and outbursts with patience, but behind his commander's back he assured the crew that Jones was more custodian than captain, that he would be replaced forthwith in France. This was a damaging presumption insofar that it raised expectations among the men that ultimately were disappointed. To them, Jones not only appeared harsh in his fussiness, and dangerous in his penchant for seeking out warships instead of fat, profitable merchantmen, but his command was also unjustly extended. In any event, it was easy to see that Lieutenant Simpson, counting more years afloat than Jones, resented the command of such a younger man.

At first, I found the company of the ship's surgeon, Ezra Green, the most agreeable of all these. Like myself, he was an army officer, gone to sea largely out of curiosity. I would most thankfully pass my idle moments with him down in the "cockpit"—a corner of the ship's hold that served as the ship's hospital. There, reclining on top of a large sea-chest that also sufficed as a surgeon's table, under the pendulous swinging of a lantern, he would expound upon his favorite subject, which was the Ladies. It was his contention that he had bedded receptive Misses from Maine to Tobago, and found that browner races—how shall I say it?—er—um—

...

Severence halted.

"Just say it." Thierry demanded, impatient.

He took a moment, wet his lips.

"I recall he put it in purely anatomical terms, this way: 'The br- browner races were gifted with a g- gr- greater ratio of . . . depth of cavity to . . . con-con-constriction of orifice.'

"He was a stutterer?"

"Just so."

"What an utterly charming crew."

"And have you found this to be true as well?" asked Gualbert.

"Mademoiselle?"

"The ratio."

"I must decline the comparison, as I have not shared the company of the duskier strain."

"None at all?"

"None—if we are speaking of the same orifice."

"*Mon dieu.* You are foul," breathed Gualbert, nonetheless amused.

"If you might resume?" Thierry reminded him.

...

Dr. Green's curiosity regarding the sea, I found, was inspired more by what he might find at port than any natural oceanic phenomena. This was harmless as far as it went, though I did on occasion wish his passion for curative medicine approached his enthusiasm for feminine anatomy.

There were others—a second lieutenant by the name of Elijah Hall, several midshipmen, all sharing a common history of never serving aboard a naval vessel before. Jones complained to me almost from the outset over this, asserting that he had been saddled with inexperienced, ill-disciplined officers purely to satisfy the gentry of Portsmouth, which demanded commissions for its sons and cronies. It was customary for a captain to have some influence on such appointments, he told me, but the only compatriot he had managed to include was . . . myself. As you can see, as of that particular conversation, I was once again his "compatriot." I was, at that time, too given to uncritical acceptance of such flattery to wonder why I, who had just met Jones a few weeks before, should count as his closest friend in the world.

No doubt concerned over his crew's limited exposure to naval discipline, Jones conceived the practice of mustering all watches on the spar deck at six bells on the forenoon watch—about 10 o'clock in the morning—for a reading from the "Rules for the Regulation of the Navy of the United Colonies." From a purely academic perspective, this was a fine idea. I found myself much enlightened of the special responsibilities of a naval, as distinguished from an army, officer. But the men resented it.

"The commanders of all ships and vessels belonging to the thirteen United Colonies," began Lieutenant Simpson one bright morning just six days out from Portsmouth, "are strictly required to show in themselves a good example of honor and virtue to their officers and men, and to be very vigilant in inspecting the behavior of all such as are under them, and to discountenance and suppress all dissolute, immoral and disorderly practices, and also such as are contrary to the rules of discipline and obedience, and to correct those who are guilty of the same, according to the usage of the sea . . . "

As the catechismal reading continued, Jones turned his back on the assembled corps and stared out across the water. A steady wind from the west had been blowing ever since the start of the morning watch, and the vessel was running free with gallants and studding sails set. With the *Ranger* comfortably before the breeze, trimmed tightly, nothing could have caught her, with the possible exception of the streaming wisps of foam blowing off the tops of the swells. The sun dogged us off the starboard rail, peeking at us from between a procession of cream-white cumuli. Above, some of our topmen were armed with telescopes, keeping up a constant watch of the horizon for prey, while others stared down from the yards, as if remote spectators in an ancient amphitheater.

"If any shall be heard to swear, curse, or blaspheme the name of God, the commander is strictly enjoined to punish them for every offense by causing them to wear a wooden collar, or some other shameful badge of distinction, for so long a time as he shall judge proper. If he be a commissioned officer, he shall forfeit one shilling for each offense, and a warrant or inferior officer six pence. He who is guilty of drunkenness, if a seaman, shall be put in irons until he is sober, but if an officer, he shall forfeit two days' pay . . . "

At last, I was offered the opportunity to inspect the greater part of the crew, collected there almost in its totality. Only a week out of port, it already seemed a haphazard, rough-hewn host. Many of the faces were bronzed and unshaven. Some men went barefoot. Most wore short, baggy pantaloons and brown woolen jackets Jones had provided, free of charge, out of his "slops chest," or ship's stores. Or so said Surgeon Green, who leaned over to whisper these facts to me. I could smell a distinct odor of rum on his breath.

"That's J-J-Jedediah Carter, in the round cap. He tried to sell me a rat he'd caught in the flour bin. The two bla-black ones—they're Scipio Africanus and Cato Carlisle. They're free Negroes, so you best have an excuse before you c-c-cuff 'em, ha!"

"Who's that talking?" Jones asked.

Green fell silent.

" . . . all ships furnished with fishing tackle, being in such places where fish is to be had," continued the indefatigable Simpson, "the captain is to employ some of the company in fishing; the fish to be distributed daily to such persons as are sick or upon recovery, provided the surgeon recommend it, and the surplus by turns amongst the messes of the officers and seamen without favor or partiality and gratis, without any deduction of their allowance on that account . . . "

I then felt Green at my ear again. "The big one there, with no shirt—," he indicated by projecting his chin toward a bare-chested giant standing, with arms crossed, near the scuttlebutt, "is Jack Sh-Sh-Sharpless, landsman. A legendary one already. The word is he—he—rode the highways to Braintree, in Massachusetts. Made a practice of per-perrrrrrrrrrrr . . . " (Green closed his eyes, snapped his head on his neck as if to shake the words loose) " . . . performing unnecessary surgery on his victims."

"Surgery? What sort?"

"On their eyes. So—so they'd not identify him . . . "

So intent had we been on Mr. Sharpless, we did not see a small blue and white form dart toward us, brandishing some dully metallic instrument. We both ducked, but it was Surgeon Green who suffered the humiliation of being bopped on the head with Captain Jones's speaking trumpet.

Many of the men turned their heads to conceal their amusement. Green blushed.

"You will kindly observe silence, will you not, Dr. Green?" inquired Jones, speaking from between clenched teeth. Green, for his part, merely stood erect, not daring to repair the tricorn cap riding crumpled on his head.

"Delighted, sir," replied the doctor.

"Thank you," said the captain, who then clop-clopped back to his perch by the starboard rail. "Lieutenant Simpson, pray proceed."

Simpson cast his eyes back down at the book before him, but hesitated. An evil expression, suggesting great self-satisfaction, came over his face.

"Every word, sir?"

"Of course, every word!"

"Captain . . . I think . . . "

Jones turned and dealt him a withering look that manifested no patience for his explanations.

Simpson continued, "The commander is never by his own authority to discharge a commission or warrant officer, nor to punish or strike him, but he may suspend or confine them, and when he comes in the way of a Commander-in-Chief, apply to him for holding a court-martial."

Simpson paused to observe Jones's response to this clear repudiation of his conduct. But the lieutenant was to have no such satisfaction. The Captain's back remained ram rod straight—his face remained inclined to sea. Simpson frowned, and read on " . . . the officer who commands by accident of the captain's or commander's absence . . . "

"Clerk!" Jones shouted suddenly.

There was some confusion, as Jones had shouted the word "clerk" very distinctly and no one responded. Jones, the man who detested yelling on deck, sucked in a prodigious breath to repeat his call . . .

"Yes, sir?" came the belated reply from the vicinity of the ladderway. O'Leary, our needle-nosed, bespectacled ship's clerk, had apparently allowed his attentions to wander during the reading of regulations.

"Make note that the captain will forfeit two days' pay," said Jones.

O'Leary's brows flew up. "Yes, sir," he said.

I then witnessed Jones look straight in Lieutenant Simpson's eye and hold his gaze. It was a look I had seen once before, in the streets of Providence when I had surprised him and he'd reached for his sword—that look of cold rage, that broadside of icicles. Already, in a matter of seconds, his coloring had darkened, the blondness of his calm chased away by oncoming clouds of combativeness. The patient Simpson, however, did not dare to rise to this evident challenge. Rather, he averted his eyes by looking back down at the text of the regulations. Having "won" this wordless argument with a mere show of force, Jones nodded slowly to himself and turned to resume his vigil.

VIII.

"IT WOULD be fruitless to continue my tale without giving you ladies some more precise notion of life aboard the man o' war. Without such knowledge, you would as soon think I was recounting the story of Paul Jones in ancient Greek . . . "

"That is well and proper," Thierry approved, "as long as you are not too detailed. We are women, after all."

"It would be the last of my intentions to overburden you, dear Miss, with facts too arcane for your sex . . . "

"You misunderstand me, Captain. As women, we don't indulge in irrelevance as freely as the male."

Severence started as if to reply, but thought the better of it.

I have already alluded to the system of watches into which the day is divided while at sea. Under normal circumstances, that portion of the crew assigned to the operation of sails and rigging stood alternating periods of four hours on duty, and four hours off, all day. These were, in order, the midwatch, from midnight to four o'clock in the morning, the morning watch to eight, the forenoon watch until twelve noon, the afternoon watch until four in the afternoon, the dog watch to eight in the evening, and the so-called first watch until midnight again.

As you might realize, the system did not much provide for the luxury of undisturbed sleep. Those resting during the morning watch were "started," sometimes with the encouragement of the whip, by half past seven. Off-hours during the day were absorbed either in repair or training, or in the essential stupors of grogging. Considering that the crew's hammocks could not be hung on the gundeck before eight PM, the mariner's rest would have been far more abbreviated than the farmer's.

I say "would have been," because our Navy adopted the common practice of dividing the dog watch, which really should be called the docked watch, or shortened watch, into two two-hour watches, the first and second dog watch . . .

···

Thierry let loose an obvious sigh. "You see, Thérèse! This is what I mean."

"Patience, Nathalie," Gualbert chided her friend.

"No. She is right," said Severence. "It is my male penchant for irrelevance again. To summarize, if one was obliged to stand, say, the first dog watch from four to six, it works out that one would only get four hours of sleep, during the midwatch. The following day, however, that same man would stand the second dog watch from six to eight at night, then immediately be permitted to sling his hammock at eight, and indulge in a total of seven and one half hours of sleep, albeit interrupted by four hours of early morning duty on the midwatch. The next day he would get the first dog watch again, and the midwatch off. Understand?"

"Not entirely. But please don't explain," begged Thierry.

Severence tossed his head, smiled a smile replete with male arrogance. He had cowed the females with a copious discharge of jargon.

···

Let it suffice for me to note that this arrangement existed for the convenience of the vessel, not the crew. If an emergency like a storm or enemy sail arose, even the seaman who had just come off watch would be obliged to rise again to answer the call to quarters. Having lived through such a circumstance myself, I can testify that there is no sensation quite like passing from sound sleep to frenzied wakefulness in a matter of a few moments —the time necessary to leap from one's hammock, dress quickly and mount the ladderway to find—what?—a typhoon blowing on deck, or our ship blundered into the center of a British squadron.

This isn't to say that life aboard the man o' war is unalloyed excitement. Once I had finally learned to sleep through the night, I discovered that a certain quality of depressive monotony was the chief enemy punctuated only by odd moments of terror or elation.

This condition was, in fact, cultivated: those grappling with the task of forging hundreds of poorly fed, undereducated, low-paid men into an efficient working unit had realized the blessing of routine as antidote to anxiety, despair, or mutiny. That the day began with a rout of meticulous cleaning—with columns of landsmen in miserable procession on their knees, sanding and wetting and scouring the decks with blocks of stone, with ship's boys polishing every square inch of brass, with seamen coiling every line and stowing every loose object—had more to do with the fact that they were all afloat on an infinite sea, and the mercy of the four winds, than with any cosmetic vanity. The young sailor's attention was diverted, time and time again, to tasks twelve inches before his nose, until he was so exhausted, his concentration so tried, he could only spend his idle time fraternizing or stealing a snooze, and look on the immensity of ocean not as a force that would kill him, but as mere backdrop.

By the turn of the forenoon watch, all men would be awakened and all hammocks unslung from below decks. The first task of this watch was to roll and stow the hammocks in the nets that ran along the ship's rail—a fine idea both for keeping them out in the fresh air, and to use them to protect the decks from enemy small arms fire. Indeed, it was common practice to inspect one's bedding after a battle, lest an unnoticed musket ball have penetrated the folds, and produced an annoying lump.

The ship's cook would have been up before sunrise, preparing breakfast for the various messes, filling the ship with an odor of boiling meal and blackened biscuits. These latter would be dissolved in water to make something called "Scotch coffee," a beverage that had the effect of banishing sleep by its extreme bitterness, and not by any particular nourishment. The oatmeal was also mixed with the ship's "fresh" water, which was usually green or brown in color, into a gruel . . .

...

"If I am not mistaken," Thierry interrupted, "you are about to boast once again of what depths of foul food were forced upon you . . . "

"And what worms you devoured, with aphids for appetizers . . . ," chimed in Gualbert.

...

Not at all. With respect to the men's rations, Jones made every effort to secure the best available provisions. Just out of Portsmouth, the men were astonished at the quantities of fresh fruits and meats their captain had seen fit to secure, apparently at his own expense! This is in addition to the new hammocks he ordered for all hands, and his gift of those smart, simple uniforms of brown I have already described. Indeed, I was startled to discover we were among the very few vessels in either the Continental or the Royal Navies to attire their men in any sort of standard fashion!

Few had any grounds for complaint when it came to Jones's consideration of the creature comforts. It was little wonder, however, as his own glory depended in large measure upon these very "creatures," Jones sought to keep them in a state of healthful efficiency. Unfortunately, as the voyage progressed, and the fresh provisions were either consumed or spoiled, the *Ranger*'s bill of fare returned to the more customary slabs of hard salt pork or beef, the cups of mashed peas and fungal potatoes, the weekly gill of vinegar . . .

In no modern navy are the officers expected to fight and die on the same fare as the men. As I was the Captain's sole personal designee among the corps of officers, I found myself at mess in his cabin quite often. There, we enjoyed, as did the junior officers in their wardroom, freshly baked scones and butter, porridge with honey and cinnamon, and fresh milk for breakfast. At the beginning of our voyage, while our livestock lasted, we dined on roast beef and suckling pig, as well as roasted goose and chickens with forcemeat, with yams and greens and cobbed corn. There was also a good selection of wine, kindly provided by our French allies, which Jones presumed to select for the table, but never indulged in himself, preferring his lime juice and water concoction.

After the crew had had some time to digest or eject their breakfasts, as the case may be, all hands were piped to the spar deck for the daily reading from the regulations, as I have already described. This was immediately followed by the day's punishment—an exercise I would just as soon have missed, though it represented the highlight of the working day for many of our more brutish brethren.

The list of offenses that warranted an appearance of the cat was lengthy, and included sleeping on duty, thievery of property and supplies, insubordination, quarreling, wagering, profanity, impiety, expression of unpatriotic sentiments, buggery and self-abuse, smoking outside the confines of the galley, and, most common of all, drunkenness.

Justice was meted out at eleven in the morning, prompt. Jones would take his usual spot on the quarter-deck, invariably draped in his most officious uniform and sword, Lieutenants Simpson and Hall and myself placed nearby, decked in comparable splendor. Jones abhorred making inefficient use of his time by doing only one thing at once, so he prefaced the proceedings with an address designed to promote the moral and spiritual improvement of the men. Some exertion of thought had clearly been put into the composition of these speeches, so fraught were they with allusions to Scripture and the classics, most prominently Plato's *Republic,* which Jones pronounced himself fortunate to study on that particular voyage. More often, however, Jones's empurpled pieties sooner assured his men's instant boredom than the perfection of their souls.

Thereafter began what I overheard some of the ables call "the good stuff." The day's offender was led forth by the master-at-arms' mates, in manacles, to the grating near the main mast. Though there had been no punishment yet, I noted his knees were already caked with flecks of dried blood. These were the wages of crawling on one's knees all morning, holystoning a deck sprinkled with sand.

Jones described the "crime" committed by the cruise's very first miscreant: the hoarding of grog rations. Jones then proceeded to make reasonable explanation of why, to prevent inebriation, the ration had been set only at a measure large enough to produce a pleasant sense of well-being, and how combining several days rations to build a single, good, roaring drunk defeated the purpose of this wise policy. Jones then asked the offender if he had anything to say. As this was none other than Ben Sharpless, the retired highwayman, Jones's voice was inflected with an extra measure of contempt. Sharpless shook his head in the negative.

"Strip that man," Jones ordered.

The manacles were removed. The mates proceeded to peel the brown *Ranger* uniform shirt from his back with some gentleness, as Sharpless was a good foot taller than any of them, and master-at-arms' mates were not immune to reprisal.

"Seize the prisoner."

Sharpless's wrists were lashed to the grating. Once he was secure, Master-at-Arms Joye turned to the Captain and nodded.

"Ten lashes," said Jones.

"Aye, sir. Ten lashes."

"Proceed."

Joye, who was shorter than Sharpless but just as thick around the chest and neck, produced the leather cord with its panoply of thick knots, and reared back. The first lash was accompanied by a whistle, like the swinging of a child's rope, followed by an unnatural pop, like a musket ball striking exposed flesh. I could see a line of purple scores on Sharpless's back. The second lash culminated in a similar pop, except a wetter one, as some of the scores had been torn open in the manner of lacerated grape-skin. The third and fourth lashes produced showers of blood droplets that peppered Sharpless's back and Joye's sleeveless arm.

The other men, meanwhile, watched in reverential fascination as Sharpless bore his pain with thuggish stolidity. His face did not appear to register the blows; there was even a hint of a smirk on his face, as if the display were the lesson not to him, but to everyone else.

The cat bit deeper on the fifth and sixth blows, and I noted a slight quiver at the corner of Sharpless's cocksure mouth. Jones, for his part, was impassive, his eyes resting not on Sharpless but on the deck, his ear cocked to the wind. I did not know what he was listening for, unless it was Sharpless's inevitable cries.

After the seventh and eighth blows, the cat was so thick with blood Joye ran the strap between his fingers to clean it between lashes. After the tenth, the Master-at-Arms stepped back and squared his shoulders, evidently much disappointed he had failed to elicit a scream from the stubborn brute. Jones looked up too, inspecting Sharpless's face, but all he was greeted with was a slight coloring on the rascal's cheeks, and that smirk.

Sharpless's eyes danced over the Captain, the officers, the rest of the crew. His silence announced his victory. He would be afraid of nothing. Unassailable, beyond punishment of mortal weaklings, he was now virtually the captain himself. Or so he thought.

"Ten lashes, sir," reported Joye.

"Ten?" replied Jones. "I believe you've lost count, Mr. Joye. What is the current total, Mr. Simpson?"

Here was an example of Jones's special genius. By adding lashes, he would pay Sharpless the wages of his bravado. By forcing Simpson to set the additional punishment, he would alienate this officer from the men. Simpson, knowing he was about to be raked, hove to and surrendered.

"I count five so far, sir."

"Continue then, Mr. Joye."

"Five more licks, nothin'! I got an even ten already!" Sharpless protested.

"Make that forty more. For insubordination."

A tremor of excitement ran through the assembly. Joye looked on the verge of bounding in happy anticipation of another chance to break Sharpless, but wisely restrained himself. Sharpless, having already fallen into Jones's trap once, held his peace.

Surgeon Green mumbled under his breath, addressed Jones.

"Captain?"

"You are excused, Mr. Green."

Green nodded, made for the ladderway. I was at first puzzled by this sudden departure. Was it some moral scruple against witnessing deliberate application of pain? Some proscription of the Hippocratic oath? In fact, it was none of these: he informed me later he was merely on his way down to the cockpit to break out his needles and cat-gut, knowing full well what forty lashes would wreak on an unprotected back.

It was this timely exit, this preparation for carnage, that finally wiped the smirk from Sharpless's face. With Joye's enthusiastic help, this expression would inevitably turn to thin-lipped resistance, followed by grimaces of discomfort, and finally scowls of agony. By lash fifteen a dull white surface appeared between the rivulets of blood on his upper back. (This was a bone Green later identified for me as the 'sca-sca-scapula'.) By lash 24 Joye's arm tired, and Jones ordered one of his mates to take over. This fresh tormentor introduced Sharpless to new depths of misery, until he was obliged to break off attempting to recite the Nicene Creed between his screams, and settled on screaming only. By lash 32 an odd silence overtook him. Only the sound of the flying cat, its ghastly whistle and pop, was audible as Sharpless's eyes rolled up inside his skull. There was a puddle of blood and corpuscles of skin and muscle on the deck beneath him. He was beyond any sensation of pain, let alone moral improvement, at that point, but the final lashes were duly served under Jones patient and legalistic supervision.

"Forty lashes, sir," said the master-at-arms' mate, out of breath.

"Cut him loose and get him down below."

As the ties around Sharpless's wrists had cut deeply, these were parted with a sharp knife. Jones was watching this operation with more than his usual attention.

"Handle him carefully," he said. "Support his head!"

The master-at-arms' mates did not take this order seriously, very probably because they believed the man who ordered such a foul beating could not possibly care if they supported Sharpless's head. They handled him more in the manner of a sack of meal on its way to the hold.

"Damnation! You're bending the wretch's neck back!" Jones cried. And he surrendered up his privileged position on the quarterdeck to dash in among the ruffians to show them how to bear a stricken man.

"Like this, you apes! Sling your forearm around—like so! Are you men watching?"

"Yes, sir," came the collective, incredulous reply.

The singular sight of the little captain, dressed in his spotlessly gilded perfection, working shoulder-to-shoulder with men clad in little more than their own sweat, rooted the rest of the crew in their spots. One hundred pairs of eyes lay on Jones and Sharpless as they approached the ladderway.

Such idleness did not sit well with Jones. He turned on his way down, frowning. "What are you rascals looking at? Lt. Simpson! All hands to quarters! Cast loose for drill!"

Simpson did not need to convey the order—it had been heard by all. Yet there was some crease of puzzlement on each brow, some slackening of pace to sort out this latest display. Was the captain's show of cruelty and kindness a warning that his wrath needed no personal animus to motivate it? Or was he, by ordering the beating, selflessly suppressing his innate sense of mercy in the name of discipline? No man could say. They all wandered off, shaking their heads, all beating their respective paths of speculation. Yet nothing was said aloud.

...

"And why did he help Sharpless?" asked Thierry.

"Once I'd learned to read Jones better, I realized the explanation was not so difficult. Quite simply, he had to be the best at everything, whether it be the application of pain or the laying on of mercy."

"Do you say he saw no distinction between the two?"

"I say he understood the distinction, and would excel at both."

...

The call for drill was the most common of the orders Jones issued in those first weeks of the crossing. Above cleanliness, gentility, and even efficiency, he held the crew's gunnery practice as essential to the achievement of his commission.

It was, alas, the sanest of his compulsions. I had already had occasion to learn at Valcour Island the bitter price to be paid for inaccurate shot-making. Jones held this question of placing the shot precisely where the gunner aimed, despite the movement of the target and the rolling of our own gun deck, as most important in the case of a running battle, where the *Ranger* enjoyed the luxury of standing off and bombarding an inferior vessel, or where she was obliged to pursue a faster one.

However, like all commanders of the melee or "open" school of tactics, his heart was not greatly attached to this sort of conflict. Instead, he preferred the straight-up exchange of iron with a superior adversary at point-blank range—the strife where Jones could see his enemy plainly and the enemy see Jones, in the glory of his courage and his impeccable pipings, as the consummate gentleman warrior he aspired to become. Even better, he relished trying conclusions with a British frigate at the end of his grappling hook, reeling it in like a fish and flooding her decks with his boarding parties. On these occasions, with the contending cannon virtually muzzle-to-muzzle, accuracy was hardly in question. Rather, it was pure speed of reload and fire, the mere difference of launching an extra broadside while the enemy paused to reload, that carried the day.

Jones was determined to have that extra shot. Specifically, he wanted to maintain a consistent rate of three discharges every five minutes. This was no mean demand, as the majority of our crew was inexperienced in the rigors of naval, as distinguished from merchant marine, gunnery. It would require many scores of drills, and the exhaustion of cask upon cask of gunpowder, to achieve such skill. But Jones was willing to wait.

Upon hearing the call to quarters, every crewman, on watch or off, was expected to race to his assigned station. For many of the landsmen, this was a position alongside one of the *Ranger*'s eighteen 9-pounder long guns. (She had originally rated twenty, but Jones left two behind in Portsmouth, to improve the sloop's sailing qualities.) With eight or nine men attached to each gun, there weren't enough hands to man all eighteen, but that was scarcely necessary as the man o'war is rarely engaged on both beams at once, and woe betide the one that is! In any case, ninety seconds after the call to quarters was piped the men were at their guns, sleeves rolled, bandannas on their heads to control their perspiration, many with cotton stuck in their ears against the shock of their guns' reports.

...

Severence paused, staring at Thierry. At length, she self-consciously crossed her right arm over her breast and fingered the teardrop-shaped lavalliere pendant at her throat. This was the last of Abrimal's gifts left in her possession.

"Is there something wrong, Captain?"

"But if I describe the task of loading, priming, aiming and firing a gun at sea it will certainly mean nothing at all to you. Much better to show you."

"I scarcely see how."

Thierry's skepticism did nothing to deflect him from this course, and he commenced to issue a list of items he would need for his demonstration. For lack of a footman, Gualbert rose and cheerily volunteered to fetch these things herself.

Soon the women were seated at the table, each with a water glass, a tin of pepper corns, a box of wooden matches, a napkin, and a dish of walnuts before them.

"First we are recounting history. Now we share recipes," remarked Thierry.

"At risk of inaccuracy," Severence began, ignoring the barb, "we shall dispense with the procedure of casting loose your guns and removing the tompions from the muzzle. As these procedures are wholly preparatory to firing, their omission will not necessarily figure in your rate of discharge . . . "

Severence then went on to describe what each of the objects before them represented aboard the man 'o war. The principles he laid before them weren't exactly difficult to comprehend—the women's slow uptake was related more to the multitude of simple things to remember, until the whole procedure appeared to them ridiculous. Severence's persistence won out over their reluctance, however, and his distaff gun crew finally stood (or, more appropriately, sat) ready to obey his commands.

"Allow these to burn and then smolder," he said, leaving two flaming matches at the lip of their dish of nuts. Then he withdrew one of his pocket watches and he laid his eye on the second hand.

"Ready?"

"Just get on with it," said Thierry.

"Now—level your guns!" he said.

The women took up their glasses and laid them on their sides.

"Load cartridge!"

Several peppercorns were tossed into the "cannons" in place of the bags of gunpowder the seamen actually used at sea. Gualbert smiled at Thierry, who was not so quick to be amused by the exercise.

"Shot your guns!"

A walnut, the cannonball, joined the peppercorns.

"Run out your guns!"

Thierry and Gualbert each slid their ordnance forward a few inches.

"Prime!"

Each woman seized an individual peppercorn and crushed it against the side of her glass. Gualbert was giggling openly now, while Thierry shook her head with the silliness of the entertainment.

"Quiet on the gun deck! Point your guns!"

They took aim, Thierry making extra effort to assure her weapon was trained on Gualbert's heart.

"FIRE!"

The women seized their smoldering matches (each representing the lye-soaked cotton wicks used aboard ship) and touched them to the "breech" of their glasses.

"BANG!" exulted Gualbert, immediately reddening with embarrassment.

"Sponge your guns!"

The glasses were cleansed with the napkin and made ready for the next "shot."

"That procedure, dear ladies, took exactly one and a half minutes to perform. A good rate, if you could maintain it."

"I have no doubt we could, as this was only our first attempt."

"Quite true. Except, you should bear in mind that the 'glasses' on the *Ranger* weigh three thousand pounds. Indeed, if they were not lashed down, and allowed to roll around a stormy deck, they would surely burst through the gunwales, or crush any number of men."

"The proverbial loose cannon!" sang Gualbert.

"Just so. Now we shall try it again. Only this time, if it amuses you, with an added element of realism . . . "

So they did it all again—this time with Severence on the floor, holding the leg of their Lacroix dining table, simulating the effect of a pitching sea. His enthusiasm soon caused a tureen and a carving knife to join him below. He also took this opportunity to make a close examination of the ladies' stockinged ankles.

"Oh, would you please get up!" Thierry implored him when they were done.

"You are a fool," Gualbert chided in a manner that would make all men grateful for their abiding foolishness.

"In a rolling sea, you took more than two and one half minutes to fire," he said as he retook his seat. "That is, I'm afraid, a recipe for defeat. Realize as well that while you operate the cannon, someone else is operating his, against you! If he is competent, there are sure to be dead and dying men all around you—blood—rigging and other detritus collapsing upon your head—"

"It was not a just test. The rocking spoiled my aim," said Gualbert.

"It is just so aboard the man o' war."

"You've made your point," Thierry sighed. "Three shots in five minutes is almost unbelievable."

...

It was a skill attained only after hundreds of hours of drills—drills for speed, drills for aim, these last at flagged buoys set afloat for the purpose. Wisely, Jones would reward the fastest crew of the day with an extra dip in the grog tub, and the fastest of the week with a doubloon. The competition fired the men's blood, until they forgot the smoke, the grit of powder between their teeth, and reports so loud they made their ears bleed. They even forgot their mistrust of Jones. Ben Sharpless, upon recovery from his injuries, became one of the quickest of the ship's shot-rammers. And no one could sponge or worm a gun faster than Scipio Africanus, the Negro.

Though it was hard work, I don't recall any more content times aboard the *Ranger* than drill. Some of the men became so attached to their guns they christened them with nicknames. The first gun on the larboard side, I recall, had a dun finish on her truck carriage, so her crew called her "Dun Bess." Anyone unfamiliar with this fact would have been puzzled to hear the men speak of the many cruelties of this lady Dun Bess, who made it her business to break many a man's heart, among other pieces of his anatomy.

The last gun on the same beam had a substantial recoil, so that one became known as "Jumping Jedediah." This gun unfortunately came to be regarded as unlucky, as "Jedediah" had a foul habit of jumping a bit too far back upon discharge, and once struck his gun captain full in the face with the butt of his cascabel—at the time the poor soul was standing a full ten feet behind! He died, of course.

My own role in these drills was no more than one of interested spectatorship. Instead, I was charged with the project of training the dozen Marines under my command in the arts of combat at sea or, in the case of several who were recruited right out of a tavern in Portsmouth, the rudiments of any sort of combat. While the cannon batteries blazed below, I would take a number of men up the main top to practice their sharp-shooting at targets in the water. By good fortune, a number of my men were raised on New England farms, and were as familiar with the musket as new recruits could ever be expected to be. Very early on, I decided to depart from custom, and permit only the best shots to do the actual firing. The rest of the men would be employed in powdering and shotting a weapon, so that the sharpshooter would always have a re-load available. In this fashion, my single gunners were able to put more balls into the target in less time than if I had employed mass-fire.

Our boarding exercises took the form of a line along the breadth of the poop deck, each Marine with a cutlass in his hand, as I acquainted them with the requisite footwork of balance in the first position, advance or retreat in the second position, and cut and thrust in the third. This drill bore some resemblance to a line-dance, provoking a rash of grins among the seamen, and self-consciousness among my own men, but these were small prices to pay. Their improvement was rapidly evident in the mock battles we organized with broom handles, and it was with some measure of pride that I showed this progress to Jones. His reaction was no more or less than I expected: a stony silence as he watched, an impatient "fair work," and the warning that their rate of improvement must be faster still.

"The enemy will not resist with broom handles," he said.

It was also my duty to oversee the sentries posted around the vessel, particularly those around the captain's door, the stores of some temptation (the grog), and, in times of battle, the guards that would stand near the ladderway to prevent shirkers from fleeing below . . .

...

"I would bear you the greatest appreciation," Thierry interrupted him, "if you would restrain your digressions to matters directly relating to your career with Paul Jones. The time . . . " And she gestured toward the mantle, assuming a glance at the clock would serve to complete her assertion.

"You need say no more, Mademoiselle. In my defense, it was merely my assumption that my taking greater care to describe life aboard the *Ranger* would serve to make further explanations unnecessary later on, as the routine is largely the same from ship to ship. By telling you, for instance, that the time between the drills and the end of the afternoon watch was, for some, consumed in the tasks of maintenance to the ship's sails, lines, wood and brasswork, and for others, an interval of leisure in conversation, crafts, or music, you may be assured that this was the case as well on the *Bonhomme Richard,* or the *Alliance,* or any of Captain Jones's other commands . . . "

"His defense takes longer than the offense," observed Gualbert. "Pray, Nathalie, let him tell it his own way . . . "

Thierry shrugged, "I don't care. The prize is his to lose."

Her reminder of this "prize" had definite effect on Severence. Suddenly, quite by impulse, his head was filled with visions of their fair and black downy locks tangled in ringleted folds of wanton abandon, of scented limbs the color of skimmed cream cocked in angles of languid receptivity, of skirts and stockings violently rent and pushed aside, of lips and napes and the best cheap passion money could buy. His editorial powers awakened.   ...

I say I was invited to mess with Captain Jones, but it would be more accurate to say that I was expected to dine with him. To Jones, supper in his cabin was as serious an affair as any state dinner in Philadelphia, and he tolerated no disrespect in its execution. In Portsmouth, he had had printed, at some expense, little gilded cards bearing his name, his rank, and his personal crest (twin dolphins and stags on a shield, undergirded by crossed cannon and the words "Pro Republica"). Every afternoon at six bells—three o'clock—Jones's steward would find the invitees for that evening and deliver their cards and respective handwritten messages, usually in the manner of "Captain Jones would be most Gratified by the Presence of Mr. Such-and-So at Table this Evening." These required the standard reply, the "Mr. Such-and-So would be most Delighted to accept the aforesaid Invitation . . . ," written on the back of the card immediately, regardless of what sort of essential ship's business the designated officer was immersed in that moment. These replies were expected to be well penned and felicitously phrased, as our captain had a passion for letters, and took a dim view of those who did not share his mania for self-improvement.

Once accepted, the captain's invitation carried a certain responsibility of carriage. Officers who appeared at his table with spots on their waistcoats or shirt ruffles uncrisp or crooked stocks and sloppy turnbacks were treated to a drubbing. Artful handling of forks and cutlery was also noted, and received appreciative comments or sharp criticism, as the circumstance demanded.

Otherwise, Jones was a fine and gracious host. He saw to it that a good table was set for his guests. He took turns speaking and respected the opinions of others. Jones was attempting to perpetuate, I realized, the illusion that he had never left the bright and witty society ashore—that he was still in some Portsmouth drawing room, albeit one much further west than the conventional town lines, taking cigars and port in company of other dashing fellows, while sumptuously flounced and hatted ladies sat and gossiped and fanned themselves prettily nearby, albeit in this case somewhere in the vicinity of middle gun deck—

And yet, even as dictator of the little world aboard the *Ranger,* he could not deceive himself. Despite the formalities, his dinners were not convocations of equals. While we discoursed on various issues, from international diplomacy to the relative merits of young ladies from the New England and the Southern colonies, I perceived his eyes searching the face of his listeners, holding his eternal vigil, as if waiting for some echo, some ricochet of vitality, to relieve him of his growing boredom with his own voice.

This was particularly evident when he saw fit to exhume the issue of the seniority list, which he brought out in the manner of a man who could not hold his spirits, but was compelled to indulge by destructive habit.

Indeed, how could he have expected this table fellowship to be anything more than a sham? To his men, he was not only a martinet, but a foreign and dangerous one. To Jones, his men were too often instruments to be sharpened or discarded, as efficiency demanded. However strongly he felt the sanctity of his dinner ritual, Jones could not alter these perceptions merely by gifting his officers with gilded cards and fine roasts. It was a puzzle of his character, this belief that he could pound a man without mercy with one hand and extend the other in collegial friendship. However stubborn or cruel he appeared in the exercise of his duty, he never seemed to believe it was possible that his most treasured self, that charming parlor raconteur and altogether fine fellow, Paul Jones, would be blamed for the excesses of the Scottish bully he let slip on deck.

The more intelligent officers seemed to suffer a more sullen sort of resentment at Jones's below-decks elegance and chivalry. They, no doubt, believed he was hinting that he was somehow superior to them. And though the refinement of his manner did indeed win him many admirers at the supper-tables of Europe, it earned him nothing but enmity in America, especially among the other captains and agents of the Navy.

Lt. Simpson, for his part, would never give his captain the satisfaction of actually engaging him in conversation, preferring instead the subtler aggression of studied passivity. Lieutenant Hall and the midshipmen would sooner have stuck their heads in the muzzle of a British long 24 than dare to dispute Jones. I would not have done so myself, despite the loneliness that now appeared to scream with each succeeding unchallenged syllable. I remembered his sudden change in disposition as soon as he had succeeded in luring me aboard. I could have ignored him.

"I think you wrong, sir, to impute such cowardice on the part of the Dutch race . . . ," I found myself uttering one evening, after Jones had taken it upon himself to trace the descent of Holland's manhood since their taking of the British factory at Bantam in 1619. He paused, momentarily out of words, in such a shock that might be expected if he had shouted down a well, and received a rejoinder instead of mere echo. He smiled, demurred: "There is much credit to be given the Dutch Indiaman in years since." For my part, I looked into my plate and cursed myself.

...

Gualbert's eyes narrowed. "Cursed yourself? Why?"

"For taking pity upon him. Pity, you could be sure, he would never show to me. It was, I own, a mistake I was to make scores of times over the ensuing months. It was the engine of our friendship."

...

IX.

I prefer a Solid to a Shining Reputation.

—JOHN PAUL JONES to M. de Sartine, 1778

～

"PITY does not strike me as a sound foundation on which to build such a relationship," Thierry remarked.

A dimple formed on Gualbert's cheek as a thought flew into her head, shook its plumage, and decided to linger a moment. "Oh, it's not so bad," she said. "It's made some of my relationships more pleasant."

"I should think pity would be indispensable in your occupation," Severence said. This remark sounded a bit insolent to Thierry's ears. She suspected he was growing too comfortable with the liberality of their talk, and fixed a cold eye on him to warn him of this offense.

"Perhaps I—er—misspoke when I called it 'pity'," he stammered, perceiving his error. "To be more accurate, it became more a matter of my implication in Jones's crimes of character. Consider, for instance, the case of a certain Midshipman Dooley, a lad not more than sixteen years old . . . "

"Midshipman? Explain."

...

A student officer, assigned aboard to learn the trade of sail and war. Almost every man o' war had a few, even ones as small as *Ranger*. Dooley was our eldest—a great, green, gangling sprout, with hands too big for his wrists and a wide moon face pocked with spots. By all accounts, he was the favorite of his mother, who drove all night down to the Piscataqua roadstead to see him off properly.

Jones, to his credit, did his best to reassure her of her son's good treatment. He came down the gangplank, took the mother's hand in his, and made a solemn personal pledge that as long as his command stayed atop the waves, then, by Jove, so would Midshipman Dooley. Yet even this could not dissuade the woman from making a disgraceful scene of weeping and wailing, and waving her handkerchief with such spastic abandon we could still make it out a half mile down the river.

For his part, Dooley suffered this separation with a quiet courage, albeit a courage of teary eyes and quivering lip! Jones got it into his head that he would favor the boy. He would take him in hand, teach him his accumulated wisdom, and turn him out a fine young version of himself. Jones took his pledges to the ladies very seriously—as long as they had nothing to do with affairs of heart.

But Dooley would not collaborate in his reinvention. Though he was clearly an intelligent boy, several delicacies of character manifested themselves rather quickly. First, he was seasick. Seasick, I mean to say, almost all of the time during that first crossing to France. While most of the lubbers managed to pull themselves vertical within a few days of their first symptoms, Dooley could not. I remember Jones emerging on the quarterdeck every morning, casting a look around, and inquiring of Lt. Simpson where Midshipman Dooley was. As the answer was always the same—sick in his bunk—Jones grew progressively more cross with every passing day of this condition. At length, Surgeon Green was charged with the task of promoting the boy's debut at any cost— ". . . even if he must wear a bucket tied around his neck!" instructed the Captain.

Soon after, Dooley was sighted up and about, though still a bit green about the gills. Jones greeted him like a long-lost father, praising the boy's pluck in the face of petty discomfort. As there was little time to delay his education, he immediately ordered him up onto the main top yards, to hand the earrings to the topmen engaged in reefing those sails. Surgeon Green's expression told me that this was not such a good idea. Jones, true to form, did not take this hint, and no one was about to gainsay him.

Dooley put on a brave face and commenced his ascent. Now, after having visited those dizzying heights myself, after a far shorter period of indisposition than poor Dooley's, I can testify that a number of uncomfortable sensations awaited him. Even with his legs braced firmly on the topgallant cross trees, his eyes closed and his thoughts focused firmly on Providence, he could not help but feel the motion of the ship exaggerated, at that extremity. Adding to this the consideration that *Ranger* was already underballasted and over-sparred, and had an unfortunate habit of heeling over far too much underway, Dooley might be forgiven for believing himself a rag doll at the end of a pike, whipped this way and that, until his head swam and his ears rang and death became a fathomable alternative.

Jones, meanwhile, believed himself imparting a valuable lesson, and shouted up encouragements to the boy to "hop-to" and "make a good show of it for the other boys." The topmen were waiting there, spread over the length of the yard, waiting for the earrings. But it was all Dooley could do to cling with both arms to the mast. Jones was down below yelling at him to "let go!", and Dooley, hearing a distant voice, made the mistake of looking down to the source of it . . .

Now, many an offensive thing has been dropped on John Paul Jones over his career, but I believe he would have preferred hot grapeshot to what bore down on him from Dooley's distressed gullet. As it was, he barely escaped a soiling. When he rose again to his feet, there was such a scowl of rage upon his face I sensed Mr. Dooley's term of education was at a sudden end.

The captain's mood darkened further when Dooley subsequently declined to climb down from his high perch. It was only with the encouragement of three topmen, and threats of laceration upon his tender back, that they were able to pry his hands from the mast and escort him, weeping with fear, to the fate that awaited him below.

It was not, dear ladies, for any lack of ordinary human compassion that Jones embarked on the program of "spine-stiffening" he formulated for the midshipman. Rather, it was a curative he sought—a way to erase the spectacle of the boy's weakness from the minds of the (otherwise amused) men. In Jones's mind, Dooley represented the future generation of the American race, and if that race needed a tempering by fire, then a tempering by fire it would be . . .

Thereafter, Dooley's fear of heights was attacked by exiling him to the farthest extremity of the mainmast (equipped, of course, with a small canvas "accident" bag). This sort of punishment was called "mastheading," and Dooley was the acknowledged master of it by the voyage's end. No other creature, except maybe the birds, saw so much of the Atlantic from such a height as he.

When further . . . susceptibilities . . . made their appearances, Jones dealt with them in like fashion. When Dooley reported that his sense of hearing was more sensitive to the insult of repeated gunfire than the other tars', Jones placed him in charge of three guns on the larboard poop. When Dooley showed some squeamishness in relieving himself like a man off the bowhawse, Jones made him "Captain of the Head," a commission that made him personally responsible for the cleanliness of the Captain's own privy closet.

Was this cruel? Judge for yourself: after two weeks of mastheading, Dooley learned how to come down with a clean bag. As captain of the three great guns on the larboard poop, Dooley overcame his sensitivity to loud noises (though at some cost, as I will detail later). He furthermore whipped those crews into the fastest ones save the team of Ben Sharpless and Scipio Africanus. As "Captain of the Head," he finally learned to meet even Jones's exacting standards.

Still, the men believed the captain was unjustly singling out the boy, and much talk was made behind his back. In the wardroom, Lieutenant Simpson muttered, "I wonder what his punishment is for a case of black vomit." Surgeon Green judged it all a "sha-sha-shameful display." The other midshipmen would hardly dare to exhale in Jones's presence. This unanimity of disapproval finally pierced Jones's consciousness: he turned to me one evening at table, after the others had left, and asked me in a voice much like the one I'd known in Portsmouth, "Say, you don't think I've led old Mrs. Dooley on, do you?"

His face showed no irony, no testing. I could only look at the sincerity of his concern for his chivalrous vow, and think about the improvements I'd undeniably seen in Dooley's seamanship, and tell him, "You have been a stern taskmaster—but you've never denied the straw to make bricks."

...

"A cowardly answer," said Thierry. "You would have helped him more if you had told the truth."

"You mean, inform on his critics?" Gualbert asked.

"Not at all."

...

I suppose I could have helped Jones to see the weaknesses of his style of command. I could have told him, for example, that stirring himself from his private cabin to dine with his officers and crew would have done more constructive good for morale than a hundred gilded invitation cards. A word of encouragement here, a "well done" there, would have made all the difference, for his men would have appreciated such morsels, and worked hard to hear more. Benjamin Franklin told him the very same, in a letter Jones read aloud to me, ostensibly in amusement, but no doubt with a sense of its truth, when he wrote in "Poor Richard" fashion that "more flies are caught with honey than with vinegar."

On the other hand, it would be unjust to indict a captain's shipboard discipline from the comfort of a drawing room. Jones humiliated men, yes. He drove them hard and he broke them, no doubt. But I never knew him to mete out such deadly punishments as were the amusement of many Royal Navy captains, such as "keel-hauling," when a man is tied by rope, dropped off the stem of a moving ship, and pulled under the keel all the way to the stern. Nor did I know Jones ever to whip a man to death, as was also known to happen in the navy of Britain.

Indeed, if Jones punished, it was most likely followed with an equal and opposite forebearance. Jones's reputation for harshness could not be sustained merely by the facts. Indeed, he was battling a far more insidious foe than the British the whole length of his career: an enemy more implacable, more difficult to run from, impossible to meet in open battle. He suffered from gossip.

Jones did not speak often of his own history. He was always far more interested in the future, unless the past included some instance of personal slight, in which case he never forgot and never tired of referring to it. I could not form a clear impression of his experiences as a boy in southwestern Scotland because his story changed every time he told it. The first time, over a bottle of Portuguese madeira on *Ranger*, he painted a picture of his childhood home at Arbigland in the rosy tints of nostalgia—of his father, the respected scion of the local Scots gentry, of the cool onshore breezes rolling up the gentle hills above Solway Firth, of his joy in running down to watch the fishing craft put in at Carsethorn. The sea, it seemed, was the natural conduit of young John's ambitions. When he looked south, he could glimpse the outlines of ships beating up or riding down out of the Solway, their prows splitting the broad avenue of wave and wind, destined (he believed) for the Continent, or such exotic parts as America, India, or China. When the weather was clear, he could glimpse the vaporous blue of the English coast opposite, some ten miles distant, and imagine he was on topmast watch aboard a great square-rigger at landfall. When the clouds blew in from the Irish Sea, he watched England grow fainter and grayer, until she disappeared entirely, and the water was traversed by columns of frowning thunderheads pouring their rains into the Firth.

When he looked north from Arbigland, though, he saw nothing more than that other sea of heather-on-moor. Though it seemed as vast as the aqueous highway, no ships ever glided on that ocean. Discounting the sheep and their drab, straggling minders, the heath looked dead to him. He could not stay there.

The next time we discussed such matters, we were at Brest, waiting for a wind to take us out of port and toward our fate in English waters. This time, he said that his wealthy father, the member of the respectable gentry, was not strictly his father at all, but rather a sort of stepparent. This distinction hardly mattered, I was told, because he was treated like a son by the man, whose name was Mr. Craik. Very early in his life, young John's heroic qualities were recognized by his social betters, who instructed him in the arts of horsemanship, the sword, and the cotillion, with an eye toward his cultivation as a hero of arms. What they could not have foreseen in his maturity, Jones noted, was his abiding love of America, and the standards of liberty and human dignity upon which he had staked his fortune and his reputation.

The third and last time he broached this subject was in a letter he wrote to me just a few months ago, when he was fulfilling his duties as Kontradmiral of the Imperial Russian Navy in that nation's struggles with the Turk. Jones's moods by this point must have been darker than I had ever known them. He seemed possessed by thoughts of opportunities, enemies, women that had slipped through his fingers over the years, and were now forever lost.

In this letter he confessed, without reference to his earlier distortions, that Mr. Craik was neither his father nor his stepfather, but merely his parents' employer. His real father, whose full name was John Paul, was Craik's gardener; his mother was washwoman and housekeeper. The name

"Jones," in fact, is an alias the junior John Paul took up some years later, for reasons I intend to make clear.

His strongest memory, he wrote, was not of the sea or of ships, but of an incident he had witnessed as a boy of ten. He had been playing on the hills near the Craik mansion, and had come running home at the time appointed by his father. As he approached the cottage Mr. Craik had built for his servant family, young John Paul was surprised to look up and see his mother there. She was, as he put it, in a position of peril with the aforesaid gentleman. That is, in his arms, leaning against the back wall of the cottage.

The boy, no doubt, was shocked and sickened by this spectacle. Until that moment, he had considered his mother's moral quality to lie somewhere between those of the Virgin Mother and Elizabeth I. Indeed, he had hardly been disabused of the notion that his own conception had been immaculate.

Imagine how his heart leapt, then, when he further saw that his father, the gardener, was approaching from around the corner, a spade slung over his shoulder, and would unavoidably lay his own eyes on the betrayal! What would his father do? the boy wondered. What mischief would he work upon Craik's soft body with that spade? Young John held his breath, as if in wait for the detonation of a cannon.

But it did not happen as he had imagined. When his father rounded the corner, he stopped short. Craik and his mother were still in their sinful embrace, *in flagrante delicto,* but young John was stunned to witness his father simply frown, turn around, and walk away—what is more, walk away on tiptoe, as if afraid his withdrawal would be noticed by the lovers!

This spectacle was more than the boy could bear. Seizing the only "weapon" at his disposal, an old broom with its comb shorn off, young John leapt into the breach, crying, "Villain, defend yourself!" Commencing then to beat his family's employer about the lower extremities with the broom, the boy had Craik at an awkward pass, as Milord's pants were at half-mast and his arms were around Mrs. Paul. Craik was down, struggling to restore his decorum in the dust, when the mother abruptly ended the attack by slapping young John, hard, across his face.

This was the episode's second and most serious shock for the boy. He stared at his mother, gape-mouthed with astonishment. Then, and only then, did he weep tears of humiliation, and ran away for many hours on the moor.

There, with his feet buried in the wet heather and his fist overhead, the boy made a vow to himself. He would, he decided, never countenance injustice when it was within his power to render it right. Indeed, he would see to this goal by increasing the range of his powers so completely, so breathtakingly, that his brilliance would forever protect him from the predations of the wealthier, the better-privileged. He would be the wisest, most powerful man he was ever likely to meet. And he would not rest until these ambitions were fulfilled.

...

"The story is pathetic, but common," Thierry remarked. "I would say most housekeepers, the pretty ones, can't be trusted. And I hardly blame them, considering the powers that lord over them."

"In France, perhaps," conceded Severence. "But Paul Jones's fighting blood did not spring out of a sinful anemia. His father, by most accounts, was an honest and spirited man; Mrs. Paul, aside from a weakness for Mr. Craik that may well have preceded her marriage, was a good and tireless mother. If such an incident had been commonplace, John Paul the Senior might have been compelled to use his spade sooner or later. But its rarity made the pass difficult—was it really worth the end of his livelihood? Instead, he made a moderate choice, a wise one. It was unfortunate only in the fact that his son, who could not yet understand the compromises of maturity, had seen it all."

"Odd, then, that he preferred to think of this Mr. Craik as his father," said Gualbert.

"But it was understandable. John Paul Jones has misspent his life believing himself superior to his fellows. He may well have wished his glory sprung from nobler loins than that of a mere gardener, and a cuckold to boot."

"Aaaaaaahhhhhhh!" Thierry blurted, holding her palms over her ears. When the eyes of her startled tablemates were turned to her, she shook her head without removing her hands from the sides of her head. "I will listen to no more of this talk! When I invited you to tell the Captain's history, I did not mean for you to conduct a vivisection! I want to hear of heroes, not specimens!"

Severence noted a crease of annoyance on Gualbert's face, as if she were growing impatient with her friend's censorious assertions. For his part, his designs on both women would oblige him to walk the middle line.

"I continually find myself making apologies to you ladies," he said. "My capacity to tell a story, unfortunately, is no greater than I have represented it to be. If it be adventure you crave, then the following might be of interest."

...

Jones was less creative in his accounts of his early career at sea, possibly because it was a tale of one success after another. He first went to sea as ship's boy at the age of fourteen. By seventeen, he was Third Mate John Paul on *King George*, a Whitehaven slaver. He soon tired of that business, owing to the fact that it was morally culpable and, in addition, that the indelible odor of slave feces in the fabric of his uniform did not betoken gentility at teas and dances.

The signal moment in his merchant marine career came when he was just 21. He was, in the summer of '68, shipping home to Kirkcudbright aboard *John*, a brig bearing pickled beef and butter from Jamaica. In mid-voyage, a fever struck both the captain and first mate. As no one else aboard held competence in navigation, there was some consternation as to who would conduct the vessel safely to port. Of course, their passenger John Paul Jr., a demonical self-improver, was fully conversant with the mysterious arts of celestial navigation. He was invited to take over command, and did so, seeing the brig to its home port in perfect order. In their gratitude, the ship's owners appointed him commander in official capacity. He had gone from ship's boy to the quarterdeck in just seven years—an impressive achievement!

John Paul Jr.'s troubles began as soon as the magnitude of his authority gave dangerous scope to his flaws of character. Less than two years after receiving his first command, he was made to answer charges of gross cruelty upon the person of one Mungo Maxwell, ship's carpenter aboard *John*.

Apparently, Maxwell had the approximate grating effect on his captain's sensibilities that midshipman Dooley did on *Ranger,* except that Maxwell could not offer the excuse of youth. Captain Paul had him trussed up on the brig's shrouds and whipped until he bled.

Unfortunately for the young commander, Maxwell was the son of a leading citizen of Kirkcudbright, and could count on powerful friends. Grievously incensed by his ill treatment, Maxwell jumped ship in Tobago and, after filing formal charges against his commander, attempted to make passage home by mail packet. On the way, he died. The reasons for his death, it is held, were the physical effects from his beating, aggravated by acute melancholia.

In any case, Paul was still obliged to answer the charges when he reached Scotland. His answers apparently were judged sufficient, as he was not officially held responsible for Mungo Maxwell's death. The verdict of the common seamen, though, was less charitable by half.

This incident was followed three years later by one that added still more notoriety to Captain John Paul's name. I warn you, in fact, to adopt some skepticism in hearing Jones's own testimony. As he was the only one I knew to witness it, I only think it wise to make adjustment for the habitual convenience of his memory.

By that time, he was commander of *Betsy,* his first ship-rigged vessel. According to Jones, he had put into the roadstead at Scarborough, at Tobago, after surviving a severe storm at sea that shredded his vessel's courses and caused him a sickness that laid him low for two weeks. What is more, the crew demanded wages in advance at Scarborough, to spend on their wives and paramours ashore. As their Captain Paul preferred to invest the ship's treasury in a lucrative spice cargo, and not to subsidize amusements, he refused the advance.

Would that this commander had had a single iota of insight into his fellow humanity at that moment! If he had, he would not have made this highly unpopular decision so blithely. Nor would he have added fuel to the blaze by making a paltry counter-offer of free socks from his slops chest. Young Paul, who did not drink, was perfectly capable of thinking a pair of woolens just compensation for a night deprived of grogging and debauchery!

Here, at last, was the end of the crew's patience with this self-important little captain. To their thinking, no doubt, they had served him more than competently through the passage and the storm, and were repaid for their heroics by an inexplicable preference for purser's minutiae.

Against his loud protests, the weakened Paul was obliged, by threats of force, to retire to a cabin below, and the crew prepared to embark for shore without his leave. Many of the mutinous gang departed believing they had acted with some measure of restraint against their impossible commander. Such uprisings were not unknown in the less disciplined atmosphere of merchant service, and were generally more injurious to the captain's pride than his real authority. And indeed, not even Jones could testify that any money or supplies were taken from his cabin by the "brutes," or that any particular harm was done to his person.

These men were surprised, therefore, to see Paul dare to reappear on deck as they cast off in the ship's launch, this time with a sword in his hand! You see, it was a peculiarity of his character that he simply could not walk away from a fight, even when there was little to win. Much later, this instinct would stand him well in battles with superior British forces. Here, his resolution became, in fact, a liability, working only to aggravate his troubles.

The less temperate characters among the mutineers cried out for someone to deal with the "pest." One fellow, a giant native to that island, returned to the deck to squash him once and for all.

Seizing a shot-rammer from one of the gun stations, this man proceeded to wield it threateningly, driving Paul backward until he teetered on the edge of an open ladderway. The brute then raised his weapon above his head, as if to strike.

Judging further retreat impossible, Paul made an impulsive stab at his adversary—and was startled to discover his blade had passed quite through the other's body! The mutineer died in minutes, after much writhing and crying out to his fellows for vengeance. Jones told me (and I believe him on this matter) that it was more in shock than in triumph that he pulled his weapon out of the corpse.

The other seamen, meanwhile, sat dumbstruck, believing themselves to have witnessed a fully wanton homicide. Screams of "Murder!" went up. The ship's launch, already filled with crewmen in anticipation of a jolly time, was cast off, every man in it a witness for Captain Paul's prosecution ashore.

Just then, he understood he had but one of two choices: either to give himself up to the island authorities willingly, or to beat a quiet retreat. Both held grave risks for the progress of his career.

...

"What did he do?" Gualbert breathed.

"He ran off like a common criminal, of course," said Thierry.

"That's curious," Severence observed, cocking his head at her. "How did you know that was what he did?"

"*Naturallement*, from my impression of his character. Aboard ship, he is fearless, impeccable. But ashore, he is lost. The subtle shades of human conduct escape him. He is not obeyed unquestioningly. In a court fight, he would not command."

An admirable appraisal. I would add but little to it—except to note that he did have influential friends ashore, including the British Lieutenant Governor! He would have had grounds to believe he would be acquitted. After all it was, strictly speaking, a clear case of mutiny.

...

Several other factors must have borne on his decision. First, the dead man was a native, and Jones may have believed an impartial judgement impossible in that hot-tempered clime. Second, the Mungo Maxwell affair still rankled his conscience, and was surely to be raised in any prospective prosecution.

Third, he had, from the first moment he saw America as a ship's boy of the brig *Friendship,* fallen quite in love with the notion of emigrating. Indeed, to my knowledge fair Columbia was the only land to which Jones had an instant affinity. He would, for other reasons, learn to dally with your France, but it was to America that he felt himself truly betrothed. Moreover, he could find refuge with a brother there, one William Paul of Fredericksburg, in the Commonwealth of Virginia. I think it quite possible that Jones, ever the opportunist, made the best of this predicament and used it to precipitate his reinvention as an American. I say, "I think," because I am not sure. If ever Jones referred to decisions made in his past, including ones as fateful as this, he rarely saw fit to justify them.

So it was to Virginia he flew, dropping his surname along the way and adopting for the first time the nondescript cognomen of "Jones." The Mungo Maxwell and Tobago affairs would always dog him, however. Men whispered of them wherever he went, and whatever victories he staked. His crews scrutinized his every action in light of them; otherwise common cruelties were held up as proofs of his abiding guilt. He was marked as clearly as Cain.

Despite all of this, Jones came to the New World bearing a goodly amount of hope in his heart. For everything about that green and untrammeled continent told him that the personal alchemy he planned for himself on that heath at Arbigland, the metamorphosis of a hot-blooded gardener's son into a cool philosopher-aristocrat, was possible—even easy!—in America.

I believe this was the freedom Jones held most dear. It was quite apart from the exaltation of the rabble beloved of French democrats, or the intellectual principles asserted by Messrs. Paine and Jefferson. It was not the disposal of elites he sought, but a meritocracy of the brilliant, the brave, the witty. And it could scarcely be said Jones fought less hard for his America than any other patriot, democratic or not, as I now will have occasion to relate.

X.

THAT FIRST ocean crossing on *Ranger* was the easiest I have ever experienced. More often than not we ran with main courses set, a quartering wind over our shoulders, with the bow pitching up and down lightly over the swells, as if the vessel had its own appointment to keep on the opposite shore. When I could not sleep, I would mount to the quarterdeck by night and observe the anonymous silhouettes on midwatch as they tended that dozing island of wood and brass, from the helmsman leaning at his wheel, his face aglow from the candlelit binnacle, to the shade braced in the main top, scanning the black of night against the profounder black of the sea. As wondrous Selene withdrew her horns, the sails seemed to stretch aloft to welcome her cold beauty, gathering her opal light until they glowed in reciprocal glory.

We saw no other sail for four weeks. Not only England but all of Europe seemed to have determined to leave the blue to the *Ranger* alone.

The crew, for their part, grew restless with the unprofitable inactivity. Men who would normally be diverted by games or crafts in their off-watch hours watched the waves instead, their eyes becoming so accustomed to a distant focus that when they turned in my direction they seemed to be looking through me. Only Jones, the campaigner, the Old Man at thirty, seemed content to wait: he knew the shipping lanes around the Continent would not, could not, fail to be teeming with fat merchantmen and, even better, scrapping warships.

It was during this lull that I was apprised of the fact, through the knowledgeable offices of Surgeon Green, that there was an additional body aboard the *Ranger* not counted on the ship's roster. Green mentioned this matter as he stood above me on the ship's head, waiting for me to finish my natural business off the bow. He eyed me as I buttoned my breeches, as if measuring me for a particularly momentous secret.

"If you like your pl-pl-pleasures on the regular, then sea life ain't for you," he said.

"What 'pleasures'?"

"The skirt-wearing kind," he replied, and then watched me again. In truth, there was no denying his point. He resumed, "Unless, you know certain parties."

"What are you coming to?" I demanded, tired of his circumlocutions. "I'll keep your secret."

This was what he was waiting for. All at once, I was informed of a certain cornfed Jezebel who had been hidden away on the orlop deck ever since Portsmouth. There, she was known to entertain all comers privileged to know of her presence. Dr. Green assured me that this numbered no more than twenty or thirty officers and men. "Her only price is her rations . . . and a share in the prize money. She keeps a book," he told me.

I was surprised. In general, sailors are superstitious men, and women were regarded as frightful carriers of bad luck, even worse than rabbits and albatrosses. True as this was ashore, as when women were seen carrying empty water buckets, or crossed a sailor's path, they were still more dangerous afloat.

With more years at sea, however, I learned that such women were not uncommon on merchant vessels, where whole economies of secret subservices could be conducted under the noses of their masters. Though the upper, more livable decks of a vessel allowed very little margin for privacy, there were, alternately, a number of dank holds and compartments that might as well have been exotic continents, so little were they visited in mid-voyage. If a determined stowaway was willing to forgo sunlight and air, he or she could escape discovery for many months, or even indulge her talent for enterprise.

"If the Captain knew . . . ," I began.

"He isn't invited. You are."

"Why me?"

"She's heard you're a Severrrrrrr'ce of New-York," he said. "She's smarter'n all of us."

...

"And did you make use of her?" asked Thierry.

"Not at first. But she will re-enter my story later, should you wish to hear it."

"Libertine. Proceed, then."

...

Jones's patience was borne out by the time we reached the lee side of the Western Islands late in November. There, not one hundred leagues from the shores of Ireland, we spoke new sails on our horizon in a more or less regular cavalcade—brigs out of Spain and Portugal, a Dutch snow, a British sloop running with a bit in her teeth. Alas, for various reasons none of these would do as prizes. The Spaniards and Portuguese were officially neutrals, and we would never have caught the sloop with the wind abeam.

Jones's eyes fell upon these ships like a wolf's searching for a straggler from the fold. He was not insensate to his men's frustrations; he would have dearly welcomed an opportunity to mete out his notion of tyrannicide at a rate of three shots every five minutes. But our infant navy, an outnumbered outlaw upon the waves, had to choose her battles with much care. The loss of *Ranger* in some ill-advised clash would have been a greater blow to the Continental Navy, in proportion to its size, than any three 74's to the Royal Navy.

"Deck! Sail ho, three points on the larboard bow!" a maintopman announced one morning, just a few day's sail north of the French headland.

"What's that ship, Mr. Simpson?" Jones asked. The captain was already standing at the larboard rail, his eyes on the described point, as if he had been scrutinizing the new sail before it had been sighted aloft. By this time I could see it too, but my novice's eyes could not distinguish what sort she was, or even whether she was coming or going.

Out came Lt. Simpson's telescope. After several moments' squinting study, he lowered the instrument.

"A brig, fully laden. Evidently making for Plymouth."

"And the Red Ensign . . . ?"

"Just as you please," came the answer.

Jones looked down, a frown upon his face. By this, I knew the prospect for action was good, as I'd learned Jones always greeted moments of opportunity with a frown.

"Mr. Cullam!" he said. "Clear new heading, two points a-larboard."

"Aye, two points a-larboard," replied Cullam, who then nodded to his helmsman. As *Ranger* was turned to a heading that would take her closer to the approaching ship, every soul aboard, busy or not, seemed to cock an ear out. In spirit, they were all standing with Simpson, behind Jones's shoulder, awaiting the inevitable, and possibly lucrative, order.

"Seize up braces, boys—step lively," Cullam told his ables. In anticipation of battle, these men were instructed to put their backs to the ropes that controlled the angle of the sail yards and, by effect, the speed of the ship.

"Beat to quarters, sir?" pressed the eager Simpson.

Jones eyed him, evidently not to be rushed. This was, after all, to be the *Ranger*'s first real proving, and by unmysterious reflection, his own debut on this much grander stage of European arms. After some moments, he finally cast a doleful eye on that faraway daub of canvas and granted, with some understatement, "That is my intention, sir."

As *Ranger* was judged too small to warrant a drummer, this much-anticipated command (such as it was) was carried through the farthest corners of the vessel by whistle and spoken relay. Yet, thanks to Jones's monomaniacal drilling, I could not imagine a quicker process if every one of the seamen had hatched the same notion in their heads simultaneously. Before the echo of the pipes had died, our topmen had scaled the shrouds and begun furling every square inch of canvas that was not customarily used in battle, and arranging the rest in that half-reefed configuration we knew as "fighting sails." Topchains and puddening were hung aloft, to snare damaged rigging before it fell to the deck, and anti-boarding nets strung along the bulwarks, to snare invaders.

These topmen were soon joined by my own marines, who took up their stations on the main-top and, in accord with my orders, had already begun to load as many surplus firepieces as they could fit through the lubber-hole. From that height, at close quarters, I trusted my marksmen would rain down God's own hellfire on anyone who dared show himself on the enemy deck. Of course, we expected a worthy opponent to attempt the same from his tops.

Meanwhile, on the main deck, the balance of my marines took up positions behind the hammock nets. Landsmen were busied with fire-buckets, spreading handfuls of sand on the deck to absorb the anticipated blood. To this frenzy was added the bleats and clucks of our surviving live stores of pigs, goats and chickens as they were tossed overboard, into the waiting arms of the men in *Ranger*'s launch. When the boat was loaded with these beasts, and with other valuables such as the captain's mahogany writing desk and the grog tub, it would repair some distance from the battle, to be retrieved by the victors.

On the gun deck, the great guns were cast loose and readied. The bulkheads defining the captain's and officers' cabins were detached and stowed, and 18-pounders rolled in. The ship's boys had gotten a head start at shuttling from the powder stores to the guns with fresh cartridges, racing serpentine around the tubs of slow-matches and of water that were set out, respectively, for detonation and for safety. Lower still, in the cockpit, I knew Surgeon Green to be laying out a stretch of canvas on his sea-chest, and preparing his instruments of amputation. No doubt he was already sampling the rum too, assuring himself of its deadening effects.

There was no real cause to believe all of these procedures would be necessary against a mere merchant brig. In all likelihood, this would surrender without a shot fired. They were, in fact, precautions against the unforeseen, such as the possibility that the brig was not a brig at all but a disguised warship, or that the sail of an escorting frigate would suddenly appear. The order to "beat to quarters" anticipated all of these eventualities, with the dividend of busying every single member of the crew and leaving no room for fear.

After the possibility of undue resistance, the next least desirable circumstance was evasion. Jones saw to this by ordering the Red Ensign of the British merchant fleet to be flown from our mast. If the brig's captain was examining *Ranger* through his own telescope at that moment (which he almost certainly was), he would see a tight, well-handled sloop, a captain dressed in limey blue and white at the rail, and a friendly flag.

When we had closed to within a mile, Lt. Simpson made an examination of the brig again.

"She's holding course. Gun ports 're opened."

"Can you count her broadside?" asked Jones.

"I see three ports to starboard . . . no bow chaser."

"Six-pounders I'd say," said Lt. Hall, staring through the blue haze of distance between *Ranger* and her quarry. "Pea-shooters, sir."

Excited, the second lieutenant had dared tender the obvious. But instead of turning to issue some chilling glance, Jones spared a rare quarterdeck smile.

"Pea-shooters to heavy timber, I'd warrant. But perdition to intemperate boys!" he exclaimed. "Steady now, Mr. Hall—mind that a bride's happiness depends on your tarrying in this world awhile."

"But sir, I have no bride."

"Trust me. You do."

"Aye sir," Hall said. Jones, Simpson and Cullam proceeded to laugh at him, though I suspected Hall knew exactly when to play the fool.

We were now close enough to the brig to see the white of the froth churning off her wake. In accord with Jones's instructions, Mr. Cullam placed us on a nonchalant heading parallel to hers. Our gun ports remained shut, to perpetuate the illusion of our friendliness. Jones also passed word around for the men to act casually, as if on an afternoon's idle cruise, and not to appear a gang of lusty marauders.

Fortunately, our quarry did not change her course. As we bore down on her, I could see she was a small vessel, with just two square-rigged masts, and a white stripe down her flanks. Her gun ports were indeed open, and many of her men were at the rail, watching us. By our British colors, Jones's faux Royal Navy uniform, and our lazy headway, we should have appeared harmless; by our topchains, boarding nets and conspicuous marines, we looked suspicious. The logical solution to this floating puzzle was that we were a Royal Navy sloop-of-war. Who else could we have been, this close to England, Mistress of Neptune?

We were approaching each other from opposite directions, *Ranger* proceeding at just five knots, the brig closer-hauled at three. The combined eight knots of speed would have taken us past her quickly, if Jones erred in timing his attack. By the time *Ranger* wore and cleared away on a pursuit heading, the brig would have made for shore, and the protection of bigger guns.

When we were less than a cable's distance (about 250 yards) apart, Jones ordered the mainsails backed and our velocity reduced. We slowed to a rolling crawl. We were then pleasantly astounded when the brig, unafraid, did the same.

"Six guns, did you say, Mr. Simpson?" whispered Jones, as puzzled as any of us by the brig's saucy behavior.

"No more, no less."

The two vessels now stood about fifty yards apart, drifting in the same direction. Jones then took up his speaking trumpet and called to the other, "Good morrow, sir! What ship is that?"

We could see a gaunt, bearded figure in a black suit, looking much like a clergyman, step to the other ship's rail and cup his hands around his mouth.

"Good morrow. This is *George,* bound for Plymouth with Spanish fruit. What ship is that?"

"H.M.S. *Mace,* of Red Squadron," Jones lied. "With whom have I the privilege of speaking?"

"You are addressing Master Whattley of Plymouth. And you, sir?"

"John Paul Jones, commander, at your service sir. Can we be of any assistance to you this afternoon, Master Whattley of Plymouth?"

"Thank you, no, Commander Jones. We may take good care of ourselves today."

"Indeed!" Jones laughed. "It is a decided pleasure to find a merchantman with such sand!"

"It is an equal pleasure to know you are here to support us, sir."

"Ah, but you must have seen one of those white-faced Yanks about, *George*?"

"As a matter of fact, yes," replied the popinjay. "A Yank privateer thought us an easy prize, but the cowards flew when we showed 'em a little British iron. Have you?"

"None at all, the blackguards!"

Smiles bloomed on our men's faces, and hardened there as they stared hungrily at the prone merchantman. Jones's foolery was a well-timed boon to morale, yet I sensed his audience was wider still. His performance upon those boards was actually directed to the further galleries, toward the seaboards of two continents, where he fancied the peoples of Europe and America gathered around the flooded Colosseum of this conflict, this great, ocean-wide naumachia. He would give them all a good show.

"Would you not say the Americans are a race without the stomach for fighting, dear Whattley?" Jones went on.

"In my experience, sir, they are a treasonous race without the stomach for anything but spawning bastards with the savages!"

There were sullen mutterings among our crew, but these were silenced. "Surely you speak the truth," Jones smiled. "But what would you say, Master Whattley of Plymouth, if I told you now that you were addressing Captain John Paul Jones of the Navy of Congress?"

"I'd say you were in jest, sir. There is no such thing as a 'Navy of Congress.'"

Jones then turned to Cullam and, in a voice deliberately frightening in its hoarse vehemence, ordered, "Helm up! Gun ports open! Up colors!"

Ranger performed a turn away from the wind, taking her on a perpendicular course behind *George*. With all of our larboard gunports open, we were then in a position to fire along the length of the brig—to rake her. This maneuver seemed to reduce Master Whattley and his crew to dumbfounded spectatorship. When the Continental Stars and Stripes went up the mast, their mouths dropped open, as if in witness of some miracle.

Thus frozen, *George* was slow to haul down her colors. Jones then called to the battery on the larboard poop, under Midshipman Dooley, to give them the spur.

"What?" came Dooley's response.

"The spur, boy! Damn you if you won't attend here!"

"What's that?" the midshipman called back, cupping his hand around his ear.

"The Devil take him, Green! Is he deaf?" Jones looked to the Surgeon.

Green crossed to Dooley's station, and made as if to stand beside him. Meanwhile, he threaded an arm behind Dooley's back, and snapped his fingers behind his right ear. The boy showed no sign of perceiving the sound. Green shrugged at Jones, who turned his back on the lad in a spirit of utter resignation to his haplessness.

That Dooley was now as deaf as a stone should not have been a surprise: the boy's ears bled after every session of gunnery drill. Even then, Jones would not excuse him from duty, obliging him to go about with a handkerchief tied around his head and the two ends of the bandage flapping above like the ears of some incarnadined rabbit.

Fortunately, a well-trained gun crew can do much to offset the weaknesses of a battery captain. Jones would have been pleased to note that Dooley's men had already seized their handspikes, inserted them under their gun breeches, and elevated them. The wedge-shaped quoin was then slid back on its bed, and the breech lowered again, so the aim of the gun was now higher, at the rigging of *George*. And all of this was conducted in a matter of seconds.

"FIRE!" Jones bellowed.

The three gun captains brought their slow-matches down upon the touch-holes, triggering simultaneous jets of blue flame from the breeches, and, as the powderbags went up, a muffled sound strangely like the shutting of a thick book. These preliminaries were followed by the triple-throated roar of *Ranger's* impatience, the arcing transit of the shots, and the much-anticipated damage.

Indeed, one of the shots went too high, passing so close to the brig's foretop gallants I could see them shiver with its passage above. The second passed through *George's* rigging with an evil whistle, but worked no more ill than the severing of a preventer stay.

But the third—that glorious third! This was aimed by none other than Dooley himself, who sought to atone for the crime of his deafness by taking the sight himself. Let God strike me from this chair, dear ladies, if Dooley's shot did not make an instantaneous hole in *George's* Red Ensign, right as it flew there from the mast! We heard the report, and the whooshing flight of the ball, and the hole was suddenly there, an aperture of sky blue in the very center of that scarlet field!

Our men cheered this miraculous blow. The effect on *George*, on the other hand, was to rouse her from her dreamy acquiescence. Master Whattley was seen to take a boarding pistol in hand, as if in preparation for a doughty fight! Every heart on *Ranger* instantly accelerated—I could hear my marines redouble their loading of extra rifles for our sharpshooters. Jones bit his lip in evident anticipation.

But our impression was incorrect. Instead of a struggle, *George's* master had only a token resistance in mind, namely a single shot, aimed deliberately at the clouds. Their colors were then immediately struck.

"Lt. Hall!" shouted Jones.

"Sir?"

"You will take the cutter to *George*, with twenty men. Lt. Simpson will help you choose your party."

The lieutenant appeared troubled by the order, but knew better than to breathe the merest hint of an objection. The choice of Hall to take command of *George,* after all, was clearly conceived as a pointed insult to Mr. Simpson. Further, Jones made it impossible for Simpson to ignore the insult by forcing the older man to help choose Hall's prize crew.

"When we are underway," Jones continued, finger in the air, "you will keep within signalling distance. If we be separated by storm or enemy action, you will make directly for Paimboeuf and await our arrival. Unless you have definite knowledge of our capture, you will not make contact with the offices of the American commissioners. Is all that clear, lieutenant?"

"Very clear, sir."

"Off with you, then."

Hall turned away with the guileless smile upon his face of a child regarding the prospect of a handful of twists. Lt. Simpson, who had stood nearby throughout this humiliation, turned to follow the young man without a hint of a "by your leave." Jones did not chose to make an issue of that. Instead, he smiled at me, and inclined his head at the brig.

"She's a pretty Molly for the price, is she not?"

I thought about what sort of response he wanted to hear and, out of nothing more than perverse impulse, ventured a potentially dangerous compliment: "Not badly done," said I, "for Number Eighteen."

Jones stared at me for a long moment, as if sifting for some noxious subtext. At length, he found none, and grinned more widely than before. "Aye, I do own it. May I live to prove myself worthy of that number!"

...

"So the hero had a sense of humor after all?" wondered Gualbert.

"At times, he threatened to develop one, yes."

Thierry gave a snorting "humpff" as she traced a moist fingertip around the circumference of her glass. "I've always found a sense of humor to be a threat to real ambition. Abrimal didn't have one."

"Nor did Busson," Gualbert assured her.

"You can't be serious. Busson was jolly next to Abrimal."

"You are mistaken, Nathalie. If there was anyone who was utterly without clue in the face of a joke, it was Busson."

"Abrimal was, I would say, grim before any occasion of levity, and scarcely took pleasure in anything but his low indulgences."

"You could not descend any lower than Busson. He was quite contemptible."

"But not, I fear, as despicable as my Abrimal."

"Ladies, ladies!" Severence interrupted them, laying a calming hand on each woman's sleeve. "If I might elevate the conversation for a moment . . . ?"

Thierry stared freezingly at Gualbert, whose eyes replied with heat of her own. For lack of a spoken reply, Severence assumed their encouragement to continue.

...

One of my last acts on that passage concerned poor Dooley, who earned a cheer with that marvelous shot at *George*'s colors, but won no special praise from Jones, who could barely stand to lay eyes on him. I regarded the boy standing there by himself, at the rail, surrounded by his whooping, celebrating fellows, yet still quite alone, and recognized in his face a lonely boy of New-York who likewise hungered vainly for the recognition of his elders. And it struck me as an unfathomable injustice, this famine of deserved esteem, this withholding of a simple hand upon a shoulder, a light squeeze, or a wink. Indeed, what project could be more important than this—the education of our future heroes and the assurance of our survival in their hands? What pride was more important? What prerogative of rank? What stubbornness?

I recalled an object in my cabin that might suit the double purpose I had in mind: to redeem the injury done to Dooley's sense of hearing, and to reward him for his role in the capture. Accordingly, I went below and retrieved for him the cherry-wood hearing trumpet that had belonged to my father.

It was of no import to me that, with my gift of it to Dooley, I would own no more reminders of my father's very existence. Instead, it was compensation enough to witness the pleasant sentiment dawn upon the boy's wide face, the recognition of kindness he had not known since he had been detached from his mother's skirts. This was followed by a puzzled arching of his eyebrow as he examined the trumpet.

"I thank ye kindly, sir . . . but . . . what is it?"

"Place it to your ear and listen."

"Excuse me?" he begged, cocking his useless ear toward me.

I took the instrument from his grasp and placed the narrow end before his ear canal. Then, bending to speak into the wide end, I made him jump with the exclamation, "How hear you now, good Captain of the Head!"

Dooley composed himself, smiled, yet insisted on returning my gift, saying, "Sir, it is a remarkable device, I'm sure, but I have no personal need of it."

"Are you quite sure of that, midshipman?"

"Huh?" he said, uncomprehending.

I pushed it back into his hands. "Just keep it, boy. Indulge me."

By that evening, Lt. Hall's prize crew was installed aboard *George,* the brig's native crew imprisoned below, and the two vessels were readied for the push on toward Nantes. We were, however, first pleasantly surprised by a present from our colleagues, sent over on the returning cutter. A crate was hauled up on our deck, and our carpenter laid it open with hammer and chisel. Inside, we beheld the wondrous sight of Spanish blood oranges. This was the first fresh fruit the crew had encountered since Portsmouth.

Jones looked down upon this lode from his pacing track on the quarterdeck, and noted well the expressions of famished anticipation on the faces of every able, every ordinary, and every landsman within his view.

"Mr. Simpson!"

"Sir?"

"May I ask what you are waiting for?"

"Waiting, sir?"

"I want one orange distributed to every man and boy on this vessel."

"With pleasure, sir."

And so it came to pass that the tars of *Ranger,* subjects of the most notorious martinet in the American Navy, pitied an ocean over, stood in the firelog red of the setting sun and besotted themselves with oranges. Most of the men missed such fare so completely that they dispensed with the propriety of peeling the fruit first: I heard the sound of rusty blades plunged into the fruit, the rip of oranges pulled apart, jets of sweet red juice sprayed upon the deck. As the jagged wedges of scarlet flesh disappeared into their mouths, great bibs of wet marked the blouse of every man, and kernels of pulp every finger. I could not say whether or not it was an illusion cast by the rays of the setting sun, but the flesh of those oranges fairly throbbed with color, and the sweetness—I can still taste it!—was such that the Gods must have known, back when Gods preferred to eat than to be eaten.

Jones did not choose to partake in this feast. Instead, I saw him keep his vigil by the rail. While I could not vouch absolutely for the thoughts that must have occupied him, I could guess they monotonously revolved about the prospect of meeting a British patrol, a frigate big enough to deprive him of *Ranger's* first prize, when we were no more than fifty leagues from the coast of Britain herself. I'd warrant the aesthetic possibilities of a blood orange, or any such useless musing, had never entered his mind, save as a way to cultivate morale among his crew. Was there ever a man more satisfied with practical things, with the ordinary business of a man's life? I say again, I pitied him—even allowing that history may remember his deeds, and my flesh rot nameless in the grave.

My disgust put me in a perverse mood. Swallowing my scruples, I indulged an impulse, and bade Surgeon Green to take me below to introduce me to his secret—the mistress of the orlop deck.

...

"You rascal!" Gualbert exclaimed.

...

I can't defend it. It is the way with men to be curious in such matters—to go and see, even if their choice is ultimately to abstain.

I followed the Surgeon down three sets of ladderways, lower and deeper into the vessel. With each step, the sound of the mortal world faded, and the groans of the *Ranger's* submarine shell rose around me. Often, bent upon my bunk, I had wondered what manner of unimagined monsters were, at that very moment, swimming within a few yards from my head. Between sleep and waking, I imagined I had heard the whisperings of the mer-men on the other side of our wooden skin, or the lamentable soundings of Leviathan, so mightily large yet so certainly lonely in his great domain. Perhaps I went below with Green to seek out the sources of these voices. After a month below, could our stowaway now be construed as anything but a creature of the deep ocean?

Other visitors from above betrayed themselves by their sounds in the darkness, some toiling, some snoring through their off-watch hours. Green would turn up to me, his face cut by a most indecent smirk, his eyes reduced to shadowy sockets by the lantern light. Really, he had no modesty at all.

The *Ranger*'s only feminine tar was a plump girl of seventeen, with a wide, ghostly pale face and a tattered white dress that testified to every day of her captivity. She was installed in a hold not far from Green's surgery, and was fed by the ship's cook out of the officer's stores. There was a pile of plate and cutlery from the captain's own table lain up in the corner of her chamber. When we showed our faces, she was bent over for Master-at-Arms Joye to introduce his member into her backside. She turned, squinting into Green's lantern, and said, "Goodness, everyone's got it now that we've taken our first prize! Put out that lamp, will you!"

Green obliged, and, as we waited, informed me that he had instructed her in the art of sodomy "for reasons of hygiene." There could be no pregnancies down here, he told me.

Our eyes adjusted to the feeble beams from the girl's single candle, and we could see Joye was already finished, and the girl sitting on an upended bucket with her frayed flounces gathered around her and a ledger-book in her lap.

"Is she a stout vessel? What's she laden with? Where's she bound for?" she was asking Joye, who appeared to be more concerned with buttoning himself up and fleeing. "How can we reach a fair settlement if you can't say what you're owed?" she asked him.

"Leave me be, trollop. The percent's plenty. Bugger off or I'll go to the captain."

"If that's your pleasure. And I'll tell 'im who's been down here three times already."

At this, Joye muttered, "Two percent."

"Four," she replied, and wrote the figure in her book.

There was no use in hiding my face from Joye as he passed. My Marines' uniform was unmistakeable. He regarded Green as he slipped by us, but said nothing.

"Who's next, then?" she looked at me. "Well, here's a pretty one. Haven't seen you before . . . " And she reversed the bucket under her and sat on it, steeling herself to expel Joye's discharge from her anus.

"And how're we d-d-doing so far, Amelia?" Green asked her, playing to the hilt the part of her cheerful procurer.

"I'll own five percent of that prize before I'm through!" she declared, a straining expression coming over her face. "And now that it's officers come to see me, well, I might be due more than the captain 'imself!"

Quite apart from her unappetizing posture, I recall being troubled by a look in her eyes. Perhaps it was a trick of the candle, or some eruption of good sense within me, but I saw on her the face of a predator. Who would do the screwing of whom here? I wondered with rising apprehension. My body suddenly began to shudder of its own volition, and the hold seemed suddenly more like a catacomb. I turned away.

"Where ye going, man?" Green called after me as I mounted the ladderway again.

"Have it your way, pretty! I'll be below if ye need me!" the girl promised from her bucket.

I climbed back above. Mounting the spar deck, I gulped at the fresh air, feeling in that instant almost as sick as my first days at sea.

As a general rule of character, I loathed myself, yes. But not so much as to share this loathing with one such as her.

Night had fallen, and a north breeze had come out of the darkness to speed our progress. I found him, of course, still on vigil, passing from one rail to the other, as *Ranger* and her sated crew gathered headway into the night, toward the future that awaited them in the France of Louis Sixteen.

XI.

YOU MUST remember how young I was. As a novice at sea, I had no knowledge of the distinction between landfall at a distant shore, and mere arrival.

...

"And what distinction would that be?" asked Thierry.

...

Arrival, such as it is, is a tedious thing—an act of exacting labor, of beating one's way in toward the coast, finding local pilots to help navigate the hidden dangers, and establishing safe and legal anchorage. In the case of our arrival at the port of Paimboeuf, near Nantes, this process took nearly fifteen hours, and did not end until we dropped anchor, exhausted, at midnight of December 2.

But prosaic as arrival might be, landfall is poetry. It is a glimmer of purple on an unsettled horizon, wafted like a banner on the collective effects of atmosphere and water. It is a convocation of expectant faces at the rail, each rippling with private ambitions, wishes, anxieties. It is a silence worked upon man, deepened by the sigh of waves upon the hull, and mocked by the hue and cry of our new companions, the gulls. For to whatever degree the nations of humanity appear dirty and sinful at proximity, these defects disappear from a longing distance, leaving the field to hope alone.

It was a landfall made doubly triumphant by our capture, some days earlier, of a second British merchantman. This was the brig *Mary,* bearing wine from Spain. The crew was then owed the proceeds from the sale of two prizes, a sum that may well have raised unrealistic expectations of the fine time they would see in gay France. And they were ultimately to be disappointed on this count, for tiny Paimboeuf boasted few of the delights of Paris.

In Jones's philosophy, time in port was not an occasion for less work, but for more. Directly upon finding anchorage, he commanded details of the crew to assist the carpenters in making alterations to *Ranger*'s rig: mainly a narrowing and shortening of the masts and spars, and the addition of gunports in the stem and stern.

To these instructions, I suggested another. When I told Jones of Our Lady of the Orlop Deck, he reddened perceptibly, certainly in embarrassment at his failure to detect her. Then he recovered, saying "This is no secret—there was no opportunity to act until now. Or would you have me pitch her into the sea?"

"No," I replied. "You would certainly have had me do it."

When he gave the order in conspicuous fashion from the quarterdeck to "get rid of the trollop," the prospect of punishment suddenly tormented the faces of her customers. The rest of the Rangers appeared even more troubled, however, by the fact that their fellows had excluded them from the secret, and that now it was too late for them to capitalize on it.

Amelia was packed off less than an hour later in a jolly boat. She wore a clean blue gown she had evidently saved for the occasion, and bore her ledger-book under her arm as she was lowered to the water, her face filled with anticipation of a fine time in France. As they rowed her away, she blew a kiss at Surgeon Green, who had been pretending her appearance was a complete surprise to him. Green shrank from the rail and vanished below, but not without passing under Jones's pitiless scrutiny.

There were, however, no punishments forthcoming from this affair. On the contrary, Jones made additional arrangements for his crew's comfort. As we were anchored some distance from shore, he contracted a small vessel to perform ferry service from *Ranger* to the wharf. Goodly amounts of fruit, fresh beef, and vegetables were brought on board at the captain's expense, in addition to many hogsheads of grog. He even lent pocket money to all the men to spend as they pleased ashore.

As for Jones himself, I saw a kind of willful repose overtake him. Though he was quite plainly burning to proceed thither to the American commissioners near Paris to learn the shape of his operations in Europe, his pride prevented him from making off without due invitation. Arrival at land therefore did not make much difference in the shipboard routines of Jones, myself, and the handful of frequent dinner guests among the corps of officers. Instead of scanning the horizon for hostile vessels, Jones stood watch over the short stretch of water between *Ranger* and the wharves, in anticipation of the boat that would deliver his message from Benjamin Franklin. The meats were a bit fresher, and there was better wine. That is all.

Ever particular with regard to his appearance, he redoubled his efforts to prepare for his Parisian debut. I saw his steward polish his buckled shoes to such a reflective brilliance they would have served equally well as high-seas signalling devices. The cut and cleanliness of his uniform passed from "impeccable" to qualities of perfection only Plato dreamt of—the very Form of Uniformness. His weapons of correspondence, including his quill pens and wax seals and inkwells, were cleaned, re-filled, and readied within their portable case. I didn't know what Jones expected to accomplish in France, but it was clear he meant not to be soon forgotten by her.

When the call did come, Jones acted with his usual tactical decisiveness. The French lieutenant who had borne the message was begged to wait for him, a delay this gentleman surely welcomed, as his eyes danced with pleasure over the spectacle of *Ranger*'s smooth efficiency, and its spit-polished Anglo-Protestant tidiness-for-its-own-sake; his tongue fairly licked his lips, as if estimable discipline actually fired his Gallic stomach with hunger.

Jones's trunk, which had been packed for days, was immediately hauled up and loaded on the Frenchman's skiff. I was nearby, my elbows resting on the larboard rail, my face turned into the breeze to sample the scents of land. I only intermittently peeked through narrowed lids to glimpse the frenzy of Jones's departure, preferring to attend to the caresses of the unseasonably warm wind, but was roused from my reverie by the sight of Jones standing a little way off, entirely still, regarding me.

What was I to make of this look? Though he said nothing, the way he stood there conveyed a spirit of puzzlement, as if he were expecting a display of some long overdue behavior. I wondered what duty I had overlooked, what sentry had not been posted, what facility had not been drilled into my troops, but could think of none. I approached him.

"On your way at last, eh?" I asked him, taking a conversational tack.

"So it would seem," came the listless reply. This was odd, considering how strongly he had anticipated this summons. "It occurs to me of late that I am not fit to answer this call . . . with my shortcomings . . . "

"Shortcomings?"

"My inadequacy of education, for one," he said, smiling an incongruous smile. "To be cast into the diplomatic lists in France without knowledge of French! I shall make a pretty statue at their state dinners!"

He shot another look at me, then absently removed and replaced his hat. It dawned upon me at last what he was asking, but was too proud to utter.

"But . . . as duty calls, I must follow! Have a pleasant holiday, Severence, and mind Providence may yet make it your last!" And he turned away from me, his face set in entirely deliberate resignation.

"Sir!" I stopped him. "If there is some purpose I could serve, I stand ready to join you, perhaps, in the capacity of translator . . . ?"

Jones stared at me, head askew, as if seeing me for the first time. He really was a very awful actor—or more precisely, an actor better trained for audiences many yards farther away, on the decks of opposing warships.

"You do speak the French, do you not?"

"A bit," said I.

"That is fortunate for you. You are superbly educated. But I cannot take you captive to my own ignorance."

"Not at all. You must have a translator. Just allow me to pack a trunk."

"If you wish," he said, waving a dismissive hand at me.

This was not as much a sacrifice on my part as Jones pretended. I had never seen Paris before, though I had heard much of the advantages of French art, cuisine, and women. Before I descended the ladderway, I heard him call to me. What followed was typical Jones:

"Severence! Your services are welcome, but I cannot tarry any longer for you. If you are not at present prepared for this journey, I must ask you to have your trunk forwarded to you at Passy!"

I had the impression that the trip from Paimboeuf to Paris should have been most pleasant, even in that blustery season. Allow me to note, at risk of digression, that your French countryside is far more logically cultivated than the American, and enveloped by that singular atmosphere of your country, so suitable to genteel contemplation.

But on the heels of John Paul Jones, there was little time to appreciate it. He travelled as if chased by the leading edge of a wildfire, stopping only for the biological necessity of the horses (usually) and the travellers (sometimes). The distance from *Ranger* to our goal was some 300 miles, or the better part of a week's journey. We traversed it in less than fifty hours.

Our actual destination, the village of Passy, I learned was a spot roughly equidistant between Paris and the royal court at Versailles, wherein Doctor Franklin and his colleagues had established themselves under the roof of a French nobleman sympathetic to our cause. When we arrived at the outskirts of this village on the 17th, I noted a complete change come over Jones. Suddenly, he became alive to the scenic diversions—the villas of the wealthy French, with their gardens mounting the hillsides in manicured tiers, their vineyards tended by proud and happy serfs, and the wide, aromatic avenues lancing down to a gentle Seine shaded by linden trees. Everywhere there were smart carriages, and litters, and smart men and women taking the sun. The dandies greeted one another with the most elaborate doffing and bowing; some bore feathered hats that were never designed to be actually worn, but instead carried out in front of them, as if these were not apparel but pet birds. Grown men tip-toed through the streets, evidently fearful of getting spots of mud or manure on their white stockings. At the sight of these, Jones slowed our carriage to scrutinize them with clear amusement.

For my part, I thought such lofty affluence to be an odd atmosphere for the directing of a popular revolution. But when I took care to note this to Jones, he only shrugged, and made an offhand reply to the effect that "It is French. No more and no less."

Our carriage turned upon a shaded path that led to a handsome hôtel set at the brow of a hill, over the water. The buff-colored edifice was composed of two symmetrical wings of four stories, connected by a colonnaded frontage larger and more splendid than the most official structure in all of little New-York.

This was Franklin's current residence, the Hôtel Valentinois. Alighting at last, we met one Dr. Edward Bancroft, a smilingly familiar gentleman who was attached to the American legation in the capacity of secretary. He was dressed, I might add, in finer French mode than many a man of means back home. And this was the assistant!

As Jones was anxious to have his interview with Doctor Franklin as soon as possible, we were led from the main hall of the *hôtel*, through the gardens with their prettily calculated view of the river down the hill, to the pavilion where the Americans were installed. The opulence of the place made a deep impression on me, used as I was to the humbler estates of America, not to mention *Ranger's* modest amenities. I can testify I saw, in that brief walk, more works of art in the foremost rank, more casts from Praxiteles, more frescoes and gilt mirrors and portraits in the celebrated style of Dupleiss, than I had in the entire span of my life to that moment.

I was, in fact, surprised by the character of the place old, plain "Ben" had chosen as his base. It appeared so entirely inconsistent with the persona he had cultivated for his public, his "Poor Richard," that I suspected the choice had been somehow forced upon him by some ostentatious but indispensable French fop. By this calculation, I expected to find him inside with a long scowl of disapproval on his face, poised to launch the short, quick, devastating barbs against the immodesty rampant around him.

Nothing could have been farther from the truth. The scene to which Jones and I were admitted was that of an impromptu concert. A multitude of chairs and small tables had been taken from their places along the walls of the pavilion's sitting room and organized in a rough semi-circle. The seats were occupied by men in silk-embroidered frock coats and stockings clocked with gold, some with swords, and by women in fabulous gowns of taffeta, satin, and velvet, their hair done up in towering artifices festooned with leaves, twigs, and small stuffed animals, their faces powdered white and marked by great red circles of painted blush on both cheeks.

Only a few faces turned at our entrance. The rest were preoccupied with a young woman playing the harpsichord for them from the other side of the room. The pretty, ribboned head bent absorbedly over the keys, I learned, was that of Madame Brillon de Juoy.

...

"Have either of you ladies had occasion to hear her?" Severence turned to them.

Thierry thought for a moment. "Myself? I don't believe so. But Abrimal had on several occasions, and believed her to be a credit to her sex."

...

I agree. Though I am no judge of such things, even I became entranced by the manifold expressions of wistfulness and joy that colored her face, and the delicacy of the hands that caressed (not poked) the keys. The melody she played was a mournful Scottish air that washed her audience in an atmosphere of doleful nostalgia—that is, the sort of expansively painful sentiment the best classes could afford in lavish scale, never having had the occasion to sample the meanness of the real thing.

Jones and I stood by the door, so as not to distract from her performance, but did not remain unnoticed. Jones closed his eyes and hummed the tune softly to himself, as he knew it from his childhood. When the piece ended, he applauded more loudly than anyone else, pounded the parquet with the bottom of his cane, and by his exuberance turned many heads.

I saw one particular gray head turn toward us, and knew immediately that this must be Doctor Franklin. I cannot say how I knew this. I knew him only through his writings and reputation, and not by any manner of portrait.

Jones strode to the head of the room with perfect confidence, extended his hand to the old Quaker, and introduced himself as "Captain John Paul Jones, Soldier of Liberty and Partisan of the Natural Sciences."

The response was measured, and measuring. Franklin touched Jones's hand and replied, "Private citizen Franklin, very much at your service, sir." Jones flushed, perhaps unprepared for the old man's self-effacing manner. But little I, so far unintroduced, kept my wits enough to make a closer examination of the giant.

He had a disappointing face, really. Unlike General Washington, whose appearance and patrician bearing lived up to the rigors of his legend, Franklin looked a drab, plain man, with a tight, small mouth, unkempt gray locks plunging to his collar, and round, tired eyes that suggested something of the character of a jaundiced turtle. He was, in fact, also the worst-dressed man in the room, with his antiquated black frock coat and old shoes with large square buckles.

Despite this, Franklin was soon surrounded by a host of bright Frenchmen and women, all calling to him affectionately as *"mon cher et venerable Docteur"* or *"ambassadeur electrique,"* and speaking much too fast for me to understand more than a phrase or two. To these Franklin replied not at all, merely nodding his head as if he understood perfectly. This scene was further enlivened by the arrival of Madame de Juoy herself, fresh from the performer's stand, her handsome features reddened with fatigue and excitement.

"Do tell me, *mon cher* Papa, did you enjoy the music?"

"Papa?" Jones and I repeated in unison, looking to each other.

"I am unfit even to praise it," Franklin told her. "If it were not for the presence of young Captain Jones here, I would beg to hear it again . . . "

"Then I shall expect payment in full?" Madame de Juoy charged, a girlish smile upon her face.

"A debt I would be the happier to discharge," said he.

With this, Madame de Juoy, a married woman, seated herself in Doctor Franklin's lap and presented her shapely neck for him to kiss. He did so with undisguised relish, and there was giddiness and laughter all around, and much clinking of champagne glasses. Madame lingered in her perch for several moments, gazing at Franklin with her arms around him. Her reverie was broken by the voice of a man in the crowd, who enjoined her to "stay just where you are, and give our dear Papa the kiss I cannot!" Later, we were introduced to this man. His name was M. de Juoy—the husband!

Has Franklin gone mad? I wondered. Had the clear licentiousness of French society overthrown his reason? Indeed, if this country could work such black arts upon a man so steadfast, what would it do to Jones, myself, and the crew of *Ranger*? Under the circumstances, such thoughts troubled me greatly, as did the suspicion that Franklin could hardly be performing his official duties well in the face of such distractions as Madame de Juoy and her powdered neck.

Then, in halting French, Franklin introduced Jones to his circle of friends. Both of us were instantly examined with wide, curious eyes, as two more half-civilized men of nature from the untamed West.

"Where is your fur-skin cap?" one young woman asked me, herself sporting a bonnet of silk flowers and real preserved bumblebees on tiny springs.

"Does Captain Jones suffer from the American climate?" asked another gentleman.

Franklin smiled at this, and turned to tell us, "The French have the impression our American climate is so bad it debases human growth. But you are Scots-raised, are you not, Captain?"

Jones nodded, ill-pleased by this talk of his "debased" stature. Franklin then explained Jones's Scottish rearing to the Frenchman, who merely replied that this further proved their theory, as Scotland had as stunting a climate as America's.

Jones, meanwhile, attempted to redirect the subject of conversation by introducing my name and rank to the assembly, at which Franklin inquired, "Severence? Are you a scion of that family of Manhattan Severences, Lieutenant?"

"Yes, I am," said I, wearily.

But I was not to be dogged by this issue for long, as the circle of Franklin's admirers quickly moved their attention back on the sage, who obliged them with only the merest of knowing nods, impish winks, and attentive scans. In short, he played them every bit as skillfully as Madame de Juoy played the harpsichord, and with no visible effort.

Two more young ladies, neither more than fifteen years old, approached, curtsied, and requested the honor of kissing the doctor. Permission was duly given, and the two fawns claimed one cheek each, and proceeded to make their wrinkly "Papa" the center of a youthful parenthesis. The crowd applauded, the fathers grinned, Franklin rolled his eyes, and I feared very deeply for the fate of my innocent country.

...

"I remember when Doctor Franklin arrived in France," Gualbert recalled. "I was in the parish school, and the sisters told us to bow our heads and pray for his mission. They believed him a very wise, virtuous man."

"He was on the right hand of Rousseau himself," said Thierry. "There was no nobler primitive."

...

It is true. Far more than I suspected at the time, Franklin understood and used the nature of his fame here to win France's help against Britain. The shape of this project became clear to me later, after he had retired from this affair to speak with Captain Jones and myself. There, behind closed doors, he bid his man to hurry and bring him some food he could digest. Then he sat in a chair with the weight of the world on his shoulders, and turned his tortoise's eyes upon us.

"It is good to see new faces from home," he sighed. "I must beg your apology for detaining you. I did not expect you until the 19th."

"The apology is mine to offer, as I have ruined your evening," replied Jones.

"That is nonsense, sir. You have brought me nothing but relief from that nest of cocksuckers."

The sudden downturn in Franklin's language momentarily defeated Jones. I, on the other hand, was not surprised, considering it part and parcel of his certain moral decline.

"Relief? From such gay times?" said I, my voice laced with censorious sarcasm. Franklin glanced at me and curled the edge of his lip in the merest smile.

"You have been speaking with that toad, Arthur Lee, haven't you?"

"I confess I don't know the gentleman."

"The third American commissioner, in addition to Silas Deane," Jones informed me, not a little impatient with my ignorance. "And permit me to add, Lt. Severence entirely understands the nature of your pleasure here is entirely none of his business."

"Oh, but it is the whole of the business, sir," Franklin said. "I don't know if you were aware of it, gentlemen, but in the span of time you stood in that room with me I was absorbed in very important negotiations with the Sieur de Chaumont, my landlord here, for the requisition of winter uniforms for the Continental Army, as well as for a new vessel—an Indiaman—for Captain Jones . . . "

Jones eyes lit up, clearly delighted at this prospect. Franklin paused as his servant returned with a plate of boiled roast beef, very thinly sliced, asparagus, and black bread.

"I find negotiations like that tire me more and more each time. Forgive my manners—would either of you like a plate?"

We refused with thanks. After watching the Doctor eat for several moments, Jones finally let his suspense get the best of him.

"And did you succeed . . . in procuring the Indian?"

Franklin frowned. "I would dearly prefer to guarantee success to you, Captain, especially after receiving word of your latest captures. Capability such as yours deserves nothing less. But . . . you must be aware that our fates are being decided in large measure on land, and to land our priority must go."

When he saw Jones's face darken, he added with a sure diplomatic touch, "It is not a matter of one or the other, exclusively, of course. Today, the uniforms are available. Tomorrow, ten tons of saltpeter. The next, a frigate . . . perhaps." And he punctuated this sentence by biting the head off a spear of asparagus, and maneuvering it within his mouth toward his remaining teeth.

"In any case, the victory at Saratoga makes the Treaty of Alliance inevitable now . . . ," he added between chews. "Unfortunately, that may not work to your advantage if the Indian becomes a gamecock between Congress and the Crown."

"I am still at a loss to understand the nature of these 'negotiations,'" said I, still too puzzled by Franklin's previous behavior to hold my tongue. "How many *livres* does the kiss of an adolescent earn you?"

Jones nudged me significantly with his elbow, but Franklin only laughed. "My dear boy," he said, "kisses from young girls are the only true currency in this country! This is fortunate for us, as I can traffic in these more easily than Continental notes. Kisses from the right mouths—in this case, the Sieur de Chaumont's two nieces—are worth more than broadsides to our cause. Mark me, gentlemen, all the truly important business in France is transacted through *les bonne femmes.* There can be no more valuable ally than the one that shares your benefactor's bed!"

I perceived then that I was being invited to swallow this morsel of wisdom, or to refuse it, according to my perception of its nourishment. The grin that dawned on Jones's face appeared to signal his readiness to learn diplomacy *à la française.* My mind, however, was still plagued with noxious memories of the dispossessed souls of burned Kingston, despairing over the charred debris of their property—the skeletons of the *Jersey*—and the sundered corpses of the patriots floating in Lake Champlain, washed in bloodstained brine. Try as I might, I simply could not hold in similar regard the "sacrifice" of being called to sip Spanish Xeres, to dance with glad ladies, or to attend sunset teas on the Seine.

...

"You judge us too harshly," protested Gualbert, who constricted her neck and shivered, as if from the coldness of his Protestantism. "Perhaps you would have less need of the real sacrifice if you indulged in more of the false."

"*Une touche,* Mademoiselle."

...

The other commissioners, Lee and Deane, shared my opinion with various degrees of virulence, but none of us could dispute the success of Franklin's efforts. Already, within two years of his arrival in France, he had a Treaty of Amity and Commerce in his pocket. Before 1778 was out, he added the formal Treaty of Alliance between America and France, in addition to unnumbered donations of funds and material. By the end of the War, he was instrumental in securing a favorable peace with the Briton. By that time, I had long achieved a pragmatist's respect for Franklin's methods, if not real sympathy.

...

"You Americans are always quite sure you know how others should live. It is one of your least admirable qualities," said Thierry. "You may thank your dull Puritan God that Doctor Franklin was wiser to foreign ways."

Severence shrugged. "We have."

...

In any case, the evening ended with our introduction to the masters of the Hôtel de Valentinois: Chaumont and his wife, Thérèse, or according to Franklin's order of things, Thérèse and her poodle, the Sieur de Chaumont. This latter was a mere wasp of a fellow, shorter than Jones, with eyes set very close together and a habit of wearing wigs that were too big for his head. He also had the pronounced habit of fingering his watchfobs anxiously as he spoke, even swinging them around and around in nervous loops, until one was seized with the temptation to strike him.

Despite this appearance, Chaumont was a reliable friend of the American cause. He was a one-man foreign ministry, in fact, for as long as France was obliged to keep her aid to us a secret. Like Jones, he was humbly born, in his case, of a shopkeeper. Also like Jones, he achieved his stature in the world by dint of his own genius, though Chaumont's battlefield was the world of speculation and investment. Before he was very old he was already fabulously rich . . .

...

"So rich, the King secured his services—meaning his money—by making him Overseer of Forests, and the Army's quartermaster," Thierry interrupted him. "His business was the East Indian trade, but the British had cost him so dearly, after the last war he pledged his fortune to their destruction. *Voilà*, his assistance to America."

"I suspect your knowledge is personal," Severence cocked his head at her.

"It is," she granted, the weariness in her voice entirely faked. Gualbert was staring at her.

"You—and Chaumont?"

"On several occasions, before Abrimal."

But Gualbert wouldn't be convinced of this coup: she knitted her brow, looked at her lap, and shook her head in obstinate silence.

Thierry laughed at her. "He was nothing very special. Really, very much the usual. But I defer on matters of substance to Captain Severence."

"Of which I am grateful," said he, "lest you tell me something I'd rather not learn!"

As a witticism this barely qualified, but Gualbert worked her revenge on Thierry by laughing more loudly at it, almost in the manner of a pouffed hyena, and attracting Severence's glance, his touch.

...

Attend: once Jones understood the importance of the two Chaumonts (with their four chins), he willed every trace of impatience, despair, and offhand disagreeableness be gone from his manner. He was gallant as he bent to kiss the glove of plain Madame de Chaumont, but held her hand a bit too long; he was the picture of heartfelt respect as he bowed for the husband, but overplayed this role so much that Chaumont grew embarrassed for him.

He never learned Franklin's adroitness in French society, which happened to stem mostly from knowing when not to speak. Jones always took the floor when it was offered. Worse for him, he simply wasn't very good at humbling himself. Though he could smile handsomely and tell a good story and behave modestly, there was always something on his face that signalled his real estimation of people. His platitudes, alas, rang flat; he was all too willing to flee at the approach of a boring or pointless anecdote. These faults of transparency were alone enough to sink him, for what great man was ever permitted to exercise his genius without first paying homage to his duller sponsors?

The women, at least, found him pleasant to look at. Both generations of Chaumont females could not remove their eyes from the dashing Captain. As Madame was, if I may be indelicate, a horse, her immodesty was particularly embarrassing. The daughter Thérèse-Elisabeth was a different case: plump, pink, cutting a fine figure in her simple cotton print dress, after the fashion of Marie Antoinette's milkmaid costume at the Petit-Trianon. Jones held the girl's hand in both of his, and remarked in

English, "And whence did this country blossom waft among us? But no—" he said, turning to Madame, "she must be a sprig of the mother bouquet!"

I translated, and Madame dismissed this reflected tribute with a polite smile. But the artless Thérèse-Elisabeth, only recently introduced to society, took Jones at his flattering word, and with quivering lip and welling tears fled the room, choking in broken English, "To excuse, there is a thing in my eye . . ."

The adults were much amused by this innocence. Jones delivered a fine quip by observing, "Alas, as beauty is bright, beauty is too quickly gone!" Chaumont laughed least, however, and was the only one to follow the girl—a fact Jones must have noted well.

So as you see, the captain landed on the French shore on his feet, and running. And despite his show of social frivolity after the meeting with Doctor Franklin, I knew the prospect of getting a bigger ship was never far from his mind. This is important to remember, if you are to understand his activities of the following weeks.

As I was exhausted from the journey, I begged Jones's leave to be shown to my room. As he had no objection (his confidence then being on the rise), I followed a valet to the pavilion's second floor, to a chamber that overlooked the terrace and the river.

This room contained a bed that was itself larger than my entire cabin on *Ranger*. It required an effort of will for to me to remove my boots before sinking into this downy universe, so incomprehensibly large I could not touch its edges with both arms outstretched. As I undressed, I stood before the window. I was there rewarded by my first view of Paris: the Field of Mars and the École Royale Militaire beyond the Seine, fringed by a bouquet of church domes.

The view below my window was no less interesting. Jones was down there, standing between the swinging boughs of an acacia tree with Thérèse-Elisabeth. He was five feet from her, his arms crossed in a pose of easy gallantry, speaking words I could not hear, but which caused the girl to dare smile, and even laugh.

He had opened his European campaign.

XII.

You certainly know a great many things. You have traveled far and wide. Honors have been heaped upon you. But you have never been inside a French girl's head! Well, I shall tell you their secret. When you want to kiss one of them, and all she will say is that the idea does not pain her, it means she's glad.

—MLLE. GENEVIEVE LE VEILLARD, in a letter to Dr. Franklin

THE NEXT weeks furnished me with a quick education in the manners of your happier classes. As I had volunteered to act as Jones's mouthpiece, I was obliged to keep up with his social calendar—no easy feat. He was, in a word, tireless, and in another, shrewd, having made a full study of Franklin's lessons in success the French way, yet with resources of energy and ambition far beyond the old doctor. He rarely declined an invitation anywhere.

My duties, therefore, included attendance at an endless series of dinners, soirées, concerts, societies of discussion, hunts, teas, anniversaries, receptions, services, luncheons, dances, after-dances, and after-after-dances. Jones navigated these with a brave enthusiasm, a ready quip or story always at his command, his lighter, blonde aspect never brighter. His success was mixed: the French men pretended to be bemused by him, but were surely challenged by his handsome valor. The women responded with either the sort of open-mouthed wonder he craved, or suggestions of the more intimate favors a wise man looked upon with caution. One Madame de Reyniére, for instance, met him first at the Hôtel and later at Dr. Bancroft's residence, and became most desperate to sacrifice her wifely fidelity to him.

Make no mistake: Jones's goal was not social renown but a new frigate. To this end, unfortunately, Madame de Reyniére could be of little use to him. Her husband's occupation, such as it was, more concerned the pleasures of shooting and card-playing than military equipage. Baron de

Reyniére was a good deal older than his wife, in fact, being not less than twice her calendar age, and seeming twice more with his sloped shoulders, gray complexion, and clothes rumpled about his bony frame.

The Reyniére courtship consisted of a dinner party given by her parents for his benefit. The subject of marriage was broached over soup, the terms of union settled over a roast goose, and the contract prepared over a fruit compote and chocolates. She was sixteen at the time.

Reyniére was already twice a widower, but his inherited properties made him an irresistible catch for ambitious bourgeoisie with pretty daughters. This was despite the rumor that the groom was more interested in their pretty sons, and his snuff, and not necessarily in that order. It should come as no surprise, then, that as the young bride blossomed into adult womanhood (and adult appetites), she turned elsewhere for company.

Even by French standards, her pursuit of Jones was shameless. She was always seated next to him during the music. She always sought to hold his hand during the quadrille, and punished her competition with pointed glances and ungracious remarks. As much a campaigner as Jones, she cultivated a tactical acquaintance with me.

But it was futile. Jones had already estimated the relative value of the women around him, and decided that Thérèse-Elisabeth, the pride of her father Chaumont, was in a better position to further his designs. This placed me in an awkward pass, as I had come to appreciate Madame de Reyniére's surprising wit and intellect, and the playful dimples about her agreeable mouth, and did not relish her humiliation.

The dumbshow reached its greatest absurdity when she appeared at the Pavilion in a wig that surpassed all others in its inventiveness. This was a great, three-foot long headpiece topped with a satin ship's hull, three beechwood masts, a full suit of sails, an ostrich feather for a bowsprit, and pearl pendants hanging from jewel-encrusted gunports! It was magnificent, if only in the effort it must have taken to keep the display balanced on her head.

"Lieutenant Severence!" she called to me, swerving in my direction with a rustle of skirts and luffing of her silken sails. She looked silly, yes, but I could not help but be softened by the sweet anxiety on her face.

"Would you be so kind, sir, to tell me where I might find Captain

Jones?" she asked me in her heavily accented schoolgirl's English.

"You will find him in astonishment, if he could see your spectacle!" I testified.

She laughed a worried laugh, tucked a lock of blonde hair under her headdress's hull. "You flatter me. But might I boast that I have had expert advice from the Ministry of Marine in the design of this . . . little thing?" And her slate-colored eyes flicked upward then, as if there could be any confusion over what her "little thing" could be.

I made a short bow. "I cannot presume to argue with such genius. Instead, allow me the pleasure of escorting you to the captain."

There was a noticeable coloring under her powdered exterior. As we linked arms and walked, I could feel the laboring of her lungs beneath the stays, and her trembling. More to ease her mind than for her information, I added, "I saw him enter the garden less than a quarter-hour ago."

"You are gallant to help me," she said in a low voice. "To be willing to be seen at the side of such—foolishness—does me more credit than I deserve."

"You do yourself an injustice."

"Not at all. I am quite aware that I look ridiculous."

"Then the word 'ridiculous' must henceforth be held to mean a charming thing."

"I warn you, Lt. Severence, I am in danger of believing your madness runs as deep as mine."

For so late in the season, it was a warm night, with a slivered moon riding high over the crease of the valley. Chaumont had a number of tall braziers set out along the garden paths, after the fashion in ancient Greek theaters, that threw forth a warm, shifting light. It was by this glow that I strolled the grounds, looking for Jones, leading a woman with an expensive miniature boat entwined in her coif. As we walked, she asked questions of me, hungering for every scrap of knowledge about the mysterious object of her affections. I answered as truthfully as I dared without diminishing her illusions of her dear Jones.

Then, in the changing light of a brazier, I saw his unmistakable figure. Jones was standing before a tree trunk, hunched over something—or embracing it.

I saw two pale arms meet across his back, two sets of fingers lacing themselves between his shoulders. Closer, and I glimpsed a feminine cheek rendered silvery by the day-old moon, a simple dress, and a pair of young eyes squeezed tightly shut. Closer still, I could see skin that was supple and clear, and trembling with the shame of innocence.

It was Thérèse-Elisabeth Chaumont.

I looked with some trepidation at the face of Madame de Reyniére, but it was a mask. She halted and, with one raised eyebrow, merely uttered a short "Oh."

It was a catastrophe, yes. But catastrophe brings forth strange heroisms: she was abruptly very resolute in the way she turned away from the horror, and pulled me with her, as if I was the one to be harmed by it. She even filled the awkward silence, adding a bright remark after the fashion of "If a kiss is stolen in the night, and no one is there to see it, is it stolen at all?"

"Perhaps it is offered," I suggested.

She performed a smile, and her hand squeezed mine. Yes, she was resolute and quick, and a good liar, but her pain still lay about her shoulders, heavier than any headdress. And though I perfectly well understood Jones had no way of anticipating our search for him, for the sake of proud Madame de Reyniére, I hated him for her.

"Sit with me for a bit," she asked, taking a bench. "I can't go in and face them all right now. Please talk with me."

I sat beside her, our arms still linked, my knees in contact with the undergirding hoops of her skirt. Looking upon her, I noted that she was never more beautiful than when such a delicious hurt shone through her eyes. After some moments of sidelong preoccupation, she saw fit to look at me, and ask of my history.

What could I tell her of my own past, dear ladies, that would not magnify her dejection over the human race? It was impossible for me to hide my own despair in the face of her example. I told her all of it: the quarrel with my father, my Aunt Hope's betrayal, the battle on the lake, the bitter story of my imprisonment. But instead of pushing her further into depression, the telling seemed to quicken her mood. I found myself basking in the sunbeams of her sympathetic astonishment, and longing for those particularly harrowing points in my tale when she would reach for me with instinctive fright and grasp my arm. I had never had such a pleasant time relating such disagreeable things.

When I was done, she shook her head, ship and all, at me as if in reproof. "Fortune has had her way with you," she told me. "But you should ask how your anger has helped her design against you."

"I own it!" I said, instantly. With this woman's hand in mine—the first woman to touch me in many months—I would own up to anything she said, even if she asserted George Washington was a Hindoo. "But what of you?" I asked. "How have you furthered your own misfortune?"

"Mine needed no help. A wife like myself is like the mown grass. My place is to lose my place. I am nothing."

"You speak from disappointment," I observed. But she laughed at me, remarking, "I speak as a realist. What do I possess, that I deserve to be happy? What arrogance of me to expect so! What perfect foolishness!"

These perplexing words left me wondering if she truly believed them, or whether she only sought reassurance that they were unfounded. To be safe, I behaved on the second assumption.

"You are beautiful," I declared. "You are witty and a good conversationalist. I understand you have a facility with the violin, and a flair with the rhyming couplet . . . "

"Please . . . stop!" she begged me, closing her eyes. By some odd convolution of the female brain, my list of her assets only saddened her, perhaps with the notion that the sum of her worth could be reduced to a mere roster of social graces. But it only required a few moments for her to regain that smiling resignation that permitted her to observe, "You have just described most of the married women in France. You prove my point."

"Most of the better women of France, perhaps . . . and I was not finished . . . "

"You were indeed, sir, for I am too tired to hear any more."

Now shut off from correcting my own blunder, I became desperate. Looking at her, I believed Madame de Reyniére was simply too undeserving of her bad luck, too accomplished, too beautiful not to be loved by . . . someone. What hand could resist a chance to smooth those golden curls back from that brave face? Who would not yearn to drink in those tears she could not shed, for lack of a gracious vessel? It was beyond my understanding, what quality of woman is traded in for snuff and brandy.

"I would love you . . . if you let me," I finally blurted, hardly believing my own words. My mind whirled about the core of my confusion, yet knew that if she accepted my proclamation I would, by God, be Heaven-bound to follow through with it forever.

Yet Madame was too wise to accept a gift so impulsively offered. Instead, with head inclined toward me, and eyes so deep as to dilute my lust to harmlessness, she said, "You flatter me again, but I am less fooled by your words than you are. Know, sir, that the woman you say you love is a common creature, schooled in charm and a musical instrument and little else. Like her million and one sisters, she has made a stab at love, mostly because she had heard of its legend, and yes, she may one day even succeed at it for a while! And when her modest measure of beauty does die, she will hide her decline behind a mature charm that will seem steadily more desperate. By then, the possibility of love will be as practical as reversing the ebb tide. The rest of her years she will spend in comfortable irrelevance. Her poets, her Lieutenants Severence, will be fled to other fields."

Madame de Reyniére paused, observing the effect of these cruel words on me, and softened, "But you should save such jewels, dear fool, to shower them upon a woman you truly love, and who loves you!"

This dismissal, again, was conducted with a most disarming good humor. My gallant assertions of her existence were rewarded with a kiss on my left cheek. Then, with a final squeeze of my hand, she rose and fled from me, her ship's headdress dipping and rolling above her as if caught in a squall at sea. Many yards from me, near the French doors and the bright and happy party within, she paused and gathered herself into a plausible imitation of frivolity. She winked at me then, and was gone.

Next I saw Madame de Reyniére, it was two weeks later, at a *petit souper* held in observance of the birthday of a minor Danish noble currently residing at Passy. Was there ever an event that was too inconsequential to merit one of their gatherings, which was usually nothing more than an excuse for vain prattle and bad poetry? I believe, had it been fashionable, this clique would have conducted balls around the birth of puppies in the barn, or the turning of the month. Doctor Franklin was obliged to go for the sake of his mission. Jones went to further his.

Though I was only two or three weeks removed from the cramped wardroom of the man o' war, I had already been corrupted by the amenities of the French table. I did not think it strange, then, to have my own footman posted behind my chair, ever ready to run the length of the room to fetch this *potage* or that *entremet* for me. I was no longer surprised by the perverse imaginations of French chefs; when I set my knife on what appeared to be a hen, it was not a shock to find it was actually a piece of sculpted rabbit meat or pork, or just an empty skin stuffed with lentils fricassée. Jones took it all as a great sport, this French cuisine, while Franklin inspected every plate placed before him with the guarded eye of a naturalist, and probably longed for his boiled roast beef and asparagus.

Neither of them succeeded in their respective tasks. Later, in the sitting room, Franklin again had to suffer being the center of a mob of jabbering, gesticulating Frenchmen who could do little to aid his real cause. Jones worked the room diligently in quest of an introduction to M. de Sartine, the French Minister of Marine. Everyone he spoke to agreed that such a meeting would be useful—even historic. They all agreed that someone should do their best to help him. But when Jones went to find this someone, he or she could not be found. Indeed, all of the possible someones insisted to the last man that they were really no one at all, but that someone else was in a much better position to assist. Jones pursued them all, in fact, until he perceived the no ones were more and more outnumbering the someone elses.

Along the way, I did see Madame de Reyniére, standing with the other flowers of matrimony, gazing forth in a state of pleasant absence. There was no headdress that day, no *coup de couture*. She seemed not to notice Jones, and betrayed only a flicker of greeting to Jones's translator.

Later she was persuaded to play one of Vivaldi's airs on the violin, an allegro from his Concerto in C Major, for the guests. This she did with tolerable skill, though her face showed no "allegro" itself. There was some irony in this, as many of the dandies in attendance found the contrast between her spritely play and her miserable face very intriguing!

Jones himself remarked on her fair appearance. "You've come to know

her, have you not?" he asked me, with a faint note of suspicion. When I
told him I had, he added, "Her ear for violin is passable, but what a great
soul behind those eyes! A poetess, I'd say, like my good Phillis Wheatley."

How could I tell him Madame de Reyniére's "poetry" was entirely cir-
cumscribed by her self-pity, and saw no farther beyond it? How to describe
a prison to someone who had never suffered in one? When I offered no
more to satisfy his curiosity, Jones merely tossed his finely groomed head,
and sighed, "There's a woman I'd befriend, if I had the leisure of a true
gentleman . . . "

And with that, he returned to the party, and his patient cultivation of
Thérèse-Elisabeth Chaumont.

In fairness, I could not say how much Jones sacrificed in pursuit of the
Chaumont girl. Only his failure was clear enough: though he succeeded
in gaining her entire admiration and trust, and did so in a manner that
(he said) kept the Mademoiselle . . . intact . . . she proved far less a resource
than Jones would have supposed.

...

"She wouldn't cooperate?" Gualbert speculated.

...

Not at all. She played her part willingly. The problem, you see, was though
Chaumont loved his daughters perhaps as much as his fortune, he simply
never listened to a word they said. Jones could drop whatever manner of
hint into the girl's ear he wanted—it didn't matter. Chaumont would listen to her suggestion that her friend Paul Jones deserved a new frigate, or
that her friend the captain's ship would certainly sail faster with a new
coppered bottom, and the man would merely laugh, finger his fobs, and
boast to his friends how clever his daughter was. When she insisted, he
would wonder aloud whether it was not time to marry her off, as she was
already growing shrewish.

At length, the poor girl grew worse than useless to Jones. He received
two or three passionate letters from her daily, and when he neglected to
reply at once, she came looking for him to assure his ardor had not cooled.
When she couldn't find him, she pounded on any door she could find,
wailing his name, crying out "My captain, my captain, stop killing me!" If
he did not attend to her enough in public, or looked at some other fawn,
she would feign swooning spells, and refuse to wake unless Jones planted

magic kisses on her lips. She carried a lock of his hair around with her like a Papist relic. She promised to kill herself if he ever stopped loving her.

Jones began to detect the whiff of scandal. To see his character and his professionalism discredited at that tender juncture would have been something worse than disastrous, not only for himself, but for his nation's cause. After all, it already required some effort to convince the French we Americans were not a race of malnourished dwarves, much less creditable allies.

His patience exhausted, Jones decided to bypass the American commissioners entirely and make a written plea for the Indiaman to Sartine, the Foreign Minister the Comte de Vergennes, and the King himself. He composed, I translated, and he recopied a volley of truly eloquent missives, full of fine phrases and unassailable logic, and closing with the deliberately modest words, "Your most obedient and humble Servant, Captain Paul Jones".

His crowning coup, he informed them, was a clever plan for a surprise attack on the Royal fleet in North American waters by the French, who would then be in a position to intercept British reinforcements and maroon the land army. It was nothing less than a prescription for making the Atlantic a French lake. Jones was confident that this clear evidence of his education and sensibility would at last clear the way to his success.

He was again disappointed. For though every one of his letters was favored with an answer, these came mostly from the desks of assistants, or else were hastily scrawled notes promising a meeting at some unnamed future date. His grand design for the destruction of the Royal Navy was hardly mentioned. Jones was incensed at this "abuse of my good name," asking, "Severence, what is wrong with this damned place, that they invite American patriots on their soil, then refuse to help them?!" As I could make no answer, and moreover Mademoiselle de Chaumont was at that moment pounding on the door to be let in, Jones fell into a brooding silence. Nothing was proceeding as he had planned.

Dr. Franklin watched over all this from a discreet but attentive distance. Finally, near the middle of January, we were summoned to his apartments.

We found him in the small parlor adjoining his bedroom, and not alone. Madame de Juoy, the Franklin partisan and renowned harpsichordist, was seated near him. She was dressed in a sharply mannish "riding suit" of forest green velvet, with a jacket lined in black and boots so pristine they must never have touched ordinary earth; her rich red hair was braided at the back and draped sinuously over her shoulder, the black bow at the end of the braid left dangling over the frankly phenomenal precipice of her bosom.

Neither she nor Franklin, dressed in his plain black usuals and grasping an ebony cane, paid us much mind on our entrance. They were absorbed instead in a game of chess at Franklin's cherrywood table (an object, he liked to note, that was of his own design). We were equally unwilling to disturb them, and so were forced to endure several uncomfortable minutes of mutual nonrecognition.

Jones nudged my arm and inclined his head toward the door leading to Franklin's private boudoir. The doctor's bed was plainly visible through the open door, and in full view from where Madame was sitting at that moment! Faced with such libertinism, I couldn't decide whether it was Franklin who was more to blame, or Madame de Juoy for not immediately removing her married self from this danger. Jones, at last, cleared his throat to announce our presence.

"You must excuse an old man for attending to one war at a time," Franklin apologized.

Jones bowed his head in reply, first to Franklin, then to his companion. But Madame de Juoy scarcely acknowledged him, locked instead in a fit of indecision over the advancement of one of her rooks to the sixth rank. At length, she snorted with a most unladylike disgust and pushed the piece forward, muttering, *"Le diable emporte lui . . . "*

Franklin responded at once: veritably chortling, he moved his queen from one end of the board to the other, captured her errant rook, and yelped *"Echec!"*

Madame de Juoy's eyes opened wide, then narrowed in indecorous frustration. She upended her own king in submission.

"A brave strategy, Madam, defeated only by a single oversight," Jones commented.

"It was no oversight, Captain," she said bitterly in good English. "It was Dr. Franklin's wiles that distracted me!"

"Thus be the prattle of the vanquished," Franklin pronounced, sitting back in his chair. "But to the victor, the promised spoils!"

At that, Madame rose from her chair, and with an expression of resolute distaste, did kiss Dr. Franklin direct upon his lips!

"Again, then?" she asked, almost before she had pulled away from him. Franklin smiled, answering, "Yet another game? Dear lady, I fear that at such a rate of advancement you will defeat me within the week!"

"That is my intention—or else my honor will be strained beyond mending," she said, stealing a glance at Jones and I.

"Then you must plight your skill again, with the same stakes."

"Yes, the same."

"But first, allow me to speak to these two patient gentlemen."

Jones bowed again, and indicated with a nudge that I should as well. Madame de Juoy sighed heavily, and with a brief nod at us, departed.

"You must excuse her enthusiasm," Franklin said. "She regards me as the only genius she is ever likely to meet, and desires to extract the maximum from our acquaintance."

"The maximum?" Jones repeated.

"If I take your innuendo, Captain, I might tell you her fidelity has never been in question. Her husband has no grounds for suspicion."

"Ah," breathed the other, outwardly satisfied. For as everyone knows, no Frenchwoman of that class may generally be thought a trollop, whatever her acts, unless her husband recognizes such, and in public.

...

"That is the practice in civilized lands," Thierry countered, "instead of leaving such powers in the hands of gossips."

"Of course," Severence patronized her, his eyes twinkling in the direction of Gualbert.

...

Franklin was thereafter intent only on the business at hand. Reaching into his pocket, he produced an envelope sealed with the stamp of the American Commission. Jones snatched it, tore it open, and scrutinized its contents with what appeared like rising pleasure.

"I trust the orders provide the latitude you desire," Franklin asked him when he looked up again.

"These are the latitudes," punned Jones with placid malice, "that will encompass the entire British nation!"

Instead of laughing at this, Franklin let out a sudden, resonant fart. Though no one appeared to want to notice this, the event asserted its own brief silence before Franklin continued.

"The orders, as written, empower Captain Jones to lead his *Ranger* against the Briton in any fashion he sees fit. What remains unwritten, however, is the call to good sense I believe you will bring to the expedition, Mr. Severence."

"I stand honored, sir," I said.

"Would that I had these orders with the proper ship!" Jones cried—most ungraciously, I believed.

"In due time," said the Doctor. "But for the present, you have only to show your natural spots."

"You need not fear of that. And if I do not appear to thank you enough for your efforts, sir, please understand that a patriot does not marvel at the permission to fight. He expects it."

I winced. In fact, Jones's taste for the unvarnished truth should have sunk him in Franklin's eyes. Fortunately for our hero, the old man chose not to take offense.

"For me, your success will be thanks enough. But if you might take a bit of advice: you should take care to learn some time, Captain, the brute utility of a gentle lie."

So much, then, for Jones at his ungracious worst. As for his best, I offer you the fate of his plan for the assault on the Royal Navy in America.

His master plan was not ignored by the French admiralty after all. Some months later, we learned, the Comte d'Estaing left with the Toulon fleet to effect a very similar scheme!

Still, no Frenchman acknowledged the role of an obscure American captain in framing the strategy. The ultimate failure of this fleet had more to do with the delay in executing the plan than with any flaw in Jones's vision.

Jones took no spiteful pleasure in the comedy that became d'Estaing's cruise in America. On the contrary, he held that the quality of one's ideas can be best judged by the class of thief that comes to snatch them. "I have a few more notions for them to steal, if they want for inspiration," he promised.

XIII.

. . . as Milton said of Adam—"The world lies all before me."
                                —JONES, in a letter to John Ross, 1778

~

WE RUSHED back to the *Ranger* as quickly as we had left her.

"And what of the girl, Thérèse-Elisabeth?" asked Gualbert.

"As I said, we left quickly. There was no parting: I translated a note from Jones to the girl, in which he begged to be excused to go fight the war, and promised to return for her if he lived. We didn't wait to see her reaction."

"His celebrated honesty, I see, does not extend to his lovers," Gualbert observed. "It doesn't matter. Go on."

Jones's manner was now worlds away from the sullen vigilance I'd seen on our arrival in France: he was conversational again. To be sure, he was still in command of a minor ship. But now he was armed with liberal orders, and faced a sea of opportunities to exercise them. He appeared willing to bide his time concerning the new frigate.

We passed the carriage ride to Paimboeuf in discussions of his plan for the coming campaign—or more exactly, in his hints at his plans and my guesses at them. Ever mindful of espionage, he would lean across the gap between our seats and ask in hushed tones, "Would you believe it worthy of a civilized race, Severence, that they would make a policy of burning all of an enemy's ports, even those having nothing to do with the business of war?"

"I would not," was my answer.

"And what would you say if I told you that is in fact the official English order?"

"I would ask how you know this?"

He thought for a moment, no doubt wondering if he could risk divulging his contacts to me. "What if I told you my knowledge comes from unimpeachable sources in the French government?"

The steadiness of his gaze demanded an answer, yet what could I say to such a question? To my mind, there was little difference between destroying the innocent merchant's warehouse with torch and explosives like the English, and seizing his property on the high seas with a privateer's commission, as America preferred. Both amounted to economic war, the coward's war. But Jones bristled at this.

"Make those arguments to the people of Kingston, or of the other towns put to the British torch. Ask if the oppressor's flames make any distinction between warehouses and the nurseries of sleeping children. Ask any merchant which fate he would choose: to suffer the loss of a ship far at sea, or to see his family burned alive in their beds!"

Jones was never more insufferable than when he was right. "Fairly put," I nodded. "But what can we do to change it? They have a hundred times our force."

Jones sat back in his seat, clucking his tongue at me.

"A thousand times. But we may still do a bit about it, I would say. Quite a bit."

There was no elaboration, but my imagination needed none. If Jones had indeed lost his taste for simple commerce-raiding, and was now set on repaying the enemy for the burning of Kingston town, then he would do well to hide it from his crew. It was absurd to believe that our little sloop could defy the greatest naval power on earth, and prevail so easily that we could proceed to her very shores and strike terror into the souls of her people.

Besides, there was no prize money in burning English cities.

"Do you ever think upon your time on the *Jersey*?" he asked me.

I shrugged. "It is beyond my power not to think about it."

Jones set his jaw and looked me in the eye. "No seaman deserves that fate. We'll see to doing something about that, too."

Clearly, absurdity would not stop Paul Jones. Moreover, I sensed he planned to make an ally of it: to use absurdity to disarm his adversary by the pure unlikelihood of his plans.

As we would have raced ahead of any posted letter, we didn't write to inform Lt. Simpson of our return. Our arrival in Paimboeuf was therefore completely unexpected.

Much can be learned in such moments of unguarded surprise. Jones could not have missed the frown that crossed Simpson's face as our cutter approached the man o' war. More stony faces looked down upon us from deck and yardarm. Of Green and Cullam, there was no sign.

In fact, Simpson had worked hard to convince the men that Captain Jones would not be returning to vex them with his inconvenient disciplines. This expectation, combined with the special dullness of Paimboeuf as a pleasure port, made Jones's reappearance something less than a triumphant occasion. He was treated to anonymous mutterings, wan salutes, and conspicuously turned backs. Notably, only Midshipman Dooley could muster a smile and a sharp salute for his commander, a gesture Jones returned with clear appreciation.

Again, Jones had an answer to Simpson's schemes. I don't know whether it was by accident or purpose, but Jones soon welcomed one Jonathan Williams, Continental prize agent in Nantes. After he and Jones had retired to the captain's cabin to dispense with a few details of business, several cloth sacks were hauled up on deck under the guard of Williams's own armed staff.

"Clerk!" shouted Jones.

"Sir?" said O'Leary, standing just behind him.

"Mr. O'Leary, please announce the distribution of prize money for brig *George!*" Jones said, loudly enough for everyone to overhear. There was a general eruption of cheers, and O'Leary wet his fingers to open his accounts book.

The prize money for the sale of the fruiterer was divided according to the standard formula, with some ten percent reserved for the captain, another forty percent shared between the officers, and the rest distributed to the seamen and marines. The cash money was not in the form of questionable Continental currency, mind, but infinitely preferable French specie. Some of the men were pleased to find that their scurvy-bitten teeth broke in their mouths as they tested the coins. With each shard of broken tooth spat over the side, Jones's stock rose.

Moody humors are easily banished by the clink of money in the pocket. The men's sentiments shifted now to impatience to have out to sea again, for more easy profits. Would that they had known the contents of Jones's mind then, as he had revealed his new strategy to me in the carriage from Passy!

Jones had resolution, but he would not be rushed. There were still a thousand details of *Ranger*'s refit to tend to, and he threw himself into his task with all the brio of battle itself. By shortening the yardarms and increasing ballast, he was determined to remedy the vessel's "crank" condition and make her a more stable platform for his gunners. As these projects would have a negative influence on her speed, Jones also ordered *Ranger*'s bottom scraped for a second time, to smooth her progress through the water. Her armament was improved with the addition of mounted pieces on the toprails, and with new gunports fore and aft to improve her chances when she was (respectively) chasing prey, or being chased. And though his campaign for Chaumont's favor had not been entirely successful, Jones did manage to wrangle a new suit of sails from the French marine stores.

The job was completed with a new coat of paint along the ship's side: a broad stripe of sky blue. It was a rare color for a naval vessel and became her nicely, but Jones had a subtler motive. According to him, the blue stripe would help conceal the size of the ship at distance when her hull flirted with the horizon, and the enemy had only her masts and rig to judge what sort of vessel she was. As most men o' war, from sloops to frigates to ships-of-the-line, were easily confounded above-decks, there was a chance we would be over-estimated, and gain some tactical advantage.

It was close by the middle of February when we were at last ready to leave. Jones overcame one last obstacle, though, when eight members of our crew, including Surgeon Green, could not be found aboard. The local gendarmerie was alerted, and with the appropriate cash inducements, succeeded in intercepting seven of the deserters on the Paris road, and delivering them back to Jones for judgment.

One of these was Ben Sharpless, the recipient of fifty lashes on the cruise over. Though he had been a dangerous man when he first stepped aboard the sloop, his punishment had worked an odd change on his personality. Lately, he had complained of all manner of stomach ailments, palsies, ringing in his ears, spots before his eyes, and the like. The expression on his face as he and his fellows were lined up on the quarterdeck, in manacles, under Jones's unsparing eye, was close to hysteria. He would not have survived another fifty lashes.

"Under the rules and regulations of the Navy of Congress," Jones began, "any officer, mariner, or others who shall basely desert their duty or station in the ship and run away shall suffer *death*, or such other punishment as a court-martial shall inflict."

He paused, waiting for his words to have their effect. Sharpless was ashen, quivering. The rest looked equally convinced the fate of Mungo Maxwell had found them, and that they would soon join him as dead men.

But Jones looked away from them, focusing instead on the space above the deserters' heads. "I, however, prefer to believe you late in returning, and not in actual desertion of this command. Tell me, am I correct in this matter?"

The condemned looked to each other, then furtively at Jones. "Yes," they said, in fair unison. "Yes," said Ben Sharpless, his voice no more than a dry croak.

"Good," said Jones. "Mr. Joye, strike your irons."

Joye frowned, then stirred himself to fulfill this remarkable order. Once free, Ben Sharpless charged toward the captain.

Jones instantly turned his shoulders oblique to the other and reached for his sword—but this was no attack. Rather, Sharpless fell to his belly, placed his arms around Jones's ankles, and proceeded to embarrass both of them by shedding his tears into Jones's stockings. Jones managed to separate himself, hissing contemptuously, "You will let go, dog! Stand up and behave like a man! You are a disgrace!"

"I can't take it, I swear it. I can't bear it, sweet Lord, good sweet Lord!" the big man whimpered, crawling forward to take hold of Jones again. The little captain evaded him by running around behind him, and with the exclamation, "So we treat our dogs!", kicked Sharpless in the seat of his pants with such force the captain's hat flew off his head.

This odd punishment continued, with Jones spewing a steady stream of foul exhortations for Sharpless to show some personal honor, some manhood, until the highwayman finally rose in shame and disappeared below. Only then did Jones become conscious of the audience all around him, watching. True to form, he ignored them all in favor of straightening his uniform and replacing his hat. That done, he turned his back on the assembled witnesses.

Despite this beating, it was remarkable Jones did not call for a formal flogging of the deserters for their crime. It was the talk of the crew for the next few days, this strange captain and his unfathomable ways. Lt. Simpson tried to prove that Jones had been merciful because able crewmen were scarce, and that he preferred not to replace them with Frenchmen. But this view was cynical.

Surgeon Green returned the following day in a state of extreme inebriation. His was apparently not a case of desertion, but mere drunken dereliction of his post—"A matter of perrrrrrsonal diplomacy," he explained to me, "with a young lady of the local de-de-demi-monde. She was practiced, I say, in the use of intimate portals but dimly unnnnnnnderstood by medical science."

"Which you were too pleased to plumb," I speculated.

"Just so," he replied.

I could only shake my head and leave him to his fate. For this crime, Jones's judgment was swift and devastating: while in deference to the Hippocratic art the doctor would be spared physical punishment, he would henceforth be deprived access to all alcoholic stores except those necessary for the comfort of his patients during amputation. Midshipman Dooley would be assigned to assure his compliance in this.

Even through his drunk, Green went as white as the *Ranger*'s new sails. "Might I suggest the more effective p-p-punishment of twenty lashes?" Green offered.

"I have dismissed you, doctor," said Jones, turning his attention back to the charts he'd laid out on his desk.

"A man like me . . . ," Green persisted, "would learn more from a little physical discommmmfort . . . "

"I will give you both the lashes and the other, if you try me further!"

The surgeon withdrew with a bow of his head. When he was gone, I looked to the exhausted Jones, who subsided into his writing chair. As he had pronounced the equivalent of a sentence of death on poor Green, I felt moved to remind Jones of some Army field wisdom: "I would not trust the bone saw to a man without his daily fortification. His hands will shake."

"He will drink despite my order. Maybe now he will hide it better, at least," said Jones, with untypical realism. "You will tell Dooley his responsibilities on this, won't you?"

When I agreed to this mild request he fell silent, with his hands shielding his eyes from the late afternoon sun pouring through the stern gallery. This was his signal for me to leave, but not before I stole a look at the charts before him.

They were maps of the British side of the Irish Sea—the very heart of the Kingdom.

Later, I found Dooley bare-eared, and reprimanded him for not using his hearing trumpet. Ashamed, he fetched it and listened very closely to my instructions to keep an eye on Surgeon Green, and to confiscate any spirits found on or near his person with the exception of those reserved for anesthesia. The boy saluted and went off right then to check on Green's lucidity, and I must confess I felt very sorry for the surgeon. This boy would be his nemesis, his Wormwood, but Green's stylish pleas for mercy would fall literally on deaf ears.

At last, we slipped with the tide out of Paimboeuf in the gray dawn of February 13. In that half-light, under setting Orion, I could see a half-dozen female figures in white gowns and overcoats gathered on the quay, watching our departure. These ghosts of love were too far for me to see their faces, but I could glimpse the effect they had on some of the men. Expressions turned dark, distracted; eyes grew red around the rims. There were no ribald work songs as lines were hauled and reefs untied. For some, this would certainly be their last cruise.

I found myself thinking about Madame de Reyniére—thinking, yet not knowing what I should think about her. For the most part, I recalled my last glimpse of her, standing among the other wives at that birthday affair. Her eyes swept over me, and I was chilled by the smallness of her recognition. Yet this was less the smallness of vanity, of aristocracy, than that of distance, like the women seeing their men off from the shore. Madame de Reyniére believed herself too remote from me, too deep within her trap, to have any hope of communication. Instead, with just a lift of an eyebrow, and a brief fixation of her eye, she waved to me as I passed her Naxos, her Ogygia, her marriage.

I turned, and saw Jones standing in his usual spot by the quarterdeck rail. It seemed impossible that he would be affected by the same sentiments that assailed his crewmen or his dour-hearted commander of Marines. Rather, we twinkling, inconstant beings reeled about the Polaris of his ambition, and from it, measured our place in the scheme of things. I could have viewed him then as I always had—as insensate, obsessive, an automaton, a living abstraction. Instead, at that moment, with his hat pulled down hard over his head against the breeze, and his shoes set their usual eighteen inches apart, Jones seemed the only force in the universe as implacable as the sea, and as dangerous as our own hearts. He was inevitable.

Before I describe the next voyage, I would beg to recount a series of incidents that threw our true relations with the French into high relief. As you ladies may know, navigating your northern waters in winter is no easy project. There are squalls, frigid temperatures, and a jagged coastline that waits to punish the careless pilot. We struck out north from Paimboeuf, picking a careful path through the reefs, sometimes standing well out to sea to weather the many treacherous points, and then to-ing and fro-ing our way back to evening anchorage. Such operations had to be conducted with speed, as no part of the Brittany coast went unvisited by British cruisers, and we were unescorted.

Our first stop was at Quiberon Bay, 75 miles as the crow flies from Paimboeuf, where we found a small force of French 74's and attending frigates. Upon inquiry, Jones was informed that this squadron was under the command of one Commodore Piquet. Breaking out his weapons of correspondence, Jones launched a salvo of compliments, one gentleman to another, along with the suggestion that they exchange an official salute of thirteen guns under our respective national flags.

Piquet's answer was in hand within the hour. This was an insultingly brief note informing the American commander that his flagship would indeed recognize Jones's thirteen-gun salute, but with only nine guns in return. I expected Jones to be miffed at this. Instead, he preferred not to believe it, speculating that Piquet had quoted only the official policy, but would in fact make an equal response if he was presented with a real opportunity to show his respect for the Stars and Stripes.

The next day we sailed conspicuously below the gallery of Piquet's ship, offering thirteen guns in tribute. The response was ceremonious and immediate: unfortunately, Simpson's running count of their salute ended at only nine guns. Jones stood on, his ear cocked, as if presuming Piquet's silence was due to oversight. The four other reports never came. They were the loudest guns of all.

Some weeks later, we repeated the exercise at L'Orient, and again at Brest. Each time we found we rated but nine guns for thirteen. Jones finally turned to the surgeon, and remarked bitterly, "Mark it well, Green. We have finally discovered a species of man as haughty as the English!" He then retired to his cabin to pen his letters of protest to the dozen or so parties he believed responsible for these insults.

Green came to me then, his eyes shot through with red, his hair wild, but otherwise more alert than I had ever seen him. Could I see to it, he asked me, that the standards of sobriety be loosened somewhat? Members of the crew had been looking with some worry on the way virtue made Green's hand tremble. Many of them had never shipped out with a surgeon who didn't drink. But Midshipman Dooley was now Green's very shadow, and even as the surgeon appealed to me, the boy haunted the background, pretending to polish some brasswork with the lapel of his frockcoat.

Under those circumstances, I could only decline this request. Still, I wondered: if chance had reserved an amputation for me, would I be better served by taking a nip for myself, or by donating it all to my doctor?

XIV.

I am not . . . a mere adventurer of Fortune. Stimulated by principles
of Reason and Philanthropy, I laid aside my enjoyments in private
Life and embarked under the Flagg of America when it was first dis-
played—in that line my desire for Fame is infinite.
                    —JONES, in a letter to Prince de Nassau-Siegen, 1778

SO BEGAN a cruise that Jones had designated a veritable orgy of destruction. After our tour of salutes in the northern French ports, we finally
pressed in toward English waters by the second week in April to earn our
extra four guns.

We were escorted part of the way by a French frigate, the captain of
which Jones entertained with great effort and enthusiasm. Here again, I
noted the increasing delight Jones appeared to take in all things French,
or more precisely, in all things formal, stylish, "refined." The crew, present
party included, disliked this French captain's fey and superior manner—
it was difficult to imagine he would allow any circumstance, battle or
otherwise, where he would risk soiling his fine silk uniform. Monsieur le
Capitaine spoke only French on board, though his knowledge of English
was clear from his habit of correcting my translations of his words. It was
with some relief for all, except Jones, that we watched him return to his
ship on the fourth day out, his frigate wear about, and at last fall off astern.

"Honestly, do you take that man's part at all?" I asked Jones later.

"Did it appear that I liked him?"

"Well . . . yes."

"Good," he said.

There was a marked surge in tension aboard as Master Cullam pointed
our prow fully toward the North, where nothing separated us and the
enemy's home islands but a few leagues of open water. Jones appointed

two official lookouts per watch, but in fact there were 150. Their vigilance was spurred by the inevitable calculations of every officer and seaman on the eve of battle: the chances of intercepting a merchantman with a truly valuable cargo and becoming rich, vs. the likelihood of stumbling upon a bigger and faster warship, in which case we were captured or quite possibly dead.

Fortune smiled on us at first. Proceeding across the English Channel, we crossed paths with a flaxseed carrier of two masts and forced her to lay to with a shot across her bow. However, as Jones didn't see fit to spare a prize crew to sail her back to France, he sent her to the bottom by exploding a charge in her hold. The prisoners would prove valuable in trade for American captives, to be sure, but there was much grumbling among the Rangers as we watched our prize shares disappear under the waves. Not to fret, Jones assured us: there are greater fish in this ocean.

Our luck held as we ran up past the Isles of Scilly, took wide berth around Bristol Channel, and entered the Irish Sea. Here Jones's strategic mind showed itself to best advantage, for this body was teeming with commerce, yet was deemed so secure by the Royal Navy that they patrolled it only with small sloops and wherries, themselves mere prey for our *Ranger*.

The hunting should have been good. We passed within sight of several tasty-looking vessels, but Jones would not move against them. He was saving his crew, I understood, for those operations he had explained only once, to me, in the carriage from Passy. When we finally spoke a little merchantman bearing porter for Dublin, pretty and irresistible, Jones cursed this "bad luck." Relenting, he took it without bloodshed, and sent it back to Brest with the smallest prize crew he dared.

It was off the northern reaches of the Isle of Man that Jones finally had a crack at the kind of game he preferred. This was a Royal cutter of fore-and-aft rig. She first took the measure of us north of Port Ayre, and came about after us so saucy and so confident, Jones could hardly wait to blow her out of the water.

As the breeze had shifted over to the north, and Cullam had been instructed not to make any sudden maneuvers, we were now sailing fairly close to the wind. This condition favored the fore-and-after, which could haul more directly upwind than our square rig would allow.

The cutter caught up with us late in the afternoon and hailed us with the usual "What ship is that?" Jones played the fool as long as it amused him, asking first for directions to Whitehaven, then for a pilot. The Englishman's patience ran out—he demanded identification, or he would "not be responsible for the disfortunate consequences." Jones shrugged, remarking "Then unfortunate they must be."

He ordered our gunports opened and our iron run out. Meanwhile, I signaled my Marines to open fire from our tops. Their aim, I knew, would be improved by the happy knowledge that the law of shares for a military capture guaranteed they would divide all the money from its sale, not just the half from a merchantman. Many of the Rangers were undoubtedly fighting with only half their wits, calculating their coming fortunes with the rest.

"Will you bring to, sir?" Jones demanded.

"Just a minute, and you will have your answer." replied the other.

The captain of this cutter was no Captain Whattley. He had already worked his quick little vessel to a position too far forward to be covered by our main guns and too far aft to train our bow chaser on her. Not to be beaten by this maneuver, Jones told Cullam to bring 'er about on the starboard tack, with the clear intention of turning the *Ranger* enough to bring an entire broadside to bear on the pest.

Cullam ordered, "Ready about!" as the driver was sheeted in, "Mainsail haul!" as the main yard was swung through 90 degrees, "Let go and haul!" as the headsail was trimmed, and all the other commands that must be made to turn a square-rigger through the eye of the wind. Unfortunately, this took all of several minutes of screaming and hauling and tramping from one end of the sloop to the other, and by that time the cutter had also beat to the starboard tack. Our aim was then no better than before. Worse, the other had cleared away faster on her new heading, and was now putting some distance between herself and the *Ranger.*

Jones had no choice but to tack again in the other direction. The cutter aped the maneuver, but this time Jones tacked farther still, allowing the wind to come almost full abeam. We lost ground again, but had a clear shot at last.

"FIRE!" cried Jones.

"FIRE!" cried the respective gun captains.

It was a gloriously thunderous broadside, yes, but it did the art of gunnery no credit. There was a pretty play of water-spouts about the cutter, and one clear hit astern that ripped a gash through her gallery. But this was not enough damage to prevent her escape.

Jones ordered us into the wind again. This was our third tack in less than ten minutes, and our afterguard performed it only at the cost of wheezing, open-mouthed exhaustion. The gun crews ran to the other side of the ship to prepare the next broadside. We came about once again on the starboard tack, but now the cutter was so distant a man could hold his hand out at arm's length and cover it with his thumb.

"Fire," Jones commanded, this time with less zest.

"Fire," came the hopeless refrain.

We hit nothing. Cullam waited for further instructions, but Jones just stood there on the quarterdeck, watching the cutter recede from his grasp. The sun was setting, its pretty rays fixing a bronze fire upon the cutter our guns could not.

"There's a trim little Miss," he said to me, nodding at the cutter. "Look how she stands up to the wind. Ballasted to a particle—she won't skate about on her wales."

Despite this apparent appreciation, I knew he had a mind to try again, to hope for some miraculous blow that would take away her tiller, or strike some poorly fortified magazine. In any case, the cutter had demonstrated the principle of her escape. It was Jones's choice whether or not to see the bitter end of the proof.

"Down ports," said Jones. "Secure from quarters."

So much for our latest fortune. The crew then had nothing more to look forward to than several hours' further toil. On that eventful cruise, this episode was Disappointment Number One.

"What a lovely turn that was!" Jones persisted in praising the enemy, much to everyone's annoyance. "It was a bit of schooling we received today, boys. It was high artistic. We didn't deserve to catch 'er."

Then Jones looked to me and remarked, "I saw your top-fire take a man, Severence. Say there, Simpson, did you see it?"

"I did," said Simpson. "Took a man right off the wheel, I think."

"Hmm. Not badly done," came the reply. "Clerk!"

O'Leary instantly stuck head up from the ladderway. This was the one place aboard that was close enough to be in earshot of Jones's call, but enough concealed from the action to be safe.

"Yes, sir?" he said.

"Record that Severence's sharpshooter . . . Marine Private Denham . . . is due one day's pay bonus."

"I will, sir."

With that, the captain took himself and his smiling facade below, and was not seen above for the rest of the evening.

The next day's wind blew up sharp from the east, complicating any further approach to the English coast. These winds were the same Jones must have known coming up off the moors of his childhood. A good nose, it was said, could smell the spring heather halfway to Ireland. But there was no Galwegian sentiment in Jones's eye that day. There was only frustration, and hunger for a commemorable success that would forever free him of this fragrance, this past.

Forgetting England for the moment, we sailed with the wind to the Irish coast to continue our predations. Jones suspected good hunting in the bay of Belfast on the northeast headlands. As these waters were tricky, we sought and seized a local fishing yawl and invited her master to strike a blow against the English. This he declined to do, though he did remark that the sloop of war H.M.S. *Drake* was anchored that very afternoon in the bay, should we want for a worthy target.

Jones thanked the Irishman for this intelligence, then apologized for being obliged to sink his yawl and hold his crew in irons until the conclusion of the day's business. He did take care, however, to see that a bucket of grog was sent below to leaven our guests' stay.

Sure enough, from the mouth of the bay we spied a low-slung Caribbean cruiser of eighteen or twenty guns which, except for the broad blonde stripe down her side, appeared every inch the twin of the *Ranger* herself!

We all saw the same vessel there, but not the same opportunity. It was Jones's plan to proceed directly into the bay, present our colors, and invite *Drake* out for a contest of broadsides. The men, however, had acquired a taste for easier game, and were terrified by the prospect of dying with unspent money in their pockets.

As no seaman could approach the captain directly with his concerns, the crew's reservations made their way first to Midshipman Dooley and Lt. Hall, and thence to Lt. Simpson. This latter then had the unenviable obligation to approach the Captain.

"Sir?"

"What is it, Simpson?" snapped Jones, perhaps already anticipating the message.

"Begging your pardon, sir, but some of the men request a meeting to discuss the attack."

Jones turned to him with such a lot of resentment in his eyes, it was a wonder Simpson did not wither in his boots.

"A meeting, eh? Tell me, Lieutenant, do you remember why we are here?"

"I do. If I might remind the captain, I only deliver the message, I don't invent it." And he said that word, "remind," with a quality of contempt that questioned whether Jones possessed any mind at all.

But Jones would not cavil with him. Instead, he swept the lieutenant aside and addressed the crew directly with his speaking trumpet, from fo'c'sle to yards to poop. "You want a meeting, do you? Scurvy apes! A meeting with the enemy, I say, would resound to our greater glory! There's history to be written this afternoon, boys! Come on now, who has the courage among you?"

This half-insult, half-exhortation was answered with a resounding silence. This, from a crew that owed the very shirts on their backs to Jones's personal largesse. He stood there, no doubt feeling more humiliated than he had cause to be. The cowardice, after all, was not his.

"Tell me, boys," he tried again, this time beginning in a much lower key. "Did we cross the ocean for this? Have we tried the deep, and put the trident to flight, for this? And if glory does not move you, what of your brothers imprisoned ashore, dying in chains because our enemy does not respect our right to contest tyranny on the seas? What of your daughters and wives at home, quivering beneath the occupier's boot? Are you Americans? Are you men? Now, who is with me?"

They made no answer. Jones let his arms droop to his sides, and the speaking trumpet fall to the deck. It bounced twice and rested against his shoe.

"I have your answer, then," he said. "I know now what sort of nation has adopted me. I am ashamed." And with that, he turned toward the ladderway. His expression was funereal as he passed me.

"Heading, sir?" asked Cullam.

Jones didn't answer. Sorely defied, he retired to his cabin to sulk.

Though they had foiled Jones's plan for an attack on the *Drake,* no one among the crew had any notion of what to do next. I suspect we all had marvelled at the swiftness of Jones's mind, and come to depend upon it more than we knew. Nor did anyone have a taste for actual mutiny . . . yet. So, for lack of any orders at all, the sloop was left to drift at the mercy of the currents.

With that, anxiety bloomed. The shipboard routine was broken. The men began to sense the fragility of their lives without Jones's bullying insistences.

Cullam, having been ignored, did nothing to control the vessel. We drifted stupidly, first aft, then broadside to the breeze, the sails luffing away until they seemed, to superstitious minds, the flapping wings of the Angel of Death. The men began to speak among themselves, exchanging whispers, insults, and, at last, nods. A consensus was struck and handed down to Lt. Hall. He communicated it to Lt. Simpson, who informed me.

At my suggestion, Jones's speaking trumpet was retrieved, and a deputation of myself, Lt. Simpson, and Mr. Cullam went down to deliver it back to the captain.

The Marine guard on duty at Jones's cabin straightened to attention as I ducked beneath the beams. I nodded to him, and he turned to knock exactly three times on the door.

"Come in."

The guard opened the door for us, and we saw Jones standing before his writing desk. His attitude was like that of a man waiting to receive the first shot in a duel: position slightly sideways, arm cocked at his side, hand grasping his coat stiffly. We all looked at him for a bit, and he at us. None of us had planned what to say.

"If it pleases the captain," Simpson began, "it would be the crew's duty to follow his plan to attack the enemy in stealth, under cover of darkness."

Jones stared at him, blinking. A crease of what seemed like relief crossed his features. I suspected, but cannot vouch, that he had been expecting a reprise of the Tobago affair.

"By night?" he repeated.

"Yes, sir."

The captain shifted, turned his attention back to the papers on his desk. Clearly, no commander would prefer to have strategy dictated to him by his subordinates. Jones's only salvation, however, lay in acknowledging that these were not subordinates, but Americans.

"We will be astride her weather bow before the moon rises," he told us at last, rekindling the martial fire in his eyes. "If they make a move, we will rake her decks. Then we will send our boarding crews and raise our colors over her."

"If it so pleases the captain," came the unimpressed Simpson.

"Mr. Cullam, would you be so kind as to retire us to the far side of Copeland Isle for now?"

"That I would, sir," he said, and was gone with what was, for him, unusual footspeed.

Simpson withdrew after him, leaving only myself and Jones's abandoned speaking trumpet. Jones stepped forward, hands clasped behind him.

"I trust you will have need of this again," I said, offering the instrument to him.

He took it, looking at me with an expression almost fatherly.

"I cannot fail with you aboard, Severence," he told me.

"I would not be so sure."

What was most surprising about this particular affair, ladies, was not the crew's distaste for needless bloodshed, but Jones's nimble capitulation. As we swung about Copeland Isle and waited for dark, he stepped about the quarterdeck with such liveliness you would have thought the night attack had been his plan from the beginning. Perhaps he saw the wisdom of the idea after all.

Some of the crew still took no pleasure in the change of tactics. A few worriedly re-practiced the dance-steps I had taught them for blade-to-blade combat. A few others, I noticed, had the definite air of grog about them; Surgeon Green had suddenly ceased his complaints on this matter, and bore a look of some relief on his face. I put all this down to attempts by some to steady their nerves before the next test. My naïveté was tremendous.

By midnight the moon had set and we proceeded back toward our appointment with the *Drake*. As we sailed the light airs, I could see the lamps of Carrickfergus town twinkle on the lee shore. The town hung like a great constellation over the vessels anchored in the roads, and made a good target for Cullam and his helmsman.

Jones ordered all crewmen with shoes to remove them, and brooked no talking as we glided under reduced courses to *Drake*'s windward. Our guns were already cast loose and shotted, and the crews waited silently with their slow matches smoking. My Marines stared down mutely from their perch, taking the measure of the enemy sloop recumbent on the water below. The *Drake* was sleepy, unsuspecting. Our surprise would be complete. Except for a loose bell rolling with the swells on some nearby coaster, there was no sound but the tread of the rising tide on the coast-line rocks.

Jones held fast until we were perfectly athwart the *Drake*'s bow, then gave a quiet order to release the anchor. The order was relayed forward, the gunners bent over their guns, the boarding parties clapped their sweating palms over their cutlasses, and . . .

Severence stopped, drank.

"And?" breathed Thierry. "What?"

Nothing. Nothing at all. The *Ranger* glided just as serenely onward, passing the best point from which to cover the *Drake*'s decks.

"The devil take it—what's wrong now?" I heard Jones demand through clenched teeth. There was some shouting ahead, and curses, until we finally heard the familiar running of the cable, and the splash of the bow anchor into the bay. We came to rest some fifty yards beyond where we were supposed to be, and entirely covered by the *Drake*'s own broadside. To the general horror, it was realized the enemy could have raked us from that position.

A crewman came back through the darkness, and on his approach we could see he was the one called Fallows, quartermaster's mate. He saluted poorly, and in a speech garbled by alcohol informed us that the anchor had unfortunately seized up, but was "all right" now.

"'All right now,'" he says!" Lt. Hall mocked him. "'All right' to see him triced up on a hatch, the sot!"

"Shut up, Hall. Simpson, go forward and cut our cable. Quickly!"

As Simpson went forward to separate us from our anchor, Jones turned sadly to the *Drake*. Even then she was dozing, despite her power over us. Still, Jones reasonably believed it was better to beat an invisible retreat now, at no cost but to our pride, than to fight on unfavorable terms.

I stepped beside the Captain, and Jones spoke to me.

"You know," he said, "I've half a mind to . . . "

"I know it," I told him. "Do we try again tomorrow?"

He nodded. "If we get away clean."

We were free after only three or four minutes at anchor, and after dropping far to the *Drake*'s lee, we began the laborious task of beating our way back out of the bay. Looking back, I could see that, for all our careful preparations, for all of our worry and bumbling incompetence, not to mention a near-mutiny, the *Drake* had never stirred. She lay at anchor, mocking us with her indomitable quiescence, driving each officer and seaman aboard the *Ranger* to ponder the fact that she had never noticed us.

...

"That should have been to your credit. You must have taken some comfort in escaping so skillfully," Thierry ventured.

Gualbert squeezed Severence's arm. Then she said to her friend "Tell me, Nathalie, have you ever had your eye on a man and pursued him with all your arts? And when he did not notice you despite your best efforts, did you pretend you never took any interest in him in the first place?"

Gualbert stared right at Thierry, dark eyes fixed on fair in that competition older than the oldest profession. Thierry frowned, not liking what her friend implied. Gualbert pressed on, "Did that stratagem, that little lie you told yourself, truly make you feel better?"

"No. I have no experience of such a case," said Thierry, with apparently seamless confidence. Then she looked out the window at the empty street, and added "But I know what you mean."

...

That fiasco was disappointment Number Two. Nature decided to add insult to our injury by stirring up a storm the next day. This was a short reprise of winter, with frigid winds, driven snow, and waves so high they broke over the stem and turned the fo'c'sle into an icy torrent. This great blow lasted two more days, and pushed us so far to the east, we lost contact with the *Drake*. I could not help but believe we were being perversely slung from one end of the Irish Sea to the other, and back again, like a shuttlecock.

When the third day dawned clear, we were again to the east of Man, in Solway Firth, between Scotland and England. As I feared, Jones's mind turned once more to his plan to humble Britannia by laying waste a city on her coast. And what better stretch of coast could he choose than this, the very one he had known as a boy dreaming of the sea?

And so, for the moment, the *Drake* was forgotten.

XV.

*I cannot but feel myself hurt by the dirty insinuations of the Enemy
that my Entrance at Whitehaven was in Consequence of a Capital
Sum paid me in hand by the Court of France. They have more visits
of the same kind to expect.*

—JONES, in a letter to Benjamin Franklin, 1778

PIPES were sounded, and the boatswain's mates went into the bowels of
the ship with starter-whips to muster all hands on the spar deck. When
the men were gathered, some half-dressed, all blowing into their hands
and stomping their feet with the cold, Jones very slowly and clearly out-
lined his plan to them. This was for a rapid, devastating night raid on the
port of Whitehaven. The expedition would coincide with the low tide,
when all the vessels there would be lying helplessly aground in the ebb,
he said. If the operation was timed correctly, and the port's defensive guns
sabotaged, and the fires set with precision, Jones predicted that a determined party could torch between two hundred and three hundred enemy
vessels.

The faces around him were mostly blank. There seemed no end to this
captain's bad ideas. Still, I could see a sort of reckless sheen in the eyes of
some. Here, in Jones's wildly imprudent scheme, would at least be a story
to tell around the hearths of their old age. For some, this was all it took.

Taking some wisdom from the resistance to his frontal attack on the
Drake, Jones made a point of asking for volunteers this time. He then leav-
ened his appeal with sober reminders of Britain's crimes against property
in America. The crew being mostly New Englanders, and New Englanders
being known for their talent at righteous indignation, Jones soon found
himself with a body of thirty enthusiastic angels of vengeance, including
myself, Lt. Hall, and Midshipman Dooley.

Well pleased, Jones tested the Fates further by drafting Ben Sharpless for the mission, with the intent to "make an honest felon out of him." Sharpless's huge form only redoubled its trembling at this order. Yet he knew better than to dispute it openly.

Notably, Lt. Simpson did not join us: faced with the prospect of losing a good fraction of the crew to Jones's unprofitable fantasy, this officer was suddenly taken with great "fatigue," and retired to his cabin to plot strategy.

The fruit of his thought, I presume, came ripe the evening before the attack was launched. I was surprised to be approached by Surgeon Green again, this time with a story that a mutiny was planned by that majority of the crew that still believed the *Ranger* was best employed in making money for her crew. Around two bells on the first watch, his story ran, Master Cullam (whose hatred of Jones made him a plausible party to the conspiracy) would remark upon the turn of the temperature. This would be the agreed-upon signal for the mutineers to seize their boarding cutlasses and make prisoners of all loyal officers and men. Jones and myself were mentioned particularly as officers "likely" to be killed in the struggle.

Jones listened to Green's account without expression. He then looked at the surgeon standing there, cap in hand, knowing full well what he expected in exchange for this intelligence.

"Severence," Jones said at last. "Please give Dooley something else to do right now. Something far from the grog tub."

I nodded. Green seemed struck dumb by his turn of fortune.

Jones's counterstroke against the conspirators was his first unmixed success of the cruise. Shortly before two bells, we sent a party of Marines up to the main top with weapons. This show of force worried a number of the men working the afterguard that night—their eyes often flitted up the shrouds nervously, aware that from that position the marines had clear command of the spar deck.

Still, the mutinous plan seemed to be carried forward by its own momentum, until Master Cullam drifted over to Jones on the quarterdeck, looked up at the moonlit sky, and remarked, with all apparent innocence, "Looks to be a chill in the offing."

At that, Cullam was surprised to find the barrel of Jones's pistol aimed squarely at the bridge of his nose. No one, seditious or loyal, dared move. Jones then asked the other, in a voice hardened by Scots flint, "Be you sure o' that forecast, Mr. Cullam?"

Though Cullam was the enthusiastic bellwether of the plot, he was far from its bravest partisan. Despite the cold, sweat stood on his wide face as he learned what it was like to be entirely at the mercy of the notorious murderer of Tobago. He swallowed, his girth heaving up and down with the reflex, and jabbered, "Nay, nay, not 't all . . . sir. Merely remarkin', that's all, ha ha. You know."

"Yes. I did know," replied Jones, casting his eyes around to deliver this message to the other mutineers. Inevitably, fists came unclenched—shadowy figures moved away from the racks of pikes and blades.

Jones stood there, constant as a stone, until all of these men had returned to their proper duties. Only this return to productivity obliged him to lower the pistol from Cullam's head.

"Back to your station!" he ordered, adding, "And let's hear nothing more about the temperature!"

Lt. Simpson, meanwhile, had never shown his face on deck, though the relative quiet up above must have told him the plot was a failure. This business settled, Jones resumed his preparations for the raid on Whitehaven.

...

"What?" asked Thierry, disbelieving. "He did not seek out the conspirators? Wring confessions? Issue punishments?"

"Nothing could be proven. Cullam had, after all, only spoken of the weather, and Green would only risk betraying gossip, not names. Furthermore, Jones needed all of his men to make the cruise a success. He would never become famous just by foiling plots among his own crew."

"*Incroyable!*" she said. "To continue to serve with known traitors . . . for a Frenchman, it would be impossible."

"But what a pit of disloyalty your navy was, *mon ami!*" added Gualbert, in a tone perhaps more appropriate for some accident of fashion. "It is very sad."

"Perhaps it was," Severence granted. "But no more than similar commands in navies the world over. I suspect your . . . uh . . . acquaintance with military matters has been confined mostly to army officers, who operate within a more immediate chain of command. In the field, the army commander is rarely more than a few hours' ride from his superior officer, if not a few minutes!

"At sea, the commander operates with all the independence of the open ocean. Within the small universe of his ship, he is the Godhead himself. It is an independence that gives a power like no other—and a danger. His isolation is also his vulnerability. With opportunity, 'accidents' can happen to unpopular captains and officers. Such things occurred far more than I knew from my experience in the Continental Army, itself no bastion of good order. It is, in any case, not a thing a navy prefers to get about."

...

After this diversion Jones took to his cabin for a turn of splendid solitude. It was already close to midnight when he emerged again, this time with his frockcoat discarded, and wearing a newly laundered white shirt, his uniform breeches, a plain tricorne, and a gilded blue sash about his waist. The other officers in the party, including myself, then rushed to adopt Jones's dashing raider's costume, knowing full well that this was what he expected of us. I gather everyone but Jones worried that the bright white shirts made excellent targets of us all.

The *Ranger*'s launch and gig were lowered away, each with fifteen men. Jones decided to take personal command of the party in the launch, and set Lt. Hall in command of the gig. The boats were each provided with incendiary bombs of old sailcloth soaked in oil, and enough small arms to make a momentary stand if the need arose.

The two boats, riding the swells under their little ship, soon sallied forth against the English Empire with but a single, weak "hip, hip, hooray" from the rest of the crew to cheer them. As the oarsmen pulled to their task and Jones took the vanguard at the prow of the launch, I found myself gazing back at the receding *Ranger,* wondering how Jones could so easily trust the conduct of officers so recently suspected of conspiracy. How could we be sure the sloop, under Simpson's command, would wait for our return? What fresh battles would we face after fighting our way out of Whitehaven?

I asked Jones later whether such fears crossed his own mind. While he accepted the possibility that some parties would dispute his tactics, he said, it was beyond his conception that Americans would ever abandon Americans to their common enemy. Truly, this was the naiveté of genius.

The airs were light that morning, with but a little offshore breeze to stir our colors. As we pulled away, the orb of the moon gleamed behind the nodding *Ranger,* nestling in among her yards and stays and throwing the vessel's penumbral shadow beyond us, toward Whitehaven. The town was there too, just then a mere cluster of faint lights on the profounder black of the shore, deep in the slumber of Empire.

So it was an hour later, still a cluster of distant lights—and an hour after that, apparently no closer. Jones took the latest of a dozen sightings through his glass, and barked for the oarsmen to lean into their work. They obeyed, but different versions of the same question now troubled the faces of Ben Sharpless and Midshipman Dooley and Cato Carlisle and all the other hands in the launch. Only the wide, beardless face of Scipio Africanus seemed at repose, if only because he appeared not to be thinking of our raid at all, but spreading his thoughts upon some more remote pleasure.

"You there! Nigger!" I called to him.

He looked at me with an expression of boredom that was just on the safe side from offensive.

"What are you thinking about?" I asked him.

I imagined, in fact, that he was sustained by some devilish black creed, some chanting echo from the dawn of his godless continent. Still more secretly, I feared perhaps that his superstition would prove a greater comfort to him than my hapless rationalism was to me.

Scipio's wide shoulders—the shoulders of an oarsman—heaved a shrug.

"Stock market," he said.

All at once, the war party erupted in a round of whooping laughter. I blushed, but was of no mind to compound my foolishness, when Jones finally snarled, "Shut your mouths, apes! Best think of your first words to your Maker!"

Three exhausting hours later, Whitehaven finally seemed at hand. Alas, so did the glow of daylight above the Cumbrian highlands. Clearly, Jones had not counted on the fact that rowing against the ebbtide would make the distance to shore seem double. There was no possibility of conducting our raid under cover of darkness then. More likely, we would exercise our nocturnal plan directly under the cheery rays of the sun.

After the *Drake* debacle, I knew Jones would never order another humiliating turnabout. We were, to choose an unfortunate word, committed.

A thought struck me then: the memory of Dr. Franklin's trust in the "good sense" I would bring to the expedition. This had the effect of throwing me into a further state of despair, as I fully knew I lacked the will to stand in Jones's way if he chose to persist in the doomed attack.

"The hour is late, boys, but we'll catch 'em napping yet, I'll warrant!" he cried out, hoping to rally his men. Their reply was a deep, resonant groan that might have been intended as some sort of cheer.

When the sun mounted the hills behind the town and parted the morning mists, we could at last see our target in detail. The town seemed to shamble down to the water in quiet, unhurried blocks. At only one point, at the taller of the town's two church steeples, did it stir its torpid self upward to greet the day.

This was, I recalled, the very town from which John Paul, ship's boy, first went to sea aboard the brig *Friendship*, nearly 20 years before. But if Jones held any regard for a place so significant to his life, he never allowed it to cloud his thinking. I believe he would have led an assault on his father's garden if he saw some advantage in the deed. I would not have discounted the possibility he had begun planning this raid while polishing his master's boots on the *Friendship*—just in case.

The harbor appeared to us to be split in two by a crude seawall of piled cobbles. The real wealth of the town lay on both sides of this wall, in its hundreds of fishing schooners, cutters, yawls, and sloops. All of these were heeled over in the shallow water, as helpless as a yard of fatted turkeys. It was too early in the season for these vessels to ply their respective trades, and the natives seemed content to while away the frigid morning in their warm bedclosets. Indeed, in their experience, what could they possibly have to fear?

Lt. Hall's gig, being the faster of the two boats, was some two cables ahead of ours. We could see Hall turn back toward us, his blond hair gathering the morning rays, and Jones responded by rising to his feet and pointing to starboard, telling him to attack the south side of the harbor.

It took another quarter hour of pulling against the tide before we tied up at the northside quay. Jones was the first to leap ashore, followed by myself and the handful of armed Marines. These fanned out to secure the immediate vicinity from the "natives," which so far consisted of a half-dozen seagulls and a black retriever who came to us with mouth smiling and tail happily churning the air.

Jones directed the pre-emptive feeding of the dog to assure it would not bark, then charged the sentries to mount a cross-fire across the approaches to our boat. This took ten minutes more, yet none of the phantom port's human inhabitants appeared.

Far from soothing our worries, this eerie absence increased them. None of us really had any notion of what to expect from the expedition; though American privateers had already entered British waters as we had, no one had dared to approach the beaches with as much impunity as the *Ranger*. The uncertainty of the entire affair twisted our minds to a state of pan-icked fascination, as if we were the first men to walk a new continent.

Jones looked to me. "Mr. Severence, if you please?"

"Gladly, sir," said I, swinging the heavy cannon-spiking tools across my back. We took a handful of men with us, including a pair of Marines, as we set off up the hill toward the port's north battery.

Our party passed along several of Whitehaven's narrow lanes on our way. There, at last, we encountered evidence of the town's human popu-lation, in the person of a thick-set housemaid sweeping a front walk with her straw broom.

By the time we saw her, we were too far exposed to withdraw—she had only to lift her eyes to sight us. She would then sound the alarm, I knew, and so precipitate our capture, our confinement, and our slow exe-cution as pirates. For England would never excuse our incursion as an enterprise of war. In payment for their navy's embarrassment, they would prefer to see us as lawless corsairs, with all the happy indulgences of vengeance such a capture would imply.

But when the maid's eyes did rise, and fixed themselves on us, it was not a skulking band of intruders she saw, but Jones, marching through the town in his well-tailored perfection, his pace purposeful, his confidence that of a haughty British post captain. We followed his lead as best we could, taking the role of a deputation from his Royal Navy command.

"John? John Paul! Ye come back a' last!" the gray-haired woman called out to him.

Jones looked at her, and, as if recognizing her in a disagreeable flash, turned away immediately. "Come along, boys," he hurried us. "We mustn't be late for our appointment!" And he doubled our pace to a fast trot up the slope.

This presumptuous woman had stopped her sweeping, and was looking to Jones with arms at her sides. "John, where ye going in such a hurry, now? Always in such a rush to be at somethin'!" she called to him in a matron's tone. "Come on back 'ere and talk to yer Nan when yer done now! Don't make 'er come an' look for ye!"

We were several streets above her, and still puzzling over this woman's familiarity with Jones, when we heard her voice calling out to him again, saying, "Yer still not too good for me to wipe yer bum, John Paul! Remember that, ye rascal!"

Lord knows, I was filled with questions after this encounter, but our attention was diverted by a terrible shouting in the streets to our south. Looking in this direction, we could see a man running away from us, stopping at every other door to pound on it and scream, "Wake up! The rebels are here! Rise if you value your lives!"

I recognized the voice and the figure.

Jones did as well. "Sharpless," he muttered.

We watched the coward's antics fearfully for some minutes. He was such a manic sight, in fact, that few of the Whitehaveners opened their doors to him. Several cursed him outright. Another dumped a full chamberpot on his head. Sharpless, it appeared, was better at annoying people than rousing them.

"Time to step lively, boys! We have an alarm to beat," Jones said, turning back to the business at hand.

Two of our party slipped away from us on the next turn. Jones saw them go, but he said nothing. I believe he would have been half-pleased to make the attack single-handed.

The north battery was situated on a hillock above the town, and commanded the harbor in such a way to cross-fire with the southern battery a mile distant. Once on that height, we could see all the vessels of Whitehaven lying about in the water and, farther off, flirting with the horizon, the reassuring outlines of the *Ranger*'s rig.

The sun's rays were working their way down the church steeple, angling ever downward, closer to bedroom windows and kitchens and dressing parlors. Our luck, by then, seemed almost unbelievable. Even after Sharpless's alarm, no one interfered as we circled the battery's ramparts, puzzling over where to enter. At length, we decided to assault the structure by scaling the fifteen-foot walls directly. A marine took position at the bottom of the wall, and I climbed up to stand on his shoulders. Then Jones, with a cutlass in his teeth, used our bodies as a human ladder and clambered over the top.

We heard him drop to the other side and then—nothing.

"Let me," I told the others. The other Marine having taken my place on the wall, I went over with two pistols stuck in my belt.

...

"Oh *cheri*, weren't you frightened?" Gualbert asked Severence, wearing such a look of admiration that the preferred answer was already clear.

...

In truth, no. I was really more concerned for Captain Jones, inside the fort all alone. When I landed, I expected to find him held at swordpoint, a hand clapped over his mouth to prevent him from warning us.

The reality was nothing so straightforward. Climbing to my feet, I was stupefied to find Jones standing before me, holding the point of his cutlass at my throat!

"Move, and I will run you through," he said plainly.

I opened my mouth in what was perhaps intended to be a question or a protest . . . I could not say. In any case, nothing issued from my lips.

A smile played about Jones's mouth then. It was his black smile—the one that implied he had a prime catch snared at the end of his tackle and would not throw me back.

"Are you the only brave man in my company?" Jones quizzed me. "Or would you mock me by following me here?"

The question meant nothing to me. In fact, I was more mindful of the possibility that we would both be captured while we sorted out Jones's mysterious new pique. Finding voice at last, I said "Have I ever made my mockeries to your back, sir? Or do you believe yourself the only knight to deliver Jerusalem?"

My words seemed to fan the flames behind Jones's eyes, but his sword did not move.

"You are too witty by half, Severence," he said, "And I will not presume to doubt Madame de Reyniére's Gentleman Conqueror!" And with that, he seemed to lower the blade and turn away from me. But when he saw that my guard was lowered, he whirled about and struck me across the face with the butt of the weapon, shouting, *"En garde!"*

In that instant, I merely stared at him as blood poured out upon my chin and down the green facings of my uniform coat.

...

"So you did not receive your scar in battle," said Gualbert, sounding a bit disappointed.

...

Not against the enemy, no. Jones stood looking back at me with an expression of curious expectancy. It was all a diverting test for him. My own foremost thought was rage, tempered by a memory of my last hours with my father. Like him, Jones would think he could break me like some dumb draft animal, merely by brute intimidation. Indeed, the more I looked at him, the more my blood rose, until I found myself fairly shivering with emotion. At last, I seized a pistol from my belt and cocked it in his face, regulations and British guard be damned.

Jones regarded the fatal aperture not three inches from his nose as if it were the eye of a lover. Wooing it, he sang Thomas Young:

> *Of tenderness let heavenly pity fall*
> *On me, more justly number'd with the dead.*
> *This is the desert, this the solitude*
> *How populous, how vital is the grave!*

With that, he took hold of my pistol-hand and lowered my arm. "Perhaps," he said, "you are no gentleman after all, my friend."

...

"Hah! Hah, hah, hah!" Gualbert erupted, raising her balled fist. "So he was jealous of you after all!"

"I would suppose he was, though one wouldn't know it from the speed with which he forgot the entire incident."

...

"A creditable response, was that," he praised me, lending me his handkerchief. "And if you forgive my surprise at your arrival, my admiration will be complete."

What nonsense! I thought, demonstrating my contempt for his games by throwing the bloody handkerchief back at him.

Still, I performed my duty in helping him search the sentry boxes for the guards. These were abandoned. Jones looked to me, mystified. I shrugged.

Only later, going door to door, did we come upon two guards sitting inside their post by the fire. By all evidence, it was customary for them to pass the mornings there at cards. These men heaped the crime of foolishness on that of dereliction by refusing to believe we were American rebels. Instead, they insisted we must be either French or Dutch:

"Come now, 'fess yer mother's a froggie," said one to me as I tied him.

For this, I secured his silence by sticking a balled-up woolen sock in his mouth.

Now safe from interruption, we set about spiking all 36 of the battery's guns. This operation consisted of hammering a soft iron spike into the touch-hole, and then breaking off the excess length above the breech to assure the spike could not be extracted by anyone but a smith. Blocking the touch-hole made it impossible to insert the priming tube into the powder bag, making the gun entirely useless. As these would be the guns the natives would work against us as we rowed away, we took care to make them all as useless as possible.

Afterward, I joined Jones as he stood up on the ramparts of the little fort, looking out over the town still largely asleep below. Though matters seemed to be in hand, there was a deep frown on his face. Following his gaze out into the harbor, I saw the reason: the gig under Lt. Hall's command was already working its way back to the *Ranger*. Meanwhile, we could see no flames on the other side of town, no smoke, no evidence that his party had achieved any of its tactical goals.

"Damn them," Jones breathed. "They've run off."

"Maybe they were driven away."

"By the gulls, no doubt."

"But they've spiked the south guns for sure," I asserted, speaking more in hope than assurance.

Jones leapt down and demanded the spiking tools. These were handed to him, and as he swung the kit over his shoulder he looked to Scipio Africanus. "You," he said, "will follow me. The rest of you will return to the launch and prepare the bombs."

"You will not disappoint me," he stated as a kind of general warning against what I presumed included incompetence, fear, and the temptation to shove off without him.

Then he came about and was gone, the Negro following the little commander as best he could. His departure was so sudden I hadn't even time to begin to dissuade him. Apparently, the south battery would be his alone to secure.

The remainder of our party proceeded back down the hill toward our boat. I would prefer to report that we went there in a proper military column, but as the heavy hand of truth is laid upon me . . .

···

"And it is indeed," Thierry warned.

···

. . . then I must confess that we stole down the hill like a pack of thieves, skulking around every corner. When we reached the launch, the sentries we had left were gone—only Midshipman Dooley was left to guard our sole means of escape. This he did with a cutlass he'd neglected to sharpen and a boarding pistol he did not know how to load. Of course, I could not give him a proper dressing-down for these lapses, as his spirit more than made up for his ordnance.

Dooley showed us to the rest of the men. They had decided to strike their blow against England by breaking down the door of a tavern close by the wharves and raiding the spirits. I arrested the six of them on the spot, but could only spare Dooley and his empty pistol to guard them. These men had already indulged so freely, in fact, that escape never entered their fogged minds.

Meanwhile, they had taken the incendiary tools into the tavern with them, and sometime during their revels, had misplaced all of our flints, strikers, and charpaper. As these were our single means of igniting our bombs, their carelessness threatened to reduce our expedition to a pointless cannon-spiking spree.

Taking the conviction that the best offense is a bold and direct one, I proceeded thither to a house, placed my hat on my heart, and knocked at the front door.

A wizened old goody appeared in response to my summons, with an ancient lace housecap on her head and spectacles, with one missing lens, on her nose. This, I judged, would be a simple provincial bumpkin, defenseless before the onslaught of my educated fictions. I addressed her, "If you please, madam, would you spare a flame?"

"A flame?" she repeated, narrowing her eyes. "What for?"

"You see, we . . . I mean, myself and my mates . . . we be mixing up a batch of ship-black, except we require two full buckets of boiled beef-pickle, and no fire to warm it—"

"Mixing ship-black? At this hour? That is nonsense, sir. And what is that uniform, might I ask? I don't place it," she declared, looking me up and down with the most frigid suspicion.

So much, thought I, for the simple trust, the unsoiled naiveté of the backwater native. "I hail from His Majesty's foot in Ireland," I lunged, perhaps more quickly than I should have, not being entirely sure if His Majesty indeed had any foot in Ireland at that time.

But there was no relief from this woman's jaundiced eye. "I reckon I have your plot fixed, then. You don't fool me," she told me ominously. "You're making cider, aren't you?"

I could only stare at her. "I . . . hesitate to say."

"Why didn't you say so at the first, young man? Boiling beef-pickle, indeed! Wait here," she commanded, closing the door after her. In a moment she was back, and handed me one of those smoldering sticks of wood that are known in New England as "poor man's candles."

"I presume you will return this to me direct," she said, " . . . along with a pint of that 'ship-black,' eh?" And she winked conspiratorially at me, shutting her door again.

Thus equipped, I posted new sentries and awaited Jones's return. This took only ten more minutes, as I saw him approaching through my spyglass at a flat run, Scipio Africanus now a few strides ahead, and at least three dozen angry Whitehaveners close at his heels! Several of these had swords, a few cudgels, and the rest wielding whatever they could find. One was swinging a rolling pin at him.

More curious, I saw that Jones was grasping a tattered Union Jack as he ran, waving it in the air over his head as if to goad his pursuers. At this, he was succeeding.

As we were powerless to help him at such a distance, I ordered our reception prepared by having several barrels of tar moved onto a bark tied up nearby, a 150-ton coaster by the name of *Londonderry*. We then piled as much cordage and inflammables around the tar as we dared, my intention being to ignite the vessel as the mob approached and either frighten or distract it from hindering our escape.

Jones was still more than fifty rods distant when he began to shout orders—"Up oars! Prepare to cast off!"—but he said it with such little breath the order sounded more like "uproars—preparacasoff!" As he neared us, I could see that even in headlong flight he bore his plain tricorne tucked neatly under his arm.

I was standing on the fo'c'sle of the *Londonderry* as Scipio and the captain passed the last cross-street and swept down toward our boat. Lighting a sailcloth bomb with the poor man's candle, I tossed this onto the tar and cordage pile and, for good measure, the candle too, and leapt from the rail of the bark.

I shudder to imagine my embarrassment had the flames not caught, but they did indeed, and very well. With all the fuel we had scattered around, the bark blossomed into a truly impressive torch.

Tragically, Midshipman Dooley had been admiring my "exploits" from too close a distance, and not withdrawn from the danger as fast as I. The tremendous heat of the blast instantly singed his eyebrows off and set his hair alight, causing him to run about the quay, screaming. His only remedy was a headlong dive into the harbor.

I was back in the boat in time to welcome Jones, who regarded the burning vessel before him with exhaustion and relief. His plan, at last, had succeeded in destroying something.

"Bless him, that Severence." He collapsed against the wales, grasping his Union Jack, for once too winded to issue orders.

The pursuing mob was a motley, unkempt bunch, some still in their nightdresses, none of them with firearms. Most of them fled backward as the *Londonderry* erupted, and a new cry of "Firebuckets! Firebuckets!" went up. This was exactly what we needed, for by the time their attentions shifted back to us, we had already fished poor Dooley out of the water and were halfway out of the harbor.

As these matters usually go, one of our tavern-revelers discovered that our flints and strikers, believed lost, had been stuck in his belt the entire time. Cursing the man, Jones seized these and lit a number of the bombs we had stored in the boat. He then stood up and threw them onto several of the fishing boats as we rowed past. As these stood well off from the shore, they would certainly burn to the water-line before any serious effort to save them could be mounted.

There was, in fact, much to celebrate as we pulled away from White-haven that morning. While we had failed to torch any of the houses or stores, the fire on the *Londonderry* was resisting the natives' efforts to quench it, and had even spread to part of the dock. Three fishermen were burning and scattering hot cinders broadcast over the port, with a promise of further damage.

Perhaps best of all, our predations had touched off a general panic in the town, which had awoken at last to find itself under rebel attack with no vaunted Royal Navy in sight to protect it. Hundreds of natives were heading toward the high ground behind the batteries, children and property in their arms, half-dressed, all running about in half-witted terror. Scores more ran toward the fire, bearing blankets, overcoats, handfuls of sand. Across the still distance, we could hear the peel of churchbells tolling the great invasion. For those of us who had seen the spiteful devastation wreaked on Danbury and Kingston and Escopus in New-York, this was all a most gratifying sight.

"Tell us, Mr. Scipio, are you thinking of the stock market now?" Jones asked, to the general delight of the party. He was standing with his flag trophy draped around his shoulders, bearing it like a triumphal toga.

"No sir. I'm checkin' all o' my parts, to see if I left any behind," said the other.

"What happened up there?" I asked him.

Scipio only turned away, shook his head. "Our cap'n—he crazy. We find all the guns spiked, but he tells me he wants a souvenir. I tell him we be killed, but that only make him more stubb'n. Then he gives me his pistol, an' climbs the flagpole hisself to tear it down! He must o' been born under th' moonlight, I say. That's the only log'cal explanation."

And we all laughed at him.

Thus far, our escape had been clean—not even a pistol had been fired on us as we worked our way back out into the Irish Sea. Thanks to Lt. Hall (and confirmed by Jones and Scipio Africanus), the south battery was as silent as the north. This was important, since just one hit from one of the 24-pound guns would have reduced our force to a scatter of bloody splinters.

At length, one of the Whitehaveners conceived the notion of bringing up a piece from one of their armed merchantmen. This they did with some speed, but we were already more than half a mile away when their first shot echoed off the surrounding hills. After that first "pop," and a short whistle, we saw the ball plunge into the water more than a hundred yards short.

Jones screwed himself into a state of mock indignation over this show of resistance, and ordered the Marines to return fire with a "broadside" of small arms. I ordered my men to shoulder their weapons, aim high, and fire. Yes, this contemptuous reply was no more effective than the Englishmen's errant insult, but it sent a message just the same: we were just as capable as they of wasting powder on vain gestures.

Our casualties were light, consisting only of Dooley's hair, (which grew back) and his eyebrows (which never did). So high was our morale at this pass that we did not care that a rainstorm came through very soon after, and put out our little inferno. Instead, we were looking in the other direction and breathing easier, as we saw the sharp-countered form of the *Ranger*, flying in on a southwest wind to gather her little lost flock.

XVI.

As the feelings of your gentle Bosom cannot but be congenial with mind—let me entreat you Madam to use your soft persuasive Arts with your Husband to endeavor to stop this Cruel and destructive War, in which Britain can never succeed. . . . Your endeavors to effect a general Exchange of Prisoners, will be an Act of Humanity, which will afford you Golden feelings on a Death bed.

—John Paul Jones, in a letter to Lady Selkirk, 1778

OUR HIGH spirits did not long survive the morning. Once the men's elation at their mere survival had ebbed, their thoughts shifted to the fact that they had left Whitehaven none the richer for their heroism.

Jones's mood soured as well, though for different reasons. No sooner had he arrived back on board than he was filled with a thousand self-recriminations, all bent upon the premise that the raid should have destroyed not four vessels but four hundred. He cursed the perverse impulse that inspired him to select the traitor Sharpless for his party. He decried that blindness that led him to misjudge the distance to shore. He lamented the precious minutes of darkness he had wasted in his cabin. He laid the heaviest burden of blame upon himself, and brought but a light scolding on Lt. Hall for quailing prematurely at Sharpless's alarm. As for myself, I was excluded from comment entirely. In Jones's vocabulary of fervent mutenesses, the lack of room for even unreasonable improvement counted as high praise.

Still, Jones had scored himself a tidy coup of publicity with his little raid. Once the news of his unprecedented invasion had spread by horse and newsprint, panic spread along every firth and mull of coastal Britain. The captured Sharpless worked to further Jones's fame by giving an identity to the little "pirate" who had mocked the Wooden Walls of the Royal Navy.

Englishmen learned to either spit his name forth like some vile humor, or swing it like a club against the partisans of Empire, depending on their political sympathies. Frenchmen and Dutchmen and Russians hoisted their glasses to his health and dared hope he cut an even wider swath of destruction before his inevitable defeat. It was the first time Europe had heard of John Paul Jones, and it was not to be the last.

But at sea that morning, sailing broad-reached on the spring airs, we flew from Whitehaven as if from the persistent legacy of our failure. The only antidote, clearly, was Jones's next scheme.

Now that he had paid the marauding Briton back in his own coin, Jones decided to civilize the Admiralty by forcing it to accede to a general exchange of naval prisoners. This he would do by taking custody of some convenient British noble, preferably a peer, and holding him captive until such time as England recognized America's God-given belligerent rights.

Here, at last, was a plan everyone could relish for their own reasons. I believe Jones could distinctly hear the strains of his beloved Clio, Muse of Everlasting Fame, coming to play his victory song. Other Rangers imagined the plundered riches of a vast estate. Still others dreamt of other sorts of booty wrested from haughty squires' daughters and luscious French maids.

Cullam was directed northwest, to stand across the neck of Solway Firth. We sighted the other side—the Scottish side—before the morning was out, and Jones relayed further orders from his cabin for us to come over to the starboard tack and cruise southwest, meanwhile keeping an eye out for a little five-acre island that guarded the mouth of the Bay of Kirkcudbright.

As these were familiar waters, there was no need to "recruit" a local pilot. We did not happen to pass Arbigland House, manor of his father's laird Mr. Craike, though I did glimpse, on the horizon, the lowering mass of the same Criffel peak that must have dominated Jones's birthplace. Green also pointed out to me, with bemusement, an excited gaggle of Galwegian schoolboys running along the cobbled shore, struggling to keep up with the sleek ghost that had materialized out of the mists guarding distant, chimerical England.

These must have been the very stuff of Jones's earliest memories. Still, he did not make his appearance on the quarterdeck until midday, when Cullam announced that an island had been sighted, exactly as the captain had described it. The master was then ordered to reef all courses but the fore and two stay-sails, and to inch our way into the bay along a channel we could never have discerned without Jones's special knowledge.

The *Ranger*'s hiding place turned out to be so close by the western shore of Kirkcudbright Bay our yards nearly kissed the boughs of the trees, and butterflies danced among the vessel's shrouds.

The Captain mustered everyone on the spar deck, and announced that a small party, led by himself, would take the launch and proceed to St. Mary's Isle, the estate and residence of the Earl of Selkirk, with the design of making him our "guest."

Jones selected myself, Mr. Joye the master-at-arms, and a half dozen other tars who had not seen action at Whitehaven, to accompany him. He also saw fit to add Lt. Hall to our little company, perhaps with an eye to allowing the lad an opportunity to redeem himself. Simpson, as usual, was checkmated by being left behind, where the extent of his options was confined to the difficult extremes of mere rumor-mongering, or mutiny.

It was by no means clear why this particular man was selected for abduction. Only much later, in fact, did Jones tell me that Selkirk had several times been shooting at Arbigland with Mr. Craik, and that young John Paul had once been charged with cleaning this gentleman's boots. This task the boy did with such thoroughness the earl remarked on his diligence. Would that Selkirk could have looked forward several decades, and seen in what manner his little boot-cleaner intended to repay his praises!

The sun was at its highest in an unsettled spring sky as the launch was again lowered to water. Aloft, the clouds had gathered themselves into a dramatic and vaprous architecture I have often noted above Europe: storied, shifting, buttressed by columns of sunlight—a prophet's sky. Even before our men had touched their oars, our boat was surrounded by a swarm of swooping, cawing seagulls, who wheeled about our launch as if convinced it hid a trove of fresh fishmeats. I confess I looked with some worry on these birds: certainly, if our purpose was stealth, the gulls would announce our presence as clearly as a cannon shot.

Jones took his place at the bow again, and with laconic efficiency piloted us up the channel toward the beach of St. Mary's Isle. When we had reached the shore, he picked just a half-dozen hands, including myself and Mr. Hall, saying, "This lot will come with me to the Palace. The rest of you—make yourselves presentable to the earl."

So ordered, we followed Jones up the hill from the beach. The others, meanwhile, set about straightening the slops-rags on their frames, disentangling the knots in their salt-caked hair, and scouring their faces with handfuls of sand.

The identical pattern of our approach by sea was followed on land, as Jones marched ahead of us through the Selkirk grounds. We passed through one of a set of two symmetrical pergolas on our way toward the manor house, each submerged in a lattice of bare wisteria. There was a gazebo, a garden of experimental herbs, and a swing hanging half-broken from a tree, but none of the splendor, the full-bore, complex exuberance of Passy. The question occurred to me, as I looked upon these pleasant but frankly modest holdings, whether England would indeed reverse her prisoner policy for what was clearly no more than a minor noble. But next to Jones's driven assurance, my misgivings would have looked very feeble indeed.

At last Selkirk's residence came into view, and what Jones recalled as a "palace" we immediately discovered was nothing more than a large, shambling house. Jones was so struck by this that he halted his march, remarking, "Those must be the servants' quarters." And he led us around the grounds again, in search of the great mansion of his memory.

Jones's puzzlement soon turned to anger, and then to embarassment, as he led us all in circles about the Selkirk estate. Yet for thirty minutes of tramping through brambles and across brown lawns, we found nothing else larger than a tool shed. In the end he was left standing before the house again, forced to concede that he had made a mistake.

A bare-headed old man in a gardener's smock rounded a hedge then, his hands thrust deep into his pockets. When he saw us, he stopped himself short, perhaps startled by the appearance of we wild and wide-eyed Rangers, all staring in apparent perplexity at the Selkirk house.

"If you will excuse me, sir," Jones addressed him, though not in his native accent, "could you tell me if the earl is taking visitors today?"

The gardener looked him up and down with that same air of flinty suspicion I'd seen in the old goody of Whitehaven. "And who're you?"

Jones removed his hat. "Captain Hoysted Hacker of brig *Concord*," ran
his instant lie, "bearing important news of the earl's overseas assets."

The other man cast a doleful eye on Jones, saying, "Well, if y'knew the
earl, y'd know he dinna be here on a Saturty. He's in London."

"Not home?" Jones said, almost plaintively.

"All day."

Jones absorbed this disappointment with a momentary wavering of his
portrayal. But he still could ask, "Is there anyone else about?"

"No one but Lady Selkirk and her babes. Lest you want to talk assets
wi' them, eh?" And the gardener proceeded to laugh a reedy Scots laugh
at Jones, and to walk away. This left us standing on the lawn before Selkirk
house, now missing a Lord as well as a Palace.

This, I might add, was Disappointment Number Three.

So, just as we came, we retreated back toward the beach. It was a deathly
silent procession, broken not even by the twittering of a bird. At length,
Mr. Joye cleared his throat, and addressed the captain.

"Sir, if you might see yer way clear to hear a word . . . ?"

"What is it, Joye?" came the joyless answer.

"Well, sir, seein' that we fought the good fight at Whitehaven, but did-
n't take no spoils, and we came here to ransom the count, and he ain'
home, by my reckonin' we be well behind the ante, if I might say so. Sir."

"What are you saying, you ape?"

"Well, uh, I only say that maybe a visit would be in order nevermind,
since there's bound to be some o' the Lordship's valuables inside, and
nobody can tell me otherwise, 'cause it's just spoils o' war, I say."

The rest of the tars then nodded their eager agreement, mumbling nonsense about "our just due" and "spoils of war."

"Can somebody please explain to me what this man is saying?" the captain appealed to Hall and myself. He was perhaps stalling for time.

"To my understanding," Hall ventured, "Mr. Joye has put forward a
motion that we descend upon Selkirk Palace in raid, to carry away such
treasures as might help our cause."

"Exac'ly!" Joye blurted, to more grunts of general approval.

"Seconded," added Drury, a waister.

"Me too," said Fallows, the quartermaster's mate.

"I see," Jones sighed, and turned his back on the rest of us. From our position atop the rise we could see the launch down below, and the guards scattered about in happily unsupervised leisure. Still farther, we could make out the masts and spars of the *Ranger* nestled in among the tall trees, distinguished by the glint of varnish in the midday sun. She seemed very far away indeed.

"Tell me your opinion, Mr. Severence," Jones asked me without turning around. Four pairs of eyes were trained on me immediately, and I wondered if Jones was attempting to shift the blame for an unpopular decision on to me.

Clearly, an act of wanton robbery, no matter how deeply couched in the excuses of war, was far from the polite visitation Jones had had in mind. It was also difficult to understand what could be gained by robbing the Selkirk house, other than a few more coins in the till and a deeper reputation for barbarity than we already possessed.

Then again, the sentiments of the men were never clearer than on this question. These could not be flouted forever. Nor did I relish meeting my end in some dubious shipboard "accident." No—Jones would have to find his own way out of the snare he had so cleverly invented for himself.

"The plan has much to recommend it," said I, adding nothing more when Jones regarded me sharply.

Attention fixed again on Jones, who sank to his haunches. When he spoke again, it was as if his voice was that of some dead thing, sealed away from humanity as surely as if it had come from a sarcophagus. His eyes were on the ground as he delivered his instructions.

"Very well—let it all be on your heads. But you will not humiliate me with your foolishness. You will comport yourselves with the strictest discipline. You will enter and secure the family plate, but you will disrupt the normal running of the house as little as possible. Your objective will be the silver only. There will be no other 'souvenirs' taken."

Joye smiled at Fallows, who smacked his chapped lips in crude anticipation. Jones noted this, and looked to me. "It will be Lieutenant

Severence's responsibility to see my orders are carried through."

"Sir?" I bridled. But Jones would not stay to hear my protests: he was already on his way down the hill, washing his hands of the whole affair. My pique was hardly soothed by Joye's detestable hand on my shoulder, and his voice telling me, "It ain't no matter, sir—we'll need an extra back to carry all th' loot!"

Drafted, then, to supervise this low chore, I resolved to at least see it through properly. I organized my party into an orderly column, and marched them down to the Selkirk house with their cutlasses on their shoulders. We passed the old gardener again on the way, and this man appeared somewhat distressed by the return of such ruffians, this time without their leader. But I only smiled at him, and nodded as if our purpose was only to take the air. A light of realization came over his face—he smiled.

"Press gang?" he asked us.

I merely placed my finger to my lips, bidding him keep our "secret." He then vanished through a narrow gate in the moss-eaten stone fence, evidently well pleased with his powers of observation.

The Selkirk house appeared no more impressive on closer inspection than it had from afar. Set on a patch of new spring green bordered by beech trees, it rose to three stories under a tarred, sloping roof, topped with four corbelled chimneys. Out of these issued curls of smoke from what smelled like a kitchen hearth. We passed before one of the ground-story windows on our way to the door, and could peep between the vines into the parlor. As there was no one in this room, I allowed discipline to lapse long enough for the men to press their noses against the panes to admire the faded designs on Lord Selkirk's wool tapestry carpet, and his gaming table with two chessmen missing.

"Yer breath's foggin' up th' glass!" complained Drury to Fallows, who wagged a finger at Drury and replied, "Watch yerself, now."

"Watch yourselves, both of you," I warned them. "Back in line, now. There's work to be done."

Once two men had been set in front of the house to serve as look-outs, we were ready to approach the front door. I organized our party to present the best-dressed of us, myself and Lt. Hall, in the van, and the haphazard, unshaven mugs of the four others to the rear. If our mission was no more than a primitive robbery, it would at least be launched with its most civilized face forward.

I used the brass knocker, and in due course the door opened. We were then looking at an elder manservant in his domestic blacks, who regarded us from under arched gray brows. This man's nose was singular in its size and in its battery of warts, one of which stood at the tip and had a thick hair growing from its center.

"Good morning," said this resonant Nose.

"Good morning," I replied, at that moment most conscious of my American accent. But I plunged on to inquire, "Is his Lordship at home to-day?"

The Nose looked me up and down in a short second, and was already stretching his neck to inspect the appearance of my men. "No, he is not . . . ," he said, and upon getting a glimpse of Joye's hungry leer and ready sabre, added in shaky tones, "Would you like to leave your card?"

"Not precisely," said I. "Is there someone else we could speak to, perhaps?"

"Lady Selkirk. May I tell her who is calling?"

I gave this question a second's thought, then shook my head, to which the Nose asked us to wait and began to close the door. I stopped it with my boot—which should have left little doubt regarding our intent.

We stood in the open doorway, waiting, until we heard a high-pitched, girlish voice ask, "Who is it, Masefield?"

"I could not say. They have no card," came the Nose's answer.

Lady Selkirk made her appearance at the top of the stairs. From her bright voice, I expected she was a young bride. Yet as she approached, and stepped out of the natural gloom of the old house and into the light, I saw a woman no less than forty years of age. Her white hair was gathered behind her neck in a chignon, and she wore a buff-colored day dress and a lace shawl about her shoulders. She held this last with hands crossed over her bosom, bearing it about the house like a judge's robes or a bishop's cassock or some other vestment of power. The details of her face were not displeasing, with eyes of shady bower green and a mouth still shapely after the assault of years.

...

"You make a science of observing women, I see," Gualbert teased.

"Of measuring women, rather," Thierry suggested.

"I plead guilty, and await the pleasure of this most beautiful Court" was his answer, to which Thierry parried, "Don't make pleas. They insure a cold ear. Go on."

...

In accord with Jones's instructions, I endeavored to present myself as more functionary than buccaneer. I bowed at Lady Selkirk, and introduced myself as an officer of the ship *Ranger* of the United Colonies, under the command of Captain John Paul Jones, Esquire. At this, she exclaimed in that tuneful voice, "Merciful God, what welcome news! I must confess, sir, that seeing you down here, with my husband gone to London, and Masefield in such a state, I feared you were a gang of Frenchmen!"

Behind me, Joye grumbled at this noxious suggestion, which was still not unreasonable considering the pointed cut of beard many Rangers had gotten at Paimboeuf. Lady Selkirk trilled on, "But you are Britons after all. We had no grounds to raise an alarm, did we, Masefield?" And she cast a chastening glare at the Nose, who stood as motionless as he could, perhaps in hopes that sheer petrification would render him beneath our notice.

"In point of fact, m'lady," I resumed, "we are here on a matter of business related to the current struggle between our two governments, which brings me with some reluctance to ask you . . . "

"Struggle? Call it a family quarrel between natural cousins, Lieutenant! But whatever the business may be, there is no reason it cannot wait until after tea."

"Tea?"

"I shall not tolerate a refusal, Lieutenant. Masefield, set seven places."

The Nose inclined his head stiffly, and the servant and I shared a glance that bespoke our mutual befuddlement at the way the raid was unfolding.

As Lady Selkirk led us to the parlor, chattering happily to me of the early arrival of spring and the Tory reverses in Parliament, addressing each successive subject apparently at random, I could hear the angry whispers of my men behind me. To their minds, the raid should have been a simple hit-and-run affair—no conversation, certainly no tea—and they were clearly correct. Yet however obvious this wisdom was to me, I simply could not rob this woman indelicately.

And so the next hour found our impatient and unscrubbed party gathered around Lady Selkirk's tea table, china cups and saucers trembling in our hands. Still, we cut a fair figure after all our weeks at sea: Fallows followed my example in spreading his linen napkin over his filthy service pantaloons, and Drury did chew his scones before he swallowed them. Joye, for his part, had his covetous eyes set on the silver tea service itself.

". . . I still don't answer to 'Lady Selkirk' after all these years," the woman was saying. "How long has it been, now? Dunbar, my husband, took me to wife in '58, so it has been close on twenty years, has it not?" And she gestured at a portrait on the wall of the portly earl, heaved astride a dappled gray with a Quaker hat in his hand. "But when I look in the glass, I still expect to see little Helen of Haddington, with dirt under her nails. Do you understand, young man?" she asked Lt. Hall.

"Yes, I do," said Hall, ever ready to oblige.

She smiled. "Of course you don't. You are a young stag in velvet, so to speak, and believe you will live forever, just the way you are now."

Her smile came almost coquettish, and seemed to settle on me. I shifted uncomfortably on the old cushions of my chair, which moved her to add, "But I appreciate your interest in humoring me. You are all gentlemen."

Just then Joye cleared his throat conspicuously. Lady Selkirk made a momentary glance in the boor's direction, opening the first silence of our interview with her. Then she bid to repair the mood by informing us that the aromatic quality we had undoubtedly noticed in her tea had been due to various rose petals she had placed in the strainer. We would-be pirates hurried to praise her innovation, but there appeared a tightness about her mouth, and a hoarseness in her voice that hinted she was beginning to despair in her role.

She soldiered on. "But now, if the tea leaves do not lie, it is time to discuss your business."

I set my cup down on the table. "Ma'am, may I say again that your tea is most fine, and your hospitality beyond what we have any right to expect. However, the imperatives of war . . . oblige me to beg your forgiveness for what we are about to request."

"And what would that be?" she asked brightly, lifting the teapot from its silver tray to fill my cup again.

"I—hesitate to say it—" I mumbled, mesmerized by the breeding evident in her elegance of pouring.

"Please, go ahead. I give you my permission to ask."

"In that case, then, I would ask you to hand over that tray, and the teapot, and any other silver plate you may have about the house."

Words hardly exist to describe how foolish I felt when I uttered this request. Even my companions, I noted, had ceased to look up at this magnificant lady, staring ashamed into their laps, or into their empty cups.

Lady Selkirk finished pouring hot water through the strainer with unlapsed grace.

"Sugar?" she asked me.

"Please."

"Two lumps?"

"Yes."

She sweetened my cup using the silver tongs, and finally remarked, "Such are the fortunes of all war, Lieutenant. You need not apologize." Then she turned to Masefield, and made a little twirling gesture with her right index finger. I suspected that, under ordinary circumstances, this was probably a signal for him to clear the table. Here, it was probably intended to convey a more permanent sort of clearing.

"But I see you haven't brought anything to carry it all," she turned to me, concerned.

"Er—no. We have not."

Lady Selkirk had a quick solution. "Masefield, do run out and take a cloth sack from the garden shed."

"But m'lady . . . ," the Nose demurred.

"And let's not keep these young men waiting."

Joye looked to me with a question in his eye, and I duly sent him out with the Nose, to assure he wouldn't run off for help.

···

"But this Lady Selkirk—she seems either very simple—or too sweetly natured possibly to exist," Gualbert wondered. "Could she ever have believed your purpose was anything but illegal?"

···

She understood our purpose very well, I suspect. Consider her position in all this, if you might: she was at home by herself, with no husband to protect her, with a pack of desperate characters on her doorstep. What could she have done but humor us, perhaps even act a bit the fool, to assure that we stuck to our material purpose only? There was no way for her to estimate what crimes could have been committed against her modesty and her life. She was really very extraordinary. To my mind, of all the characters I met in the *Ranger* campaign, she was Jones's sole equal in pure nerve.

Was there ever such a perfectly pleasant act of larceny? The Nose led Joye around with his sack to collect the rest of the silver in the kitchen and pantry, Lady Selkirk kept the scones and jam coming, and I was spared the indignity of leaving my chair to supervise my crime.

As with Madame de Reyniére, I suddenly found myself a favored receptacle of women's misery. We passed half an hour in airing her Ladyship's fears of loneliness and boredom, with her leading me to believe, in oblique fashion of course, that Lord Selkirk was hardly significant enough, and still more importantly, not companion or conversationalist enough, to warrant a sea change in England's prisoner policy. I sought to comfort her by praising her husband (whom I had never met), but she only brushed my words aside as further evidence of my basic gallantry.

Soon she was probing me with small, innocent-sounding questions about myself, my ship, Captain Jones, and our exact heading out to sea. My answers were appropriately evasive at first, but considering the refreshment of true feminine company, there was no telling how much enemy intelligence she would have gathered in the end.

We were interrupted by Joye, who chose that moment to re-enter the room and claim the teapot for our collection. Worse, he commenced to empty everything—tea, rose-petals and all—onto the carpet, causing Lady Selkirk such evident pain I immediately stood and ordered him to fetch a rag and bucket.

"That's not necessary," our canny hostess said through watering eyes, " . . . except, perhaps, if you could provide me with a receipt for what you have taken? . . . "

"Of course," said chivalrous, unthinking I, who immediately took pen and paper from the Nose, and commenced to write "I, Lieutenant John Christopher Severence of the Marine Forces of the United States Congress, do hereby swear and attest that the following items . . . "

Just then I felt young Hall's hand on my arm. And while I could not say a surfeit of wisdom was always exhibited on his young face, he was far wiser than I with regard to the subtler sex. Looking at him, I knew the full foolishness of what I had been about to do.

I tore up the receipt and handed the pen back to the Nose. Then, having collected all of my men, I bade them to reverse their pockets in front of her Ladyship, so as to confirm to her that no other "souvenirs" had been taken. That settled, I bowed to kiss her Ladyship's hand, and said my farewell to her. I recall her expression was mostly one of relief—but not entirely.

"I suppose you'll have to run off back to your ship now," she frowned, slow to retrieve her hand from me.

"I fear so."

"I have been fortunate to be robbed by the likes of you," she added, leading me to suspect our arrival had, after all, turned out to be a welcome recess in her otherwise empty career as a domestic ornament.

We emerged in the waning light of early evening, hearts thumping and stomachs warmed by rose tea, and proceeded down the hill toward our boat. As we escaped, I heard the clanking of the silver plate on Joye's back as he ran—a heaving, rhythmical crunching, punctuated suddenly by a "slam."

This noise was the closing of a door at the side of the Selkirk house. Turning, I saw someone I did not recognize, possibly a scullery boy who had hidden from us, flee down the way, no doubt to warn the general neighborhood that a gang of vaguely French-looking American marauders had alighted on these quiet shores, aiming to burgle everyone's homes and eat their cakes.

A different boat, the ship's gig, was waiting for us on the beach. Jones, it appeared, had been too embarrassed by the spectacle to remain on land, and had sent the smaller craft back to retrieve us.

For all our trouble, the captain would barely have the stomach to look at the loot we had liberated: for him, the only worthy prize was Lord Selkirk himself, preferably resplendent in the same hunting clothes Jones had glimpsed as a boy at Arbigland. As a guest of the adult John Paul, the captured Selkirk would no doubt be awarded the quarters of some lower-ranking officer, and often receive gilded invitation cards to sup in the captain's company. This would require his Lordship's boots be cleaned again, and Jones would oblige, again. The difference, of course, is that this time Jones would order it done by his own steward. The circle of this old humiliation would, at last, be closed.

I saw him standing at the rail as we pulled around the spit of scrubland between the *Ranger* and the beach. He seemed to examine us for a long minute, as if in hopes that, by some miracle, his Lordship had returned during our raid, and we had secured him after all. But he was only to be disappointed by the sight of Joye, seated with his knees around the white canvas garden sack, fingers stroking the hoard with tender affection. Jones turned his back on us.

We escaped to sea without meeting another vessel, and set courses to proceed west again. When we were some miles from St. Mary's Isle, we heard the report of a gun fired from the vicinity of the high ground above the Selkirk house. Examining the isle through a glass, Simpson told us, "They're firing at a rock."

"A rock?" aped Green, whose recent sobriety had done much to dull his thinking.

"A rock in the water," said Simpson, pointing at a peaked crag in Kirkcudbright Bay.

"The militia has gotten up some old piece, probably from someone's cellar," Jones told us. "They've dragged it up to that hill, and have mistaken that rock for us. They make that very same mistake every war."

Looking at the formation, and squinting my eyes, I could perhaps imagine how the effects of water and atmosphere could make a rigged ship out of the rock. The error would demand more zeal than acuity.

"I see," said Green, who waited until another shot had sounded and fallen into the bay before he told Jones, "You certainly do understand these people."

XVII.

For they, t'was THEY unsheath'd the ruthless blade,
And Heav'n shall ask the Havock it has made.

— JONES, in a letter to Lady Selkirk, 1778

~

BEFORE hearing any more, Thierry excused herself from the table. When she had gone to her dressing room and shut the door, Severence looked to Gualbert, who drank in the full measure of his gaze with her own eyes.

They both leaned forward, over their linen napkins, and mingled the paint on each other's lips once, and again, harder. Then Thierry's door opened and they were forced to stop.

"Am I proper?" Gualbert whispered, fearing she appeared disheveled.

"Unfortunately, yes . . . for now," he answered.

Thierry returned with something he did not expect: an ivory smoking pipe, with a foot-long stem and tiny carved cherubs laboring to support the bowl. On seeing this, Gualbert's pretty little nose retreated up her nasal bone, giving it the texture of a walnut shell.

Thierry went about filling her pipe anyway, using tobacco she kept in an embroidered sachet bag. She had instantly noticed some of the powder from Gualbert's face was caked above Severence's nostril.

"Have you any objections?" she asked him, showing him the pipe.

"I do," interjected her friend. "It's not your most becoming habit."

"Don't be naive, Thérèse. For Captain Severence, what is most becoming in a woman is the way she opens her legs. Isn't that so?"

Thierry was looking at him with an expression of such girlish sweetness it could have been served as a dessert. That is, until she indulged her bent for sluttish perversity by touching the long stem of her pipe with her tongue as she placed it between her lips.

"You make fun of me," Severence answered. "But your pipe doesn't trouble me at all."

"Thank you," she said, lighting it from a candle flame. And as Gualbert had feared, the room was soon filled with an odor not unlike that of burning vanilla.

...

As I have described, the *Ranger* had already succeeded in twice landing upon the enemy homeland, burned her shipping, and taken the war literally to Britannia's very doorstep. Nothing but the resistance of his own crew, I believe, would have prevented Jones from sailing straight up the Thames and planting the Stars and Stripes right on the brow of Wren's great Dome.

Still, he was not satisfied. By the turn of the first dog watch, the wind blew steady and cold from the northwest, and Jones ordered Cullam to put the helm down once again, and steer us a course back across the Irish Sea. The captain's intention was no mystery to any of us: had he not vowed to return to Carrickfergus roads, and finally have his way with the once-lucky *Drake*?

Jones devoted the night's passage to hearing my account of the events at Selkirk house. True to his character, he required precision and efficiency in my report. He demanded repeated assurances that his party had done nothing to embarrass his country and himself before Lady Selkirk, the servants, the neighbors, or that wider circle of nearby gentry that must have included Mr. Craik of Arbigland.

He brooked no irrelevant details, but couldn't hear enough about Lady Selkirk, who had managed the invasion of her home and hearth with such grace. Her genius at diversion, and her subtle efforts to secure information from me, amused him greatly. He asked me how I had presented his name to her, and when I told him, asked again if I had been sure to append the word "Esquire" to his name. He then required an exact account of her autumnal beauty, down to the sort of fragrance she had worn, and the way she had arranged her hair.

...

"And being such a keen observer of women, you were amply equipped to oblige him," Thierry presumed.

...

I am not unfamiliar with the weapons ladies wield in their campaigns of attraction, yes. But Paul Jones—now there was a man who knew his way around the *cabinet de toilette.* Since men mistrusted him, Jones saw women as his natural allies. He studied the sex like he studied poetry, or celestial navigation, or any subject that was likely to magnify his advantages. He knew them as well as any ship under his command.

His questions answered, Jones unsealed his sea-chest to re-examine Lady Selkirk's teapot and strainer. Opening the latter, and inhaling the lingering airs of tea and rose petals, a surge of sentimentality moved him, and he swore, "As the Lord bears witness, I will see our insult atoned! I will see her property returned." And then his expression grew grave under the swinging lantern light, and he felt the smooth silver with his fingers.

"You believe I will do it, don't you?"

"Yes, I do," I answered him.

...

"And did he? Return the teapot?"

...

In time. But first he sat down to write a letter to Lady Selkirk that was full of finely turned phrases and philosophies, and proclaimed himself to be her devoted servant. "Let not the Amiable Countess of Selkirk regard me as an enemy," he wrote. "I am ambitious of her Esteem and Friendship."

...

"The fool," came Thierry's voice from behind her veil of smoke.

...

So fully did he expect that her Ladyship would make a reply to this graceful missive, dear ladies, that he had multiple copies made and distributed to all of his acquaintances, as a testament to his gallantry. Europe, he resolved, would stand to be impressed by at least one exemplary American, who could seek peace with as much vigor and effect as he could prosecute war.

He still awaited her response years later. It was only one of the many unanswered letters that would darken Jones's days, and fill him with the same fear of unworth that I glimpsed that night on the *Ranger,* when he turned to me to ask, "You believe I will do it, don't you?"

There was, of course, no way to know whether the envelope was ever permitted to reach the lady's hands: I reminded the captain of this whenever the subject arose. But despite logic, I do believe her silence wounded him more deeply than any British or Turkish weapon ever would, in all the battles he would ever wage. Even as he stood upon the grandest heights of his fame, I could watch his face when the mail pouch arrived, and know that some small part of him still anticipated the arrival of Lady Selkirk's reply.

We weathered the mouth of the Bay of Belfast by sunrise. This time, the *Drake* was not dozing. She appeared to be waiting for us, in fact, and beat out to meet us as we stood off Carrickfergus roads. On the presumption that no word of his activities in England and Scotland had preceded the swift *Ranger*, Jones gambled that the *Drake* was merely curious. Therefore, he bid most of the sloop's crew retire to the gun deck, where they couldn't be seen, and made all impression that the *Ranger* was nothing more than a lazy merchantman of the Caribbean trade. Jones's blue stripe down his vessel's side added to the illusion, as this color increased the difficulty of making an accurate count of her broadside, especially at a distance, with her ports sealed tight.

This ruse succeeded in puzzling the enemy, whose commander saw fit to launch a boat to inspect us before making any further approach. Jones witnessed this confusion with great delight, and made preparations to capture the scout.

Meanwhile, the assembly on the gun deck had given Lieutenant Simpson another instance to agitate against this latest unprofitable "adventure." As I was standing on the spar deck near a hatch, I was well placed to gauge the rate of the enemy boat's approach against the crescendo of indignation building below, and to wonder which potential doom would visit us first.

"The earl's plate's plenty enough for me!" insisted a waister.

"Remember Mungo Maxwell!" said another.

As a precaution, I posted two Marines at every ladderway. At this Jones only commented, with an odd lilt in his voice, "If they move against me now, it will be that blonde ghost who will rule this bay!", and indicated across the water at the *Drake*. He then ordered my Marines out of sight below, where they too could imbibe Simpson's poison.

Fortunately for us, the enemy boat won the race with mutiny. There were just six men in it, including the four oarsmen, a midshipman of no more than fifteen years old, and a lieutenant. This latter was stood up in the boat, clad in the blue frockcoat and white breeches of his navy, with a broad scowl on his face as he counted the *Ranger*'s most unpeaceable host of gunports. Jones looked down upon them from the quarterdeck, nodding. The lieutenant nodded back, and not a word was exchanged as our launch came out to accept his sword and his surrender.

There could be no doubt that the Old Man of the *Drake* had been watching through his glass, and that he had seen his men taken into custody. Meanwhile, the prospect of carnage brought a swarm of Irish coasters out from Carrickfergus to admire the spectacle. I could see the jackals there on their boats, unwisely close to us, taking wagers between themselves on the outcome.

Jones made certain the six new prisoners were marched through the angry crowd on the gun deck. This demonstration seemed to have the desired effect on the crew, distracting them from making solid plans of their vague grievances. The perfume of easy money suddenly permeated the chamber.

Fallows, the quartermaster's mate, begged to speak, and was granted the floor. "That's six pris'ners we got already. Maybe this *Drake* isn't as stout as all that," I heard him say. "An' don't we get full share for a captured ship 'o war?"

"We do indeed," concurred Joye, who had become a Jones apologist after the commander had accepted his plan to loot the Selkirk house.

"Do we put it to a vote, then? Do we fight?" Fallows asked.

"Seconded," said Cato Carlisle, who reclined against the carriage of "Dun Bess," whittling a piece of bone-hard salt horse with his knife.

"Any seconds that count?" added Simpson in a low tone that rolled as ominously as a black cloud. He did not like the direction of this discourse, and was determined to slow its progress.

Joye seconded, and Fallows moved to make the formal motion to fight, but Simpson objected that only the chairman of the meeting could frame such resolutions, at which the assembled began to argue amongst themselves over who was the chairman, and the gathering dissolved into inert acrimony.

These parliamentary proceedings occurred, I remind you, while the *Drake* had set herself before the wind, flying down on us with her topgallants set. In a very few moments she would be upon us, and opposed only by Jones, his loyal officers, and my one sharpshooter.

Jones, however, made no further move to influence the decision being made below. All his attention was fixed instead on his "blonde ghost," and that special sort of kiss he sought to give her. I was trapped, therefore, between the reciprocal insanities of captain and crew, and facing the imminent prospect of capture again.

At length, order was restored below, and Joye seconded Fallows's motion to make a vote to fight. Simpson delayed the proceedings further by opening a discussion of whether this should be an open, voice vote, or a secret written one. Arguments flew on behalf of both for some minutes, with the former prevailing on the virtue that most of the crew could not write their names. The motion was announced again, lest anyone had forgotten it, and the vote conducted. The "ayes" won.

So it came to be that the *Ranger*'s crew deigned to lend their aid in opposing the *Drake*. And though they were a mutinous lot, they had not forgotten their drills: we were cleared for action with a few seconds to spare. Cullam stood at the wheel with the helmsman, tapping his foot upon the deck in evident nervousness, until he addressed Jones, "Heading, sir?"

The captain had leapt atop the ship's rail to get a better view of matters. Unsatisfied, he climbed still higher up the mizzen shroud, with one elbow hooked around a ratline. At just five or six cables' distance it was alarmingly clear that the *Drake* was very heavily manned. She had fighters with cutlasses hanging from her shrouds, men brandishing pikes on her fo'c'sle, and other boarders, with short swords and no discernible uniform, drawn up in lines along her rail.

"She means to ram us and grapple," Simpson warned.

For the *Drake*, a deck fight was a fair plan, considering her advantage in numbers, and the fact that Jones had already allowed her in so close. Moreover, we were presenting our stern to the enemy, covering her only with our single stern gun. *Drake* would put her bowsprit over our starboard quarter, lash our vessels together, and send forth her hordes to hack through our boarding nets. Or so she believed.

Still grasping the ratlines, Jones swung inboard and dropped to the deck. We were all quite anxious to hear what his counterstroke would be.

"Word to gunners. Load cannister," he said.

This was a call for a special kind of ammunition: a tin vessel filled with one-inch musket shot. Once fired, the cannister shattered, releasing a swarm of leaden balls that were very effective against human flesh.

...

"*Mon dieu,*" breathed Thierry.

...

However, cannister was effective only at short ranges, suggesting that Jones would permit the *Drake* and her horde as close as he dared.

His next order was "Mr. Cullam, will you show them the mains'l?", to which the other responded, "With pleasure," and turned to order his waisters to clap onto their lines and haul away. The wind filled these courses, and the *Ranger* at last began to gather headway. It was not a moment too soon, as the *Drake*'s topmen had begun to play small arms on us.

"Up helm," said Jones.

The *Drake* was now less than fifty yards astern, and driving at us at close to eight knots. Yet so precisely trimmed was our sloop that she turned as if on a pivot, and instantly "crossed the T" on the enemy. Through their ports, our gunners should have seen a perfect target—coming at us bow first—become centered in their sights.

The *Drake,* surprised, put her helm up as well. But she was seconds too slow. Now at point-blank range, Jones gave the order to fire, and we raked those gleaming decks with their legion of eager young men. The cannister worked with frankly sickening effect, producing a blizzard of deadly projectiles like the fusillade of an entire infantry column. When the thunder of this first broadside had ceased resounding off the stony shores of Belfast Bay, and the smoke finally blew away in the stiff airs, we saw the enemy's decks were covered with men who were either hiding, dying, or dead.

The *Ranger*'s starboard nine-pounders were ready for re-fire in less than two minutes. In that time Jones passed an order to the gun captains to load with chain-and-bar shot, and aim their guns high. His idea, no doubt, was to immobilize the enemy by shredding her sails and rigging, leaving the more expensive (and less replaceable) parts of the vessel to be claimed as our trophy.

The message was delivered and understood. Our second broadside made a devil's rain through the *Drake*'s courses, shrouds and stays. British Marines fell in twos and threes from her devastated tops. The *Drake*'s momentum, however, had cleared her through her turn, and she brought forth her own first blast. By the grace of God, she was to windward of us, and a bit crank in that wind, so that she was heaved too much to starboard, and discharged most of her shot into the water a few yards abeam of us.

Our Irish audience, by the way, lost its wagering zest when chain-and-bar shot suddenly littered the sea around them. The spectator fleet turned about and fled, en masse, back to Carrickfergus.

The action went on like this, the vessels abreast one another, trading our nine-pounders for their sixes, for close to an hour. Our crews were left to fire at their own rates, virtually stripping the *Drake* of her usable canvas and cordage. The enemy continued to play their long-guns and sniper fire on us, and we were saddened to see three of our number, including Midshipman Dooley, struck down.

...

"The boy? How sad!" exclaimed Gualbert.

...

He was standing on the fo'c'sle when a ball struck the foremast. Splinters shot everywhere. Indeed, the shivering of wood produces many of the injuries in this sort of fight; the shards are as dangerous as gunfire. I went to him when I saw him fall, and steadied him as he appeared to sink into shock. His right arm was shattered at the elbow, and this limb was splayed upon the bloody deck at a twistedly unnatural angle.

"To perdition with you, boy! Don't you know to step aside when a body's got a bead on you?" I tasked him. I recall his eyes were suddenly very wide open as he looked up at me and smiled.

"I can hear you, sir!" he breathed. "I can hear you as plain as you're standing there!"

My father's hearing trumpet was still lying beside him, hardly scratched by the explosion.

"Simpson! Get that boy . . ." Jones began, and was interrupted when his cocked hat was shot off. He completed his thought, saying "Get that boy below! Step to it!" before he bent to retrieve the hat, and placed that perfect target once again upon his stubborn head. Before the *Drake* fired again, Dooley was carried down the ladderway, toward Surgeon Green's cockpit.

All circumstances being equal, the vessels were twins of one another, and quite well matched. But the circumstances were not equal. In that oceanic *pas de deux* it was Jones, with Master Cullam's collaboration, that kept the enemy lagging behind us by just a few critical seconds. The accumulation of damage aloft slowed the *Drake* in her evolutions. She became easy to beat 'round the corner, and we began to rake her at will.

But the *Drake* was a fine ship, and still reserved a surprise for us. We were but a cable's distance apart, with the wind blowing great guns through us both, when her helm was thrown up and she turned on us in a desperate charge. She had placed herself in a position to be raked again, but with the hope that she would catch us at last, and seize us with her grappling hooks.

We applied another broadside down the length of her as her bowsprit sliced over our rail. Her stem heaved against our starboard beam, and she came to rest with her keel exactly perpendicular to ours. We were now too close to her to cover her decks with our guns—I could see her men emerge from their cover, some readying their weapons, others with grappling tackle in their hands, still more (her crew was limitless!) hauling the ship's braces to turn her yards, in hopes the wind would push her side-on-side to us.

The *Drake*'s captain was visible there too, standing on her quarterdeck, hands clasped behind him. And though I could see his hair was gray, and the buttons of his frockcoat could not be secured over his ample stomach, he stood there in the same manner as Jones, oblivious to the possibility that he would meet a piece of cast iron for all his trouble.

The wind had become the *Drake*'s ally at last, as her keel began to come parallel with ours. Her boarding parties were forming up now, one at her bow, one astern. They appeared to be very well equipped, and very angry at having to crouch under cover for so much of the battle. Several of the Drakes had also inched out along the bowsprit and boomkin, and were swinging and stabbing their pikes savagely at anything within their reach. Most of our men stood clear, except for Joye, who had seized the opposite end of a pike and engaged in a tug o' war over the weapon.

The enemy threw grappling hooks aboard the *Ranger*, in hopes of preventing our escape. On seeing these, our men would rush to either throw the barbed implements overboard, or sever them from their lines. As you might guess, it was far easier to throw a hook than it was to extricate one.

"Hands to the braces! Put yer backs to it, boys!" Jones cried. As our sails were in better condition than the enemy's, the wind moved us farther, and faster, when our yards were turned at last. Open water appeared between the sloops again—the *Drake*'s grappling hooks were thrown out, but hooked only water. Her gambit had failed.

Just then my Marines gave a great cheer. I asked the reason, and learned that my sharpshooter had picked off a man in officer's uniform.

Our concentrated fire had by now rendered the *Drake* completely unmanageable. We shot ahead again, to lie athwart her bows, but she could do nothing to follow, and keep her broadside to us. *The Ranger's* gun crews worked like automatons, keeping up a steady rate of fire as our enemy's discharge became progressively more ragged. Our barrage was so hot and quick, in fact, that our guns fairly glowed with the heat of repeated fire, and many Rangers were burned when their naked skin brushed against the trunnions. "Dun Bess," her crew later boasted, had fired eighteen times in less than an hour. "Jumping Jedediah" marked fourteen, and in a further miracle she was worked the entire battle without killing a single one of her own operators.

At length, we began to feel pity for the poor devils on the *Drake*. To fight on through this sort of carnage was too much to wring out of any crew.

"Why don't they give up?" Hall asked with all the innocence of his age.

It was a quarter hour later before we finally heard a voice call out to us across the water. It said, "Quarter, quarter, for the love of Heaven! Our captain is dead!"

To this Jones replied, "Strike your colors, or I will fire again!"

This was an unanswerable argument. The British ensign was hauled down, and such a riot of celebration went up on the *Ranger* that no one could hear Jones shout for boarding parties to hurry over to claim our new prize. For this, at last, was no fisherman or saucy fruiterer. It was the Royal Navy we had fought, and pound-for-pound, we had proven ourselves the better.

The senior officer left aboard the *Drake* was brought to the captain. This turned out to be the sailing master: a man who looked very much frighted by the whole affair, yet tall, so that he towered above his conqueror. He had lost his hat in the battle, and carried no sword, so Jones was deprived of the ritual of accepting the blade of the vanquished.

The dignity of the scene was marred further by the fact that we had all been subjected to the steady roar of sixty minutes of gunnery, and our ears were ringing. Jones could hardly hear the master, and the other had to bend his ear down to hear Jones.

"Captain Burden is dead," the man said.

"What?" Jones cried.

"Captain Burden is dead, and his lieutenant too!" the master repeated.

"That is unfortunate."

"Sir?"

"I grieve the loss of two such brave officers!" Jones yelled. "But tell me, why was it you waited so long to strike? You were beaten when we bore away the last time!"

The *Drake*'s master thought for a moment, and shrugged. "How could we strike before a Yankee privateer?" he asked us.

The victory was the capstone of that eventful cruise. In the first flush of jubilation over it, it was widely asked whether any other Continental Navy vessel had ever bested the Briton in a straight-up, ship-to-ship duel. To our definite gratification, none of us could think of a single instance.

"There should have been seventeen such victories before this," noted our dry Captain Eighteen.

Later, before the trip back to Brest, I took the occasion to inspect the deck of our prize. Like us, the Royals made a practice of spreading out sand to prevent their men from slipping on a bloody deck. In this instance, I was sobered to discover that their sand was soaked through in many spots, and that there were still some remnants of flesh (skin, muscle, and several fingers) lying about uncollected, on which some of the gulls had begun to feast.

Shooing the scavengers away, I happened upon a stretch of deck that was caked not with blood, but with some more sweet-smelling humor. Kneeling, I found that this substance was brandy. Indeed, standing nearby were the remains of a large cask that appeared to have been shivered by one of our cannister blasts.

"They broke out a hogshead for their victory party," Hall told me with a smile, to which Simpson chimed in, "Then they do not drill as we do, for they would know that Jones's gunners hit barrels first of all!"

I was pleased to find Midshipman Dooley alive and recuperating under Green's care. It was reported (and I think it plausible, given the boy's character) that while the surgeon was hacking Dooley's arm off at his shoulder, his patient spat the rag from his mouth and upbraided the doctor for daring to take a "wee nip" to fortify himself for the operation.

From deep in his befogged brain, Dooley summoned the lucidity to report the transgression to Jones and me when we visited him, along with a strong recommendation that his doctor be disciplined. The captain assured him that it would be done, and attempted some other soothing words, but surely he did not hear them, as his good ear was lying against the folded material of Jones's frockcoat, which then served as his pillow.

...

Thierry shook her head. "The poor child. First, he is deprived of his hearing, then burned, then rendered misshapen. What could his mother have thought?"   ...

I was not present when Dooley was at last returned home to Portsmouth later that season. And though the captain had kept his promise and returned him to her alive, Jones learned that the mother fainted straight away when she first glimpsed her deaf, burned, and one-armed little warrior. Yet it could not be dismissed how much Jones had done for him, how much grown in maturity and the manly virtues he was after just a few months at sea. Mrs. Dooley finally wrote Jones a letter to that effect, relating that she accepted the ear, arm, and lost eyebrows as fit tuition for such an education.

...

"Barbaric!" declared Gualbert, who was nonetheless held rapt by all the talk of amputations and blood and fighting.

Severence shrugged.   ...

Yes, it is. You will be glad to hear, then, that Jones struggled to make a gallant punctuation to this carnage. Every practical assistance was extended to the *Drake*'s surgeon in his struggle to contend with his injured. Before we set sail for Brest, Jones insisted upon giving Captain Burden and Mr. Dobbs, his first lieutenant, the honor of formal interment in the sea, according to the Burial Service of their own Navy.

The service was held at one bell on the second dog watch. With Venus lingering in the sky above the Irish heath, our prisoners were let out of the hold, and allowed to stand shoulder-to-shoulder with their colonial brethren as Jones read the appropriate pieties from Scripture.

He then paid tribute in his own words, most large-mindedly, to "these brave servants of their King, so late our countrymen. With their deaths they commend to us the maintenance of that quality of dignity that makes brothers of us all. For in this profession of the sea, the labels of country are mere pretensions, and ones that we sanctify only at our own peril. We may well be the victors this day—but we cannot presume to be more than the equals of these good men."

With that the signal was given, and the boards, wrapped in the *Drake's* own tattered ensign, were inclined to free the dead for their journey to their reward. Just as they sank, Venus bent to the horizon and sealed their earthly struggles at last with her kiss.

"Three cheers for Cap'n Jones!" Joye cried. With our richest prize in our grasp, and prisoners under our boot, there seemed no disputing the suggestion; for the first time, the Rangers cheered their captain.

"Hip, hip, hooray!" we all shouted, waving our hats and bandanas in the dying light. "Hip, hip, hooray!"

Jones looked at the deck, shielding his eyes from us with the brim of his hat. For all his ambition as a parlor raconteur, this was the sort of praise he understood best. When he looked up again, and the third "hooray" dissolved over the surface of the sea, a tear was standing on his cheek. Of course, fine warriors never cried. Only the best ones, like Achilles, did.

The prisoners honored themselves by remaining silent during the cheer. After the ceremony, they put themselves in irons again and returned to their hole. The sound of hammering and sawing resumed from the *Drake*, as our carpenters hurried their repairs for the return to Brest. There was no doubt by this time that Royal Navy frigates had been sent forth to search for us. It would require a further, very long stretch of good fortune for us to evade them, and reach France with our prize.

With the advantage of hindsight, I say this of Jones: that as he watched those two British officers sink beneath the waves from his quarterdeck, and the cheers of the crew echoed in his ears, he was, with only a single exception, upon as high a promontory of success as he would ever know. He had reached it sooner than he might have expected, and probably did not fully appreciate his position there until he had lost it.

XVIII.

There are Ships in various ports of France to whom no Commanders are appointed—Give me the Command of what will Sail and if possible of what is calculated to fight—At any rate pray them to remove my doubts—I will exercize my patience but after so many changings this suspense is Hell itself.

—JONES, in a letter to Dr. Edward Bancroft, 1778

~

THIS TIME Jones thought it best to separate Lt. Simpson from his ready audience on the *Ranger*. Therefore, he was named as Prize Captain on the *Drake* for the trip back to Brest, under strict instructions to lay by Jones's starboard quarter the entire way back. Meanwhile, the Irish prisoners—the fishermen who had done us the favor of first alerting us to the *Drake*—were released with money and a gig, and in their gratitude offered up three cheers to Jones before they rowed away. For like our Scot, these fishermen bore no great love for the Royal Navy, and with their release Jones was fast on his way to being as much a hero in Ireland as he was a villain in England.

Word of Jones's activities had already spread the length and breadth of Britain. As the Bristol channel was no doubt already under close watch, Jones opted to take a circuitous route back to France, counter-clockwise around Ireland. We first sailed north, barely weathering the Mull of Kintyre in the late winter storms, and cleared Malin Head in good order. As we turned south again, we saw nothing of the Red Ensign. Lieutenant Simpson fulfilled his prize orders to the letter, and the cruise seemed destined to come to a happy end.

I beg you now, patient ladies, to attend to the details of what happened next. For though the facts may seem trivial now, they had a profound effect on the end of my relationship with Jones.

We were within a day's sail of France when our lookout sighted what appeared to be a ship-rigged merchantman. She was running east off our starboard beam, and bound on a course that would cross our wake barely a league astern of us. Though he was jealous to protect his prize warship, Jones found this vessel too tempting a plum to resist, especially in light of the perennial complaint that his cruises were unprofitable.

This impulsive decision to give chase to the merchantman surprised us all, not the least prizemaster Simpson. When I had the opportunity later to interview other members of the prize crew regarding the events of that puzzling day, they were unanimous in declaring that Jones's announcement of his intention was not understood. Jones had commanded Simpson to wear ship and follow in the attack, but he neglected to use his speaking trumpet, making it a task for those aboard the *Drake* to apprehend his words over the sound of wave and wind. As the *Ranger* came about and squared away on the opposite heading, Simpson duly begged clarification of the obscure order. To this, Lieutenant Hall, equally uncomprehending at the widening distance, merely signalled a general assent. This still left Simpson the problem of divining exactly what Hall had confirmed.

Faced with the deplorable condition of the *Drake*'s rig, and assuming Jones was also well aware of this, Simpson made the fateful presumption that he had been ordered to run for Brest and safety.

When Jones returned to the quarterdeck, he was of course much incensed to see that the *Drake* had disobeyed his order to follow, but had instead wandered off on its own, unescorted. The errand was made doubly useless by the discovery that the merchantman was not British, and therefore not a lawful target. Jones ordered us about again, and bade Cullam clap on sail to intercept the *Drake* and her impudent prizemaster.

Now, as you have heard, it was not altogether unreasonable to call Lieutenant Simpson mutinous in light of his many attempts to undermine Jones's authority. Unfortunately, this did not happen to be one of those actions.

"Damn you, Simpson!" Jones fumed as he leapt from the launch and scaled the ladder to the *Drake*'s spar deck. "You will stand down, you rascal!"

Simpson, for his part, was utterly innocent. From where he stood, it appeared his crazy little captain was on the rant again, this time merely because he had obeyed orders to continue on to Brest.

"I gave no such order!" Jones shouted up at him from a distance shorter than the combined lengths of their noses. Indeed, Jones appeared to be speaking directly to the white silk stock buttoned at Simpson's throat. Under such attack Simpson's natural conceit only redoubled in its intensity, and he retaliated against Jones's ferocity with an air of superior calm. He said, very simply, "I have witnesses."

"You are relieved, sir. And you will own up to your treachery."

Simpson met Jones's eyes. There was no softening in them.

"I will stand down. But I will own up to nothing," he said, biting off the last word.

"Mark me—this'll be yer last defiance, ye skinkin' caire!" the captain cursed him.

Upon hearing this last utterance, everyone looked to each other. Clearly, the intensity of his passion was causing Jones to lapse back into his Galwegian burr. Jones, aware of his accent's effect, reddened visibly, and became still more enraged.

"I am not defying you," Simpson said, calmly.

"It's a mutiny yer been aboon, an' a list o' charges as lang's my arm," sputtered Jones, sounding more Scottish by the second. Flagrant giggles sounded from hidden quarters. Many of the men were now hiding smiles behind their hands, or were so amused by this they were compelled to turn their faces away. Jones, however, became unnerved by the evident thinness of his Continental facade. Out came the sword.

"Gie me ye submission, or taste a bit o' this!"

But the men were not frightened. Instead, Jones was now greeted with great rolling gales of laughter. He moved toward Simpson—and found his way suddenly blocked by a half-dozen of the *Drake*'s prize crew.

The look on their faces was faintly apologetic, yes, but wholly convinced that Simpson was in the right. "Sorry, Cap'n . . . that it shoulda come to this . . . ," one of Simpson's men told him. "We don't mean nothin' but to be good tars, sir, but we do believe it poss'ble you're mistook."

This, at last, was the worst case. We had reached that fateful point where the clash of these men's personalities would—or would not—be magnified into a clash of shipboard factions. Unfortunately, as I stood behind Jones, no Marine guard stood behind me. Jones had rushed over far too fast for me to organize a meaningful force.

The captain looked at his adversaries in turn, calculations of attack and defense undoubtedly flying through his brain. Who could say, indeed, that memories of Tobago, and the almost disastrous effect that it had had on his career, did not work to cool his temper? That was, at least, my hope.

He returned his sword to its scabbard, then drew himself to as full a height as he could muster. "Lt. Simpson, am I to understand you refuse to accept my orders?" he asked, correcting his accent.

"Not at all. I stand down this very moment."

Simpson then stepped out from behind his protectors. Jones bit his lip, knowing a well-executed strategical withdrawal when he saw one.

Lt. Hall was placed in command of the prize crew, and Simpson retired to his quarters for the rest of the run into Brest. But in fact, the miserable Jones confined himself as well, leaving Cullam in charge of what should have been the *Ranger*'s triumphal return.

For although it appeared that Simpson had relented, even the dullest of us understood that his concession was more honorable than Jones's "victory." Jones had, after all, demanded his satisfaction, and Simpson had not given it to him. Moreover, he had demonstrated that Jones was both unreasonable and foreign, two prejudices Jones had worked all of his life to erase. Thus humiliated, he could hope to accomplish no more with this crew.

All of this turmoil, I remind you, was over a single misunderstood order shouted over a cable's stretch of howling sea.

...

Thierry shook her head as she tapped the exhausted embers from her pipe.

"That story . . . ," she began, with Severence smiling broadly at her consistent, alluring skepticism and herself frowning back, " . . . is nonsense. I don't believe it. I don't believe you would have simply stood there, patiently noting other people's reactions while your dubious little hero was humiliated."

"Nathalie. Recall that he is our guest," Gualbert warned her.

"The story, alas, is true," said the guest. "And you are correct to sense that I put aside many of my own sentiments in the telling, with a view to finishing my story before the sun rises." And he checked his watches again.

"Oh, the arrogance of him! Really, Thérèse, need we hear more?"

Thierry hurried from her seat, crossing to look into the mirror above her oaken console table. She was experiencing one of those uncomfortable moments when she could feel the condition of her hair, and the new lines around her eyes, and the flesh around her neck, and believed she was unattractive.

Gualbert told him, "Well, I want to hear the rest." Severence obliged her, perhaps in hopes that their ménage was not entirely beyond repair. Thierry, meanwhile, pretended not to listen from across the room, absorbing herself instead in looking for flecks of tobacco under her lips and between her teeth.

...

We reached Brest by the second week of May, with the *Drake* in tow. It was not a typical day when any vessel entered a French port with a Royal Navy ship as prize. Your own navy had not carried a significant sea engagement against British arms in a decade. We therefore expected some measure of recognition for our eventful month of conquering, and were disappointed to find that our hosts largely carried on with their usual frivolities. As a test, Jones offered thirteen guns to a French 64 anchored in the roads. We still only merited nine guns in return.

With this began another long season of disappointment for Jones. To him, it seemed that nothing he did, no matter how singular, would win him the attention he needed to succeed. He therefore preferred to believe he had simply not achieved enough. This, at least, was a problem further victories could solve. The alternative—namely, that powerful forces far beyond his influence were at work to frustrate his plans and belittle his accomplishments—was too dispiriting to contemplate.

The first, and worst, of these forces was England herself. Having identified Jones as a positive irritant, she worked the levers of diplomacy to keep him bottled up in port. The ship Franklin had had in mind for him, the Indian, was still at Amsterdam, and extraordinary measures were surely taken to warn the Dutch of His Majesty's displeasure should that fast, powerful vessel be sold to America. The craven Dutch vacillated, delaying their aid to a sister republic in her birth-struggle. I began to believe Jones spoke the truth, when he traced the decay of Dutch manhood around his supper table on the *Ranger*.

Second, he was in France—a country with an abiding hatred of the Briton, to be sure, but one that was not officially at war with him. As such, Marine Minister Sartine was under no formal obligation to find Jones a ship, nor to help feed and secure Jones's British prisoners. Indeed, any such efforts had to be discreet, lest the British plausibly claim themselves the aggrieved party. In short, the wheels of French bureaucracy were sure to grind exceedingly slow for Jones, and not to grind very finely either.

This did not prevent him from begging for a ship, again and again, in letters (which I translated) to Sartine, Chaumont, Franklin, even to the King. And for every noncommittal or lukewarm answer, Jones's next letter grew ever more shrill and frustrated, until Sartine thought to end his sufferings by offering him an opportunity to beg in person. They would meet at the residence of his friend Monsieur Le Veillard, in Passy.

Jones looked forward to this interview as one of the more important of his career. His uniform, already impeccable, was cleaned and brightened again, and he purchased a new bagwig for the occasion. As I would translate for him, Jones insisted on the same program of preparation for me, and paid for it himself.

At last the day arrived. We were offered one of Chaumont's coaches to take us to Le Veillard's, and Franklin rode with us to prepare Jones for this particular Minister of Marine, who would listen with infinite patience to his supplicants, but who (it was said) made his decision yea or nay within two minutes of their introduction.

The coach let us off before Le Veillard's villa, and Franklin waved to us from the departing carrosse as it conveyed him back to the Chaumonts'. We were then shown to the villa's sitting room by a footman, who informed us that the Monsieur and the Minister were out shooting for the day and were expected to return soon. Meanwhile, we were offered glasses of porter and the run of Monsieur's books and instruments.

So we waited. And we waited, scratching our heads under our new wigs. And we waited still longer, drinking, while Le Veillard's daughter, a five-and-a-half-foot tall, fourteen-year old Amazon named Genevieve, came out to scandalize us with her secret ambition to be an actress, and to run away with her hero-love, the Electric Doctor Franklin.

"What's wrong with him?" she asked me, nodding at the glum Jones.
"He's been made unhappy," said I, uninformatively.

Genevieve thought for a moment. "Does he want to hear my recitation?"

I would have answered in the negative, but she had already launched into her portrayal of Antigone in her defiance of Creon, and was not to be interrupted. We had heard ten minutes of this, with the girl declaiming and the liquor running low and Sartine nowhere in sight, when Jones could take no more.

We returned to the Hôtel Valentinois by evening. Of course, by the next morning, Le Veillard's footman followed us with Minister Sartine's profuse apologies, the explanation that he had been "detained by an unfortunate accident afield", and the promise that he would be pleased to see the Captain again "at some time to be mutually decided."

"The shooting must have been very good," was Jones's only comment.

The third force opposing his progress was America herself. With our nation at that moment engaged in a struggle for her very existence, one would think we could not afford the indulgence of petty political gamesmanship. Yet it went on, and as men fought and died on the sea to capture the *Drake*, the schemes and maneuvers of other men ashore worked to nullify their sacrifice.

...

"Please don't preach to us," Thierry said as she reclaimed her seat.
"Just tell us what happened."   ...

What happened, then: the regular naval adjutant at Brest had been a man called Williams, a likeable young fellow whom we had met at Passy and got on with quite well. While we were at sea, however, Williams's job fell victim to the ongoing tug o' war between Franklin and Arthur Lee, and it was filled by a Swiss named Schweingruber or Schweinhauser, who bore an immediate and inexplicable dislike for Jones. Our prizes, which included the *Drake* and the two merchantmen we had seized on our way from America, were sold at disgracefully low prices, largely through the offices of this Schweingruber, whom we'd presumed to be working on our behalf. Of course, his behavior was explained by the fact that he was closely associated with Commissioner Lee, who hated Franklin and, accordingly, anyone whom Franklin happened to sponsor. This, sadly, included Captain Jones.

Jones could have used more money, what with the distribution of shares to his men to assure, and the care of his British prisoners to worry about. The American Commission could spare only token sums to this latter task. Chaumont would not condescend to deal with this issue, and Sartine could lend only quiet assistance in imprisoning foreign nationals taken on the high seas. The responsibility therefore fell to Jones to guarantee the feeding, care, and security of some 150 prisoners at Brest. It was a task he took on grudgingly, but performed as thoroughly as any of his projects. It had been, after all, his firm intention to use these prisoners as currency to free American seamen languishing without hope in the British gaol.

His foresight was vindicated in the end. A full nine months later, after much foot-dragging on the north side of the Channel, and diplomatic high-handedness on the part of our French hosts, Jones's prisoners were released aboard a British channel packet, and another bearing an equal number of Yankee sailors arrived from Plymouth.

But when these desperate men stumbled ashore that gray Brittany morning and kissed the free soil beneath them, it was the agents of the French crown they saw first, not Jones. Only a handful of the prisoners found their way to their real liberator. When they did, however, their gratitude tended to be as firm and undying as mine had been.

Jones's most important prisoner was Simpson. And though this officer had tested the captain's authority at every turn, these crimes were as nothing compared to the headaches he caused after Jones had finally arrested him. A court martial was indicated, clearly, but such a proceeding required the judgment of three officers of command grade. It was Jones's misfortune that there were only two American captains in French ports at that time, not including Jones himself. While we waited for a third to arrive, Simpson stood a prisoner of Jones's acquaintance, the French Admiral D'Orvilliers. This arrangement was convenient for Jones, but the fact that he was under a French jailor helped Simpson immeasurably as he campaigned for the sympathy of the *Ranger*'s crew.

We were at Passy, in Franklin's apartments, when the issue at last gathered to a head. Jones was inquiring after the same Indian that had bewitched him since his arrival in France, when a messenger arrived with a packet from Brest. Franklin unsealed it in front of us, his ancient fingers trembling as he wielded the opener. He read the contents through to himself first, touching his chin lightly with his fingertips as he peered through the bottoms of his bifocals. Jones sat watching with his agitation barely concealed.

"This appears to be a petition," Franklin said slowly, "that lays out in some detail what the writers regard as the most shameful episode in their captain's career. It raises . . . questions." And he looked steadily at Jones, waiting for him to elaborate or defend himself, at which Jones inspected the Chinese carpet at his feet, and launched his defense:

"That episode is a matter of record. It was a justified killing, I have said, under an occasion of severe mutiny. As for my decision to leave Tobago before trial, I say again that I would do the same under similar circumstances. The court of Providence will be my sole judge in this matter, sir, and I trust it will be a fairer instrument than the organs of that island. Call me a martinet, yes, and even ruthless in the face of sedition, but I am no murderer."

Franklin listened to Jones's account of his actions at Tobago without interruption, studying him as if he were a bug wiggling on a specimen pin. When the captain was finished, the Doctor lifted the packet from Brest and pronounced calmly, "This petition holds that your Lieutenant Simpson was a victim of some misunderstanding. Do you regard that issue as a matter of record as well?"

For making a foolish presumption, and defending himself for the wrong "crime," Jones flushed a deep red. Recovering, he snapped, "I ask who has signed such a petition. In fact, I demand to know."

"You will—but not just yet. The preamble tells a different tale." The old man prolonged the ordeal with his damnable precision. "It maintains that the instance upon which you arrested the Lieutenant was a matter of misapprehension, not treachery. Is it true, for instance, that you delivered your order for the *Drake* to follow only once? Over a rough sea?"

Jones bounded to his feet and bore down on Franklin's desk. Despite himself, the doctor flinched a bit before Jones's advance. "I refuse," the captain said, leaning forward, "to entertain any charges against my conduct from anonymous accusers!"

Franklin's reptilian eyes lay coldly on Jones. "This petition is signed by more than half your officers and men."

Jones stood up straight. Again, he looked surprised to learn the depths of his own unpopularity, even after he had worked so long and completely at insuring it. He turned about diffidently and retook his chair, but apparently could think of nothing to say.

Franklin placed the petition on his desk and set about straightening the pile of papers with his long, unwashed fingernails.

"Captain, you must believe me when I tell you I have complete confidence in your version of the events on the prize ship. Honestly, this man Simpson has been a problem not only for you, but for our French friends as well—Admiral d'Orvilliers has assured me that his ill-discipline is as contagious among his French prisoners as it was in your crew . . . "

"That is the measure of the man. He breeds impudence . . . "

" . . . which the wise man must not discount in his calculations," said Franklin, cutting Jones's argument off at its knees. "For whatever you know this Simpson to be, he is nothing but a master of semblance. And this . . . ," Franklin waved the *Ranger* petition, "is his knife at your throat."

"I see your object, sir, and I tell you again I will not abide it . . . "

Jones paused as an expression of acute discomfort suddenly appeared on Franklin's face. Then, just as abruptly, the pain seemed to subside. It was a most disquieting display, made worse by the fact that Franklin did not explain or excuse it. Instead, he continued, "Such a man as you, who can call the very winds to heel in battle, can understand these simple matters. This Simpson affair could reduce your expeditionary force to squabbling factions. Is this the face we wish to present to our friends here?"

"Perhaps our friends will respect our passion for discipline," Jones parried.

"More likely, they will believe us incapable of unity, even under threat of destruction. And they would have grounds for thinking so. Not to forget that there would be no guarantee a Court Martial would find against him."

Jones opened his mouth to answer, but checked himself. Captain Eighteen needed no further reminders of his unpopularity among the other captains of the Continental Navy. Franklin continued, saying, "An acquittal would be worse than a capitulation. It would erase everything you've accomplished here. Why give him such a chance? Why not checkmate him now?"

"Checkmate!" came Jones's sarcastic refrain. "Giving him a stretch in the gaol would satisfy me, entirely."

"Mark it—semblance is a subtle weapon, but it is easily turned. Why hope for victory, when you can simply claim it? Mr. Severence, tell him."

Franklin was looking to me. And although Jones was not, I presumed his ears were primed to hear my answer. In this case, the decision was easy: "I say Simpson is not worth the slightest risk to a distinguished career."

My advice drew no response from Jones. Franklin took this to signal agreement. He leaned back in his chair, clasping his fingers over his wide belly. "We must make this controversy go away in the manner most flattering to our good captain here. An impression of magnanimity—of forgiveness proper to a good Christian—would be the antidote to Simpson's poison. A parole, perhaps, releasing him from prison until an accommodation is reached. To turn the other cheek. That would fix him."

"Of course, the decision is yours," Franklin ended, after his pronouncements had already rendered Jones's position foregone.

Jones stood and cocked his hat on his head. I stood too, not without some trepidation that Jones would walk out on Franklin forthwith. But instead, he added a provision: "I agree, but only on condition that Simpson, on his honor, will not approach within two cables of the *Ranger* or any of her crew."

"A reasonable precaution," said the other.

The captain offered a short bow, saying, "You know where to find my signature." And the interview was over.

He was silent as we walked out though the conspicuous splendor of the building's vestibule. Still, I knew Jones's brief moment of retreat before Franklin would very soon have to be purchased with blood and bluster. Surely enough, he turned to me outside, and with a tightness around his mouth, told me, "The fault is yours if this Simpson affair recoils on me."

With that, he walked away. I didn't see him for the rest of evening or most of the next day. Nor did I seek him out, in fact. Though I had only known Jones for less than a year, I felt I had already suffered through a lifetime of his grudges, his insatiable enthusiasms, and his foul humor. For the first time, I began to sense I had finally discharged my debt of freedom to him.

XIX.

For God's sake let's hear from you by return of Post if you are able to write or to dictate a line . . . !

—JONES, in a letter to Dr. Bancroft, 1778

~

WHEN HE sent for me again, it was of course an invitation sweetened with an apology: "I know not by what misguided Reason," his note read, "that I was moved to direct the Passions intended for the usurper Simpson instead upon you, my dear Friend. Perhaps it may be understood as an index of my sentiments in this affair that Justice be served." And he ended his missive with a request for my indulgence, not the least because the demands of diplomacy required my services as translator: that is, that Patriotism itself demanded my forgiveness!

We had stayed on at Passy for close on a fortnight. Brest, you see, had become too painful for him. This was despite the fact that the Admiral d'Orvilliers' fleet lay at anchor there, and promised a veritable academy for our captain's professional curiosity. When we finally did return, we found more than thirty ships-of-the-line at the port. I believe Jones sought to examine each one, taking care to make notes regarding their rig, armament, and crews.

I had expected D'Orvilliers to be a typical French long-nose, and he was indeed, but he also proved to have a surprisingly receptive ear for good ideas. Jones, of course, was full of them. And though he never tired of communicating his strategical fantasias to the Admiral, the older man apparently recognized in them a refreshing keenness of mind. The French Navy, apparently, was every bit the sinkhole of patronage and nepotism as the Royal and Continental Navies, and equally famished for real imagination.

At length, the Continental victory at Saratoga worked its happy effect on Franklin's mission, and the official Treaty of Alliance between America and France was signed. Orders came down to Brest for d'Orvilliers to take his fleet into the Atlantic, in hopes of intercepting a convoy of British merchantmen expected to arrive in those waters from the East Indies. This plan was suspiciously similar to one of Jones's own "modest suggestions," but Jones pleaded no credit for thus instructing the French admiralty. Rather, he asked only to stand by as a passenger on d'Orvilliers' 110-gun flagship *Bretagne,* in hopes of improving his knowledge of fleet tactics.

I was witness to d'Orvilliers' reaction to this very reasonable request (indeed, I translated Jones's words for him). The bibbed, powder-faced aristocrat stared at Jones over his dish of crayfish cooked in sauterne, and appeared suffused by an air of paternal warmth for his young American guest. He then gushed to the effect of "But are you not the most perfect little treasure of a captain! I would not go without you. And when the Minister sends his approval, you will occupy the day cabin beside mine!"

Jones dutifully thanked his host, and sat back in good humor, for he presumed that though Minister Sartine had done little to secure the Indian for him, he could scarcely fail to grant such a small favor.

Jones's chest and writing materials were packed with typical dispatch, and he expected not many days would pass before he could send his things on to the *Bretagne.*

He hadn't counted on the peculiar "efficiency" of the French naval bureaucracy. By all accounts, d'Orvilliers did indeed send his inquiry to the ministry the following day, and by military post-courier the envelope should have reached Paris in less than three days—or by June the 30th. Assuming it took the same time for the reply to pass from the capital to Brest, Sartine would have had all of four days to pen his simple "oui" before d'Orvilliers was scheduled to sail. Jones therefore had his chest delivered to the day cabin aboard the flagship.

More than half a week was apparently not enough, for by the eighth of July d'Orvilliers could wait no longer. With the wind and tide favorable and fine weather in the offing, d'Orvilliers was forced, with evident regret, to invite Jones to re-pack his chest and disembark. To his credit, the admiral waited until the last possible moment, keeping a special watch up in his tops for the messenger bearing Sartine's leave. But it was not to be.

D'Orvilliers kissed Jones twice, once on each cheek, before delivering him back to Brest. Jones's promised education in fleet evolutions was reduced to watching the vessels of the admiral's great armada fall out with the tide in order, unfurled their courses, and disappear over the horizon.

Two hours later, Sartine's letter arrived from the Ministry. Jones would not read it, but I did: it was a full approval, and even expressed some surprise that d'Orvilliers had not merely assumed the minister's assent.

Jones suffered this missed opportunity stoically. Still, he could not help but voice the suspicion to me that Sartine had had reservations about an Anglo observer, so recently a subject of the Georges, taking notes aboard a French fleet. As the minister lacked the integrity to issue an open denial, he had merely delayed his answer just long enough for the admiral to sail without Jones.

"That scoundrel is playing about with me," the captain said, adding ominously, "and he may discover my limit before he supposes!"

This bitterness proved justified, as the cruise with d'Orvilliers would have been every bit the object lesson he had hoped. Though the admiral had failed to fall in with the East Indian convoy, he did try conclusions with the British Admiral Keppel and his Channel force of thirty ships-of-the-line. This was an enormous set-piece battle, involving some 40,000 men and 5,000 guns between the fleets, and opposing lines that each ran across several miles of ocean. D'Orvilliers succeeded in positioning his line upwind of Keppel's, and ran his entire armada across the British line, trading broadsides as they passed. More than 1,000 seamen were killed in this first engagement. And despite the fact that d'Orvilliers immediately returned to port, and had not sunk a single British vessel, he had likewise lost none. The French had again failed to prove they could win a battle, but at least had shown that they needn't always lose.

Jones's reaction to this so-called "Battle of Ushant" (it had in fact occurred more than 250 miles west of Ushant island) was an insatiable thirst for the details, coupled with distaste for such a "gentleman's draw." Retiring so early rendered the sacrifice of so many good men meaningless: if it was worth 500 men simply to annoy the British fleet, he held, certainly it was worth a few more to defeat it outright.

Smashing Keppel would have had the further consequences of delivering the East Indian convoy into French hands, and forcing the Royal Navy to reinforce her Channel fleet, possibly with forces otherwise engaged in harassing American commerce and burning American cities. "I fear we will do well to survive these 'allies,'" Jones complained.

He consoled himself by throwing himself into the social lists at Passy. Young Thérèse-Elisabeth Chaumont was, alas, gone to her aunt's in Boulogne, so he could do this happily without the threat of further scandal.

I was scarcely of the same value to him in the banquet hall and ballroom as I had been during our first visit. First, his confidence (if not his skills) in French had improved, and he began to sally forth on his expeditions without insisting that his translator remain over on his starboard beam. I was glad of this, as I had noted the conspicuous absence of Madame de Reynière from the scene. Indeed, I looked for her, half-hoping always to see that outlandish headdress again, hovering uncertainly over the hedges and sweetmeat tables of the hôtel. At several affairs I glimpsed gowns and plumed hats that might contain her, and on approaching these, was disappointed when their occupants turned around, and they were strangers. Puzzled, I approached Madame de Chaumont to inquire after our mutual acquaintance's health.

"I could not say," she told me, meanwhile exhibiting that transparently false regret some ladies affect when men ask after prettier ladies. "We've not exchanged a line in weeks and weeks—I fear it may be her melancholia again."

"But the baron is here," she brightened. "Why don't we ask him?"

She then seized my hand without asking and pulled me through her crowded parlor to Baron de Reynière. This man was deposited on the settee with one of his gaunt legs dangling over the other, the stem of a pipe stuck between the sharp points of his teeth. He was wearing a suit of embroidered green silk that made it appear as if a clump of sea-kelp had washed up on the cushions.

"Baron, this man is very much missing your wife," Madame de Chaumont announced. "Might you ease his fears?"

He had been laughing with another gentleman standing beside him in a French army general's uniform. Reynière listened to Madame de Chaumont's taunt without turning his head entirely toward her, and did

not answer her immediately. Instead, he introduced his companion as
Général de Brigade le Comte de Lowendahl.

This man displayed a frame which told of many assaults on plates of
bon-bons, but few battles. He drew his rotundity erect and bowed his head
smartly at his hostess. Madame de Chaumont then did me the honor of
remembering my name and rank and nationality (she never forgot names
and ranks), to which the Général de Brigade le Comte seemed to respond
bodily, surging toward me with sudden enthusiasm.

"But you are an ally of ours now, aren't you?" he asked me.

"Apparently, yes."

"When you return to America, you must send my compliments to General Washington. Please offer my services to him in our mutual struggle,"
Lowendahl said, thereby making the typical French assumption that America was so small that everyone there was acquainted with everyone else.

...

"They aren't?" Gualbert teased.

...

They aren't. The baron, meanwhile, finally resorted to answering
Madame de Chaumont's question, saying, "My wife has taken to her room
for the time being. It is not unusual."

"She is delicate," said Lowendahl, admiring.

"Yes, she is," said Reynière, proud.

"So, you see, you need not worry." Madame de Chaumont turned to
me. "She is no sicker than usual."

The General smiled. "A condition easily remedied by the making of
love."

To which the Baron replied: "But I assure you, Lowendahl, that I do
not make love. I purchase it ready-made!"

This was an old joke. I chose the moment to retreat, wondering perhaps if my continued ignorance would have been better than learning of
Madame de Reynière's illness. But I wasn't allowed to ponder this for long
before Jones appeared at my side again. He looked to me much agitated.

"If you would be so kind as to humor me, Lieutenant . . . ?" He bade
me follow him, meanwhile leaning close to speak in my ear. "I have just
been introduced to her, and her English is only as good as my French. And
she's most definitely worth understanding fully, is she not . . . ?"

"Who is?" I asked.

But we had already reached Jones's new friend—a woman.

"Madame La Vendahl, permit me to present my compatriot, Lieutenant Severence," the captain said immediately. I bowed, still dizzy from my rapid transit across the room, as the lady corrected Jones's pronunciation of her name by uttering the single word—"Lowendahl."

She was a young lady of very pleasing appearance, with a finely pointed chin, cheekbones worthy of an artist's model, and a wide brow. Indeed, the proportions of these features gave her face a fairly triangular shape, constraining her fairness within a geometrical severity. She was too beautiful, really, to inspire any comfort, an effect made worse by her lack of a particular feminine discretion: she had a habit of looking men straight in their eyes. Could this be the woman married to Baron de Reynière's friend, the soft general?

"Madame de Lowendahl, you said?" I asked her in French. "Is it possible I have just met your husband?"

"Ah, but my secret is spoiled!" she replied, laughing. "And I was just becoming acquainted with your Captain Jones."

"It is not spoiled. He doesn't understand."

"What is that? What are you saying?" Jones demanded, to which I assured him, "Just the pleasantries."

Looking on her, her allure for Jones was obvious. She was standing by the window, reserving for herself the last rays of twilight, attired all in white gauze, with a brown silk sash around her waist and a faux-shepherdess's staff in her right hand. In keeping with this "natural" style, she dared show her own hair. This was hardly a risk, for its color was that quality of dusky blonde that lent the curls a patently metallic shine. Much of her breast was exposed by her wide, fringed Medici collar, and despite her modiste's skill, her gift in this department was clearly not prodigious. She was compensated, however, by a neck of perfect grace.

Our introduction was only an interruption in a long flirtation between the captain and the married woman. To give you the sense of this, I leave out my contribution to their exchange and convey it as if they were speaking directly to one other. This is a fair distortion, I might add, because their attentions were locked upon one another so greedily, with Jones drinking her in unreservedly and Madame staring back just as fearlessly, that I might as well not have been present.

"Is it so, as I have heard, that the captain of the ocean sea is a lord unto himself, and holds the power of life and death over his inferiors?" she asked him.

"Aye, it is true indeed," Jones confessed, his face flushed with an unmistakable pride in this distinction. "Moreover, his ship is a country, and his rank a throne, against which treason is harshly punished."

Madame took his arm, causing him to start, as she implored him, "But how can you justify it, when Monsieur Rousseau taught us that Man is born in freedom, and such fetters you describe only degrade and defile him?"

"Be assured, dear Lady, that I have consented to command only at the price of my peaceful pursuits of love and learning, and consecrate my life to the perfection of that freedom to which you allude."

"Perfection of freedom! What an extraordinary object for a little despotism on the water! What freedom could be more perfect than a community of men governing themselves, with none more sovereign than the whole?"

At this Jones could only close his mouth and stare at Madame, who dared assault the foundation of his authority, yet grew ever more beautiful as she did so. In fairness, Jones was at a disadvantage with her, having never read Rousseau. He preferred such poets as Shakespeare and Young— men who had, in his words, "vanquished the dust"—and therefore left himself ignorant before devotees of the new and fashionably radical. All the while she kept her hand on his sleeve, holding on to him as she sensed his defense stiffen.

"But what time does a man of war have for idle philosophies!" she exclaimed brightly. "They are for women and thinking men. No revolution was launched from a parlor."

"Not launched. Only financed," remarked Jones, to which Madame de Lowendahl offered up an artificially girlish giggle that propelled her against him again. There was more contact. Jones was already charmed out of his pique of twenty seconds before.

His deficiency so plainly laid bare, Jones sought later to remedy his ignorance of modern political thought. He requested and received copies of Rousseau's *First* and *Second Discourses* from Franklin's own library. Up in his room, far into the night, I was obliged to translate these works by candlelight for him.

This was not easy. Jones was an intelligent man and bore the intelligent man's admixture of contempt and inferiority before career intellectuals. He could conceive and interject his criticisms of the text, but did so impulsively, as if he feared he would soon forget them. When, in the *Second Discourse,* Rousseau asserted that the natural man was "wandering the forests, without industry, without speech, without domicile, without war and without liaisons, with no need of his fellow-men, likewise with no desire to harm them," the captain leapt from his seat as if it was in flames, and scampered across the room in a poor imitation of a thoughtful stroll.

"What entire rot, to make a hero of the savage without sensibility!" he declared. "What then would be the purpose of civility and faith? Why educate, when it only places us a greater distance from the virtuous animal?"

"Perhaps it is his purpose to make criticism of those instruments of culture," I told him. "Sophistication is the misery of the soul, not its perfection."

But he talked on as if he had not heard me, saying, "Yet *she* seems to take all this most seriously, doesn't she? Curious. At any rate, we must maintain an open mind, my friend. Read on." And he was back on his chair again, ready for me to resume.

...

Thierry nodded, "Your Jones was right to loathe Rousseau. Was there ever a sophistry so odious, so toxic to the rational order? These mobs of Paris love his nonsense. Really, then, if savagery was so pleasant, why did men consent to give it up?"

"Maybe it wasn't a matter of consent," offered Gualbert.

Considering the source, neither Thierry nor Severence bothered to respond to this remark, and Gualbert lacked the confidence to press it.

...

In accord with Jones's new fascination with Madame de Lowendahl, I was charged to learn as much as I could about herself and her husband, to ascertain if there was any use he could make of them. For this, I found I need go no farther than Madame de Chaumont.

She was but 26 years old, I learned. Her *prenom* was Charlotte-Marguerite, and her diversions included singing, philosophy, and the painting of miniatures. She had been married to the General Lowendahl for eight years, and it was generally held that she was far too beautiful a match for him, and therefore desperately unhappy. Most intriguing for Jones, I found, was her royal pedigree, which fanned his ardor more than her pretty face. For if there was one thing that could be as exciting as taking a prize at sea, it was taking a Bourbon to bed.

This, apparently, would be his next project. It was surprising to me, I confess, because Madame de Lowendahl was not at all well placed to forward his career. On the contrary, the Général de Brigade le Comte was widely known to be underemployed himself, and frequented Passy in search of a command in the American war.

Knowing Jones as I did, and how much he sought to learn from defeat, I can speculate. Perhaps his missed opportunity with Madame de Reynière inspired him at last to act out of his passions instead of his ambitions. Such lust for a woman for her own sake was most unlike him. He may have discovered his heart at last.

XX.

You have made me in Love with my own Picture because you have
condescended to Draw it. If it is possible for you also to bestow the
portrait (of you) I have solicited I will wear it round my Neck and
always think how I may merit so great an obligation.

— JONES, in a letter to Madame la Comtesse de Lowendahl

~

THE SPRING took hold, and the trees on the Seine bent new rigs of delicate, green sails over the river. By their cultivator's unnatural arts, the
parterres of Passy were coaxed into an early advance of crocus, daffodil
and lilac, flanked by auxiliaries of doughty forsythia.

The new fashion of clothing, meanwhile, began in earnest with the
arrival of the season's "fashion dolls" from Versailles—those life-size man-
nequins attired after the dictates of Marie Antoinette and her advisor Mlle.
Rose Bertin, and distributed for the convenience of ladies from Lisbon to
St. Petersburg. Ladies from as far as Rouen came to the Hôtel Valentinois
to pay homage to Madame de Chaumont's version.

The doll's influence was apparent very soon after, when the women
suddenly began to eschew exotic fabrics and gemstones, and to prefer subtler, simpler cotton or light silk chemises. Jones, ever the student of the
feminine arts, credited "La Vendahl" (would he ever pronounce that name
correctly?) for anticipating this trend toward modesty and simplicity, taking for evidence the shepherdess costume she had worn on the night of
their first meeting.

Meanwhile, that other object of Jones's ambitions, the Indian, at last
appeared to be within his grasp. According to Franklin, the vessel was at
anchor in Amsterdam, and only awaited the final consent of the Dutch
authorities to proceed to sea under our flag. From our agents in that country, Jones learned that the ship was a most singular East Indiaman, with
low, fast lines and a unique convex stem. She would skim over the waves

like a dragonfly, Jones was assured, and with a good crew (that perennial catch!) could intercept or escape from anything afloat.

France was now a signed and official ally in the war against Britain, and the time for subterfuge was past. Sartine at last forwarded the sum to purchase the vessel outright, and sent forth his acquaintance, one Prince de Nassau-Siegen, to dispose of the details. Suitable armaments were discussed, and Franklin expressed confidence Jones would be back at sea by the autumn.

...

"Sartine! Now I recall where I've heard that name before!" interrupted Gualbert. She looked to Thierry, whose expression bid her continue.

"According to an acquaintance of Busson's, Sartine took it upon himself to entertain Louis XV by hiring DuBarry to scour the brothels of Paris and make detailed reports of the abominations he witnessed there. When the week's accounts were not remarkable enough to entertain, Sartine would dictate his own fictions to DuBarry. His specialty, I understand, was the ruination of virgins with oblong implements. The King appreciated the service, as he reimbursed Sartine over three million louis for it."

"And this was your Minister of Marine," Severence sighed.

Thierry flared at him again. "More American sanctimony. Is it not true that half the members of your Congress take pleasure of their household blacks?"

"No doubt. The difference, of course, is that Americans leave such stories under the bedclothes, while the French hang them out to dry."

...

In any case, Jones's star continued to rise through the summer. Jones was intrigued when Franklin conceived a scheme for another amphibious attack, this time on a more substantial British coastal city, and under the joint command of Jones and the Marquis de Lafayette. The three of them met informally at Passy, just before one of the Chaumonts' lawn parties. I was present as translator.

Lafayette was persistently odd. Everything about his appearance, from the receding slope of his brow to his patrician nose and beginnings of a double chin, spoke of unabashed nobility. Everything he said, however, revolved around the virtues of "freedom," "revolt," "independence," and "fair struggle." Really, he was taking the platitudes right out of Jones's mouth. Jones countered by claiming (yet again) that he had put aside the peaceful pursuits of love and gentlemanly repose to don the uniform of freedom, such and so forth—you know the rest. Franklin sought to forge their rivalry into a powerful partnership, with Jones in command of the sea and Lafayette the land force. This was speedily resolved.

The matter of the expedition's target was next on the agenda, and that took a great deal more time. I suspect this was because the contemplation of bringing a British city to its knees was too much of a pleasure to rush. After an hour of indulging more or less pure fantasy, the three resolved that demanding an indemnity would be preferable to actually burning a city to the ground.

...

"'Indemnity?' *C'est es se?*" asked Gualbert.

"A bribe to go away," said Thierry.

...

Franklin took out pen and paper and compiled a list of municipalities and their ransoms, which he read out by the end of our meeting: "48 million livres for Bristol and Liverpool, 40 millions for Edinburgh, 20 millions for Plymouth, 12 millions for Bath and Whitehaven, 6 millions for Lancaster . . ."

At which Lafayette turned to Jones: "What a delight to think of how much 48 millions could help your countrymen's cause!"

Jones offered a tight-lipped smile.

"What a delight, yes."

Franklin then invited the two heroes to stand and solemnize their plan over glasses of porter. Lafayette kissed Jones on both cheeks, and swore to support the project at Versailles. Jones promised to build Lafayette his very own tower on the deck of the Indian.

"Let the matter we have discussed today remain in confidence," warned Franklin, "lest you land and find yourselves opposed by half the British home army!"

"Of course," promised the younger men, and the meeting was over.

On our way down to the party, however, Jones regarded Lafayette's narrow back and leaned toward me.

"A climber," he said, "even with a title."

We descended to the garden by dusk, in time for the Chaumonts' dinner by torchlight. All faces turned toward us as Franklin and Lafayette appeared. The Marquis greeted these strangers with perfect poise and perfect enthusiasm for his pet cause. Franklin groaned at the prospect of yet another French feast.

Madame de Lowendahl had failed to notice Jones when he first emerged in the garden. Yet when she saw he was seated between Lafayette on one hand, and Madame de Chaumont on the other, she sought the captain's eyes deliberately, and found them. He offered her a short nod, which she acknowledged with a fearless wink.

"I will have that woman!" Jones hissed at me.

"Sheet out, now."

The menu that evening was exquisite, and highlighted still more by the spectacle of Madame de Lowendahl eating it. First, a pheasant consommé, enlivened, for Jones, by Madame's pursed lips as she spooned down the clear liquor. Next, cucumbers stuffed with beef marrow (she crudely licked out the marrow first, but no one seemed to mind). She took little bites of the partridge filets, the eel with tartar sauce, and burbot liver pastries, putting on a show of some delicacy while, in fact, she ate as much as any man at the table. A constant stream of compliments, meanwhile, were made to Franklin and Lafayette and George Washington (whose popularity in France, I suspected, was fortified by the fact that he was more than a thousand leagues away). The eating halted for glasses to be lifted, pieties to be uttered. Jones toasted Madame de Chaumont. She toasted the North American continent.

It seemed Général de Brigade le Comte de Lowendahl was absolutely determined not to notice his wife's flirtations. To me, this was a bad omen, but Jones chose to take it as evidence of their failing marriage. Madame de Chaumont only encouraged this impression when, over a dessert course of strawberries maraschino, she bent Jones's ear with whispered tales of the Lowendahls' misery. Not the least of these was the entirely unconfirmed horror of their wedding night, when the General so stuffed himself with a large variety of West Indian escargot that he was loathe to consummate the match. Once he'd mounted her (and it seems her maidenhead was, in fact, preserved for him), the Général de Brigade le Comte found himself greatly nauseated by the rhythm of love, and deposited two dozen semi-digested snails directly on his bride's breast.

"The ass!" uttered Jones, a bit too loudly.

According to Madame de Chaumont, the bride was so unnerved by this mishap she avoided her conjugal duties whenever she could, and when she couldn't, took care to lay a smock over her chest in bed. This ludicrous ordeal gave Jones excuse to pity as well as desire the woman. Unfortunately, Madame de Chaumont had altered her account slightly for the captain's sake. Baron de Reyniére himself informed me later, with the air of certainty, that the escargot accident had not "unnerved" the pretty wife at all. On the contrary, Madame de Lowendahl discovered that she was one of that class of sexual deviant who enjoyed feeling her skin defiled by all sorts of noxious things! Further details, he said, would be "hunting talk" (that is, not for the parlor).

...

"Though I don't sympathize with the Baron's version," said Thierry, "I know there are men and women who have instructed their spouses in providing this sort of service. There have been times I've been asked to provide it myself."

"And did you accept?" asked Gualbert.

"Never as recipient."   ...

By this time I feared Jones to be very much in danger of corruption from this Frenchwoman. But he would hear none of my warnings. He was, it seemed, still jealous of my presumed liaison with Madame de Reyniére, and believed I was merely attempting to spoil his triumph.

"So you believe my sensibility to be that small?" I asked him.

"Not small. Devious, perhaps."

"Then go to her. And go to the Devil, too," I retorted, and left him. Of course, with her husband's well-timed absence, he went off with her immediately for a stroll around the perimeter of the garden. The substance of their conversation I couldn't imagine, as they bore no common language. They remained out there in the gathering dark for quite some time, until only his white uniform breeches and her pink and white striped summer coat were still visible from a distance.

The couple was, of course, the subject of much speculation among the other guests.

...

Thierry raised her hand to stop him, saying, "You cannot imagine what they were saying to one another. Based on the gambits common to our sex, would you allow me to tell you, then?"

"Please, yes," granted Severence, intrigued.

"Ah, the contortions the intelligent woman must strike for a man! First, she speaks and understands English far better than you suppose. She reveals this skill only gradually, though, so as not to surprise or embarrass the gentleman with the sharpness of her mind. She apologizes for her momentary infatuation with Rousseau . . . she is impressionable, she confesses. Secure behind the mask of her beauty, she pretends unconcern for how she appears. Meanwhile, she compliments the captain, telling him how different he is, what a pleasant surprise he is, how free she feels to speak with him in confidence. She tells him a few minor secrets—some money she keeps of her own, for instance, or her ambition to write novels. Your captain feels privileged to know things about her that her husband does not . . . "

Thierry looked to her friend to continue.

Gualbert obliged: "She continues to touch him, but in such a way that her meaning is familial, as if being his sister would be a greater pleasure to her than being his lover. She hugs him tightly to her body, but turns her mouth away from his kiss. She wants her fragrance to permeate his clothes, his hair, so that he will think of her. She wants to be thought about."

"I am eternally amazed," Severence remarked, "at the misogyny of women. You presume motives in Madame de Lowendahl that would fairly be called Machiavellian, where I believed her merely hungry for the attention of a charming young man."

"That is because you and Machiavelli are men, and underestimate woman's power for both evil and good."

"You say she is a singer. Perhaps she promised to sing him a song later," ventured Gualbert.

Severence looked down, smiled. "Not precisely. But you are not far wrong in assuming that promise."

"Continue, then," Thierry commanded.

...

My disapproval and Jones's pride served to keep us apart for the next two days. When he finally sent for me, it was in the capacity of translator, not as friend.

I found him in his sitting room facing his visitor . . . General Lowendahl!

Under any other circumstances, I would have presumed the husband had observed Jones's attentions to his wife, and paid a visit to remind the interloper politely of his conjugal interests. Either that, or to ask for Jones's choice of weapon. Jones waved me in.

"Lieutenant, would you be so kind . . . "

"Of course."

Until my arrival they had stumbled along as best they could, Jones with his boudoir French, the Général de Brigade le Comte with an English so heavily accented it was hardly recognizable. Now matters moved more speedily. Lowendahl reached into the pocket of his coat and removed not a weapon, but a small, flat, oval object wrapped in a piece of linen whitecloth.

"This is for you, Captain, from the hand of the Comtesse," he said with faint pride, and handed the present to Jones.

Rightly suspecting the duplicity of a jealous husband, Jones unwrapped it carefully. Lowendahl added, "She devoted herself to this project for the better part of a week. I've never seen her so inspired by a subject—"

Madame's gift, via her husband, was a miniature portrait of Jones himself. His first reaction was, of course, to be flattered: he blushed like a lovelorn whelp from the circumference of his collar to the roots of his hair. "It really is . . . clearly is . . . remarkable . . . ," he went on, distracted by the spectacle of himself refracted through the imagination of a beautiful woman.

"And quite the likeness!" Lowendahl exclaimed, as if he were attempting to sell it.

Jones held the miniature up to me, cocking it next to his cheek. "And what do you think now, Mr. Severence?"

If Jones's question referred only to the work at hand, I could have called Madame's skills very well and good. The resemblance was clear, if somewhat womanly in its refinement. The artist had captured all of Jones's pretensions, but few of his virtues. Her version of his face was handsome, but only in the manner of a handsome watch, or a handsome pillbox. The powdered rolls she set athwart his ears made him seem like a perfumed poodle.

This, however, was not the question Jones was asking. Rather, he was bidding me to eat my words regarding Madame de Lowendahl's mixed motives. This I would not do.

"It is a handsome likeness, yes," I said. Meanwhile, I shifted my eyes suspiciously to the Général de Brigade le Comte's back, implying my real meaning, namely, "But why is he sent to bring it?"

Jones would not allow my skepticism to invade his fantasy. He set the miniature down on the desk before him as he continued his talk with Lowendahl, but he never took his eyes off of it for long.

"I fear my wife means to be as deep a friend of yours as you will tolerate," the other said, using the word *amie*, which, in the French, could equally well mean "friend" or something else more intimate. His perversity filled me with loathing and wonder. Did Jones understand the danger he was in?

"Then my tolerance will be very high," said Jones, the last word of which I translated a bit more coldly as *altier*, which more properly meant "high-minded" or "generous."

But the other merely wiped the air with his hands. "That is between you and her."

He then seemed to change the subject by asking after the prospect of his alliance with Lafayette. Jones, at last, resumed his normal character with his apology, "I know nothing about the alliance you mention. It sounds most intriguing, I'll admit, but if such a project were under plan, I would be honor-bound to keep it in confidence."

"Yes, yes, that is prudent. There are many spies about, many pieces of intelligence that may be obtained through informal channels. I assure you, no details will escape my lips."

And, upon offering this odd promise, he rose and dangled his hand for Jones to shake. This Jones did, looking uncertainly at the Général de Brigade le Comte, until the latter returned to the more pleasant subject by saying, "I shall tell the Comtesse you approve of her gift."

"I do more than approve," Jones declared. "I treasure it. It will follow me to the four corners of the earth, or wherever the cause of liberty shall take me."

"That is far. And please understand, good Captain, that the Comtesse's affections are entirely spontaneous. I believe she would be embarrassed to learn that you and I are friends. I assume I can expect your confidence."

The men stared at each other: the Uncomprehending facing the Unspeakable.

"Shall I tell her you will call on her soon?" asked the General.

Jones blinked at the man, perhaps still suspecting the sort of trap such liberal French husbands would probably find laughable. "Yes, I will," the Captain ventured.

...

"This Lowendahl sounds the dullest sort of clod," Thierry interjected. "Really, to be so indelicate about such a proposal! It is really the first skill of the professional: how to make a transaction not a transaction at all but a friendship. Or an alliance. Or if need be, a love."

"The Madame was no professional. Her skills suggest the level of devoted amateur," said Gualbert.

"Truthfully, that is the most dangerous sort of enchanteresse, the amateur. Lacking practical experience, she can either make herself foolish, as did your Madame de Reyniére, or apply too much persuasion where a little will do, and thereby invite the unexpected, the uncontrollable. She may half-believe her wiles herself. That is how hearts are broken."

Severence laughed. "Madamoiselle, forgive my shock at your sudden compassion for men's broken hearts!"

"Then you understand nothing, Monsieur. Broken hearts are the poison of this profession, as they make it all the more difficult for the next woman to apply her arts, as ill-used men are already marked by prior misuse, and on their guard. Doesn't common courtesy demand that the outgoing occupant leave the toilet hospitable and tidy for the next? It is the same with the use of men. Oh, how the field is ruined by these young girls! Really, there ought to be a law against them!"

...

Knowing her as I did, I would hold that you judge Madame de Lowendahl too harshly. At the worst, she was only employing her charm in the service of her husband's career. There was no way to tell if she would allow the project to compromise her.

For all the geography Jones had plied and memorized, he was now nearing shoals of which he was entirely ignorant. Against my proper advice, he proceeded to the Lowendahl villa the next day, ostensibly for the purpose of "presenting his card."

This time, my translation was not needed, as Madame had acquired a working English with admirable speed. Her pidgin was marked, he was amused to find, by an identical trace of Scottish inflection as his own. From this, he gathered he had been her teacher.

...

"Please, this is terribly too much . . . !" Thierry exclaimed.

"Upon Jones's return, I learned that 'presenting his card' had taken some five hours," said Severence, "and entailed the taking of an afternoon boat ride with her on the Seine. Jones later recounted this event with all the relished precision of a combat report. I will tell it all to you, ladies, with the warning that I do intentionally embroider events to further your entertainment.

"But you shall embroider only the truth."

...

The Lowendahls' sitting room, he told me, was modest in comparison to the splendors of the Hôtel Valentinois. There were narcissus blooms on the candlestand, and the consoles, and the serving table, which collectively filled the room with a pungent odor somewhere between the sweet and the rank. Jones was allergic to narcissus.

Madame was sitting on the settée, and had just left off reading a book. She wore a daydress of cream silk and satin and, on her feet, slippers lined with kid. Her head was bare and her unpowdered hair wended like molten platinum down along her neck and shoulders, behind the back of the sofa and, for all he knew, along the floor and out the door. She held out her hand to him as he was admitted, saying in perfect English, "My sweet Ulysses, you have found your Calypso at last!"

His answer was a sniffle. He apologized, kissed her hand . . . and nearly sneezed on her fingers.

"But you are sick!" she fretted.

"I beg your pardon, but there are certain species of blossom that have no love for me, though I have done them no ill . . . ARRRGG-HUMPFFF!"

Madame held the captain's hand as he launched into a fit of sneezes, her face a triangle of sunny compassion. "I'm so sorry. I feel as if at fault."

"That is nonsense, madame. This sensitivity was unknown to me until this instant."

"Then I must apologize for indulging my florist. I am something of a sensualist, as you might see . . . I will have them all removed."

"Not at all. It doesn't concern me."

From there, Jones persisted in playing the hero for her while his nose twitched and his eyes ran with tears. But it was no use—he was speaking more into his handkerchief than to her.

"But the afternoon is perfect," she announced, rising. Then, with a hopeless glance out of doors, she paced the carpet, finally confiding, "François orders me to promenade along the riverbank, as if I were his trophy! I won't do it, but perhaps with you . . . I can turn the excursion to my own purpose. Yes?"

For Jones there was no choice. After a brief interlude of twenty minutes, during which Madame rushed to attire herself for the out-of-doors and Jones suffered with his head stuck out the window, she came down in a silk gown of white with tiny embroidered bluebells, a summer coat of cobweb transparency, and a wide-brimmed straw hat trimmed with ostrich plumes. Her face, in accord with her natural custom, was left mostly unpainted, with only her lips brushed red and a light powder on her cheeks.

"Am I presentable?" Madame asked.

She got no answer, as her suitor was too busy blowing his nose.

Madame took his arm as they strolled across the back lawns of the villa and down to the river. As she was very nearly Jones's height, one imagines him standing very straight and tall as they stood together, as if with a rod down his back. She accommodated him by stooping a bit—but not enough to spoil her poise.

It was (parenthetically) as perfect a June day as ever had dawned, with a sky of flawless blue lit by a cheering but discreet spring sun. Above, the town steeples supported the Heavens and rising skylarks sang their songs of freedom and altitude. Below, there were young aristocratic boys in white dresses with bows in their hair playing "graces" under the trees, and Jones, ever the part of a perfect landscape in his gold-fringed blues and whites, walking the lawns with a profound validation attached to his arm.

The water offered up a humble rowboat at the foot of the villa's short dock. Jones jumped in first and, balancing himself, extended a hand to help the lady gain purchase with her heeled boot. He then said something like, "Though a master at sea, I declare this cruise is yours. What does Madame La Vendahl command?"

"Lowendahl," she corrected him.

"Forgive me," he begged, very certainly alarmed she would take offense. She soothed him with a smile, and an order "To the center! As far from the fools around us as we can be!"

"Aye, Captain!"

Jones leaned to the oars, laboring to bring them out to the middle of the Seine. He had taken only ten strokes when he looked to her, and saw her wipe away a tear with her glove.

"Madame, are you ill?"

Though clearly miserable, she attempted to smile, saying, "I know you but joke with me, but you can't guess how you gratify me. Most gentlemen would prefer to offer me the rank of figurehead."

"That is a compliment, is it not?"

"It has a head made of wood."

As the river is more than a quarter-mile wide at Passy, and flows with enough haste to carry a boat two yards downstream for every one across, I presume Madame's wish was not fulfilled without effort. Jones removed his hat and gave it to her to hold. As they spoke, she traced with her fingertip the white Bourbon cockade he had fixed to its brim. She was working quite hard to regain her buoyancy of mood.

"Would it be a matter of insult if I told you I am surprised at you, Captain Jones?"

"Surprised?"

"Most of we French are ignorant about Americans. We know only the clichés, or the stories of French soldiers who fought in the Indian War, in the forest."

"Then you have much to learn. America is a prodigious land—some

say even larger than Russia. Yet in some places, in the cities mainly, one
would as well be in Europe."

"A prodigious land, you say, but not the fairest too?" she stared at him.
He composed his answer carefully, saying, "By all available evidence, France
is the fairest of nations. But her wilder cousin has yet to mature."

She smiled into the blue. "A tantalizing answer, sir. You make me anticipate a visit."

"That," he replied, "would be my fondest pleasure."

What fancies must have infected the captain's brain at that moment!
What visions of Madame fleeing her loutish general for him, pining
patiently for him while he won the war at sea for America, and then emigrating to Virginia with him to adorn his squire's estate with her
sophistications! And how easy would it be for a discerning eye like Madame
de Lowendahl's to perceive these thoughts in his eyes!

"And I would be . . . oh, what is your word? . . . ecstatic . . . to be conducted under your guidance."

Jones swallowed. "That is the word."

From this point Jones reported very little of their exact conversation.
Madame went on to complain at length at the poverty of satisfying company in her husband's circle, and the dearth of any profitable activity for
her active mind, save her hobby of painting.

He then opened his frockcoat to her to reveal Madame's own miniature of Jones tucked there, next to his heart.

"I am flattered," she said, "but I will have you know, I parted with
that portrait only reluctantly, as I like to keep the faces of my friends close
to me."

"But you will always have the original close at hand, as I intend never
to stray far from you."

With that, Madame de Lowendahl's face contorted with the full brunt
of her misery. She cried like a little child, in long wails of utter wretched-
ness, and her glove was quickly soaked through with her tears. Jones
hurried to offer her a 'kerchief, for which she thanked him with a proper
"Merci," a charming smile, and then resumed crying.

As you might imagine, Jones was beside himself with confusion, for
he believed he had just attempted to reassure her of his feelings. More

practically, he felt helpless to console her, as even he would not dare take another man's wife in his arms so soon in their acquaintance.

"You must forgive me," she said at length, collecting herself. "It is only my disease, this sobbing. I've done it always, since before the beginning."

"But you are talented. You are beautiful."

She placed a hand upon his knee then, as if in return payment.

"Do you know, my dear Ulysses, that you are the first man ever to compliment my painting?" she said.

"That is incomprehensible. Your husband must."

"He hates it—but can do nothing to stop me. My Mama and Papa would not suffer to see me draw. They would punish me for it. And when I persisted, they wrapped my hands in bandages to still my fingers. They wrapped the gauze so tight, my hands could not grow. Aren't they small?" she asked, holding her hands up to him for inspection.

"Yes," said Jones, lost in lover's sympathy.

"But they could not bandage my imagination. I would draw in my mind—I would draw people, clouds, whole cities! I practiced so much in my imagination, that when the bandages finally came off, I drew even better than before!"

"Astounding!"

"But even today, my hands hurt me. It is painful to hold the brush."

"Do they hurt you now?" Jones asked her. She nodded, and with genuine tenderness, he commenced to stroke her palms with his fingertips.

"I would gladly endure the pain to be the artist I might have been," she continued. "To be recognized by the Academy, like Vigée le Brun." She sighed. "But it is useless to fret. I have lost my chance, and must take pleasure in the praises of my good friends."

With that, she fixed him with her irresistible eyes, leaving Jones with only the power to babble something about hearing of le Brun also, and his admiration of that woman's talents.

After this, he recalled they talked not at all, but floated together on the stream as if they were already lovers of long acquaintance, and everything had been said. Madame rested with her head bent back over the bows, her palms caressed, her face turned up to be warmed by the descending sun. She was a figurehead after all, albeit one faced in reverse.

I saw them floating by, in fact, as I looked through the windows of the Chaumont's music room. Madame de Chaumont was watching too, with a gaggle of her friends, and those servants with a pretext to appear busy in her sitting room next door. There was no discussion, just the drinking of tea, the resting of eyes on the distant adulterers, and, I sensed, the faint cynicism of the righteous and the bored.

I heard Jones's account of this day later that week, at the Hôtel Valentinois. He insisted on sharing his adventure with me because, he swore, I was his own dearest brother, and further, there was no one else to tell. Soon, I was also privileged to hear of their next meeting at the Palais Royale in Paris, where Madame had permitted herself to be surprised before a mirror, and had not resisted when Jones took her hand in his, and lifted it to his lips to inhale her fragrance, and offered his first kiss in the very palm of her painting hand.

To her credit, Madame de Lowendahl had worked a change on the captain. His ambitions now had a different thrust. I was now no longer useful in composing letters to notables in the French government; as of that day, I was called on to take the woman's point of view, and make objective judgment of his latest waft of romantic air. In essence, this love letter began, "Nothing short of my duty to the Glorious cause of Freedom in which I have the honor to be engaged could have induced me to leave your company. I will not attempt to describe here the sentiments that you have inspired in my Mind; Words would not do Justice to the affections of a Breast like mine that is all alive to the divine feelings of Gratitude and Sensibility . . . "

As Jones read this adolescent's panegyric to me, I noted that, for the first time since I'd known him, he'd forgotten to tend fully to his own appearance. Unshaven, he went about without his uniform coat, and there were spots of ink on his sleeves. His hair hung loose, untied and untamed, with a substantial lock missing at the back. This had been cut off as a gift for Madame de Lowendahl, it appeared, to be wrapped in a white ribbon with the apology, "I only regret that it is now eighteen inches shorter than it was three months ago."

Honestly, the changes in him were unnerving. Yet who was I to spoil such an uncharacteristic tenderness? I could only sit and watch him, knowing full well how I had myself very nearly donated my life to Madame de Reyniére.

Our next project would be to devise a cypher—or code system—that he would propose to Madame in order to keep their private correspondence secure. This consisted of the substitution of numerals for key words in a document, which could only be decoded by someone in possession of the key dictionary. Jones used cypher in his sensitive diplomatic letters, and never tired of inventing new barriers against prying eyes. A recent innovation was to send out six dictionaries, one for each planet, and to instruct his correspondent to use the one identified with the orb highest in the zodiac at dawn the next day.

In this case, he judged Madame to be unfamiliar with such machinations and restricted himself to only two full dictionaries, one for letters dated on days whose names began with odd-numbered letters (assuming a=1, b=2, etc., this meant Mondays, Saturdays, Sundays, Wednesdays) and another for even-lettered days (Tuesdays, Thursdays, and Fridays).

We had just had the pleasure of defining the word "esteem" as "99" on Mondays and "46" on Tuesdays when the mails arrived, and Jones received a note from Brest. Reading it, he dropped the message on his desk and rubbed his eyes.

"It hurts me to read poor English," he said. "Especially as poor as Mr. Joye writes it."

"Joye? What does he want?"

"'It is whit scat pleashore that I write to you in connection to the Mister Simpson,'" Jones read, "'the same off-cer we was informed to be out-o-bounds whit-in two cables of the *Ranger* but I myself would see milling whit the tars not a hop from our slip and causing trouble . . .'"

"Then clap him back into prison," I suggested.

Jones rose, walked to his window. He cast his eyes down on the river below, that wide midwife of his current happiness. It was on that water, I understood, that he had stumbled, for once, upon a pleasure that did not stem from his success. Rather, in his joke, in "serving" on Madame de Lowendahl's little flagship, he'd discovered the bliss of climbing down from the quarterdeck at last, and placing trust in a new Master. He'd signed his letter to her, "Your ladyship's most obedient and most obliged

Servant." I believe this was more than a polite platitude. He meant it.

"Franklin was right. What a fool I've been about this Simpson affair!" he declared. "When the Indian is mine, there'll be no time for pests."

And right at that moment, he took out his knife, sharpened his pen, and wrote a letter to the American Commission extending full pardon to Lt. Simpson for all offenses, with the added provision that he be sent back to America on the next available vessel, naval or private.

He wrote this astonishing instrument quickly, without his usual first draft, and after allowing me to read it, he sealed it with a carelessly large splash of wax. Then he rang for a footman and left the pardon at the corner of his writing desk for the man to take away.

With that, all thought of Simpson apparently flew from his mind.

"Let's take care to make the code for 'love' a low numeral . . . ," he said, taking up the cypher again.

XXI.

*. . . some time passed, however, before any steps were taken to
employ him in a manner agreeable to him . . . [with] many difficul-
ties attending any attempt of introducing a foreign officer into the
French marine, as it disturbs the order of their promotions, and he
himself choosing to act rather under the commission of Congress.*
        —FRANKLIN to the Board of Admiralty, Philadelphia, 1781

"I SHOULD assure you, dear ladies, that I have not only been telling
you my account, I have been listening to it as well. And on occasion
I have been puzzled over a quality of perverse pleasure that has crept
into my voice as I've sketched Captain Jones's travails. This is not just.
I could not protest if you rejected me, on that score, as a criminal
against compassion.

"But if you wish to understand it, think of it perhaps as a reflection
of my own story, not Jones's. For what man deserves to be the butt of
sordid mirth, when like Jones, his ambitions are merely to serve his
country, bring honor to his name, and, perhaps, to fall in love? And
what man deserves scorn more than the man who, like me, is the
stranger to noble ambition, who sees corruption everywhere, and is
motivated by nothing but spite?"

Severence paused to stare at the windows, into the morning light.
Neither woman challenged his assertion.

...

Any day we expected to receive word of the Indian's release from exile in
Amsterdam. Upon this news, we expected to proceed directly to its point
of arrival in France, where the re-fit and drafting of a crew would com-
mence. There was much to do—the procuring of new armaments, the
construction of General Lafayette's tower, Jones's inevitable tinkerings with
rig and ballast—but with the open assistance of our French allies these

preparations would have proceeded faster than they had back in block-aded Portsmouth.

Meanwhile, Louis's spies in London (or more precisely, the socialites who pursued their rounds across the Channel whether the countries were at war or not) had passed along the intelligence that the Admiralty was indeed expecting Jones to return to British waters, this time with a squadron of no less than four ships under his command! This must have appeared somewhat bewildering to Jones, considering the difficulty he had seen procuring just one vessel. Still he held, in his words, that "We must try not to disappoint them."

My next communication, however, was not from the Netherlands but from New-York. It was a small, folded letter, waxed without an identify-ing seal, and addressed merely to "Mr. Jn Severence, Navy of Congress, France." Though I did not welcome a message from that quarter, it was remarkable that it had found its way to me at all. I retired to my room, locked the door, and broke the seal.

From the handwriting I would never have guessed it was from Esmer-alda. Nor from the language, which appeared to have been somewhat "cleaned up" by the party that had written it out for her. In any case, it was undated, and read:

YOUNG BOSS:

> *I did not know where you are or whether you be alive to read this,*
> *but you have the news coming anyway, so here it is: your Aunt*
> *Hope has taken to her bed. The Physic was there, but he says he can*
> *do nothing, because she won't eat, and her heart's all broke, on*
> *account of that Affair between you and Old Boss. I've been sitting*
> *with her on the odd day, and seen her whisper your name in her*
> *sleep. When she wakes, she does nothing but pine for you, and*
> *moan that she sent you to your death in the Sea, because she was*
> *too much the coward to stand up to your father. And I think she*
> *means to die for it. So there you are. I won't tell you what to do*
> *about this Matter, except to remind you that she's got nobody else. I*
> *hope you're finding success where you are, and found what you*
> *wanted to find, whatever it was. I don't expect to be writing to you*

again. I haven't received a line from you since you left me, so I don't expect one, neither.

GOODBYE.

P.S. I long moved out of the old house. I'm by the Collect Pond now—on the north bank. Goodbye again, for good.

E.

I read the note again, looking perhaps for some clue to when it was written. In the least it could not have been any more recent than five weeks' sea passage, even if it had found its way to Passy directly. I folded it and put it aside, but found I could not take my thoughts from it.

The house on Broad-Way, apparently, had been sold outside the family. This would scarcely be a surprise, considering that my parents had no living siblings, and I was an only son. Indeed, the fantasy of my dear Esmeralda living on there, waiting for her scarred warrior to return covered in glory, had quite unreasonably distorted my presumptions on this matter. She was living in the slums near the Collect Pond now, quite possibly doing day-work for strangers, or piece-work to survive. Her new freedom, such as it was, did not appear to bear mentioning.

Aunt Hope taken to her bed, possibly to die! In truth, it gratified me, for I had meant her to be hurt as deeply as she had hurt me. Yet, though I had no intent of seeing her again, I would rather our estrangement had been by my choice, not by the intercession of eternity. With her death, she would escape my affliction—leaving no one else for me to pain, except perhaps myself.

She may well have been dead already.

But what was the foolishness of these women to me? In their weakness, they had both been complicit in my humiliation. To both of them, their just rewards! I burned Esmeralda's letter with a candle and washed my hands of them. And I cursed them and washed my hands of them for many hours and days afterward.

It was at about this time, meanwhile, that I presume Louis XVI rose from his locksmith's bench at Versailles, removed His Most High Royal Work Apron, and sought out the Queen Marie Antoinette. He found her, I imagine, in some faux-barn at the Petit-Trianon, milking a cow. (For both Louis and the Queen were so ill-fitted to the drudgery of rule, they

sought escape by fancying themselves common laborers. Those knowledgeable about such things held Louis to be a better locksmith than King,
and the Queen's skill at the teats was much remarked.)

He may well have asked her if she believed in his new war with England. Marie, for her part, was given to leave men's games to men, and not
presume to deny them their amusements. However, this business about
landing Lafayette on British soil was more stupid than brave, she said. For
the Englishman would surely retaliate and his Royal Navy give him the
capacity to attack anywhere, on terms of his own choosing.

Louis would think further on this, and perceive that the Queen was
correct. France had more to lose than to win in such an amphibious war.
A few words would then be exchanged with Sartine, very much in passing of course, very privately, as if what was recently the official crown
policy was suddenly not worthy of open discussion. Lafayette's landing
was, from that moment, a dead letter.

Still, there were compensations to be made. Benjamin Franklin would
be satisfied with some other favor, such as a French expedition overseas
to support George Washington. General Lafayette would be pacified in
assembling and launching such a force. And the Scottish captain—what
was his name?—would still think himself fortunate to get his Indian.

Louis then returned to his workbench.

The decision reached Passy at an unhurried pace, and when Jones
finally learned of it, it was Chaumont who told him, casually, over coffee
and pipes. Franklin himself was surprised to hear it: I believe he had been
more taken with the buccaneering scheme than anyone. Jones only
slouched deeply on his chair, his chin sunk into the fabric of his stock.

"So much for Lafayette's friends at Versailles," he muttered.

"My dear Captain, do not blame Lafayette," said Chaumont, in English.
"After all, the King had only said 'yes' to your plan."

"By appearances, 'oui' is not sufficient."

Chaumont laughed, saying, "At Versailles, a 'yes' is barely a 'perhaps!'"

This eventuality had, at least, simplified Jones's plan for refitting the
Indian for her cruise. He would not be obliged, after all, to honor his
promise to obstruct his deck with a tower for Lafayette and his lieutenants.
Nor would he be required to permit the French general to lead the land
force. There would be no sharing of the glory.

This French *oui* plagued us again with the next bit of intelligence to disturb our hilltop retreat: a visit from Arthur Lee, Franklin's fellow (and competing) commissioner to France. Jones, myself, Dr. Franklin, and Madame de Juoy were using the Chaumonts' playing cards (which the lady of the house had, after the recent fashion, stunk up with perfume) when this gentleman interrupted us. This was remarkable insofar that Lee usually avoided Franklin when he could, and had been known to toast the Doctor's "legacy" when he more likely meant the old man's imminent death.

Lee was a trim, severe man and appeared, like his rival, to prefer to be clad in the same provincial weeds he would have worn inspecting his barn in America. In relative plainness, at least, they were colleagues.

"Captain Jones, is it true that you have been compassionate enough to forgive Lieutenant Simpson of all charges against him?"

Lee had asked the question in a tone of apparent admiration. Jones chose to accept it at face value, boasting, "Yes. I did it only in service of the Greater Cause, which would be unquestionably harmed by any appearance of disunity."

"Unquestionably," hissed the snake. "In that case, I assume you would have no objection to our appointment of Lt. Simpson as master of the *Ranger* for the cruise back to Portsmouth?"

Jones virtually choked at this. He replied, with smoldering hoarseness, "That would be a very grievous error, sir, as Lt. Simpson is the most disloyal sort of officer!"

"Really? I understand he is very popular with the rest of the crew. And at any rate, you have pardoned him. Mr. Deane and I are in close agreement on this score."

This last assertion was directed at Franklin. The older man, however, would not rise to the bait. He continued to count the diamonds on his scented trump card, sparing only a single, brief glance at Jones.

"What is it to me? Do what you will," Jones finally said, his voice laced with disgust.

"As I thought." Lee paused. And when he had judged his claws had sunk sufficently deep into his rivals, he asked another apparently innocent question: "Say, can it be you've heard from your Prince Nassau-Siegen?"

Jones raised his head again.

"No. I haven't," Franklin said.

"As of yesterday he was playing the shepherd to the Queen's goat-milker. He wore pantaloons."

"Then his business is done in Amsterdam?" asked Jones.

"After a fashion. Yorke, the British ambassador, made notice that His Majesty would not look kindly on any aid to the Colonies. A clever writer, that Yorke! He turned the Dutch Orangists quite effectively. He turned them right away."

"That," replied the skeptical Franklin, "was expected. What of the Republicans?"

"The Prince saw to them, I presume, when he tired of all their dull parties, and had insulted all of their daughters. Then he quit the field, they say."

"Who says?"

"They all do," Lee said, rising. "But I have delayed your game long enough." His mischief done and looking very well pleased with himself, he then bowed his head in our direction, and was gone.

Our game, alas, had been forgotten.

"Could it be true?" I asked the doctor.

"Consider the source."

"With the Prince de Nassau-Siegen," said the Madame, "there is no question of his conforming to the most extraordinary rumors. I would believe them all."

"Then why send him to Amsterdam?" I asked her.

"Why, Monsieur, he is a prince."

Jones folded his cards. "Then the Indian . . . "

But he stopped. There was no purpose served in saying the words. To learn such a disappointment that way, from the lips of a swaggering rival, and to know his humiliation would be wholly broadcast amounted to the crucifixion of his dignity. He stood inflexibly, apologizing. "If you'll excuse me, I have neglected a bit of business . . . "

"Oh, sit down," Franklin chastened him. "Don't be such a boob. At least, not until we confirm his story."

...

Gualbert frowned. "But why was he so intent on that particular ship? Weren't there many others?"   ...

There were, though few quite so fast. For a raider, there are no capacities more essential than to be able to catch one's prey, and to run from one's superiors. The Indian was perfect for the purpose he intended.

But there was more at stake than Jones's ideal command. There was the matter that he had gone several months already with no command at all. He was, of course, finished with the *Ranger* and her disloyal gang, which had chosen the execrable Simpson over him. He had won victories and frightened all of Britain, yet he was a man without a ship, rotting ashore, while lesser men were at sea wasting good ships and stout crews. Would not Simpson's victory appear total now, risen as he was to claim Jones's command?

Franklin consulted his sources to confirm or refute Lee's account. We heard nothing more about the affair thereafter. Franklin's deafening silence was, in fact, more dispiriting to us than any of Lee's spiteful gossip.

Jones found his only solace in pouring his frustrations out at the slippered feet of Madame de Lowendahl. As this woman had temporarily retired to Paris with her husband, he composed long letters to her in English, with what he regarded as the more "difficult" passages translated into French (by me) for Madame's convenience. At one point I was called upon to render (and I paraphrase), "How the sun of your Esteem warms me in this still waste! How fortunate I am to look beyond this perfect Torture and aspire to becoming Worthy of your smiles at last! Though I will never cause the matter of our Exchange in our little Boat to become a subject for Malicious Prattle, my heart does wish to sing it aloud, and I am obliged to whisper it to my pillows by night. I speak my sentiments to no one, yet hope your own pillows are equally well informed. Oh my Lady Captain! I am made to appear useless and laid aside, and still have so many battles to win for you and for Liberty . . . "

This letter crossed in the post with an affectionate missive from the Comtesse, in French, dated just several days earlier. Here she confessed herself "quite delirious with the knowledge of Friendship with a man of such Strength and Compassion. Your Understanding, your Sensitivity to the dilemma of my Sex, has quite brought me to tears, so much that my husband thinks me ill! Do promise that upon our return to Passy we will steal a few more hours together in Spiritual Congress. Can you know how much I depend upon you . . . ?"

This note did much to lighten Jones's mood in that dark time. From resignation, he rallied back to indignation and fired off another salvo of letters to Sartine, the Dutch Republican leader Van der Capellen in Amsterdam, and to Louis. Nor did he wring his hands waiting for responses: instead, he mused publicly about retiring from military service, buying a farm in Virginia, and taking a wife (or, in the present case, someone else's wife).

Such talk fairly alarmed Franklin, who alerted his contacts in Brest, Paimboeuf, and L'Orient to redouble their efforts to find Jones a suitable ship. In this emergency, the hero was regrettably offered a string of truly awful vessels—ancient converted merchantmen, British men o' war so feeble and slow they were captured by the French—and Jones was obliged to reject them all.

Finally, in some exasperation, and at Franklin's behest, Sartine authorized an officer's commission for Jones in the French Marine. This undoubtedly would have smoothed Jones's progress, and would not necessarily have precluded a flag rank in the Continental Navy after the war (assuming any Continental Navy would survive). I imagine the French bureaucrats were most satisfied with this jiggering, which required only that Jones renounce his Congressional commission and temporarily hail the flag of another country.

Jones would have none of it. Before Chaumont and Franklin, he tore the proffered French commission in half, calling it "a dirty piece of parchment," and swearing before God, "I will never betray the flag of America, who adopted me, and under whose colors I would rather lay up as a private citizen than win the greatest glory for another!"

Chaumont snorted at this bullheadedness, muttering as he departed, "Then the devil with you!" Even Franklin, who understood loyalty, was growing discernibly grayer dealing with Jones.

Not that Jones blamed Franklin for the "insult." Rather, he took it to be yet another slap from Minister Sartine. "I fear that one more insult from that quarter will poison the well forever," he told me, darkly.

XXII.

*The Comtesse de Lavendahl [sic] was very pretty, and very young,
and very sentimental, something of a flirt, and a little, it will appear,
of a wag.*

—J.H. Sherburne, *Life and Character of
the Chevalier Paul Jones*, 1825

. . . (Sartine) is bound in honor to give me the Indian!
—Jones, in a letter to the Duc de la Rochefoucauld, 1778

~

AT LENGTH Jones and I completed the cypher dictionary he intended to provide Madame de Lowendahl. This had grown to be a document of fourteen closely written pages, with numerals standing not only for such elementary terms as "love" and "forever" but for such things as "avenue," "lunch," "ennui," and "brigantine."

This last was hardly copied and sealed before Madame's latest arrived at the Hôtel Valentinois. I was immediately summoned, and found Jones seated behind his writing desk, in his uniform, with her open packet before him. There was, I saw, a lock of hair lying by his cuff, and though at first glance I supposed it to be hers, closer examination revealed it to be otherwise.

He looked up at me, and I started at what I saw in his eyes. There was more fear in them at that moment than I had seen before, even in combat.

"Lieutenant . . . John . . . if you please?" he asked me, holding the note out to me. He had evidently been trying to puzzle out the contents without my help. His unfortunate mood showed he had perhaps succeeded too well, and now only required to learn the literal sense.

On the outside of the paper I could see that yet again Jones had failed to grasp her name correctly. This time he paid dearly, for she began coldly,

> SIR,
>
> *I am in receipt of a letter in your hand, and know not why, as I am acquainted with no 'Madame de La Vendahl.' I return it to you forthwith, in order that its goodwill be spread upon its proper object . . .*

I paused here, and noted that Jones had taken to his feet. His stiffened, half turned-about attitude appeared much like it did that day off the Irish coast, when, under the pall of mutiny, Simpson, Cullam, and I had confronted him regarding the first attack on the *Drake*.

"Go on," he ordered.

> *I must apologize for inadvertently reading the contents of your letter. The flatteries expressed there would indeed gladden any woman's heart. However, as your correspondent is evidently constrained by the bonds of matrimony, might I advise you, as a friend, to direct your poetry in a more availing direction?*

I folded the note. "Is that all?" Jones asked.

> *"P.S., I also return the enclosed items forthwith. Your sincere and admiring servant, Madame de Général de Brigade le Comte François-Xavier de Lowendahl."*

These "items" were the cypher dictionary, and the lock of Jones's hair.

He looked out the window for some moments, watching the barge of some wealthy Passien glide downstream under the linden boughs. From somewhere nearby, a mourning dove had the perverse bent just then to cry *coo-ah coo, coo, coo*. Yet, oddly, the sound only caused Jones to laugh.

"An extraordinary woman, that," he shook his head. "She is sensitive. I have displeased her with my poor spelling. Would you mind, Lieutenant . . . ?"

He stopped himself, and looked to me. "Would you mind, *John*, helping me to clear up this little matter? A short note will do, I'd think . . . "

I couldn't refuse him, though I sensed it was useless. I took up the pen and **Jones** dictated a gentle reply to me. This message was very much more formal in tone this time, presuming nothing from her. "The Madame de Lowendahl is fair to be cross with her Captain, as he has had ample opportunity to master the spelling of her name," he began—

> *As for the matter of your wedlock, I would not be a gentleman to discount it. We are friends without regard to Sex. But what would be the harm, then, in accepting a gift of sentiment from a friend? Can it be that you hold the nature of foulest Mankind against me? I think not, as our very pleasant conversation on the Seine should have proven to you beyond doubting that our acquaintance is cut of much finer cloth.*
>
> *I beseech you, therefore, to accept the enclosed Cypher, and to use it in the spirit for which it was always intended, to safeguard your virtue from the waggings of malicious Tongues. I also ask your leave to attend you in Paris, so that we may Converse. You have only to suggest a place and time of appointment, and I shall fly to you directly.*

It was a plausible strategy for Jones in the face of her new resistance. In a sense, he was retreating to the conventional tactic of the ulterior motive—of the suitor disguising himself as a mere friend. This shift cost him some degree of pain, however, as this was the approach he employed most of the time, and with women he cared far less about.

He need not have bothered. Madame had suffered a change, though whether a change of heart or purely of mind who could say? She immediately replied:

> *I regret dear Captain that I must again return your Cypher within, as I have no use for such an instrument. Indeed, your friend finds herself embarrassed by the manner in which she has misled you. What she said in that boat, alas, was no more than a matter of fun.*

(Here she used the word *badinage*, which implied a discomfiting notion of child's play.)

> *Her error is doubly grievous, as it has thrown a gallant man into*

moral peril and has shaken the bedrock of her marriage trust,
which is the source of all her happiness. Her foolishness so oppresses
her heart she may only complete this letter in Tearful Mortification,
well knowing the ruin which she very nearly visited upon herself,
her husband, and the good Paul Jones. The sole balm and remedy to
her spirit, therefore, is the Hope that she and her captain may
remain True Friends. Of this she is sure, as much from her estima-
tion of his Character as from the testimony of his own words.

    Alas, though I find only delight in the prospect of meeting with
the Captain again, I am saddened to discover that my husband's
duties next take him to Versailles, and that we shall have no oppor-
tunity to pause at Passy on the way . . .

There was more, but this was all that was necessary. Jones sat like a
dead man, his head no longer appearing set upon his shoulders, but posed
there, like a flask poised on the edge of a shelf.

"This place has killed me," he observed. "I have had my cup filled to
the brim."

I thought furiously to find something to say to him, but failed. For what
commiseration of Man can ever remedy even the most casual cruelty of
Woman?

     ...

"Some women," corrected Gualbert.

     ...

Quite right—some women. Or more precisely, the ones we cannot have.
At any rate, Jones was enough aware of his own crimes against Love to
make a show of philosophy.

"The breaker of hearts is himself broken," he observed, lips curling with
relish around this morsel of self-styled irony. "Tell me, Severence, do you
believe I deserved it?"

"Completely."

This surprised him. He set his eyes on me, searching my face.

"You have never approved of me," he said at last.

"Not at all."

"You can't approve. You have always been a Manhattan Severence; what
can you know of how the unprivileged struggle?"

"That is an impertinent remark, sir."

He had dropped the phony mirth, and I, in my turn, had abandoned all attempt to flatter his pretensions. Our conversation therefore lacked its familiar ground.

"Very well, then," he rose.

I was thanked for my kind translation and shown the door. And though he presented an air no darker than usual, I sensed that Madame de Lowendahl had finally stove him in—and that I was failing him.

I never learned what he did or what he felt behind his closed door.

This interview still preoccupied my mind as I passed to the ground floor of the Hôtel, meaning perhaps to settle my thoughts with a solitary turn around the gardens by the river.

···

"You worried for him," suggested Gualbert.

···

Perhaps, later. At the time I felt myself much aggrieved, as I had warned him about the woman from the very beginning, and he had ignored me. I had gained a clearer view of the strategical situation than he (the first time, I own) and found my wisdom dismissed summarily! I was not smug, and yet . . . I feared I had no compassion left for him. I had had my fill of fearing and lying and fighting for John Paul Jones. Was he not as disappointingly human as myself—or Aunt Hope—or, I shuddered, as my father had been?

In truth, my mind had settled with some measure of fondness on the prospect of returning to New-York. But I had scarcely had time to reject the thought when I spied, with a surge of fear, a face and a figure I had hoped not to see again.

She was standing out on the cobblestone way with her father, the commissioner Arthur Lee, and another man, whose back was turned, in the blues of a Continental Navy captain. Unfortunately, Thérèse-Elisabeth saw me before I could slip away to warn Jones, and waved at me, the wide sleeves of her gown flapping on her pale forearms.

"Oh, there's Monsieur Severence! Say, won't you come over and chat with us?"

Lee and Chaumont turned to look on me, and under their scrutiny I knew I couldn't flee a teenaged girl. Striving to appear unruffled, I strode toward her, inwardly dreading the inevitable questions about her dear captain, and the challenge of finding lies that would not also work to insult her father.

"Mademoiselle—what a pleasure to see you," said I.

"You've been hiding from me," she said, offering her cheek. "I've been back for an entire hour and a half!"

"I've been at business."

I pressed my cheek against hers. She continued, "And you must know Captain Simpson, I presume?"

I turned, my heart foundering.

He was standing there, gleaming in the French sun and his new uniform from Paris. There was a smug assurance on his face as he held his hand out to me.

"Severence," he said, simply.

I don't recollect actually shaking the man's hand: perhaps I slapped at it. In any case, Lee was at Simpson's side, his smile fairly whipping at me.

"Simpson. I didn't know Brest was done with you," I said, to which he replied, "It was not, but I am done with Brest! I take the *Ranger* out by the end of the month."

As he said this, I noted on Thérèse-Elisabeth's face a particular expression—a scrutinizing, and a gathering appreciation. If she did not yet love the "miracle" of Simpson's features, or the "music" of his voice, she was threatening such.

"We were standing here thinking that the *Ranger* still cries out for her commander of Marines," said Lee. "Should we assume you'll be available?"

To this, Simpson added, "Yes! Our complement would not be complete without old Severence. What do you say, man?"

"Oh, you must say yes, Lieutenant! There'll be such glories for you!" urged the girl.

"I . . . must decline . . . because Captain Jones . . . ," And I did not finish my excuse, as I could think of no reason other than the one they surely would not comprehend: foolish loyalty to Jones and to my debt to him.

Simpson shook his head sadly. "Jones! A good sailor, yes. But useless in a scrap, I'm afraid."

"And how is Captain Jones?" asked Lee, as if inquiring after a sick man.

"Yes," Simpson chimed, "I hope the little Scotsman is still fighting on our side!"

They all laughed then, even Chaumont.

Knowing Jones's plight at that moment, and the circumstances of his pardon of Simpson, I could simply bear no more. I bowed my head in courtesy to the girl, and showed them all my back.

From their silence I guessed that they stared after me in incredulity for some time. Then Simpson shouted, "He is finished, you know! Virtue has defeated him!"

"Think upon it, Lieutenant, if you bear any ambition at all in this Navy!" added Lee.

I neither paused nor looked back.

XXIII.

The Minister . . . has treated me like a Child five times successively by
leading me on from Great to little and from little to less . . .
        —JONES, in a letter to the Duc de la Rochefoucauld, 1778

Whoever considers the trivial pursuits that have ended in hostile
meetings between gentlemen, will recall the story told of a Neapolitan
nobleman, who fought fourteen duels to prove that Dante was a
greater poet than Ariosto, and who, on his death-bed, admitted to his
confessor that he had never read the works of either.
        —LORENZO SABINE, *Notes on Duels and Duelling*, 1855

∾

FOR THE first time in many hours, Severence stood, stretched, and
walked to the window. The women observed him quietly as he leaned
against the wall to watch the first stirrings of the day on the Rue de
Petits Augustins. He could see, on the opposite corner, a coffee woman
standing with her tin urn slung on her back, selling breakfast to passing workmen for two sous a cup. Waiters from the more enterprising
cafés were running about with trays, delivering tea and hot buttered
muffins to private apartments. It occurred to Severence that his throat
was dry from speaking so long, and that he was hungry, and that he
barely cared if he bedded these women or not. Or at least, he thought
he barely cared at that moment.

...

There is really not much left for me to tell. There were no further direct
communications with Madame de Lowendahl. Jones did not write to her,
though I suspect that he took her rebuff as only a temporary setback,
somewhat as he did his first attempt to take H.M.S. *Drake*. Like the man
o' war, she would offer him his chance again. Or so he believed.

Madame de Chaumont had never lost her admiration for Jones, despite
the fact that she was fully aware of what had transpired between himself

and Madame de Lowendahl. In fact, she pitied him. It was through her good offices that I learned an interesting fact. Stopping me on the stairs one morning, she engaged me in small conversation, and complained that the collapse of the Lafayette expedition had upset her social calendar, as some guests had suddenly realized prior engagements. One of these was the "Lowendahl duo" (she called them this, as if they were a team). Indeed, their letter of regret to Madame de Chaumont appeared to correspond exactly with the day the King had changed his mind about the landing with Lafayette!

My suspicions were vindicated. Taking this intelligence to Jones, I told him (albeit bluntly) that when he had lost his capacity to further her husband's career, Madame had simply reneged on her promise of love. There was no other explanation.

But this theory only angered him. Instead, he insisted that she had been restrained by the despotic Général de Brigade le Comte when her love for Jones had at last become manifest.

"Then you are completely blind," I told him.

"Take care, now," he warned, bristling.

Now with no crew to overwork, and our friendship strained, Jones would have to find someone to pay for all of his foul luck. Who this someone was, and what Jones did to him, forms the epilogue of my tale.

To his credit, Sartine had not been unmindful of the frustrations of Jones and his sponsor Franklin, and apparently sought to make amends with a letter offering the captain free passage home on a French frigate. This was only a further mistake, however, as Jones's sense of honor would never allow him to return to America until he was a success in Europe— a success Sartine had, he was convinced, barely lifted a finger to assure. Yet again, Jones believed himself deliberately insulted by the minister.

This was the last straw. Jones appeared in Franklin's office the next day, and demanded the old man's leave to "take the field" against Sartine! Fortunately, Franklin must have managed to dissuade the captain by explaining the political consequences of such a barbarous challenge, for his anger soon sought another object. Specifically, he marched directly downstairs, and found Simpson in the music room regaling Thérèse-Elisabeth with tales of the sea.

After making a show of bowing to the lady, he addressed Simpson thus: "I'm sure that we are agreed, sir, that there is but little good fellowship wasted between us. I had rather hoped that our business together was finally concluded, until yesterday, when a rumor came to my attention that certain words were spoken by you in insult of my loyal honor. If, however, you would disown the offense, I would be pleased to forget I have heard it."

To which Simpson replied, "You are correct to observe that there is little on which we can agree. Sadly, I cannot deny the rumor, but only clarify it, if it be your pleasure that I do so."

"Then please do."

Simpson turned to face Jones directly, and said, quite slowly and deliberately, "I judged that you are a very good sailor, but entirely useless in a scrap. Then I questioned whether you were still on the just side of the war, and called you 'a little Scotsman' as well."

Jones smiled. "Then I assume you are prepared to take the field with me, sir."

"That would be my greatest pleasure."

"Take care lest it be your last."

"Monsieurs, there is no need to fight over a mere girl!" exclaimed Thérèse-Elisabeth, who was nonetheless clearly delighted by the prospect. There could be no doubt that she was the source of the rumors that had reached Jones's ear.

"Find your second, then," invited the Captain, "and send him here to meet mine."

"You may be sure of it."

At last, Jones had succeeded in assuring a battle for himself.

...

"And what did he mean by asking for 'a second?'" asked Gualbert.

...

For this sort of project, the combatants each required a "second" to help arrange the details, to stand by their compatriots on the field, and if need be, take the principal's place should he suddenly be unable to uphold his good name.

He came to me the next day in my room and asked if I might do him the honor of service.

"Your second?" I asked him, "For your contest with a man you did not regard worth the risking of your career?"

"He is worth no man's career. But this is a point of honor . . . "

"And what of equality between the antagonists? Where is the honor in plight with a junior officer?"

"He is no junior. He commands the *Ranger* now."

"But he does so without a captain's commission."

"Damn your ratiocinations, Severence! I risk nothing more here than my life. And my good name . . . "

" . . . is your misfortune, and the sorrow of your friends."

Jones looked at me curiously for a moment. Then his expression became stern again.

"Then I shall presume your answer is no?"

"My answer is yes," I said, adding, "And may I ask something of you in return?"

"Of course."

"Approve my transfer."

The clouds settled more thickly around him. "Is that your price, then?"

"Call it what you will. This delay is hellish. I've heard of a war to be fought at home."

"How unfortunate." Though he was suddenly quite pale, there was little prospect he would reveal any more fraternal distress than this. He turned on his heel and told me over his shoulder, "I expect Simpson's second to contact you direct."

"Good," I returned, not looking at him.

After this interview, we had no contact until the Sunday morning he was to meet Simpson. As part of his duties, Simpson's "second" did indeed call on me; when I saw this man standing in the parlor of the Hôtel, shaved and neatly attired in a frock coat of pink satin with fastenings of mother-of-pearl, I was shocked to recognize him.

"Joye?" I looked him up and down, disbelieving. "You are Simpson's man?"

He tossed his head. "Ahh, it ain't such a bleedin' big deal, sir. They asked me out o' mere formlty, between you an' I."

"And this new wardrobe?"

"Can't very well travel about lookin' like a steward's rag, could I?"

"No . . . I suppose not," I said, knowing full well that this "formlty" had entirely purchased Joye's loyalty from Jones. Save for me, the Captain now had precious few allies left among the Rangers.

"How's about our business, then . . . ?" he asked me.

Thereafter, we conducted our meeting over cups of West Indian cocoa in the garden. Joye took this occasion to demonstrate his new, cultivated persona, handling the cup with a real attempt at delicacy, and restraining his tendency to slurp.

As Simpson was the challenged party, it was his right, under the customary rules, to propose the weapons, the time, and the site. It required but a few moments to settle these questions: as the wager of battle was officially banned in France, the two officers would meet in secret, at dawn, one week hence, in a pasture somewhat off the Avenue de Pont de Sèvres, a few miles southwest of Passy. Simpson, well aware of Jones's reputation with the rapier, had expressed his preference for pistols. Jones, I knew, would be equally happy to work his revenge by pistol, sword and buckler, dagger, or bare hands.

All that remained, then, was the problem of how many paces we would measure between them, and the exchange of the gifts.

...

"Gifts?" the women asked, in a chorus.

...

An occasional custom, chiefly among cultivated men who happened to want to kill one other. The practice originated for the purpose of providing for bereaved wives, who might be left with nothing after a contest except a dead husband. The gift would always be happily accepted. In this case, Simpson gave to Jones a handsome watch of English manufacture, with a case of gold plate and numerals of semi-precious jewels. Jones ordered for Simpson a bronze telescope with eyepiece of polished ivory, intending the barely veiled insult that the latter required help to see the flag signals of his commanding officers.

The problem of firing distance took more time to settle. Simpson's suggestion was ten paces. This was a sensible choice, and reasonably safe, considering the capricious accuracy of the weapons. Jones, however, held out for just four paces. Joye returned with the objection that this distance was suicidal, and bid eight. Again, Jones insisted on four paces, with the additional proposal to give Simpson the right of first shot!

Simpson was well disposed to this arrangement, but Joye and I forbade it, as there was no "right of first shot" under civilized rules. As the combatants could not agree, we therefore moved to declare the challenge null and void.

Jones acceded to eight paces.

The duel was possibly the worst-kept secret in the entire French kingdom that week. Wherever Jones or Simpson appeared, whispers followed them. Franklin called both men into his cabinet to swear such a barbarity would not be committed while America's sons would be more properly engaged in fighting the common enemy. The duellists wholly agreed, begged the Doctor's pardon, and of course resumed their preparations.

In due course the day was at hand, and I spent the night before pacing my chamber, fully at a loss to imagine a future for myself. Whether he emerged victorious or not, I had severed my attachment to Jones, and must, by my own honor, return to America to face—what? The prospect of returning home to a city with no relations or friends filled me with despair. It was clear that my absence from New-York had made this sacrifice all too easy for me, and that scorning Aunt Hope from a visitable distance would be a great deal more painful. Yet what was there to do? Neither loneliness nor apology suited me.

At last the gray cast of the appointed dawn crept over the village. The parties left the Hôtel at different times, and travelled toward the Pont de Sèvres out of sight of each other. The cabriolets rolled through the sleeping hamlet of Auteuil as the mist rose to swirl about the treetops, and the first rays of the sun shone on the heights of Passy behind us. Of spectators we saw none, though they surely were behind and all around, for as much as France legislated against the ritual (her laws condemned the surviving party to death, confiscation of his property, and official blackening of his coat of arms) privately she thrilled to it.

Jones and I said nothing to each other on the way, and nothing as we mounted the crest of the pasture where Simpson, Joye, and a surgeon waited for us. As the vapors receded, the trees were revealed all around us, alive with crows determined to keep up a steady din. There were cattle some quarter of a mile distant, but they tired of looking at us quickly, and contented themselves with a quiet chew. The Seine was as yet invisible below.

The antagonists had both chosen to dress in full naval uniform, each entirely clean and bright, with Jones going bare-headed. They separately met the surgeon, a Dr. Clément of Auteuil, whom Joye had discovered by reputation to be accomplished at treating field wounds. Widely known as discreet and proficient, he appeared perfect for the job, except for his urgent moral calling to end the practice of duelling. To this end, he ministered to every duel he could, in order to lessen their ravages.

"There is still time for a more civilized solution," the doctor told the Americans in turn. Unfortunately, he said it in French, and neither man was disposed to hear my translation.

Jones and Simpson then shook each other's hand, and waited shoulder to shoulder as Joye paced off the agreed eight paces on the grass. On Simpson's face I could see fortitude masking fear. On Jones's, only a bland tranquillity.

Dr. Clément suggested that, as a precaution against the infection of wounds, the contestants should void their bladders before they begin. This they did on opposite sides of the same tree, avoiding each other's eyes as they did so. As their urine ran along the ground, however, their respective discharges pooled toward a common spot, and began to mingle. Clearly, this would not do. They each turned to piss farther apart.

Meanwhile, I did idly cast my eyes across the field, back where we had come, and marked a strange black horse tied up not far from our carriages. Above the road, I could see a female figure watching from the opposite promontory, very much distant, but clad in black and apparently with a dark veil concealing her features.

...

"Madame de Lowendahl?" suggested Gualbert.

Thierry made a face as if she doubted this idea.

...

Just then, I could not know. There was no time. Joye and I flipped a coin, and Simpson called it correctly, winning the right to select his ground. He chose the right-hand, slightly downhill spot. Jones took the opposite, and as he waited for us to load the two sets of guns, called out to Simpson, "I trust you know that we meet purely on a point of honor, and that I bear you no abiding antagonism."

Simpson replied, "Though I have often found myself differing from you, I have never doubted your evident courage."

"Then I stand honored to oppose you."

"And I, you."

Having demonstrated their higher sensibilities, the two took their positions. As Jones had lost the coin toss, it was his consolation to take first pick of arms. He examined both pistols, staring along their barrels, examining their hammers, and generally ensuring that they were in good working order. He made his selection, and Simpson received the other weapon accordingly. Joye stepped out of the line of fire.

"I will call the first shot," I declared. "Is there an objection?"

There was none.

"Before we begin, I am obliged to ask the challenged if he is prepared at this time to offer his apology," I said. "Lieutenant Simpson, what say you?"

Simpson was standing with his pistol across his chest. Though a certain constriction was evident around his mouth, and he was wiping his palm across the back of his breeches, he remained silent.

"Then we will proceed to the first shot," I announced.

"And God help you both," muttered Dr. Clément.

"Gentlemen, the signal will be, Present, one, two, three. On the first word you will raise and train your weapons. You will not fire until the count reaches three, after which you will fire at your pleasure. Should one of you fire first, the other must return fire within the next count of three, as called by Mr. Joye, or that party will forfeit his shot. Do you understand?"

The duellists nodded, Simpson perhaps more stiffly than Jones.

"Mr. Joye, do you stand ready?"

"I do."

"Very well. We begin . . . "

I paused, hopeful that the rising tension would set upon the men's nerves, and perhaps spoil their aim. Somewhere near at hand a cow bell pealed lazily as its owner shifted to some fresh bit of turf.

"Present . . . !"

Jones and Simpson raised their pistols, both holding the heavy weapons at full arm's length. Even for a strong man, such a position was fatiguing. I held them there by design, and surely enough, Simpson's hand began to shake, and his pistol with it. Jones's commenced to rise and fall in the air, as if it were afloat on the sea.

"One . . . "

Simpson turned his body so as to present his right flank to Jones's fire. The captain also turned, but less obliquely.

"Two . . . "

Unfortunately, my tactics of delay were having a marked effect on myself as well, and I found the next word difficult to pronounce. Upon its utterance, after all, a life or lives might suddenly cease.

"Three!"

At first, I thought they fired together. I heard but one report, and an eruption of smoke that was frankly prodigious.

The echo of this shot reverberated along the hillsides, scattering the crows. Simpson peered anxiously through the black powder vapor and heavy air, trying to ascertain Jones's condition.

What he saw could not have pleased him. Jones was still standing there, having apparently been blessed with a clean miss. What's more, he had not fired back!

Simpson looked to his gun. "I have had a misfire!" he exclaimed, holding the weapon out to us in a spirit half disgusted, half beseeching.

The rules in such a case were most explicit. There was no redress: his misfire was his misfortune.

This established, Joye commenced his own three count, before the end of which Jones would have to fire or sacrifice his shot. He cleared his throat, and began, "Captain Jones, one . . . "

Joye, the sadistic devil, saw fit to draw his count out even longer than I had mine. I looked to Jones, and saw that his aspect was in its darkest cunning now—his hand was a rock. His chief irritant was now fully within his sights.

The fear was now flying out of Simpson unchecked. His face grew red, his eyes watered, and his entire body shook more severely than his arm had moments before. I believe he was in danger of opening his bladder again.

"Jones . . . I . . . ," he began. But when he saw the rage increase in Jones's eye, he stopped speaking.

"Joye, damn you . . . !" I growled at him.

"Two . . . ," said the other.

Suddenly, Jones's aim shifted. It rose and seemed to rest not on Simpson's heart, but his head!

"Hat," Jones stated.

And with that, he fired. Simpson's cocked hat instantly flew from his head, and did not land until it had flown twenty yards.

Simpson opened his eyes. And when he saw that he had not yet entered the next world, he seemed filled with a sudden confusion, as if he was the victim of some perverse trick. Sportingly, Jones had chosen to square the odds again.

Joye fairly slapped his thigh with delight in this. Clearly anxious for further "fun," he then strode up to the Lieutenant bearing the second set of loaded pistols.

"Mister Sim'son, you have the pick for the second shot."

Simpson, still shaken from the last exchange of fire, only stared at them, as if unsure of what to do.

"Just pick one, sir," said Joye, with an almost fatherly gentleness.

He chose. Jones took the other, gave it a brief examination, then set his eye on his prey again. Simpson appeared to be captivated by a spot on the ground midway between the two men.

"Once again, custom extends to Lieutenant Simpson the opportunity to make his apology now, before the second shot," I told them.

Simpson had had enough. He looked up at Jones. "If it is the Captain's pleasure, I withdraw my—observations—and stand in hope that he will accept my sincere regrets."

With that, and no blood, Jones had won the battle. His heart, however, was set upon winning the war. "I will accept your apology," he sneered, "on the condition that you acknowledge, in view of the public, that you were entirely in error when you disobeyed my orders, and in addition, that you surrender your command of the *Ranger* to another officer."

At this, even Joye sputtered. Simpson, who had been loath to apologize for making mere criticism, found his pride resurrected.

"Surely, sir, you are not serious."

"I demand these things with no view toward personal gain," Jones credited himself. "I do not personally seek command of the *Ranger* again. But I will not see you, nor anyone, rewarded for deliberate disregard of the chain of command. For the good of our service, I require your complete and willing surrender."

Simpson's pistol, which had been hanging listlessly at his side, was lifted to rest against his chest again. He gave his answer: "As I cannot truly claim fault that is not mine, I would be dishonest to comply with such demands."

"Then I recommend," Jones said, "that you shoot me down on your next opportunity. I give you first shot. But mark me, if I survive, I will kill you this time."

"The parties will fire together!" I corrected him. "Those are the rules."

"Of course," Jones replied, meanwhile not making a move to lift his weapon.

"I'll call this time," said Joye. "Any objections?"

"None," said Simpson, now rejuvenated at the prospect of a free first shot. And though I had warned him, I knew Jones would keep his word, and give Simpson every chance to kill him first, possibly upon the assumption that he would miss, and that the attempt would make Simpson's subsequent destruction all the sweeter. Meanwhile, I was yet again sorry ever to have been rescued from the *Jersey,* and ever to have met the walking exasperation that was Paul Jones.

"Good. We'll start then: Present . . . !"

This time, Simpson took until the very last moment to aim well. With apparent disdain for Simpson's skill as a marksman, Jones had not even troubled himself to present his side to the other's fire.

"Three," said Joye.

At last, there was a hit. Jones's shoulder was propelled backward, and he almost toppled from his feet. After regaining his balance, Jones looked curiously to his shoulder, as if inspecting the damage to some inanimate machinery. Simpson stepped forward in desperate expectation.

"Keep your place, Mr. Simpson," I warned him.

Jones reached up with his left hand and touched the torn remnants of his epaulet. There was no bleeding. Simpson's shot had torn this emblem of rank from Jones's uniform, but worked no deeper harm.

...

"What a terrible shot he was!" Thierry exclaimed.

"Or maybe a nervous one," Gualbert suggested, looking to Severence.

...

You are both wrong: this "miss" was deliberate. After performing this trick of marksmanship, Simpson dared stare Jones straight in his eye. In sparing the captain, he had proven himself every bit the man of magnanimous sensibility as Jones—that, and perhaps the better shot, too. It was a foolish point to make, I warrant, considering the promise Jones had made to kill him at his next opportunity. But it worked its effect, as Jones was, for the first time, clearly impressed with Simpson's courage.

Joye then asked, as he was supposed to, "Cap'n Jones, are you able to continue?"

"Yes," he replied, taking the measure of Simpson again. He must have seen there, on the target's face, a resignation of the soul beyond fear, beyond simple sadness. The lieutenant had turned his face up to the sky, which was brightening with the mist's ebb, and closed his eyes.

Still, Jones took aim, and announced his target "the heart" in the same way he had said "hat" before. I made the count with merciful quickness this time. Simpson still did not look at Jones, who, with an expression of narrow deliberateness on his face, cocked his pistol and shut one eye.

At the count of two I expected him to fire. At three, it was his last chance. And then my count was over . . . and Jones had not fired!

"I accept your apology, sir," he suddenly said, lowering his weapon.

The other opened his eyes, but said nothing. Reversing the pistol in his hand, Jones handed it back to Joye.

"And the conditions for this apology?" asked Simpson, voice firm, still rooted in the spot he had expected to die.

"No conditions," Jones replied as he retrieved the larger pieces of his epaulet. "Except, perhaps, that you approach me, that we might greet one another as new friends . . . "

And they did so, embracing each other like comrades. As they descended the hill to the road together, matched stride for stride, arm in arm, it seemed that there was no bond tighter between two gentlemen than the holy sacrament of shooting at each other.

"*Magnifique,*" trilled the Surgeon, apparently pleased his services were not needed.

I kept some distance behind as I followed them all down. Below, the morning fog had finally parted to reveal the Seine, and farther, the towers of "Sodom." The crows were returning to the trees in detachments of three and four, and the battleground was fast becoming a mere pasture again.

I expect there were also scores of eyes watching us from the surrounding hills and forest, puzzling over what had just happened. Unfortunately, at that moment I could have done nothing to enlighten them, except to say that the only casualties were several pieces of apparel.

"Thank you for your indulgence, Lieutenant." Jones looked to me as we neared the carriage: "Will you take breakfast with me?"

I shook my head, and he sighed.

"Your papers of transfer are ready. Please collect them from my desk today. I don't intend to be there myself this afternoon."

I heard his words as he said them, but my attention was seized by the figure of the woman in black riding toward me, mounted side-saddle on her huge black mount. Her face was still all but covered by her veil, with barely a square inch of her skin exposed, and that entirely on her cheeks and brow.

Was this one of Jones's prior conquests? Had she come to see him live, or to see him die? We stared at her, interrogating that half-face, and learning nothing.

"Good morning," Jones said to her as she rode by.

She didn't answer. However, there was a certain movement of her amber-hued eye, and a particular sideways glance, that I knew I had seen before . . . but with whom? Under such circumstances, with such a brief impression, the memory is quite useless.

"Odd," said the captain.

I stood a bit longer to watch this woman's back recede from me, preferring to think she was Madame de Reynière. But I never learned the truth.

XXIV.

SEVERENCE poured water for himself and drank. Thierry was embarrassed that they lacked the resources to offer him a breakfast. She decided her best strategy to conceal this was to keep him talking.

...

"So you went through with your transfer?" she asked him.

Yes. I own it much pained me to abandon Jones then, with no prospects to console him, but no one could argue that anyone had shown him more patience, more of the purest Christianity than I. It was really quite unusual for a Severence, this loyalty to another.

Through the offices of Dr. Bancroft, I learned of an American privateer, the 18-gun sloop *Tremendous,* that was due to cross from Brest in early September. The fact that her American destination was "undisclosed" did not matter to me. Any port would do.

I wrote to her master, one Peter Broadnough, and he agreed to meet with me at the Hôtel de Ville in Paris several weeks thence. I met him without notifying Jones, and proceeded into the city with only the darkest presumptions, as I had heard much from Jones regarding the venality and incompetence of privateer masters.

Of his competence I learned nothing that day, but a bright and loquacious soul like Broadnough's could easily have given "venality" a good name. This well-fed and cherry-cheeked master went about without a hint of a uniform, affecting instead the style of a wide-eyed, monied tourist. On our meeting, I was pleased to find he showed no recognition of my family's name. Rather, he showed more interest in exploring the Tuileries, and in purchasing dresses for his wife and daughters. Later we strolled across the Pont Royale, where we bought glacés and paused to watch the convicts downstream dig the pilings for the new Pont de Louis XVI.

Broadnough knew no French, but he made courageous attempts. To John Paul Jones he wished only the best, and regarded his placement on the Navy seniority list "a blanked shame" for which Jones had every justification to "pitch hell." It would be his honor, furthermore, to offer passage to a man who had served on the *Ranger.*

What a revelation this was, this exchange with an unhaunted individual, someone who spoke not in declamations but in normal questions and answers, and who knew how to take turns in conversation! A man, by all appearances, doing exactly what he wanted to do, and comfortable with the portion Fate had dealt to him. It was with bitter joy that I recalled that my life with Paul Jones was not the whole of the world, but indeed only an exceptional interlude, and fortunately very near its end.

I spent my last two weeks before meeting the *Tremendous* at the usual frolics at the Hôtel de Valentinois. The summer was dying: an occasion that, in the Chaumonts' circle, called for still more pompous *soupers* and garden parties. Franklin did his duty to attend almost every one, and very near the end tore himself from Madame de Juoy's protective clutch to speak to me privately.

"I have wagered the Madame five sous you will change your mind," he told me. "You would not make her any richer, would you?"

"Does Poor Richard wager? I'm astonished."

"Yes, he does, I'm afraid. Alas, diplomatic immunity corrupts absolutely," said he. And then, growing serious, he added, "This war has changed us all. And there is more changing to be done."

He paused as we looked at Jones across the lawn, very successfully charming three military wives just up from Brest. Despite his many setbacks of late, his social offensives had never ceased.

"I'm uncertain for him without you," Franklin said in low tones. "With one less reasonable voice, how shall he be controlled?"

This question, I believed, verged on the noxious.

"I have never 'controlled' Paul Jones, sir. In fact, I would more likely claim the reverse."

"I'm sorry," Franklin retreated. "Forgive my poor choice of that word. I meant, rather, how shall he be humanized until his luck is turned?"

"Humanized?"

But Madame de Juoy would wait no longer. "Papa, come meet someone!" she pulled at him.

"Goodbye," the old man told me, allowing himself to be towed away. "May we meet again under freer circumstances."

"Of that we are sure, as Heaven has no tyrant," I replied, but I don't believe he heard me.

My leavetaking of Jones was a bit less hurried. We had avoided each other, and subsequently the issue of my departure, for days. On the very last day, I descended the stairs from the Hôtel into the lower terrace of the garden, where I would meet my boat on the river below. Jones was standing on the marble landing, his hat perched back on his head, apparently admiring the masonry. I paused behind him.

"The Devil with you, Severence!" he said without turning around. "Why must you leave now? What can you accomplish back there that you can't with me?"

"Nothing, I'm afraid," I told him.

He faced me. "Remain, then. Franklin is on to a frigate, he promises me."

I shook my head. "I couldn't stay if he were on to a 64."

"I said, 'Pray remain.' I warn you, I beg before no man. But I need you."

I started at this unwonted desperation. Proud Jones certainly perceived this, for he added, "You're too valuable to my progress to lose now."

"*Your* progress, eh?" replied I, adding, "Your offer is most tempting, sir, but I regret I must decline."

"Then this is rank betrayal," he seethed. "You stab me in the back, though I lifted you from mediocrity. From obscurity. From your petty grudges. As far as you are a man and a soldier, you owe it to me."

At this I merely continued my descent without another word. Of course, Jones could not bear ending an argument with an insult that would leave him possibly disliked. Though I walked quickly, I soon heard his voice immediately behind me again.

"The *Tremendous.* Your conveyance is beneath you."

I paused, answered, "I would rather my conveyance be beneath me, than be beneath my conveyance."

We faced each other again and, after a moment of mutual scrutiny, embraced. Jones then surprised me with a parting kiss on my cheek. This gesture seemed hardly like him. I had never seen him do so with anyone but a useful female. It was a soldier's kiss, I might add. Free of the exigencies of physical desire, it was a sort of gift much sweeter and softer than the ones we launch against women.

"We shall meet again on the other side," he pronounced, "when my business here is done."

"You lie, sir, for your sort of business is never finished."

"Perhaps—but I fear I may run out of war to exercise it."

We exchanged salutes, and I resumed my descent. After a dozen steps I turned, and saw that Jones was still looking after me. There was no small sadness in his eyes, and he quickly looked away from me.

"In any case, you are no Captain Eighteen!" I told him.

He clearly lit up at this. But then he grumbled something inaudible and turned away.

And that, dear ladies, was the last I saw of Jones in France.

Of my journey back to America there is little to say, except that Master Broadnough turned out to be a better tourist than commander. As it was late in the season, and as he had taken a total of three lightly armed prizes over four months in European waters, he and his crew were far more interested in dashing home with their loot than in punishing the enemy. The first time we sighted a convoy of fat merchantmen, waddling along under the Red Ensign with their wales barely out of the water, Broadnough examined it only long enough to note its escort—a sloop of just ten guns—and to reject any notion of attack. When I pointed out how far out of position the escort was for a weather-gauge approach, Broadnough looked at me as if I'd suggested throwing their treasure overboard.

"Look here, we have a true fighter's fighter," he said finally with some amusement, pointing at me. Then he looked to his officers, asking, "Well then, fellows, shall we do as Lieutenant Severence suggests?"

His first mate shrugged.

"Why?" he asked.

"Your order, sir?" asked one of his ables.

Broadnough tossed his head. "I don't know. Take 'em or leave 'em be—it's all the same to me."

After such a rousing call to arms, it was no surprise the crew preferred to lay about the deck sunning themselves, or working at their various hobbies of craft.

I therefore made no further tactical suggestions. Rather, I kept to my cabin for most of the passage, and only came up at night and in the early mornings for a walk and a smoke, or else to sit at Broadnough's supper table.

The latter was, as long as the French provisions held out, as fine as anything I'd seen on the *Ranger*. Unfortunately, the conversation was not, as Broadnough brought no artistry to his role as host. For him, the meal was not a ritual of portable civilization, but mere food. His conversation revolved around real estate investments. He had nothing to prove.

In those weeks I had ample time for reflection, and in my anger at Jones and disappointment in Broadnough, I discovered I had little room left for juvenile resentments. I allowed myself to think fondly of my childhood with Aunt Hope again. With this, my resistance broke completely, and I took up pen and paper to write to her. I had begun—

> *I know you must be surprised in hearing from me again, after the wrong you have done to me—*

—when I recalled, with a shiver, that she might well have died since I'd received Esmeralda's last. With that I could write no more, as I had been seized with an acute guilt. For my punishment, I allowed myself to think of little else through the long weeks. Instead, I drew a dark mood over myself, and set my length of punishment at the width of an ocean.

By mid-November we lay off Rhode Island, waiting for an opportunity to slip through the Royal Navy blockade. Broadnough took no chances at this, preferring to wait for exactly the most fortuitous combination of tide, wind, moon, and enemy deployment to attempt a dash into the harbor. We flitted off the coast for two, four, eight days, in which time I sighted only a single enemy frigate. I paced the deck with rising exasperation, impatient at the very least, but more deeply concerned that Aunt Hope would die while I remained a prisoner of Master Broadnough's caution.

At last he gave the order, and I quit the *Tremendous* almost as her anchor struck bottom in Providence harbor. From there I purchased a horse and rode the poor beast to exhaustion along the Post Road, reaching New Haven in just four days. From the sale of that horse and the rest of my French currency, I bought a still-poorer animal, rode through the rain to the outskirts of Throgs Farm, and proceeded the rest of the way on foot.

As New-York was still under occupation and rife with Loyalists, I traded this second horse for a suit of field hand's clothes. Then I buried my uniform in a pasture in Bloomingdale Village and entered the city proper in disguise. I was, after all, still a "Manhattan Severence."

My first stop was near the Collect Pond, where I made inquiries after a certain party. This personage was, alas, very well known to her neighbors, and it took no time at all for me to find her. She was kneeling by a creek, sleeves rolled up over leathery elbows, with a mountain of strangers' washings by her side.

Esmeralda did not recognize me at first. I scrutinized her from the corner of my eye as I sat beside her, swabbing my neck with the dirty water. She was wearing spectacles, I noted, held in place over her nose by two strings looped over her ears. She looked not less than a decade older and no longer sang over her washing as she had in my father's house. Rather, she grunted with the effort of lifting her washing stone, and dropped it several times in the water for the pain of grasping it. Each time this happened, she splashed herself, and cursed in her island tongue. This talk had always amused me as a child, and I laughed out loud at it.

She looked at me, then fairly sprang to her feet as she exclaimed, "You!"

"Yes, it is me, my dear Esmeralda!" I replied, falling back upon my elbows. And as she stood there staring at me, I feigned insult, asking her, "And is this your best greeting for your returned warrior?"

When she had governed her shock, she surprised me by kneeling again at her washing. "What're you 'ere, young boss? I'd thought ya swore to stay afar."

This question cut me deeply. I allowed myself to become stony, asked her, "Perhaps Aunt Hope would be more disposed to a proper welcome."

At this she did not look at me. "I wouldna be that sure o' dat."

"And what would that mean?"

"It means nothin'," she said, "except what'd says."

"Then I'll go see her myself, and good day to you." I rose, brushing the dirt from my rags.

She allowed me to go some fifty yards when she followed me, and offered to take me to Aunt Hope, once her washing was complete. I agreed to this and further accelerated the process by kneeling beside her to help.

She looked askance at me for this favor, and indeed would not allow me to wash more than one stocking, as I did "the devil'wn job" cleaning a garment thoroughly. So instead, I rinsed, my arms plunged in the same frigid water as hers, sharing the same work, and thinking that perhaps this was not as elegant as high tea with Phillis Wheatley, but far less awkward.

"Y'shouldna come back like dis, young boss." she was telling me. "Writin' first would've done ya better a good sight."

"Why? Is she recovered? Or . . . ," and I allowed the rest of this question to wash away with the soap suds.

This seemed to anger her. "Why do Esmeralda got to fix it all? Why cant'nt all ya Severences go 'way fer good?"

"Come now Emmie, what's all this?" I asked her, pretending to make light of it all.

She looked away from me, and rising to her feet, told the ground with some disgust, "I'll take ya to 'er if ya want."

"I do. Where is she?"

"Just where ya left 'er."

So I allowed myself to be guided through the remnants of the stockade at Wall Street, into the town of Manhattan proper. It was only a few hundred yards to Aunt Hope's old house on the Post Road, across from the Common, and I was delighted with how little several years of British occupation had changed my mother city. When we reached her address at last, the only change seemed to be the gentler ravages of benign neglect.

"Why didn't she hire a man to work for her?" I asked.

"I'd not say," Esmeralda said, shrugging.

There was smoke in the kitchen flue, and the odor of fresh baking in the air. Was she still at making those mischievous gingerbreads, I wondered, giving them all away to the children in the streets? It appeared to me that the same curtains were yet in the window: the muslin ones through which I'd seen her looking down at me in the street, after I'd quit my father's house, years before.

At that moment, it was my firm intent to take back the poisonous utterances I'd made to her. Charged with a vague excitement, I reached for the door. Esmeralda stopped me.

"No, young boss. She's dis way . . . "

"What?"

Unaccountably, she led me away from the house on the Post Road, across the street again.

Our destination was a gravestone stood in the little churchyard abutting the Common. It was topped by a Death's Head, and beneath it, the name Hope Sarah Severence, with the dates October 12, 1728 to August 23, 1779. There was no other inscription.

The stone marked a plot closest to the road, and to her house. It lay precisely at the place where I had slept that night, waiting in vain for her to take me in, and where I had flung my indignation at her.

"She wanted no oder place t' rest'n," Esmeralda went on. "The men even 'ad ta move a body off o' it, afder she bough't from the fam'ly. When she got't, she wouldn't eat nothin', and die straight away. So you see, I 'oped ya never come back while I was livin', young boss, so I'd 'ave to tell ya no sad tales."

So as you can see, dear ladies, my flight across the Atlantic and down to New-York had been unnecessary. I had been too late even months before, when I had danced the quadrilles in France with feathered ladies and played the games of influence with which we filled our days. For while I'd done these things, she was cold in the ground.

She had died, and I recalled feeling nothing extraordinary in my soul on that August day in Passy, the twenty-third. There had been no quickening of the ether, no scent of memory descending upon me. I had been oblivious. I had proven the principle that Jones and I had held as the very foundation of our plans: that distance is stronger than love, and that we may even fashion ourselves into automatons without hearts, or more precisely, mold our hearts to love only the powerful, and the beautiful.

"So much for idle sentiment," I told Esmeralda.

···

Gualbert would have allowed Severence the solitude of his thoughts for a moment, but Thierry was impatient.

"And what of Paul Jones?" she asked. "Was your association with him really at an end?"

"Not entirely. There was a fairly consistent correspondence until several years ago."

"You have still not told how he ends up here, in Paris, now."

···

That, I fear, is a much longer story than I have told so far, and one I know only by hearsay. Let it suffice for me to say that he did get to sea again, to great effect. And when the war ended, and America had no further use for Paul Jones or a Navy, he proved flexible enough to seek his destiny elsewhere, fighting the Turk for the Empress Catherine. He even achieved the rank of admiral in that service.

But the principle of his success, which was equally alloyed with failure, never changed. Wherever he went, he found lovers, and admirers, and enemies, but few true friends. This continued to baffle him through the years, the basic indifference of the world to him, though he would have scattered his own vitals to fill it with color and combat and romance. The least indifferent part of the world to him, I gather, was the place where he had known Franklin, and myself, and Madame de Lowendahl. He therefore always returned to Paris, and always for the same reason: to await, in the midst of even the grossest chaos, the descent of the *deus ex machina* that would restore his faith in his meritocracy. He awaits it still, over on the Rue de Tournon, I believe.

For my part, I can't bear to see him. Rather, I prefer to send my thoughts wending back to the two cruises on the *Ranger*. Typically, as time passes I think less and less on the details of privations and disappointments in those times, and more on the broad outlines of what we had accomplished. Surgeon Green seems less the scalpeled drunk than a kind of jolly friar of our watery wilderness. The unmerry Cullam and Joye and Hall do fewer pirouettes in allegiance, and Simpson softens from arbitrary villain to loyal, even necessary, opposition. Young Dooley stays just as he was.

As the memories alter, so do my emotional reflections, until it all appears to me a sort of glowing moment. That is utter fiction, of course. I still remember all the true details. But I remember them as a service to our children, who might yet hear of John Paul Jones. Phillis Wheatley called him an "artist of battle," whose major work might be called "The Creation of a Legendary Career." This masterpiece is mostly done now, but it may well excel for nought, as it appears destined to hang in an obscure corner of the gallery.

XXV.

THE TELLING done, Severence poured himself another glass of tepid water from the pitcher on the table, then drank it down in three great gulps. The time by the Venus clock was nine o'clock, the morning hour indicated by the gold-foil sun ascendant on the mechanism's face. The candles in the room had long since burned down, and the women's faces were less well served by the brutish sunshine barging through the windows.

The women had wilted badly. Gualbert had virtually sweated the powder from her face, and without their color, her lips looked scarcely so festive. In the brighter light, Severence could also see that Thierry was not so beautiful as she had seemed: she had clearly spent too much of her life frowning.

"And so, what is your verdict?" he asked, soldiering on as men are wont to do.

Gualbert rubbed her chin in an appraising air, looking to Thierry, who looked at neither of the others. As Gualbert's inclination had always been clear, the decision evidently lay with her friend.

"When we asked you to tell a hero's tale," she began, "this was not what we intended. Isn't that so, Thérèse?"

Gualbert had no answer. She would have accepted the Lord's Prayer as adventure enough from a man such as him. Thierry read her face and shrugged.

"But as we see we are in the minority, we mustn't disappoint." And she got up from the table then, gathered her skirts up a bit to ease her progress, and moved toward the bedroom.

Severence was surprised. He would have contented himself with Gualbert alone. But Thierry's capitulation, despite her abiding skepticism, was stunning to him.

"You are coming, aren't you?" she asked him, turning.

"Now?" the others asked, in unison.

"Now," Thierry replied.

The heavy drapes in Thierry's bedroom restored the precious gloom. This left Severence to watch the women disrobe by the light of a single candle on the table. They did so with an economy of effort that reminded him of top-men in a ship's rig: that is, effective and quick, with no more grace than necessary to avoid disaster.

Disaster for these women was, in fact, a tear in their costly stockings, chemises, and gowns. Gualbert at least spared him a smile as she freed her breasts from their whalebone niches. Otherwise, his hostesses stripped directly down to their skins, and flopped into bed with him like fresh fish dumped from a net.

"Well, here we are," Gualbert told him, spreading her fingers through her raven hair to disentangle it.

"How shall it be?" demanded Thierry.

"Mmm?" responded Severence, busy now kissing the soft parabola beneath her left aureole.

"Shall we love you as women—or as whores?" Gualbert rephrased.

Severence paused to think about this for a moment.

"As whores," he decided.

Thierry frowned as she offered her breast for him to resume. "You are a cold man, sir," she told him. "But before we begin, may I ask you a final favor?"

"Of course," he mumbled, engrossed.

"Do you know where I can find Jones?"

By noon Severence rose and dressed again. Though he had succeeded in the evening's plan, he was conscious of a definite dissatisfaction. He was, for instance, fairly sure his "prize" had not been worth the exertion, since the women had later become very pointedly bored in their giving. At heart he was no real sexual adventurer, and lacked the courage to push their cynical coupling toward its logical fruition: namely, to give himself over to complete and honest depravity.

Worse, he had finally become conscious of the fact that he had exposed himself before these women not only in body, but in soul, by telling them his history. He feared blackmail, though he could not imagine exactly how it could be done. Thierry had asked for Jones's address—had he made a mistake in telling her what he knew?

Such questions dogged him as he bid them courteous goodbyes at the door. Why, indeed, was Thierry so ready to see him off? Why were tears standing in Gualbert's eyes, when he believed he had spent as much time inside her as in her friend? Why could the three of them barely stand to look at one another?

Turning into the street, he adjusted his Pennsylvania hat, switched his cane to the other fist, and checked the synchrony of his fine watches, all because he felt at that moment a chill that penetrated him through and through.

"I'll be married," he told himself. "Yes, that will do nicely."

Armed with this prescription, his hope was momentarily restored. He then turned his attention to the coming day at the Hôtel de Ville, where he would gladly lose himself in the comforting oblivion of money and influence.

The women were perhaps only slightly less cool with each other after Severence's departure. Though their recent frugality had forced them to start bathing together, they did not speak. Gliding a sponge over Thierry's back, Gualbert pitied herself and wished the rest of the world could love as fully as she. Thierry, as she wrapped Gualbert in a sheet, despised her friend's regard for Severence. He, after all, had not been the prize, but only the messenger of a finer sort of manhood.

She could not stop thinking about Paul Jones. The fact that he was on the Rue de Tournon, mere steps away, increased her temptation. She would go to see him.

"To the milliner's today?" Gualbert asked her, adopting the fractured speech of the all too familiar.

"Mmm," was Thierry's response, as she stood before her closet. She removed a canary yellow circassienne—one she could not have resold in those days if she had tried—and held it against her body. Gualbert saw her and laughed.

"Nathalie, that gown is ten years old! You can't be thinking of wearing it!"

Thierry cocked her head in the glass. "You're right. It's too yellow." And she put the dress back.

"Too yellow for what?"

She finally settled on a more modest redingote, a tasseled velvet jacket of red with satin reverses, and a pretty lingerie tie, all more than ten years old. As she could scarcely wear such retrograde fashions openly, she covered herself with a simple overcoat of cloth and a suitably modest hat for her wigless head. As a further precaution, she also ripped the tassels off her wicker walking cane.

It occurred to her, as she crossed the Rue du Colombier and allowed her eyes to scale the walls of the Abbey de Germain on her left, that Paul Jones might not be home when she knocked on his door. As she was used to being called upon, not calling on others, she had no card to leave him.

Nathalie-Anne Thierry was of that species of mind, however, that was not stopped by minor obstacles. Instead, she interpreted them as evidence of the preference of Fate. If Jones wasn't there, she would leave no card, no message. Nor would she return. She would accept that she had tried, and sustain herself with that.

She found the Rue de Tournon to be a fine avenue, cooled by spreading elm trees, and lined with respectable properties probably rented out by minor merchants and government functionaries. It seemed hardly awake at 11 o'clock on a weekday morning: the residents, it seemed, were either all out tending to their various businesses in the city, out strolling in the Palace du Luxembourg gardens at the end of the street, or else living quietly on their stipends and legacies behind their handsome, sealed doors.

Severence had not known Jones's exact house number. She needed to inquire only once, however, of a knife-sharpener set up by the trunk of a tree. This man only grimaced, saying, "You mean the 'Admiral,' eh?", and, after indicating the correct house, laughed with his customers at her. She repaid him with a freezing stare, and swinging her hips in a contemptuous show of power, crossed the street to number 52.

No one stopped her as she entered the six-storied townhouse and, by reading the names on the doorplates, pursued her search up to the third floor. That was where she found the name "JN. P. Jones" on the otherwise undistinguished door to a front apartment.

Her strategy next called for her to remove her plain overcoat. After assuring herself that the satin turnbacks in her jacket were folded properly outward, and that a single pleasing lock curled over her forehead from beneath her bonnet, she took several deep breaths and knocked.

Nothing. She knocked again, louder this time, and drew what sounded like a hacking cough from within.

She heard steps, and saw a shadow occlude the light under the door. The knob turned—and there Jones stood.

"Madame?" he asked.

As Thierry had her back to the hallway window, and Jones was standing in its full glare, she had an opportunity to appraise him first. Though Severence had told her numerous times that he was a short man, she had not imagined him short and was startled to find her head level with his. The smoky blond hair she had expected was faded, shot through now with tendrils of gray. He was not wearing his American uniform, but rather a pair of plain blue breeches, and blouse of unbleached white.

"Monsieur Captain, do you not recognize me?" she asked him in English, taking several steps so the light would fall on her good side.

"Recognize? No," he said, blinking.

Now her appearance was revealed to him, in the full glory of fashion from half a generation previous. His eyes dipped up and down to seize her lure. She pressed on, "You knew my mother—the Madame de Reyniére." And she punctuated her fib by extending her gloved hand to him.

"You . . . are *her* daughter?" he stumbled, taking her hand.

"Nathalie," she told him. And when he said nothing, she asked, "Do you disbelieve me?"

"No," he said, bending finally to kiss her fingers. "I'm taken aback. It's been a very long time." And as he continued to hold her hand, she could feel his arm quivering. She withdrew her hand.

"It hasn't been so long that you would not honor me with your time, Monsieur Captain?"

He smiled then. It was the first clearly attractive thing he had done. "Not at all," he assured her.

XXVI.

I'm nobody! Who are you?
Are you nobody, too?
Then there's a pair of us—don't
Tell!
They'd banish us, you know.
How dreary to be somebody!
How public, like a frog
To tell your name the livelong
June
To an admiring bog!

— EMILY DICKINSON

JONES'S apartment, though tidy, was unbearably impersonal and mannish. There was only a single comfortable chair in his sitting room, and by the lack of books or a writing table, Jones looked to have been sitting in it for hours, doing nothing. This was depressing, and Thierry could only stand to spend a few minutes there. She creatively parried a question regarding her "mother," by asking, "Shall we stroll outside? It's very pleasant out today."

He glanced toward the window. This was a mere mannerism, as his shutters were shut tight. "Yes, I suppose it is. Of course, let's go outside," he said.

Out in the world again, Thierry attempted to do him honor by attaching herself to his arm like a trophy. If he did at last suspect what sort of woman she was, his sallow and salt-blasted face didn't show it. Instead, in a gesture of automatic chivalry, he cocked his arm out for her to take.

"So faded a man, so wasted and alone," thought Thierry as she curled her arm around his. "Still, to the last, he remains a gentleman."

She drank deep from the dregs of his refinement, daring to shut her eyes and pretend she was back beneath the sweet sunbeams of the Old Regime. In such an evening she would no doubt be engaged in an assignation, wearing her own blue satin *pelisse* in the streets without fear of being beaten by roving egalitarians, about to be fed and flattered and bedded properly like the high-class goods she knew she was. If she opened her eyes, she knew she would again be confronted with the reality of the year 1792, which for her was not *"Liberté, Ègalité, Fraternité"* but a hare-lipped rent collector's assistant, tossing her roughly over her bedrail and picking open the crevice of her sex with his chapped fingers. Knowing what she would see, she therefore did not open her eyes. Instead, she felt Jones's lips on her ear, the rush of exhaled air, and his voice beside her, whispering, *"La Vendahl, je t'aime, je t'aime . . . "*

He was no longer sane. And yet, what quality of insanity was this, that mistook her for a witty and beautiful Comtesse? What sort of madness could compel a man to believe Thierry could be his muse, the woman that possessed his heart and haunted his delirium? She kept her eyes closed and asked herself, Why not? Would she not make a better "La Vendahl" than "La Vendahl" herself? Would Thierry not spread more happiness than she, with her pride and airs and coldness of carved stone, like the rest of her family's unfeeling bone chinas and alabasters? Could Thierry ever be so patriotically irresponsible as to deny her love to a man like Paul Jones, who had humbled the enemy of France?

Thierry felt herself very close to allowing herself the weakness of a long cry. She would cry, she planned, because she might have to grant that she was perhaps not so well cut out for her profession. Either her heart or a razor in the bathtub would soon catch up with her. If it was the first, it would cost her no end of trouble.

She kept her eyes closed, letting Jones lead her.

Thierry could hear the street around her, on the other side of her eyelids. Though pleasant, it was, after all, a typical street. To her right, the rag picker was plying his trade as his lame horse struggled on three-and-a-half clip-clops on the cobbled pavement. Farther on, she could hear the rustle of hollow shells as customers picked over the nutseller's poor inventory. There was a squabble as a boy seized a handful of nuts and attempted to run off—the seller cursed, called for some honest Citizen to catch the felon. The boy ran into the street in his bare feet, in front of the ragpicker's wagon, which hauled to a stop after only two-and-a-half clip-clops. Several Citizens made half-hearted attempts to grab the boy. But he evaded them all and escaped into an alley, no one following because one of his pursuers had sprained an ankle slipping on a pile of horse manure and was now demanding compensation from the nutseller, who denied liability. A small crowd rubbernecked, grew bored, dispersed. Somewhere, a churchbell rang five.

There was a little girl clomping about in her father's shoes nearby, playing with a cooper's discarded barrel hoop. Above, a housewife slid a window open on its scratchy frame, held some newly washed bedclothes out over the street, and gave them a hard "snap." Thierry could feel drops of dirty wash-water fall upon her cheeks and cling there, very much like the tears she was crying at that moment out of her pity for Paul Jones, for herself, and for what her Paris had become.

Then something unexpected happened. She felt something being swung around her shoulders and looked to Jones. He was draping his own coat over hers.

"There's a chill coming in. A *tramontana*," he told her. Then he paused, and with no trace of indictment in his voice, asked, "Who are you, really?"

Thierry turned to him. Her finger felt the hard wool lapel of his old Russian admiral's uniform coat, and she felt a sudden hunger for him to answer his question for her—to tell her, quickly, if she was a Comtesse, or a friend, or just a whore.

"Who am I?" she demanded of him. And when Jones only looked back, uncomprehending, she repeated, "Who would you have me be? Tell me."

Instead, he placed his hand on her arm and asked banally, "Are you all right?"

A bolt of indignation shot through her. Saying nothing to him, Thierry turned and sought out the little girl playing with the barrel hoop. Thierry offered the child her last *sou* in exchange for the tricolor rosette pinned to her little smock. A smart trader, the girl accepted the sale and skipped off to buy herself a handful of twists. Thierry fixed the rosette to her tulle and taffeta bonnet—her plain, depressingly Republican tulle and taffeta bonnet—and stood up on a wooden crate lying beside the nutseller's cart.

The second she mounted above the rest of the crowd, Thierry saw hundreds of eyes turn immediately toward her. It was not that the passersby exactly knew or cared what she intended to announce. More likely, they hoped for a session of bracing demagoguery to exercise their dormant passions. It had become a sort of national sport, with all the purely academic seriousness that word implied. She had scarcely assured her balance on the crate when she looked up and saw a mob gathering in a semicircle around her, looks of critical expectation on all the people's faces, as if they expected to grade her performance.

A little way off, Jones stood watching, uncertain, shivering without his uniform coat.

"Citizens!" she began, a bit too hoarsely. Her voice broke on the next word—she coughed. Several in the crowd shuffled their feet impatiently. "Citizens!" she resumed, frightened to her core, but determined. "I am crying for you. I am crying for France. I stand here before you, an ignorant woman, but knowing full well that our Motherland's best days are behind her. I cry because I know the armies of foreign kings will soon scar our beloved ground with the hooves and wheels of their armies. Nothing can stop the invaders now. Even now they plot the division of loot—the Loire to this Prussian baron, Ile de France to that whey-faced British lord, the gardens of Versailles turned into a field for their polo ponies. It is inevitable. It is too late . . . "

The second she opened her mouth she lost twenty percent of her audience. Most of the rest looked on skeptically, granting her momentary manipulation of their prejudices. A smaller minority stood agape, genuinely frightened by the picture she was painting.

"You ask me how I know these things, how I can be so sure in consigning France to the ranks of the servile nations? I might ask you a question first: how long may a nation live if she neglects her legacy? How long, if she bears contempt for the greater part of her patrimony—the men who have sustained her, lifted her, brought luster to her name? Poets sing of glory eternal, but there is no such thing in France. Indeed, why bring such glory to France if it will not live out a single season in the hearts of men? Better to work a trade, or attend to a desk or, better yet, fight for France's enemies!"

Somewhere in the crowd a man shouted, "No!" A number of her more gullible listeners seconded the denial. Meanwhile, the great majority of the mildly interested, the marginally entertained, opted to perpetuate this vacation from the dull afternoon by playing along.

Jones watched in what seemed like increasing horror. As Severence had informed her, the admiral clearly abhorred the Mob. Yet he looked unable to tear himself away, possibly anticipating that he would soon be called upon to do the gallant thing and rescue Thierry from several hundred coarse and unwashed *sans culottes*.

"Do you need proof of what I say?" Thierry asked, her confidence rising. "You need not look beyond this street. Among us right now, you ignore a man who once brought a smile of satisfaction to all your faces. An ally he was, fighting for a republic across the sea—the very republic that proved to us that the spirit of liberty must prevail! By his courage and by his brilliance, he humbled haughty Britannia in her own chosen arena! His victory came at the expense of knight and aristocrats, though he was no more than a low-born gardener's son. Men admired him, women aspired to be near him, and boys took to playing sea captain just to be like him! Composers from all of Europe dedicated songs to him. Can it be you've already forgotten his name? Is Paris a city of hypocrites? When you honored him, you honored the best in yourselves. Can you remember his name even now, after I've reminded you?"

No one seemed to know the man she spoke about.

"Do you remember . . . Paul Jones?" Thierry asked.

The question was not necessary, because the name didn't matter. Suddenly a litter of boys reared their heads back and veritably screamed the name: "Paul Jones!" Girls linked arms and took turns chanting first "Paul," then "Jones," back and forth, over and over. Even the skeptical majority, finally realizing the identity of the mystery hero, took up the chorus. A man wearing carpenter's overalls and a torn canvas feed bag on his head leapt forward and demanded, "Where is he?" The question reverberated through the mob, until it was being shot at her from all sides.

Thierry extended her hand in the direction of the dumbfounded Jones.

"See him there, already accepting his ill-served fate bravely, without complaint, wishing nothing more for himself but the dignity of his memories. Can we allow him to settle for that, Citizens?"

"No!"

"Will it serve France to forget Paul Jones?"

"No!"

"Then what will we do?"

"GET HIM!" they screamed, surging forward in a mass. The mob surrounded Jones and crowded upon him, all of them struggling to reach him and give him a pat on the shoulder, a kiss, or a word of tardy thanks for his unspecified exploits. His initial steps toward escape now blocked, Jones stood stock still, his arms stiffly at his sides.

Thierry watched it all from her box, taking particular note of Jones's reactions. All this unregulated goodwill gravely unnerved the hero. The acclaim might only have served to remind him of subsequent disappointments—the Simpson debacle, his failure with "La Vendahl," his lack of recognition from Empress Catherine, the years of boredom and inactivity. When they lifted him on their shoulders, Jones's expression was sour, impatient, anxious; the face of a man who believed he was a fraud and awaited apprehension. His eye met hers and seemed to ask her, "Why?"

Her answer, if she'd offered it, would have been that his private feelings didn't matter. She had done it all to ennoble the Parisians, not him—to turn their thoughts to old-style adventure, heroism, and history again, beyond that diminished republican world of wages, bread, fornication. It was actually Jones who was elevating the Mob, not the reverse. She merely hoped he could enjoy it.

He wasn't. The welter of hands, fingers, lips, elbows, all jabbing toward him in affectionate proximity had disheveled his carefully groomed appearance. His sword was gone. His hat was knocked off and trampled. His hair came loose from its ribbon and fell around his shoulders. In their love for him, the merchants and farmers who lifted him skyward had not thought to support him adequately, and the maneuver had twisted the small of his back.

"Take your hands off me!" he ordered in his loudest quarterdeck voice.

"You rascals will pay the piper, I'll warrant!" But they all laughed at him, believing him modest, and chanted his name so loudly no one could hear his protests.

Jones looked more a flopping effigy than a living monument as they carried him down the street. To his credit, he held on tenaciously, served well by instincts honed in years of riding out storms at sea. His face set, his arms splayed out to brace himself, his body bent over toward the good side of his back, he waited grimly for his apotheosis to end.

They took him first down the Rue de Tournon toward the Palais du Luxembourg, shouting, "*Vive* Paul Jones!", "*Vive* America!" With Thierry following, herself entirely forgotten, they turned right on the Rue de Vaugirard, skirted the palace gardens, and went right again on the Rue Garanciere, toward the Church of Saint Sulpice. Passersby stopped, gawked at the procession, asked after the little man being carried aloft. When some heard the name, they nodded, hailed the hero from afar, and went about their business. Others joined the mob. Still others had never heard of him, but that didn't prevent them from participating. The well-wishers soon carried him too close to a row of small shops on Rue Garanciere—Jones struck his head twice, first on a millinery sign, then on the painted plaster figure of a smiling boar, in front of a tavern. He cursed, demanded to be released. Thierry couldn't hear him.

The parade reached the close of St. Sulpice and curled around, making for the Rue du Vieux Colombier. Several enterprising fellows had already begun to reap profit from the event, selling tricolor rosettes and ribbons bearing the Stars and Stripes from rucksacks. Hobos from all over the district converged in hopes of capitalizing on this minor patriotic ejaculation. A bugler had materialized from somewhere, trumpeting rousing anthems and doffing his cap for contributions.

Jones's impromptu triumph had gotten off to a good start. However, when it reached the Croix Rouge Square, someone recognized a figure in a cocked hat and cloak, walking by himself. A name was shouted out— the Marquis de Sade—and all eyes turned to the solitary figure. The Jones procession stopped in its tracks. Many bent to their neighbors to ask who de Sade was, but when they learned his significance they were fired with excitement. Thierry knew who he was: he was a notorious child molester and profligate, who happened to be one of the handful of inmates rescued by the storming of the Bastille.

Her worst fears were realized when Jones was abruptly dropped to the ground and everyone made off to honor this most famous former prisoner (or more precisely, one of the most famous) in all of France. When de Sade saw them coming, he froze like an animal about to be shot. Like Jones, his cane and hat were lost as the people jockeyed him up on their shoulders, then made off in the direction of the river. The bugler-for-hire launched into a spirited rendition of "La Marseillaise." In just two minutes, the echo of the song had melted away into the ambient din of the city. Thierry and Jones were virtually alone on the square.

He had hit the ground on his knees. The dust from the unswept pavement had soiled his clothes. He rose painfully to his feet, struggling to reconcile his shattered dignity with the task of nursing his wrenched back. When she reached him, she could see the hurt in his face, but the fool would not surrender his gentility. Thierry offered a hand to steady him.

"Admiral Jones, are you all right?" she asked him, in English.

He pushed her hand away, albeit gently. "I would request your leave, Mademoiselle," he said evenly. "I think the weather unfavorable for a walk just now."

She thought just then to embrace him, to kiss away the dirt from his face, and perhaps even to apologize. But she knew this was not her character. Instead, she nodded courteously.

"I understand," she said. "Perhaps another time?"

"Another time. You do not think me remiss not to walk you to your door?"

She laughed at him. "Of course not. Please take your coat back—"

"No. Have it sent around later."

"Are you quite sure?"

"Yes."

"Good afternoon, then."

"Good afternoon."

With a short inclination of his head (but no kiss on her hand), Jones hobbled past her, back in the direction of his apartment. On the way he found his hat, and farther on, his sword, now bent almost in half. This he hid under his arm rather than compound his indignity by attempting to straighten it in the street. The last she saw of him he was still walking with a pronounced list.

Thierry returned to Rue des Petits Augustins and set about drinking too much wine. Unfortunately, she felt bloated before she felt drunk, and she had to abandon the project. Besides, there was business to attend to: a gentleman caller referred to her by Gualbert. Sitting in front of her mirror, she commenced to give her long hair one hundred strokes of the brush, counting each one out loud until the numbers crowded out every other thought. In fifteen minutes she managed to forget Paul Jones.

AUTHOR'S AFTERWORD

IN *The Eighteenth Captain* I have not been afraid to resort to historical facts, but it is not history. It is a life portrait of the younger John Paul Jones, but it certainly isn't biography. And while it is fashionable recently to take such distinctions lightly, I suspect some readers might still appreciate learning where the known facts leave off and my fictions (or, as appropriately, my lies, exaggerations, and errors) begin. Jones himself, no doubt, would have welcomed such a clarification.

My foil and narrator, John Severence, is an invention. But many aspects of his experience, including his ordeal on the prison hulk *Jersey*, and the battle at Valcour Island, are based squarely on contemporary accounts. Jones did happen to befriend the Continental Army Major John Grizzard Frazer before his first departure for France and did attempt to secure for him a Marine officer's commission. Unlike my character, however, Frazer never got the title, and sailed aboard the *Ranger* purely as a passenger. Frazer went through much of that cruise in an alcoholic haze, and the teetolaler Jones ended their relationship very soon after.

The broad factual outlines of Jones's military career are a matter of record. Where I have embroidered these facts, I have done so with a mind toward clarity and amplification of his life's themes. In some cases, as in the raid on Selkirk Manor or the attack on Whitehaven, the reality was really far more entertaining than anything I could have made up.

Jones's ongoing war with Lieutenant Thomas Simpson was, unfortunately, no fiction. Nor was the lieutenant alone: among the gallery of Jones's real or perceived enemies, there was always one true Prince of

Darkness in every period of his life. Later, during and after his cruise on the *Bonhommme Richard*, it would be Captain Pierre Landais. Later still, in Russia, it would be the Prince de Nassau-Siegen. There was never any real (that is to say, physical) pistol duel between Jones and Simpson.

Of the women, Jones was indeed proud to be acquainted with poet Phillis Wheatley (though he knew her in Boston, not Portsmouth). Madame de Reyniére is an amalgam of his many feminine admirers in Passy. Madame de Lowendahl, however, was a very real distraction: Samuel Eliot Morison wrote of her "She should have been our Commodore's Lady Hamilton. She had position, wit, intelligence, and beauty. He was never to have a mistress like her." My main crime against fact here was to set their abortive affair two years early, in the summer of 1778.

Invaluable contemporary sources include Jones's own reminiscence of his career for the benefit of King Louis XVI, circa 1786 (written pretty much as a elaborate job resumé, and to be credited with that in mind); also, the *Narrative of Nathaniel Fanning*, a midshipman who served under Jones on the *Bonhomme Richard*, and who suffered a spell in a British prison camp. Among the official biographies are Morison's *John Paul Jones: A Sailor's Biography* (the best), and John Henry Sherburne's *The Life and Character of the Chevalier John Paul Jones* (the earliest).

Those wishing to find the best scholarship available are urged to go to the historians. As for historical romances like this one, we embroider only the truth.